GUIDE ON HOW TO FAIL AT ONLINE DATING
Published originally under the title of 《网恋翻车指南》
Author © 酱子贝 (Jiang Zi Bei)
English publishing rights authorised by 北京晋江原创网络科技有限公司
(Beijing Jinjiang Original Network Technology Co., Ltd.)
English edition copyright © 2025 HT Books, LLC
Website: haitangbooks.org
Follow us on Twitter: @haitangbooks
All Rights Reserved.

No portion of this book may be reproduced or transmitted in any form or by any electronic or mechanical means without written permission from the publisher. This is a work of fiction. Names, characters, places, and incidents are the products of the author's imagination or are used fictitiously. Any resemblance to actual events, locales, or persons, living or dead, is entirely coincidental and not intended by the author.

——

Translation: Juurensha
Translation Editor: Divetus
Translation Checker: Shukun Xue
Rewriter: Nineteen
Proofreader: Nineteen, Alicia Zhou
In-House Editor: In

Art Director: Zhong Dian
Designer: Zhong Dian
Cover Art: Fueki
Interior Illustration: Jessie L.
Photographer: Zhao

——

ISBN: 978-1-966870-01-2
First Printing: Jun 2025
Printed and Bound in China

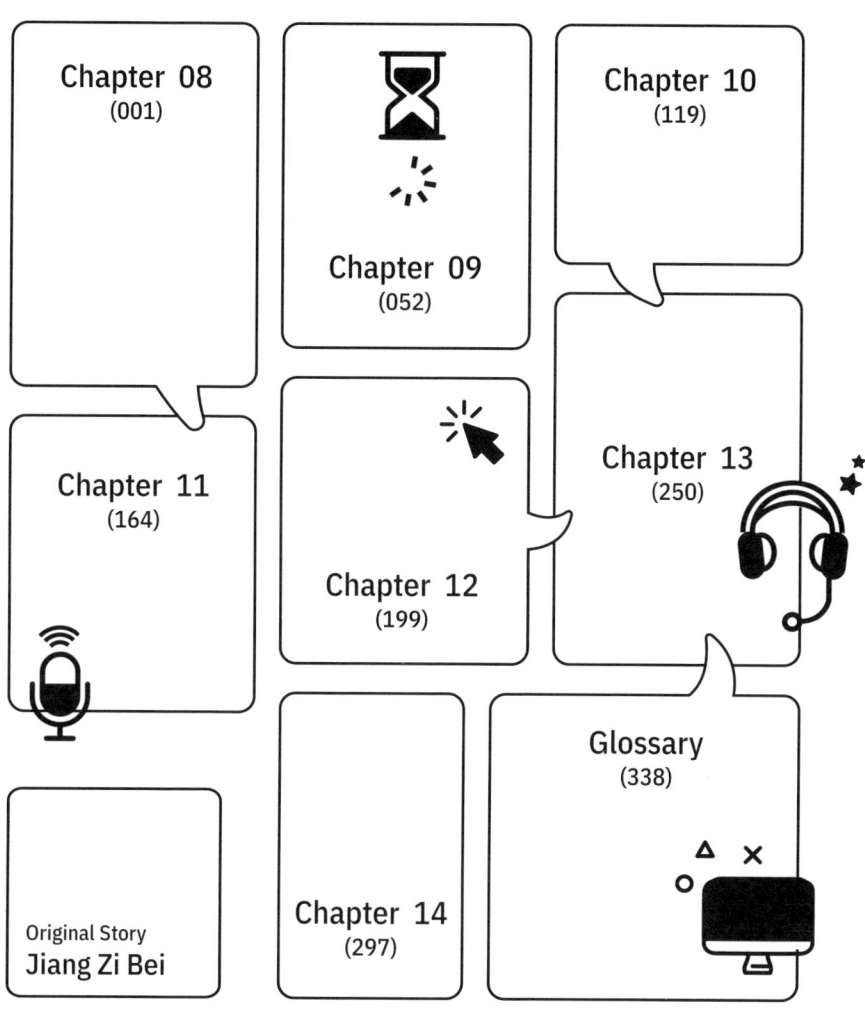

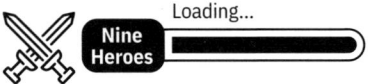

Chapter 08

Jing Huan waited until the day of their departure to start packing.

They had no other plans besides enjoying the hotel's signature hot springs during their three-day, two-night trip. According to Gao Zixiang, there were more than seventy hot spring pools, which would be more than enough for everyone to soak to their heart's content.

Since guys weren't that particular about packing their luggage, Jing Huan brought two sets of clothes, a facial cleanser, his laptop bag, and that was about it. Before leaving, he sent Yearning For a good morning message.

Lu Wenhao's car, a Volkswagen, was parked downstairs at the apartment building. His mother had bought it for him, insisting he should keep a low profile while going to school and promising she would get him a better car after he graduated. However, Lu Wenhao rarely drove; it was only because they were going to the hot springs today that he had gotten up early, gone home, and brought the car over.

It was a while before the pair seated in the car saw Jing Huan emerge. Lu Wenhao rolled the car window down and asked, "Huan-

 Chapter 08

huan, aren't you dawdling too much? And why did you bring so little?"

"I was packing," Jing Huan said. "Open up the trunk."

After stowing his belongings, Jing Huan threw himself into the back seat. "Are you two moving? We're only going for three days, why are you bringing two enormous suitcases?"

Gao Zixiang peeked out from the passenger seat and winked at him. "They contain treasures."

Having no interest in these treasures, Jing Huan casted his laptop bag to the side and yawned.

Lu Wenhao peered at him through the rearview mirror. "Huan-huan, what's been up with you lately? It's like you've been pulling all-nighters every single day. You're like this in our morning classes too, yawning at least ten times a class. Seeing you makes *me* sleepy."

Jing Huan had been running quests every night for the past few days. Fighting in the arena was addictive. The more he played, the more he felt that his equipment was utter trash. Every wrong move he made led to an easy kill; he didn't even know how many resurrection items Yearning For had wasted on him. As the equipment for sale in the marketplace wasn't to his liking, he had to gather the materials himself to see if he could craft some high-tier items.

Suspicious, Gao Zixiang asked, "You're not secretly dating someone behind our backs, are you?"

Lu Wenhao's eyes widened. "That must be it! Before, when I asked to stay at your place for two days, you refused! Damn! Huan-huan, are you living with a girl?!"

Gao Zixiang nodded knowingly. "No wonder you're always so sleepy in the mornings."

Where is this conversation going?

"Living with a girl my ass." He put on his headphones. "It's just insomnia."

Jing Huan checked his phone constantly. Twenty minutes had gone by, and still radio silence from Yearning For.

Saying he'd reply if he was free—Lies. All lies. Damn lying liar.

"I heard that the hotel has all kinds of facilities—a gym, an internet café, and karaoke. There's even a small bar." Lu Wenhao started the car. "We can go to the internet café, find some seats for the three of us, grab a gaming companion[1], and play a *PUBG* squad match. After that, we can go soak in the hot springs. Wouldn't that be awesome?"

If only Lu Wenhao hadn't brought it up. But now that he had, Jing Huan was eager to play. After quitting *Nine Heroes* two years ago, he had been surviving on *PUBG*, though he hadn't had much time to play recently.

He shifted into a more comfortable position and clicked on the live stream app on his cellphone. When he saw that the only streamer he followed wasn't live, he opened the app's main page to find other streams to watch.

【CQB[2] Goddess Little Luomi: Send Mimi gifts and I'll be super sweet, so sweet you'll want to date me~】

---

1   Gaming companions are hired players who provide in-game support or social companionship. These companions may offer skill coaching, gameplay support (carries), emotional support, etc. In this context, Lu Wenhao is saying to get a companion who will carry them.
2   Close-quarters battle (CQB) refers to tactical combat situations conducted at short ranges, typically involving guns or melee weapons. Her name implies she's a "goddess" at fighting face-to-face as opposed to sniping from afar.

Chapter 08

The live stream title immediately caught Jing Huan's attention. He glanced at the streamer's profile. Despite not having many fans on this live stream platform, she still ranked amongst the top ten of the gift leaderboards last week. Clearly, she was good at attracting the local whales[3] and flattering them into willingly spending money on her.

Full of admiration, Jing Huan joined the live stream, hoping to take a leaf out of her book.

A good amount of the girl's fair skin was exposed due to her camisole. She had delicate makeup on, and a voice so sweet that honey was virtually dripping from it. "Thank you, Want Milk Tea-gege for the itty-bitty star! I'll use gege's star to buy milk tea later!"

The streamer got shot in the head by an enemy in the game. "Aaah! These prone campers[4] are so annoying. They're too sneaky, but it's not because I'm noob! You guys aren't allowed to laugh at me! Aaah, I'll be mad if you do!"

The streamer switched to the gun that she picked up from an airdrop. In the midst of reloading, she squealed playfully, "The evil dragon roars! *Awooo!*"

When the streamer's rich whale fan entered the stream, she

---

3   A whale, in gaming and streaming, means someone who spends disproportionately large sums of money on microtransactions. In streaming, whales frequently donate substantial amounts to the streamer to secure top ranks on the donation leaderboards.
4   Prone campers, derived from 伏地魔 (Fú Dì Mó), is the direct translation of "Lord Voldemort," the antagonist in the Harry Potter series. In tactical multiplayer games like PUBG, it describes players who exploit terrain by lying prone to blend into the environment to camp and ambush players. It conflates passive gameplay tactics with the evil of Voldemort.

asked, "Is Qiu-gege here? Good morning gege, did you just wake up?"

[Public] Qiu-gege (Big Star Ambassador): Mm, just opened my eyes, but I came here immediately. Give me a good morning kiss.

Just as Jing Huan wondered how she would bestow said morning kiss, he saw the female streamer smile shyly, and then purse her lips toward the microphone. "Qiu-gege, mwah!"

The simulated kissing sound was slightly sticky, and the streamer deliberately drew out her breathy tone, making her sound especially suggestive.

Jing Huan took a deep breath, goosebumps threatening to break out from her fake smooches, and quickly exited the live stream. He took off his headphones, still shaken up, and finally understood why Yearning For didn't like him.

Compared to truly cute, coquettish, and sweet-voiced girls, I'm nothing!!!

If he remembered correctly, Fae Bae's and his cousin's voices were especially sweet. They were both complete loli voices, meaning that had to be Yearning For's type. Unfortunately, he had been too hasty and carelessly bought the voice changer. There was no way he could produce a loli voice in this lifetime.

Jing Huan closed the live stream app and looked out the window with a face full of sorrow.

Two hours later, they finally arrived at their destination. He had booked a room with a king-sized bed on the twentieth floor while Lu Wenhao and Gao Zixiang had reserved a deluxe double-bed room a few floors above his.

After checking in, Lu Wenhao wasted no time in asking, "When

Chapter 08

are we going to hit the hot springs? Huanhuan, how about you get changed and come out? Let's soak once at noon and then again at night."

"Aren't you afraid of your head spinning?" Jing Huan asked. "You guys can go ahead. I'm not going at noon; I'm taking a nap. Ask me again in the evening."

Just then, the elevator reached the twentieth floor. Jing Huan waved at them and left, hitching his backpack higher.

This resort was built in the mountains with not a single restaurant nearby. Most guests who stayed here were tourists looking to enjoy themselves without having to leave the comfort of their hotel. To attract visitors, the resort had perfected everything—from the decor to its indoor entertainment facilities.

Jing Huan swiped his card to open the door and was immediately greeted with a mountain view from the balcony. Instantly, he felt much more relaxed.

He stepped out onto the balcony, taking a moment to savor the crisp mountain air before heading back in, turning on the computer, and quickly logging into *Nine Heroes*. Since he had stayed up too late last night, he was going to take a nap first before continuing to grind his quests. For now, he'd have his character AFK in Penglai and figure out the rest later.

[Friend] Bishop Wood: You there?

[Friend] Sweet Little Jing: Yeah, what's up?

[Friend] Bishop Wood: Want to do a dungeon together? [Cute]

[Friend] Sweet Little Jing: Nah~ I already have a fixed team for dungeons.

[Friend] Bishop Wood: I know, but Long Road Ahead and Yearning

For aren't here for the next few days, right? Come grind with me, I'm a very good party leader. [Shy]

[Friend] Sweet Little Jing: ...Nope, I'm good with just doing solo quests!

[Friend] Bishop Wood: Okay then, just remember to look back when you have time.

[Friend] Sweet Little Jing: Look back at what?

[Friend] Bishop Wood: At me. [Shy]

Jing Huan's fingers hovered over his keyboard.

Since his last megaphone confessing to Yearning For, the people who used to crowd around him had completely vanished. Only Bishop Wood remained, and on occasion, he'd drop a few sentences here and there to tease him.

After some thinking, Jing Huan typed.

[Friend] Sweet Little Jing: Okay~! I'm going to AFK in Penglai now. The scenery where I am is so pretty, I want to take some pictures to show gege. >.< TTYL, bye-bye.

When Jing Huan woke up from his short nap, it was to the sun setting right outside his window. He lay on his side and watched it for a long while, before slowly raising his hand and groping for his cellphone under his pillow.

When he saw the bright red "1" on the upper right of the WeChat icon, half of his drowsiness dissipated, and he instantly clicked on it.

【Bishop Wood has sent you a friend request with a message: Little Jingjing, can you show me the scenery photos too?】

His delight faded right away. He lazily accepted.

Jing Huan opened his chat with Yearning For. At the bottom

Chapter 08

was still his "Good morning, gege" message from the morning.

Fuck.

Using his other hand, he poked Yearning For's profile picture several times.

You know, replying to messages is basic social etiquette, you shitty little didi!!

After his ranting session, he started typing on his cellphone.

Little Jing~: Did gege find a new meimei in the mountains? Why aren't you replying to me? T.T

Lu Wenhao called him to head over to the hotel's buffet restaurant at dinner time. By the time Jing Huan arrived, Lu Wenhao had already polished off his third plate of food.

"If you came any later, I would've finished all these dishes." Lu Wenhao patted his stomach.

Jing Huan put his plate of food on the table and sat down. "Eat a little less. At the current rate, you won't even be able to run during basketball anymore."

"Bullshit," said Lu Wenhao. "I'm still going to bring glory to our class at the athletic competition!"

Laughing, Jing Huan asked, "Where's Xiang'er?"

"He's on the phone with his girlfriend and said he'd eat later. He told us not to wait for him." Just as Lu Wenhao finished speaking, his cellphone rang. He picked it up, his face immediately cracking into a wide smile. He quickly put down his chopsticks to reply with both hands.

Jing Huan took a sip of orange juice. "Can you stop smiling so lewdly? People who don't know what's going on will think you're watching porn in public."

"Stop talking crap," Lu Wenhao said. "I'm chatting with my goddess."

"Which goddess?"

"The number one Putuo Mountain in the server," Lu Wenhao said proudly. "We're getting married next Wednesday. How about it? Want me to give you an alt character so you can attend the ceremony?"

Jing Huan didn't know what to say for a moment. "What, now that your wound has healed, you've forgotten the pain? Aren't you afraid it'll be an old geezer this time?"

"*Ptui ptui ptui*, don't say that shit. She video-called me before; she's beautiful and has a sweet voice. She's my baby."

Jing Huan felt nauseated at him for using the word "baby." He was about to say more when he turned around, catching a glimpse of Lu Wenhao's blissful expression. Suddenly, a flash of inspiration struck him.

Wasn't there an online dating expert sitting right beside him? Why was he trying to get tips from someone else?!

Jing Huan seized Lu Wenhao's chubby wrist. "Hao'er, put down your phone first. I want to ask you something."

Startled, Lu Wenhao stopped typing. "What's going on that's so serious?"

"It's just... I have a friend," Jing Huan said. "She likes a guy in a game and has been pursuing him for over a month now, but the guy hasn't shown much interest. Have any good ideas?"

Lu Wenhao frowned. "Is your friend hideous?"

Jing Huan paused. "Not really?"

"Then why can't she get him?" Lu Wenhao asked. "Have they ever voice-chatted?"

 Chapter 08

Jing Huan nodded. "Of course! My friend's voice might not sound sweet, but it's still nice, plus she's really good at acting cute! She courts that guy daily and calls him gege! But the guy is like a rock—completely unresponsive to her flirting."

Lu Wenhao blinked. "You seem to have a really clear idea of their situation?"

"With her complaining to me about it all the time, how could I not know?" Jing Huan coughed. "Anyway, do you have any ideas or not?"

Lu Wenhao thought for a bit. "Did your friend ever send the guy a photo?"

"No," Jing Huan said. "She's shy."

"Well, no wonder." Lu Wenhao slapped his thigh. "Tell her not to be shy! Send the guy a photo, and it'll be a sure win!"

Where am I supposed to get a photo to send?!

"...She's not exactly good-looking either," Jing Huan hedged. "Um, she's maybe a five."

"Five is enough! Just take a random photo, do a little photoshopping, and she'll shoot up to an eight. She knows about Photoshop, right? Don't worry about looking bad in person; just trick the person, get 'em hooked first! Once the feelings have developed, looks won't matter as much." Lu Wenhao added, "Oh, and she can also act a bit seductive when taking the pictures."

Jing Huan shot him a strange look. *Why are you so good at this?*

"...Seductive how?"

"Don't look at me like that! That's not what I meant!" Lu Wenhao said. "It doesn't have to be too much, just...show some thigh? A bit of arm? Or maybe her collarbone. She can handle that much, right?"

Jing Huan's face was utterly indecipherable. "Nope, not at all."

"How will you know if you don't ask her?"

"She's not that kind of girl."

Lu Wenhao stared at him, at a loss for words.

After dinner, Jing Huan went back to his room, changed into a pair of loose swimming trunks, draped on a bathrobe, and soak himself in the hot springs.

The resort indeed had dozens of hot spring pools, but some were very small. The pool would get crowded with just a few people in it, to the point where they wouldn't be able to even stretch out their legs. So, after a discussion in front of the entrance, the three of them decided to soak separately.

Jing Huan picked out a hot spring pool in a corner and sank into it, soaking in the scalding hot water. As the water lapped against his skin, it felt equal parts painful and refreshing.

Jing Huan sat in the hot spring and couldn't help sneaking glances at his cellphone that he had placed to the side. Ten hours had passed, and still no reply from Yearning For.

Jing Huan closed his eyes and thought calmly, *Maybe he's dead.*

A few seconds later, he opened his eyes, seemingly having arrived at a major decision, slowly reaching out and picking up his cellphone.

Xiang Huaizhi retrieved his cellphone from the lost and found office.

He and Lu Hang had been shopping at the city supermarket, wanting to buy supplies and food for tomorrow's hike, and somehow, he had lost his phone. The supermarket security guard had

Chapter 08

contacted him in the evening and informed him that the cellphone had been found.

In the car back to the hotel, Lu Hang said, "Turn it on and check if anyone has messed around with it."

The cellphone showed no signs of use or being forcibly unlocked. As soon as Xiang Huaizhi turned it on, several WeChat notifications popped up on the screen. He skimmed through the message notifications, hesitated for a few seconds, and then clicked on Sweet Little Jing's messages first.

Little Jing~: Good morning gege. ^^

Little Jing~: Did gege find a new meimei in the mountains? Why aren't you replying to me. T.T

Little Jing~: [Photo]

Little Jing~: [Voice message]

Xiang Huaizhi automatically played the voice message first, then enlarged the picture.

"Gege, I just went to soak in the hot springs." Sweet Little Jing's voice sounded in the car. "Remember to eat dinner on time! Mwah!"

In the photo, the girl had her thighs soaking in the hot spring water. They were pale and slender with small, rounded knees. Sweet Little Jing's cellphone had a high resolution, so he could even see a small mole on the outside of her thigh—a delectable feast for the eyes.

Lu Hang, who was sitting beside him, was stunned. He started scooting over. "What did Little Jingjing say? I didn't catch it."

Xiang Huaizhi calmly locked his phone. "Nothing. Don't come over."

Guide on How to Fail at Online Dating

Jing Huan sat in front of the computer, anxiously clicking on and replaying the voice message he had sent out again.

If he listened closely, the girl's voice sounded somewhat muffled and forced; he had recorded himself using the voice changer in advance and then played it through the laptop speakers before sending it on WeChat.

Did it sound a bit fake? Maybe he shouldn't have added the "mwah"?

Jing Huan hesitated for a long time before deciding to recall his voice message. However, two minutes had already passed since he sent it so the recall button had disappeared.

Confidence dwindling with every passing second, he opened the photo of his photoshopped legs again.

Jing Huan liked playing basketball, so his legs were fairly muscular. In any case, they didn't look like a girl's legs at all. In order to take this photo, he'd pretty much pulled his swimming trunks up to the base of his thighs; fortunately, he didn't have much leg hair, so all he had to do was photoshop his thighs slightly slimmer to make it look decent.

He thought for a moment, long-pressed the photo, and then forwarded it to Lu Wenhao.

Lu Wenhao: ?

Lu Wenhao: ???

Lu Wenhao: What the fuck, I already have a wife, why are you sending me lewd pictures? Do I look like someone who would look at this kind of photo??

Lu Wenhao: Whose legs are these? Is she from our school? Share her WeChat, I just want to check her Moments, nothing else.

Jing Huan raised his eyebrows. Looked like his photoshopping skills weren't too shabby.

His phone vibrated. The person who had been missing all day had finally replied.

Xiang: ...

Xiang: Don't send these photos to random people in the future.

Jing Huan let out a derisive snort, and all the nervousness and shame he had just felt immediately spread its wings and disappeared without a trace.

Trying to act all righteous in front of me even though all it took was a bare-legged pic for you to reply right away?

Little Jing~: T.T I didn't send it to random strangers! I only sent it to gege!

At this moment, Xiang Huaizhi was sitting in a barbecue restaurant, and at the top of the chat screen was Sweet Little Jing's leg photo. To avoid others seeing it, he covered his phone as he messaged her. He was acting no differently than a thief.

He raised his hand and, without any hesitation, deleted the photo from their chat history before he continued typing.

Xiang: I lost my phone today and just found it.

Jing Huan's lips curled in disgust. *Scumbags have all the excuses.*

Little Jing~: Oh, so that's what happened. You scared me to death, I thought gege was ignoring me. [Hugging self while crying]

Little Jing~: Did gege go hiking today?

Xiang: No, that's tomorrow.

Little Jing~: Ohhh, then gege should be careful.

Little Jing~: [Kiss][Lips]

Xiang Huaizhi stared at the big red lips emoticon, and for some reason, he remembered that voice message from earlier.

Choosing not to reply, he locked the phone and put it away, turning his attention back to grilling the meat.

"Sweet Little Jing sent you quite a few messages, didn't she?" Lu Hang teased, swallowing the meat in his mouth. He might not have heard everything Sweet Little Jing had said very clearly, but he certainly caught the kissing sound at the end.

Xiang Huaizhi replied, "No."

"Yeah right, I heard it all, she even gave you a kiss." Lu Hang flipped the meat over and shook his head. "She's really devoted."

Xiang Huaizhi paused. "We met in-game; it's not as exaggerated as how you're making it out to be."

"So what if you met in-game? Real feelings can't come out of the game?"

Xiang Huaizhi chuckled and said, "We've never even met in person, and you're bringing up real feelings after exchanging a couple words and playing a few PK matches together? I think you're obsessed with online dating."

Lu Hang stopped moving around. "Let's just cut to the chase: you're worried that Little Jingjing is actually extremely ugly in real life? That's valid; they say that statistically, eighty percent of girls with nice voices aren't good-looking, and some are even fat. But solution's simple though: just ask her for a photo. Oh wait, photos aren't reliable enough, you need a video call."

Xiang Huaizhi looked up lazily and said, "Do you think I'm you?"

"Stop with the personal attacks." Lu Hang suddenly thought of

 Chapter 08

something and laughed. "Or do you think Little Jingjing is just after your good equipment and money?"

Xiang Huaizhi couldn't be bothered with him and got up to get some dipping sauce. When he returned, he saw Lu Hang holding his phone and laughing. As soon as he sat down, Lu Hang hurriedly held his phone out to him and said, "Xiangxiang, look."

On the screen was the chat between Lu Hang and Sweet Little Jing.

Long Road Ahead: Little Jingjing, what are you doing? [Sticking head out]

Little Jing~: I'm grinding some quests for materials, what's up~

Long Road Ahead: [Photo] Xiangxiang and I are eating BBQ.

Little Jing~: Looks so yummy. [Drooling]

Long Road Ahead: He he, it is very yummy.

Long Road Ahead: Do you want to see a photo of your Xiang-gege?

Little Jing~: !!!

Little Jing~: Yes, yes! I want to! Can I? Do I really have the right to see gege's magnificent beauty?!

Little Jing~: [Kneeling and kowtowing]

Long Road Ahead: Ha ha ha, you do! But you can't tell him about this.

Little Jing~: [Chick pecking at rice]

Long Road Ahead: [Photo]

After seeing the photo Lu Hang had sent, Xiang Huaizhi's expression immediately darkened.

Lu Hang obviously hadn't sent a photo of him, and instead had sent one of a young man with small eyes behind a pair of glasses,

thick lips, and a skin tone that matched the cooked beef in front of them. He had a simple and silly smile, looking no older than twenty.

"Are you out of your mind with boredom?" Xiang Huaizhi's voice was cool. "Who is this?"

"My cousin," Lu Hang said. "Aw, it's just a joke. How come she hasn't replied? Did the photo scare her away?"

Xiang Huaizhi didn't respond and instead moved to recall the photo, all the while typing an explanation. It was one thing to joke around, but sending fake photos was crossing the line. Before he could explain though, Sweet Little Jing replied.

Little Jing~: [Crazily licking screen]

Little Jing~: Schlurp, schlurp, schlurp!

Silently, Xiang Huaizhi deleted his response and sent a question mark instead.

Little Jing~: AAAAAH! MY GEGE IS SO HOT! I'M LICKING THE SCREEN!

Long Road Ahead: ...Hot?

Little Jing~: Sooooo hot [Swooning], especially his charming little eyes!

Long Road Ahead: Eyes?

Little Jing~: There's a hint of indifference, a hint of heartlessness, a hint of devil-may-care in them.

Little Jing~: I love him. I want to print out the photo and stick it on my bedside. [Shy]

Ever since he met Sweet Little Jing, Xiang Huaizhi realized he seemed to only be able to use the question mark punctuation.

Long Road Ahead: That's not me. Long Road Ahead was messing around and just sent a random photo.

Little Jing~: ...

Little Jing~: ?

【Little Jing~ recalled a message.】

【Little Jing~ recalled a message.】

She even recalled the licking the screen sticker.

Xiang Huaizhi's lips couldn't resist curling, laughing briefly at the recalled message notifications.

Little Jing~: QAQ Long Road Ahead is so bad...

Long Road Ahead: Mm, I will talk to him.

After explaining things to Sweet Little Jing, Xiang Huaizhi tossed the cellphone back. "Don't play these kinds of pointless pranks on her anymore."

The next day, they sat side by side in the internet café below the hotel as planned.

Although they had claimed they were here to play co-op together, both Gao Zixiang and Lu Wenhao opened up *Nine Heroes*. One did his dailies while the other took his wife to go enjoy the scenery.

Jing Huan didn't like playing *PUBG* solo, so he opened up *League of Legends* for the first time in a while. However, because his skills had deteriorated, he was flamed by his four teammates and called an ultimate orphan[5].

He irritably ran his fingers through his hair. He wanted to start cussing, but the girl seated next to him suddenly tapped his shoulder.

5　　In LoL, ultimate orphan (绝 世 孤 儿 - jué shì gū ér) is a pejorative Chinese gaming slang to mock players perceived as overly isolated. Typically, it refers to top laners that farm independently, but it has spread broadly to mean players who ignore team fights or map objectives, which ultimately cause the team to lose.

Guide on How to Fail at Online Dating

The girl had long eyelashes framing her especially cute doe eyes. In a soft voice, she asked, "Little gege, want to play together?"

Jing Huan glanced at her *LoL* client, and then pointed at his match screen with a laugh. "Probably not, I'm very noob."

"That's okay, it's just a game. I only know how to play support too," the girl insisted.

Jing Huan closed the *LoL* client. "Maybe next time. I'm about to play *PUBG* now."

How could there be a next time? The girl felt a little abashed when she realized he was rejecting her. She sat there for a while before logging off and leaving.

After she left, Gao Zixiang hissed, "Huanhuan, what's wrong with you? It's only a game of *LoL*; it's not like she's asking you out, and you just rejected her like that?"

Lu Wenhao nodded. "He's right, and that girl was pretty cute too. You're too heartless."

Jing Huan scoffed. "You two have some real balls to say that. Who were the ones who said we should go to the internet café to play co-op together? And then left me sitting here watching you guys play *Nine Heroes*?" He would've been better off staying in his room to grind the event himself.

"Aaah, it's because our guild leader suddenly said we needed to do the twenty-man five-star difficulty dungeon that opens up in five minutes." Lu Wenhao led his wife to the dungeon NPC. "It'll be quick, and then after this dungeon, we'll play *PUBG*."

Jing Huan glanced at his screen. "Screw that; this dungeon will take you at least three hours."

"Three hours?" Gao Zixiang shook his head. "You're too

Chapter 08

optimistic. With Lu Wenhao, it'll be a minimum of four hours."

Lu Wenhao retorted, "Screw you guys! I'm way better now!"

Since he had already come out, Jing Huan couldn't be bothered to go back to his room. With a twitch of his fingers, he hired three male gaming companions, opened *PUBG*, and went to experience the joy of being doted on.

Lu Wenhao asked, "Is something wrong with you? Spending money to hire male gaming companions to play with you?"

"I feel embarrassed asking girls for items," Jing Huan said succinctly.

After two hours of play, Jing Huan glanced over and discovered that Lu Wenhao had already been punched to death by the boss and was now a corpse lying in a corner of the dungeon. A few seconds later, his in-game wife resurrected him. Lu Wenhao tried to set a Healing Spring for Gao Zixiang but placed it too far in the back, and therefore failed to heal him, causing Gao Zixiang to fall back to the ground.

Gao Zixiang was about to explode from rage. "You've been playing your Spirit Fox Den like shit. I could put a chicken on the keyboard and it'd play better than you."

Lu Wenhao said defensively, "It's the sect that's weak. How is that my fault?"

"Weak my ass." Jing Huan couldn't take it anymore. "You're just too used to playing DPS and not used to the casting range for the sect's spells."

Lu Wenhao protested, "It's really not that. Huanhuan, you've never played a Spirit Fox Den before, so you don't know how goddamn hard this sect is to play."

"Who said I haven't played it before?" Seeing Lu Wenhao getting pummeled to death once more, Jing Huan couldn't watch any longer. He stood up and said, "Get up, switch places. You play *PUBG*."

Ten minutes passed. Lu Wenhao's mind wasn't on *PUBG* at all. He ran away from the blue zone while simultaneously watching Jing Huan play. "What the fuck? That didn't hit you? That must be a bug, right?"

Jing Huan said, "It didn't hit me to begin with; I dodged it."

Lu Wenhao's game character was a Demon race with a tiger's head and a human body. He watched as the tiger rolled, quickly healing the party's DPS with a Healing Spring, with nary a pause in between.

Lu Wenhao was puzzled. They were obviously using the same skills, but why could Jing Huan land them all?

Gao Zixiang was healed to full health. "Holy shit, this feels great. Lu Wenhao, you better learn from him. Start taking notes!"

Lu Wenhao clicked his tongue. "Shut up, I am."

Half an hour later, the boss fell to the floor with a crash. Jing Huan released a long breath, unable to resist stretching his fingers.

He had gotten used to running dungeons with Yearning For and was accustomed to his explosive DPS, so running a high-level dungeon with others felt particularly exhausting.

"Huanhuan, you're too good," Gao Zixiang said. "Hurry up and buy a character, then come back as my dedicated healer!"

Jing Huan drank a sip of water. "I'm not that great, I just look good compared to you guys."

"Don't be so modest."

 Chapter 08

Suddenly, a voice that carried a hint of laughter resounded from behind. "You're pretty good at playing Spirit Fox Den."

Jing Huan froze and instinctively spun around.

At some point, two guys had come to stand behind him. Jing Huan wasn't familiar with the first who wore a plaid shirt and a gentle smile. The other had drooping eyelids. Due to his height and long legs, the simple black T-shirt he wore gave off a name-brand feel. It was the person Jing Huan had recently met: Xiang Huaizhi.

Both of their hair and clothes were drenched as if they had just been in a rainstorm.

Jing Huan felt slightly off balance.

He didn't know if it was because he had been running dungeons with Yearning For for too long, but he kept mishearing other peoples' voices. The girl from earlier had sounded like Love is Sharing Noms, and now this guy... He sounded a bit like Long Road Ahead.

Jing Huan snapped back to reality. He was just about to greet them when Lu Wenhao beside him stood up first.

"Lu-ge? What a coincidence, what are you doing here?" Lu Wenhao gave them a once-over. "Why are you guys...so wet?"

Lu Hang sighed, reaching out a hand to flick the water off his bangs. "Don't get me started. The two of us got caught in the rainstorm while we were hiking. We wanted to drive down the mountain, but the rain was so heavy that we couldn't see the road, so we were left with no choice but to take shelter here."

"Today's weather forecast did say it would rain," Lu Wenhao said. "Why did you guys choose this hour of all times to hike?"

Lu Hang grumbled, "Didn't look at it."

Jing Huan grabbed some tissues off the table and handed them to Xiang Huaizhi. "Senior, wipe yourself off with these."

Xiang Huaizhi accepted them. "Thank you."

Lu Hang's eyes flicked between the two of them. "You two know each other?" He'd heard of Jing Huan. Jing Huan was kind of famous at their school; a lot of girls in their department liked to watch this little underclassman play basketball.

"We met before," Xiang Huaizhi said.

Gao Zixiang did some quick introductions. "Huanhuan, this is also our upperclassman, Lu Hang. He's Senior Xiang's roommate. He's the one I met at that in-person player event. Senior, this is our roommate Jing Huan."

"I know, I've heard about him." Lu Hang asked eagerly, "You talked about me before? What'd you say?"

Jing Huan handed Lu Hang a tissue as well. "They said that you're very good at *Nine Heroes*."

"Thanks." Lu Hang dried his arms. "You play *Nine Heroes* too? Which server? I saw you handle Spirit Fox Den really well—you're just as good as the one in our party."

Jing Huan shook his head. "I used to play, but I've quit for a few years now."

"Your party also has a Spirit Fox Den, Senior?" Lu Wenhao's curiosity was piqued. "How good are they?"

"What's the point in asking?" Gao Zixiang remarked. "All you need to know is that they're better than you."

"Would it fucking kill you not to put me down?!" Lu Wenhao snapped.

Lu Hang thought of something and laughed. "Our party's Spirit Fox Den..." He raised his chin and jerked it at Xiang Huaizhi, "...is very good. Especially with him."

Ever so considerate, Xiang Huaizhi asked, "Didn't get enough of the rain?"

Lu Hang shut up.

For some reason, Jing Huan felt a bit flustered. The back of his neck felt prickly and uncomfortable.

I shouldn't wear headphones while gaming anymore, he thought. *Otherwise, everyone I hear is going to sound like Yearning For, and that would be horrible.*

"Well then, Lu-ge, are you guys here to use the internet?" Lu Wenhao asked. "Or are you also staying at this resort?"

"No, our hotel is in the city. We booked late so this resort was already full." Lu Hang scanned his surroundings. "We didn't know when the rain would stop, and we heard there was an internet café nearby, so we came here to kill some time."

The internet café's computers were arranged in rows of four. The only seat that was empty in their row was the one beside Jing Huan. It wouldn't fit them both, however, all four seats at the other end were free.

"All right, you guys have fun, we're going to go use the PC." Lu Hang gravitated to the other end and turned on a computer. Xiang Huaizhi glanced over and sat across from Jing Huan.

Jing Huan put on his headphones and started another *PUBG* match.

The three male gaming companions were chattering nonstop in his headphones, and Jing Huan's game character sat in the car without moving. His gaze unconsciously fell onto Xiang Huaizhi's hand gripping the mouse.

Xiang Huaizhi's palm was very large, and his long and slender fingers had wrapped around the entire mouse, making one unable to resist taking a second look.

Having looked his fill, Jing Huan was about to turn away when Xiang Huaizhi suddenly cocked his head, gazing at him through the gap between the two computers, expression nonchalant. "What are you looking at?"

Despite getting caught peeking, Jing Huan didn't feel an ounce of embarrassment. He slid off one side of his headphones and smiled. "Senior, you have really big hands and nice-looking fingers."

No sooner had the words left Jing Huan's mouth than the sound of intense gunfire erupted from his headphones, and he quickly shrank back and put them on again. "I'm here, I'm here, I was just talking to a friend... Someone at that spot? Okay, I see them."

Having heard his nonsensical compliment, the corner of Xiang Huaizhi's mouth twitched. He then straightened up and logged into *Nine Heroes*.

Lu Hang asked, "Wanna run a dungeon? A simple five-man one. Is Little Jingjing here? I see her character AFKing in Penglai."

Xiang Huaizhi didn't need to check his friend list before immediately saying, "She's not here."

He had been online for two whole minutes without receiving any friend messages, so she definitely wasn't in front of her computer.

"All right, come to the main city, I'll grab a random player."

Chapter 08

After winning three matches of *PUBG* in a row, Jing Huan grew bored and waved his hand to dismiss the three gaming companions. He leaned back in his chair and put his chin in his hand as he watched Lu Wenhao clear a dungeon.

"Go grab the magic relic," Lu Hang's voice carried over. "Then let's meet at the teleporter."

Xiang Huaizhi replied, "Mm."

Their discussion was very succinct, and the more Jing Huan listened, the more distracted he became. His attention was no longer on Lu Wenhao's screen at all.

The voices and conversations were...really similar.

His phone let out a soft chime, pulling Jing Huan out of his musings. He took his phone out and unlocked it.

Nomnom: How is it? Aren't tampons the most miraculous things in this world?

Little Jing~: ...

Little Jing~: I haven't used them yet...

Nomnom: What? It still hasn't arrived? Do you have irregular periods?

Jing Huan smothered his face, wondering when this topic would end. He couldn't bring himself to discuss...these things...with a girl.

Little Jing~: No...I haven't gone to soak in the hot springs yet.

Nomnom: Ohhh, okay. This treasure was also something my friend recommended to me when I was on a trip before and I've loved it ever since.

Something suddenly occurred to Jing Huan as he held his phone. He straightened up and speedily typed.

Little Jing~: Nomnom, where are you right now?

Guide on How to Fail at Online Dating

Nomnom: Ah? I'm clearing a dungeon.

Little Jing~: No, where are you in real life?

Nomnom: ...At home, why?

Little Jing~: Your family doesn't happen to own a resort in Mancheng, right?

Nomnom: ...What kind of bullshit are you spouting? I'm from Jiangcheng. If my family owned a resort, why would I still go to work and take crap from my stupid boss every day?!

Jing Huan stared at her reply, then let out a small sigh of relief, suddenly finding it funny.

There were so many similar-sounding voices in the world; he must've been crazy to think the girl he just met was Nomnom.

The five of them stayed at the internet café until it was dinner time. It was still pouring outside. Numerous cars had their emergency blinkers on as they turned into the resort's parking lot seeking refuge from the rain.

Lu Hang sussed out the situation and then came back. "This rain is even heavier than when Zhao Wei went to ask her dad for money[6]."

Jing Huan corrected him, "Her name was Yiping."

"Same thing." Lu Hang sighed. "What the hell can we do? It's so rare for us to go on a vacation, are we just going to spend it eating instant noodles and sleeping at the internet café?"

Xiang Huaizhi glanced at the menu on the computer screen. "Not necessarily, this internet café sells set meals."

Lu Wenhao checked the weather forecast. "This storm is going

---

6   This rain scene from the 2001 Chinese-Taiwanese Drama *Romance in the Rain* (Yiping portrayed by actress Zhao Wei) is often referenced in memes for being heavily sentimental and emotional.

 Chapter 08

to last until tomorrow. Even if it stops tonight, do you guys really want to drive down the mountain when it's pitch-black and the roads being this slippery?"

"What else can we do? We'll just have to drive slowly. I can't stand sleeping in a chair." Lu Hang stretched. "Besides, I just asked; forget empty rooms, the lobby doesn't even have any empty seats."

An idea hit Gao Zixiang. "Hey, Lu-ge, how about you guys sleep in our rooms?"

Everyone was stunned.

"Oh yeah," Lu Wenhao agreed. "We booked two rooms, so we'll definitely all fit."

The thought had also come to Jing Huan. "Mine's a king bed, so I can fit another person."

Lu Hang was slightly surprised. After all, he wasn't that close with these underclassmen; they had chatted only a little bit during the in-person player meetup. "You're okay with that?"

Lu Wenhao laughed. "It's fine. We're all guys, why wouldn't it be?"

Lu Hang looked at his roommate, raised an eyebrow, and sent out a questioning signal.

Xiang Huaizhi wasn't used to sharing a bed with anyone, especially strangers whom he had just met. But this internet café's chairs were terrible, and after sitting in them for a long time, his whole body ached. In addition, a faint smell of rainwater still clung to his clothes, making him feel uncomfortable.

"Come on, Senior." The boy sitting across from him suddenly leaned over, and his eyes curved as he enthusiastically invited him. "Just think of it as repayment for saving my life before."

The elevator stopped on the twentieth floor. Xiang Huaizhi followed Jing Huan out of it.

"Then I'm going to bring Senior up to shower and change his clothes first." Jing Huan checked his watch. "See you at the restaurant at seven?"

"Okay," Lu Wenhao agreed.

As Xiang Huaizhi stood by his side, he felt as though he was a kindergartener getting picked up by Jing Huan from school. It wasn't until they reached the room that Xiang Huaizhi realized there was a problem.

"I didn't bring any extra clothes."

"That's fine." Jing Huan pointed at the wardrobe. "You can wear a bathrobe for now. After you wash up and run your clothes through the dryer, you can wear them again."

Xiang Huaizhi pursed his lips. His choices were pretty limited at the moment, and this really was the only solution.

He nodded. "Okay."

Once Xiang Huaizhi went into the bathroom, Jing Huan brought his laptop over to the sofa. Seeing that Yearning For wasn't online, he leisurely opened the friend messages he had received while AFK.

Bishop Wood had sent him several greetings. Jing Huan thought about it, then decided to pretend he was still AFK and not reply.

Echoes of Spring had also sent him a message, saying that they had distributed the first kill rewards for the guild dungeon, reminding him to collect them from the guild treasury.

Jing Huan replied with an acknowledgment and then had the little spirit fox skip over to the guild.

Chapter 08

【Guild Announcement: Sweet Little Jing has obtained 100 gold as a guild reward for the first clear dungeon bonus!】

[Guild] Bishop Wood: ?

[Guild] Bishop Wood: [Crying] You actually didn't reply to my messages…

Shit, he forgot that claiming the guild reward would trigger a guild announcement.

[Guild] Sweet Little Jing: I just came back. I wasn't ignoring you on purpose. >.<

[Guild] Bishop Wood: Then, want to clear a dungeon? How about the Liusha River dungeon, since Yearning For and Lu Hang cleared it this afternoon? If you don't come, you'll have to join a PUG party.

Yearning For was online this afternoon?

When he had sent Yearning For a message this morning, the other party replied that he was going to go hiking today. The two of them hadn't talked since.

After some thought, Jing Huan sent him a message on WeChat.

When Xiang Huaizhi came out of the bathroom, Jing Huan was sitting cross-legged on the sofa. His computer was nestled in his lap where he was clattering away on the keyboard.

Jing Huan was a bit paler than other boys, and sitting on a brown sofa, the part of his calves exposed below his pants stood in stark contrast. For some reason, Xiang Huaizhi remembered Sweet Little Jing's thigh photo.

A few seconds later, though, he brushed the image out of his mind. "I'm done, are you going to wash up?"

Staring at the message that had been sent into the void, Jing Huan absentmindedly said, "Mhm. Very soon."

Xiang Huaizhi was unconcerned. He walked over to the front of the bed, picked up his phone, and saw he had a few unread WeChat messages.

Little Jing~: Is gege done hiking?

Little Jing~: Gege, were you clearing dungeons this afternoon?

Xiang Huaizhi's fingers moved. "Mm."

Ding!

The laptop on Jing Huan's lap suddenly sounded with a WeChat notification.

Xiang Huaizhi's eyes flitted over to the source of the sound, then, just as quickly, away. A few seconds later, his phone vibrated in his hand.

Little Jing~: [I'm crying so loudly] Why didn't gege call me over for the dungeons...

Xiang: You weren't on.

Ding!

The second he sent the message, another sound came from the sofa.

Xiang Huaizhi couldn't help glancing over, and he just so happened to see Jing Huan type something and then hit the send key. At the same time, his cellphone vibrated again.

Little Jing~: You could've sent me a WeChat message. QAQ

Xiang: Next time.

Ding!

Xiang Huaizhi paused.

Little Jing~: Okay, is gege going to fight in the arena tonight?

Xiang Huaizhi hesitated for a moment then tentatively typed.

Xiang: No.

 Chapter 08

Ding!

Xiang: Something came up.

Ding!

Xiang: Can't come.

Ding!

Xiang Huaizhi's breath caught in his throat as he heard the keyboard clacking over by the sofa. The second the typing stopped, his phone vibrated again.

Little Jing~: AAAH!! GEGE REPLIED TO ME WITH THREE MESSAGES IN A ROW!!! [Rolling around]

Xiang Huaizhi silently let out the breath he had been holding, then opened up his sticker menu, and sent three at random.

Xiang: [Hugging]

Xiang: [Rose]

Xiang: [Kiss kiss]

Ding! Ding! Ding!

Xiang Huaizhi stilled, then slowly raised his head, his expression extremely conflicted as he looked over at the person sitting on the sofa. He wanted to speak but something held him back.

Jing Huan stared at the three stickers in shock, suspecting that Long Road Ahead was messing with him again. Sensing the gaze from the bed, he looked up and blinked dazedly. "What's up, Senior?"

Xiang Huaizhi frowned, staring at the laptop resting on Jing Huan's lap. It took a long time for him to squeeze out, "... Nothing."

Xiang Huaizhi had an absurd thought, so absurd that he found it funny.

He pursed his lips and turned around so his back was facing the person on the sofa, then opened the WeChat function list, his finger hovering over the voice call icon. Before he could tap on it, he heard that laptop chime again.

Ding! Ding! Ding!

Then, the sound of Jing Huan typing started once more.

Xiang Huaizhi stared at his screen which still had the three stickers on it. He hadn't sent any more messages, and Sweet Little Jing hadn't replied to him either.

There were no words in the world that could describe what Xiang Huaizhi was feeling in that moment. He breathed a sigh of relief and wiped his damp hair with his towel. He must've been crazy to have such a thought.

Lu Wenhao was the one messaging Jing Huan because he wanted to know how to use the washing machine downstairs, even sending him a photo for good measure. After a quick explanation from Jing Huan, Lu Wenhao sent him a thumbs up.

Lu Wenhao: Huanhuan is such a clever wife and virtuous mother, have a kiss. [Red lips]

Lu Wenhao: If you were a woman, this lord would definitely send a lavish sedan chair to marry you.

Little Jing~: Fuck off, how much did you drink to get this drunk?

Little Jing~: Even if I were a woman, I would be way out of your league. Hurry up and wash your clothes.

Only after cursing him out did Jing Huan switch back to his conversation with Yearning For.

Little Jing~: ...QAQ. Are you Long Road Ahead!!

Xiang: Mm, he just grabbed my cellphone from me.

Chapter 08

Little Jing~: I just knew it! So hateful! [Pounding table]

Jing Huan closed the laptop, effectively ending his conversation with Yearning For, and peeked at the person standing by the bed.

Xiang Huaizhi had listened to his suggestion and slipped on a bathrobe. He was currently drying his hair with a towel, his back facing him. From behind, the superiority of his broad shoulders and tall stature was even more obvious.

"Pass me your clothes, Senior. I'll put them in the washing machine with everything else." Rain dashed against the windows relentlessly, and the glass was completely drenched. When Jing Huan tried to peer out, all he could see was a blurry green haze. He said, "Just setting it out to dry won't work. Let's put it in the dryer."

Xiang Huaizhi paused. "No need, I can do it myself."

"It's fine, I have to do it anyway. Let's just wash it all in one load." As Jing Huan pulled out his clothes from the suitcase, a thought occurred to him. "Or are you a germaphobe?"

Xiang Huaizhi shook his head. He was merely embarrassed that not only did he have to stay in someone's room, he also had to ask for their help washing his clothes. After all, they had only met a handful of times and weren't very close.

Jing Huan knew exactly what Xiang Huaizhi was thinking and laughed, his arms full of clothes. "Since you're not a germaphobe, I'll wash everything together."

Jing Huan had been rather careless when he was gathering up all the clothes, so Xiang Huaizhi happened to spot a pair of black underwear dangling on the outside of the pile.

Xiang Huaizhi looked away. "Okay, thank you."

Very soon, the sound of running water came from the bathroom. Xiang Huaizhi perched himself on the edge of the bed, eyes constantly darting over to the sofa as if possessed. The laptop lay there quietly on the sofa, staring back at him.

Xiang Huaizhi broke the staring contest first, shoving those inexplicable thoughts to the back of his mind.

He dried his hair as he sat at the desk, picked up his cellphone, and scrolled through WeChat Moments. He dithered for a while before finally landing on the post Sweet Little Jing had made this morning.

【Little Jing~: The weather is just right. [Picture]】

It was a landscape photo, but before Xiang Huaizhi could take a closer look, the sound of running water from the bathroom stopped. The door opened and out walked the boy.

Jing Huan had changed into a black hoodie and flaxen-colored shorts that ended right above his knees. His legs were straight and pale. Although they were a bit thinner than other boys' legs, they boasted a hint of muscle when he walked.

Xiang Huaizhi's eyes couldn't help shifting upward to Jing Huan's thighs, which were covered so thoroughly by his loose shorts that he couldn't even make out their outline.

Jing Huan felt Xiang Huaizhi's gaze on him as soon as he came out, so he also ducked his head to scrutinize his own legs for a few seconds. "...Is something wrong?"

Xiang Huaizhi snapped out of it and responded calmly, "Your shorts are wet."

"Oh," Jing Huan said. "I accidentally brushed against the sink just now."

Chapter 08

After drying their clothes, they went to the hotel's restaurant where Lu Wenhao and the others had been lounging around for some time now. Having their table by the window meant they could eat while they admired the rain, adding to the atmosphere.

Seeing the two men walk into the restaurant side by side, Lu Wenhao muttered, "See that? The two of them together look like models on a catwalk. Tsk, even the girl pouring water over there is sneaking looks at them. I suspect that the reason why no girl has ever courted me since I started university is because Jing Huan overshadowed my brilliance."

Gao Zixiang didn't even raise his head. "You're overthinking it. Being single is a you problem, it has nothing to do with Huanhuan."

Jing Huan caught the tail end of the conversation just as he approached. He casually plopped down in an empty seat. "What are you saying about me?"

"That you're so very handsome." Lu Wenhao sucked up to him.

Jing Huan smiled and ignored him. Seeing Xiang Huaizhi walk over with a cup of warm milk, he reached over, smoothly pulling out the chair beside him for the other party's convenience.

Xiang Huaizhi, who originally wanted to sit next to Lu Hang, paused and simply sat down in the proffered seat.

"Do you want some milk?" he asked.

Jing Huan was stupefied. "You got this for me?"

This was the last cup of hot milk in the restaurant's buffet. Without saying a word, Xiang Huaizhi placed the cup directly in front of Jing Huan.

Don't mind if I do. Jing Huan picked it up and chugged most of

Guide on How to Fail at Online Dating

it down. His gaze then swept over the black bag at Lu Wenhao's feet, and he asked, "What's that?"

Lu Wenhao snickered. "Treasures."

Jing Huan gingerly opened the bag and peered inside. It turned out to be several bottles of red wine.

He was speechless. "So those two big suitcases were used to just store all this? "

"Yep, I stole them from my family's wine cellar and hid them in my suitcase. I was worried about them breaking during the trip here, so I used a lot of padding."

"You're not afraid of your dad beating you?"

"That'll be a problem for when I get home. Anyway, who cares? Let's enjoy ourselves first, and we'll cross that bridge when we get there," Lu Wenhao said proudly. "I've already booked a karaoke room. We'll go straight there after we're done eating."

Jing Huan thought about it. Since his fixed dungeon party wasn't going to be running tonight, he nodded. "Okay."

Xiang Huaizhi said, "You guys go ahead, I'll pass."

"Come on." Lu Hang swallowed his food. "Let's go together. You didn't bring a computer with you anyway, so what's the point of going back to the room?"

Xiang Huaizhi didn't like singing or those kinds of places. His lips moved, refusal at the tip of his tongue.

"Come on, Senior." Jing Huan quickly glanced sideways at him, chin propped up. "I promise I won't let them force you to drink."

Jing Huan had standard double eyelids with long and thick eyelashes. His eyes seemed to glitter from the light reflected from the hotel's ornate chandelier.

Chapter 08

Xiang Huaizhi met his gaze for a few seconds before getting up. "Fine. I'm going to grab some food."

Jing Huan also stood up. "I'll go with you."

The two of them came and left in the same way: together. Lu Hang stared at their backs and couldn't help but ask, "Are they really that close?"

"Nah, Xiang-ge just helped Huanhuan out that one time on the stairs." Lu Wenhao wasn't interested in the friendship between two men. He leaned closer to Lu Hang. "Lu-ge, hurry up and continue with that story. What happened to that notorious female scammer in your server?"

Jing Huan was true to his word: not a single wine glass was placed in front of Xiang Huaizhi.

Random music played in the background, the volume turned very low. Xiang Huaizhi sat casually on the sofa, watching the person next to him play the finger-guessing game[7] with Lu Hang.

It seemed that Jing Huan frequented bars quite often; he knew all the tricks of finger-guessing games, and regardless of which one Lu Hang switched to, Jing Huan could keep up.

Xiang Huaizhi had thought that Jing Huan was a very well-behaved guy. *Looks are truly deceiving.*

However, Jing Huan's extensive knowledge base didn't translate

---

7   A drinking game where two people simultaneously stretch out their fingers and shout out a numerical guess (e.g., 1-20). If there is a correct guess, the loser takes a drink. The winner is the one who correctly predicts either the total sum of both players' fingers or their opponent's displayed number, depending on regional group rules.

into skill, having already lost three rounds in a row to Lu Hang.

"Fuck." Despite losing another round, he was all smiles as he cursed, pouring himself another glass of wine.

Lu Hang had also drunk a lot. "Can you handle it, Underclassman? If not, I'll have the person next to you drink a glass on your behalf."

His mouth claimed he was concerned, but his hands were not idle: he helped Jing Huan overturn the wine bottle, making sure his glass was filled to the brim.

"Me?" Lu Wenhao asked. "No problem, Huanhuan, this ge will drink this glass for you."

"No, not you." Lu Hang stopped him and pointed to Xiang Huaizhi with his chin. "I meant the one on his right."

Xiang Huaizhi raised his eyebrows, shooting a glare at Lu Hang, warning him to not go too far. He then shifted, intending to get up and drink for Jing Huan, but the latter beat him to it, raising his glass and downing it all in one go. He wiped his mouth and said, "Done. Let's keep going."

Jing Huan started going to bars at the beginning of his freshman year. Lu Wenhao taught him nothing good and showed him only the bad; there were several times that Jing Huan went to sleep in a hotel instead of his dorm because Lu Wenhao dragged him out to the bar where he would drink until near collapse.

However, drinking certainly helped them decompress, and as long as they didn't do it too often, it would be fine. This was actually the first time since the start of their sophomore year that they drank together.

Half an hour later, Jing Huan's cheeks were a little flushed.

"I'm taking a break." He plopped down onto the sofa, bumping into Xiang Huaizhi's shoulder. "Ah, bumped into you again, why do I keep bumping into you?" Jing Huan turned his head. They were now very close to each other. "Senior, you don't sing?"

The combined smell of wine and his shower gel wafted into Xiang Huaizhi's nose.

"No. Don't drink anymore, your face is already red."

Jing Huan patted his cheeks. "It's kinda hot, but it's okay; my alcohol tolerance's pretty good." No sooner had he finished saying that the background music suddenly crescendoed, followed by a familiar, imposing prelude.

Lu Wenhao sat in front of the karaoke machine and shouted, "Huanhuan! Your song is up!"

Jing Huan took a look at the display screen: "Loyalty to the Country."

He sneered. "Lu Wenhao, do you want to get beaten up?"

"Hurry up, hurry up." Gao Zixiang handed over the microphone. "Last time, I said that you sang better than that woman, but that dumbass Lu Wenhao didn't believe it. You have to sing today and convince him once and for all!"

Usually, when he went to karaoke with them, they picked some goofy songs. Jing Huan fired off a few curses at him, but he ultimately took the mic and started singing along with the music. Two lines later, he lumbered over to Lu Wenhao and nudged him with his leg, indicating that he wanted to pick a song himself.

Taking advantage of Jing Huan's absence, Lu Hang jumped to Xiang Huaizhi's side.

"What the fuck, it's this song again. Why is this song everywhere

I go lately?" Lu Hang said. "Although Huanhuan sings it quite well, I have to say I still prefer Little Jingjing's version."

When he didn't get a response, he looked up, puzzled. "Old Xiang?"

Xiang Huaizhi's eyebrows were furrowed, various emotions swirling in his eyes, his gaze locked on Jing Huan. He did not utter a single word.

After singing for a while, Lu Wenhao gathered them all together to play dice.

Xiang Huaizhi discovered that this underclassman was not only horrible at finger-guessing games, he was also bad at dice. With such lousy dice rolls, where did he get the confidence to fight head-to-head with other people?

Sure enough, after losing several rounds, Jing Huan couldn't take it anymore. They were drinking both red wine and beer, and he drank the most. By the end of the game, he was dizzy, his hands trembling when he picked up the glass.

Lu Hang also noticed. "Forget it, Huanhuan, I won't make you drink this time."

He didn't even get to finish his sentence because Jing Huan had already finished his glass. He waved dismissively. "It's okay… I'm okay. I'm going to the restroom, you guys can keep playing. I'll rejoin you when I come back."

Using the table to support himself, he staggered to his feet, but because he wasn't stable, he nearly fell onto Xiang Huaizhi.

"I'll go with you," Xiang Huaizhi said.

"N-no need." Jing Huan stepped on Xiang Huaizhi's shoes on his way out, muttering, "I can do it myself…"

 Chapter 08

Xiang Huaizhi stood up to help him, but Jing Huan's hand shot out and pressed his shoulder down. He stepped on his shoes again. "Senior! You really don't need to come!"

Xiang Huaizhi wasn't sure how to react. Watching Jing Huan drunkenly stumble out, he debated whether to go with him when he heard Lu Wenhao say, "It's okay. Drunk Huanhuan is almost the same as normal Huanhuan. He doesn't cause trouble and even knows his way back. The last time he got drunk, he was able to walk back from the hotel to the school all by himself, and didn't even go crazy on the way. Isn't that awesome?"

Xiang Huaizhi *really* didn't know how to respond to that bit of information. *That's a pretty formidable talent.*

Ten minutes later, Lu Wenhao scratched his head. "Oh crap, why hasn't Huanhuan come back yet?"

Lu Hang asked offhandedly, "Could he be trying to walk back to school from the resort?"

The room instantly fell silent.

Xiang Huaizhi got up. "I'll go check."

The karaoke rooms were operated by the resort itself and could only be booked through room reservations, so it wasn't a shady place. The hallway decor was exquisite and luxurious, making it look like a high-end hotel.

Xiang Huaizhi asked a staff member for directions and hurried to the restroom, already planning where to look next if no one was there.

As it turned out, he didn't need to go running around at all. The boy was lying on the sofa outside the restroom with his eyes closed, his shoulders rising and falling gently with each breath.

Xiang Huaizhi strolled up to his side and wordlessly slung one of Jing Huan's arms over his shoulder and then wrapped his hand around Jing Huan's waist, pulling him up to stand.

Jing Huan seemed to notice his movements. He slumped completely against Xiang Huaizhi, a frown on his face. "I can walk by myself."

Hearing that, Xiang Huaizhi loosened his grip, and Jing Huan collapsed on the sofa again, his head tipped slightly forward.

Bemused, Xiang Huaizhi glanced down at the person leaning against his thigh. "Didn't you say you could walk?"

Jing Huan silently rubbed against his leg. It took Xiang Huaizhi ten full seconds to realize Jing Huan was using his leg as a pillow. He silently bent over and once again propped him up.

Lu Wenhao hadn't lied—Jing Huan didn't make much of a ruckus when he was drunk. Xiang Huaizhi smoothly helped him over to the elevator, freeing one hand to call Lu Hang. "I'll take him back to the room first."

Lu Hang said, "All right. We're also going to head back soon. Nothing happened, right?"

"No." Xiang Huaizhi lowered his head to look down at Jing Huan and said, "He's just drunk."

The elevator arrived right after he finished the call. Xiang Huaizhi walked in and pressed the twentieth floor.

"Who were you talking to?" the man leaning on his shoulder suddenly murmured. In a sugary sweet voice, he called out to him, "Gege."

The quiet sound of the elevator door closing muffled Jing Huan's words. Xiang Huaizhi didn't hear him clearly, and he asked, frowning, "What?"

The effects of the alcohol were getting stronger and stronger, and Jing Huan was already feeling a bit lightheaded. He closed his eyes; only Yearning For's voice remained in his mind.

"Next time you have to wait for me, gege," Jing Huan said.

Xiang Huaizhi heard him clearly this time.

Jing Huan was calling him "gege." The boy had deliberately lowered his voice, making it sound especially soft.

Xiang Huaizhi took a deep breath and he asked again, "What did you call me?"

Jing Huan frowned, a little impatient, but he very obediently called him again, "Gege."

Having been stuck with Sweet Little Jing for so long, Xiang Huaizhi was well aware that there was a big difference between calling someone "ge" and calling them "gege."

"Why are you calling me that?"

Confused, Jing Huan asked, "I... Haven't I always called you that?" He let out a small drunken hiccup.

No. Jing Huan has never called him "gege" before.

Xiang Huaizhi frowned. "You told me to wait for you just now?"

Jing Huan weakly bobbed his head twice, before realizing that Yearning For wouldn't be able to see him nodding, and he spoke up. In a low voice, he grumbled, "If you don't bring me along to clear dungeons, I'll have to play with PUG parties.... I...I don't like PUG parties, and I also don't want to run dungeons with Bishop Wood's party either."

Xiang Huaizhi was struck silent for a while and could only dumbly repeat, "...Bishop Wood?"

 Chapter 08

"He already told me," Jing Huan said. "You...went to do the Havoc in Heaven dungeon this afternoon and you didn't call me."

Xiang Huaizhi slowly lowered his head and gazed down at the person resting his head on his shoulder. He had just received an overload of information, and in a rare moment, he found himself reeling.

"Jing..." Xiang Huaizhi wanted to call his name, but ultimately, he restrained himself. "Who am I?"

"Huh?" Jing Huan mumbled.

"Who am I?"

"You..." As drunk as Jing Huan was, he didn't forget to flatter Yearning For. "You are electricity, you are light, you are my superstar[8]."

Xiang Huaizhi felt that he didn't need to ask anymore, but deep down, he thought it was impossible. "I meant, what's my name?"

What the hell is this scumbag up to now? My head is about to split apart. Can he not ask such childish and nonsensical questions?!

Jing Huan drawled, "You're my No. 1. You are..." Then he dealt a heavy blow to Xiang Huaizhi. "You're Yearning For... You're gege."

The elevator door opened, then closed, then opened again, but the people inside still did not come out.

The guest staying in room 2012 stepped out of her room, and noticing the elevator doors opening, quickened her pace to enter—only to be startled by the two people standing inside.

She saw a tall guy staring down in confusion at the person leaning against him, his face full of bewilderment. Meanwhile, the other guy had already fallen asleep without a care in the world.

---

8   Jing Huan is quoting the 2003 S.H.E. hit song "Super Star."

Guide on How to Fail at Online Dating

The two men's handsome visages weren't enough to distract her from the frightening situation. Just before she walked over, she caught a glimpse of a warm light coming from the elevator. At first, she thought her eyes were playing tricks on her, but in retrospect, it was probably just the elevator light spilling out when the door opened.

The woman stood frozen outside the door, too scared to enter or even speak. She was careful with her breathing, unaware that one of the men inside was just as terrified as she was.

Xiang Huaizhi came to his senses and adjusted his grip, steadying the person slumped against him. He walked out of the elevator without a word. When they reached their door, Xiang Huaizhi whispered, "Where's the room card?"

The person leaning on him didn't so much as twitch. Xiang Huaizhi sighed. He bent down, found the room card in Jing Huan's pocket, and swiped it to open the door.

As soon as he entered the room, Jing Huan opened his eyes. He was parched and hot all over from the alcohol. Taking advantage of Xiang Huaizhi's preoccupation with closing the door, he sagged to the side and went into the bathroom.

Xiang Huaizhi grabbed him. "What are you doing?"

"Don't feel good." Jing Huan felt extremely miserable. "Want to drink water and wash my face…"

Xiang Huaizhi's mind was in turmoil right now, so he let him go—only to watch Jing Huan completely bypass the sink and head straight for the shower. By the time Xiang Huaizhi rushed in, it was already too late. Water gushed out from the shower head, soaking and darkening half of Jing Huan's pants.

Xiang Huaizhi stood frozen, at a loss for words in such a scene.

047

Chapter 08

After that bout of chaos settled, Xiang Huaizhi carried Jing Huan out of the bathroom and tossed him onto the bed.

Jing Huan groaned a few times, feeling uncomfortable with his pants glued to his body, and began to wriggle left and right.

Xiang Huaizhi was using a paper towel to wipe off all the water that had sprayed onto him, his face grim, when he suddenly heard the crisp sound of a zipper behind him.

He froze, then turned around to see Jing Huan swiftly kicking his pants off. He kicked them under the bed and then proceeded to tug the quilt over to cover himself. Afterward, he was still.

While Jing Huan slept soundly, Xiang Huaizhi was left with a whirlwind of thoughts he couldn't make sense of.

The facts were right in front of him, but Xiang Huaizhi still... He still couldn't believe it.

How could the girl who clung to him every day, who confessed her feelings in-game, suddenly turn into this drunk-as-a-skunk boy in front of him?

Forget everything else; the gender alone didn't match!

Xiang Huaizhi's gaze unconsciously swept to the quilt wrapped around Jing Huan. His Adam's apple moved slightly, and an idea came to him.

No. It was inappropriate.

If the genders were swapped, the person lying on the bed could accuse him of sexual harassment or being a peeping Tom.

All of those thoughts rushed through Xiang Huaizhi's mind, but his hand was already on the quilt. He gently pulled up a corner and, like a pervert, peeked underneath—

Beneath the quilt, Jing Huan's long pale legs were splayed

haphazardly. His legs had very little hair, and there wasn't a single blemish on his thighs. Yet from the lines of his legs, Xiang Huaizhi was still able to tell these legs belonged to a man. In short, they weren't as slender as the ones he had seen in the photo. But this did little to bring relief to Xiang Huaizhi.

Because on the outside of Jing Huan's thigh, Xiang Huaizhi saw a teeny, tiny mole.

He stared fixedly at the mole for a long time, until Jing Huan started to feel cold and flopped around twice.

Ding.

Xiang Huaizhi heard the laptop on the sofa gently chime. Jing Huan hadn't turned off his laptop.

At this point, Xiang Huaizhi could care less about respecting anyone's privacy. He went to the sofa and opened the laptop.

Not only was the laptop on, there were also programs still running on it, one of which was a client called *Nine Heroes*.

Xiang Huaizhi maximized the game and was immediately greeted by the little spirit fox who had been pestering him this entire time. Her tail casually fanned across the ground, she was sitting gracefully in Penglai beside the green trees and red flowers where Xiang Huaizhi most commonly AFKed.

At this point, Xiang Huaizhi had no choice but to admit it: Jing Huan was Sweet Little Jing. Now that he thought about it, even the name matched.

But just as Xiang Huaizhi solved one problem, another immediately sprung up.

Why is Jing Huan pretending to be a girl in front of me? And even flirting with me? Does Jing Huan know that I'm Yearning For? After

all, our voices are so similar... Or did Jing Huan know it was my character from the beginning and deliberately used a female character to find me?

Xiang Huaizhi had always kept his gaming life firmly separated from his real life. For the past few years, no one except Lu Hang knew his game ID. He got up and picked up his cellphone, going into the bathroom to call Lu Hang.

His call was quickly picked up. There was no background noise which meant Lu Hang should be back in his room.

"What's up?" Lu Hang had drunk a lot, his head currently spinning.

Xiang Huaizhi lowered his voice. "Have you ever told anyone my game ID?"

Lu Hang was taken aback. "No, you said you didn't like mixing games with real life. What's wrong?"

"Nothing." Xiang Huaizhi mentally ruled out the second possibility. "I'm going to sleep now."

"Hey, wait a minute—"

Before Lu Hang could finish speaking, Xiang Huaizhi had already hung up.

He walked out of the bathroom. The man on the bed hadn't moved from his position, breathing steadily without even a snore.

A calm suddenly settled over Xiang Huaizhi.

What was there for him to worry about when this little liar was sleeping so soundly? Besides, it wasn't like Xiang Huaizhi could wake him up to clear up the situation. Moreover, if the one Jing Huan liked was actually in-game Yearning For... Then, did that mean Jing Huan liked men?

The more he thought about it, the more his thoughts wandered. Xiang Huaizhi curbed his train of thought, hesitated for a bit, then put the laptop back in its original place.

Chapter 09

Chapter 09

Jing Huan woke up to a dull throbbing pain in his head.

He had a habit of being in a daze for a while before getting up, and today was no different. He lay on his side, staring at the bedside lamp, feeling extremely annoyed for no other reason than that he had been plagued with dreams all night.

The worst part was that the subject of his dreams was Yearning For. The scumbag constantly pestered Jing Huan in his dreams to call him "gege." There really wasn't much difference between him and a pervert.

He didn't know how much time had passed when he realized there was another person in the room.

Afraid of waking them, Jing Huan carefully and slowly turned his head, only to unexpectedly meet the open gaze of the person behind him.

Xiang Huaizhi was lying on his side with his chin propped in his hand, quietly looking at Jing Huan for who knows how long since he had been up. Jing Huan didn't know if it was just his imagination, but there seemed to be a storm of emotions churning in Xiang Huaizhi's eyes.

Jing Huan also noticed that there was a military demarcation line between them. The extra space between them was enough to fit Lu Wenhao.

"Um…" Jing Huan deliberated then asked, "Last night… Did I go crazy drunk?"

"No."

"Then did I sleepwalk? Sleep talk? Grind my teeth?"

"No."

Then why are you so far away from me?

The question seemed a little strange to ask though, so after a moment's thought, Jing Huan opted not to. He sat up, ruffled his hair, and said, "I'm sorry, Senior. I think I drank a bit too much last night."

He had never been good at judging his own alcohol tolerance. Now that he thought about it, he couldn't even remember when he got drunk.

Xiang Huaizhi's expression was complex. "Did you…forget what you said yesterday?"

Jing Huan tried to remember. "What did I say?"

Xiang Huaizhi's Adam's apple bobbed a few times before he finally said, "Nothing."

Jing Huan glanced at his cellphone, and noticed it was already almost time to check out. Lu Wenhao had left him a message saying that they wanted to soak in the hot springs one more time before leaving.

He lifted the quilt and felt a sudden chill. He realized that, apart from a pair of underpants, he was naked.

He rolled over, got out of bed, and picked up his pants, using

Chapter 09

them to halfheartedly cover himself. Turning unconcernedly around, he said, "Senior, I'm going to use the bathroom first, okay?"

"Mm," Xiang Huaizhi murmured.

Looking at Jing Huan saunter nonchalantly into the bathroom with his bare legs, Xiang Huaizhi couldn't help but wonder, *Are all gay people so open now? I thought they'd feel shy in front of someone of the same sex.*

Jing Huan felt alive again after his shower. While packing his luggage, he called out, "Senior, they're soaking in the hot springs now. Do you want to take a dip too? It's pretty nice."

"No." Xiang Huaizhi was on the sofa replying to messages, looking casual and indifferent. He asked, "I remember them saying that you played *Nine Heroes* before?"

Jing Huan nodded. "Yeah, for about five to six years."

"Why did you stop playing?" Xiang Huaizhi asked.

"My family was strict," Jing Huan said lightly. "My mom said that if I kept playing, the only career I'd have after high school was a garbageman. She said she didn't want to become the mother of a garbage king, so she cut off my internet."

Recalling Sweet Little Jing's miserable life story, Xiang Huaizhi paused and decided not to delve further into the topic of quitting the game. "Have you thought about coming back to the game again now that you have time?"

"Yeah, but maybe not for a while." Jing Huan hesitated before jerking his head up to ask, "Senior, which *Nine Heroes* server are you in?"

Don't you know the answer to that better than anyone else?

Xiang Huaizhi replied, "Full Moon Blossom."

Jing Huan grinned. "*Nine Heroes'* developers are really tacky; these server names either have flowers or moons."

The boy's expression was very relaxed, showing no surprise nor suspicion over Xiang Huaizhi giving the wrong server name.

Xiang Huaizhi nodded and agreed, "Yes, it's quite tacky."

After packing their bags, they went downstairs to check out, and it was there that Jing Huan remembered something and took out his cellphone from his pocket.

"Let's add each other on WeChat, Senior," Jing Huan said with a smile. "We can play ball together in the future."

Xiang Huaizhi hesitated for a beat before taking out his cellphone. Jing Huan quickly opened his QR Code. "You scan me?"

Staring at the familiar pink profile picture, Xiang Huaizhi expressionlessly opened his alt WeChat account and added him.

The rain had already ceased. After the heavy downpour, even the air seemed fresher. Lu Wenhao and the others had already checked out and were waiting for them in the lobby.

"See, Huanhuan? Didn't I say you couldn't outdrink me?" Lu Wenhao snickered.

Jing Huan scoffed. "What are you acting so proud for? We'll battle it out again next time."

Once Jing Huan and Xiang Huaizhi had checked out, Lu Hang said, "Thanks guys for taking us in last night. When we get back, this senior will treat you to something delicious."

"No problem." Gao Zixiang clapped his shoulder. "Alcohol is a must though!"

Lu Hang winked. "It's a deal."

Chapter 09

They walked to the parking lot together. Lu Hang headed over to a Land Rover and slipped inside. Car started, he rolled down the window. "How did you guys get here? Do you need me to take you back?"

"Nope, no need." Lu Wenhao shook his head. "We also drove here."

"All right then." Lu Hang waved to them. "We're off. See ya later."

Xiang Huaizhi remained silent the entire time, only raising his hand at the people outside the window when they were about to leave, which could count as a farewell of sorts.

Lu Wenhao ogled the back of Lu Wenhao's car as it drove out of the parking lot, sighing with a shake of his head. "That dude's car is a Land Rover, while mine is just a Volkswagen."

"Be content with that. Neither Huanhuan nor I have a car," Gao Zixiang said.

Lu Wenhao retorted, "That's only because you two are lazy, always making me the chauffeur."

Chattering and laughing, the three of them got in the car and began making their way back to school. During the drive, Gao Zixiang turned to the person in the back seat, a thought having suddenly hit him. "Huanhuan, did you go crazy last night because of the alcohol?"

Jing Huan covered his mouth and yawned. "I don't think so?"

"Then why did Xiang Huaizhi look exhausted? He even had dark circles under his eyes."

"I noticed that too." Lu Wenhao's eyes flicked over to Jing Huan from the rearview mirror. "But you… You're brimming with energy.

When the two of you came down to the lobby, I even questioned my memory of last night. Be honest, did you secretly suck out all of Xiang Huaizhi's essence yesterday?"

"Fuck off." Jing Huan laughed and scolded, "Your daddy here doesn't 'suck out' people's essence, he just kills them."

Meanwhile, Xiang Huaizhi was sitting in the front passenger seat with his eyes closed, pretending to nap.

"What's wrong with you?" Lu Hang noticed his fatigue. "Didn't sleep well last night?"

Forget sleeping well, I barely slept at all. An air of early morning weariness enshrouded Xiang Huaizhi, and he said lightly, "Mm."

Not daring to bother him, Lu Hang said nothing more.

The cellphone in his pocket vibrated. Xiang Huaizhi frowned and slowly opened his eyes.

Little Jing~: Good~ morning~ gege~

Little Jing~: I super love gege today as well! *^0^*/

Xiang: ...

By the time Jing Huan got home, it was already afternoon. After putting the carbonated drinks and fruit he had bought on the way home into the refrigerator, he went to turn on his computer.

The last couple of days had been spent with Lu Wenhao and Gao Zixiang, so he hadn't cleared any of this week's dungeons. He opened his friend list and saw that Yearning For and Long Road Ahead were both offline. Instead of idling around like a slug, he might as well join a PUG party to make up for the dungeons he missed earlier.

He clicked on the dungeon interface, randomly applied to a few

Chapter 09

parties, and within seconds, the system prompt popped up saying a party had accepted him. He ran to the dungeon entrance and waited for his party members.

【Bishop Wood has invited you to join his party. Yes, No.】

Jing Huan instinctively clicked "No," however, after the pop-up disappeared, he realized that Bishop Wood was standing right next to him.

[Current] Sweet Little Jing: [Question]

[Current] Bishop Wood: Let's clear the dungeon~

Surprised, Jing Huan opened the dungeon participant list and, sure enough, there was Bishop Wood. Jing Huan had done a cursory scan when applying for parties earlier, and only now realized that everyone in this dungeon was from their guild, with BrbOrNot as the dungeon initiator.

Bishop Wood sent him another party invite. Reluctantly, Jing Huan slowly clicked to accept, finally joined Bishop Wood's party.

[Party] Sweet Little Jing: Didn't you clear this dungeon yesterday? O.O

"You didn't come so I didn't do it," Bishop Wood said. "Can you talk right now?"

He could, but Jing Huan didn't feel like wearing his headset at the moment. He'd had them on for several hours a day for the past few days, and his ears were sore.

[Party] Sweet Little Jing: Nope, there are people around so it's not convenient.

Bishop Wood understood. "It's okay, you can just type then."

Bishop Wood's voice was actually rather pleasant—deep and magnetic in a way that would be attractive to girls. Unfortunately for him, Jing Huan was a guy and didn't fall for it. He even found Bishop Wood noisy and callously turned down his computer volume.

Havoc in Heaven was a low-difficulty dungeon. It was simple, easy to clear, and didn't award much experience. Jing Huan was planning on going AFK once he entered; it would probably take about half an hour at most.

Bishop Wood obviously had a different plan in mind. As soon as they went in the dungeon, Bishop Wood bombarded him with messages. "Little Jingjing, what are you going to do after clearing this dungeon?"

[Party] Sweet Little Jing: …Go AFK, I guess.

"You spent tens of thousands of yuan to buy this character just to go AFK?" Bishop Wood laughed. "I'll take you out to have some fun once we clear this."

[Party] Sweet Little Jing: What sort of fun?

"Some sightseeing, do some quests, dungeons, whatever you want," Bishop Wood said. "Or I can take you to open some Fate Stones?"

Fate Stones were special items in *Nine Heroes*. Each stone cost twenty yuan and, similar to a lottery, contained all sorts of things—both good and bad, but mostly bad. Many players bought hundreds of them for the thrill of it and to indulge themselves only to end up losing all their money.

Jing Huan had already played with them before and swore that he'd never again touch Fate Stones in this life.

[Party] Sweet Little Jing: [Shaking head] No!

"Why?" Bishop Wood asked. "I'll buy a hundred for you to play with, and you can get a quick buzz."

 Chapter 09

[Party] BrbOrNot: [Thumbs up]

[Party] Peach Cheese Stan: [Thumbs up] So generous.

[Party] Sweet Little Jing: >.< I really don't want to. I don't like playing with Fate Stones, it's just handing money over to the devs.

Bishop Wood hesitated. "Then…"

[Party] Sweet Little Jing: Ah! Some stuff just came up, can I go AFK for a bit?

[Party] BrbOrNot: That's fine, go ahead.

BrbOrNot had barely hit "send" on this message before he saw three words hanging over Sweet Little Jing's head: AFK. Bishop Wood was left with his mouth hanging.

As soon as he returned to his dorm, Xiang Huaizhi slept for a full six hours. When he woke up, it was already dark. He picked up his cellphone to check the time and happened to see a WeChat notification.

Little Jing~: Senior, let's play ball next time.

It shocked Xiang Huaizhi at first but then he remembered he had logged into his alt account on the way back and changed the personal info to match his main account.

His main account had been hacked before, and it had taken him a long time to recover it. During that period, he had created this account, and solely used it to contact his professors and family. After he got his main account back, he never went back to the alt account.

Xiang Huaizhi replied with an "okay," before switching back to his main account. His cellphone vibrated gently, and the same WeChat profile picture appeared at the top of his messages.

Little Jing~: Gege! You're under arrest!

The message was from four hours ago.

Xiang: ?

The name at the top of his screen immediately switched to "Typing..."

Little Jing~: Your crime is being a heart~ stealing~ thief~

Little Jing~: o (///v///) o

Xiang: ...

Little Jing~: Gege replied to me so late. T.T

Little Jing~: Gege must've met a new meimei in the mountains. :(

Xiang: Just woke up.

Little Jing~: [Pig head] So lazy!

...And whose fault is that?

Thinking of his utterly abysmal sleep quality last night, Xiang Huaizhi couldn't help massaging his temples.

If it wasn't for all the irrefutable evidence, he almost wouldn't believe that Jing Huan was the one typing all these words. This underclassman's personality wasn't bad, but he really couldn't be described as "soft and cute"—except when drunk.

Little Jing~: Is gege fighting in the arena today, or do you want to keep sleeping? [Wiggling feet]

Xiang: Do you want to go fight?

Little Jing~: I'm fine either way! If gege doesn't come, I'll just do some 1V1.

Xiang: Got it, wait for me.

Xiang Huaizhi got out of bed to wash up. Lu Hang turned to watch him while his hands flew across his keyboard. "Awake now,

huh? You can really sleep. If I didn't know any better, I would've thought that you pulled an all-nighter."

Xiang Huaizhi glanced briefly at his computer screen and asked, "Have you started the God of War quest?"

The process of creating a divine artifact was to gather materials, complete the actual God of War quest, and then challenge the God of War. The quest itself had ninety-nine steps in total, all of which had to be completed within a week. It was considerably difficult.

"Yeah, a big merchant just came by and sold me a lot of materials, so I finally have them all now," Lu Hang was elated. "Quick, how should we set up the party? What sects do we need? Name them and I'll find the people."

"The four of us," Xiang Huaizhi casually said, "plus a Warlock or a Mage. Just pick a random one."

Lu Hang nodded. "All right, I won't be clearing dungeons with you guys for the next few days. I need to focus on running through these quests first."

After he finished washing up, Xiang Huaizhi turned on his computer and saw the little spirit fox standing beside him as usual. This time she was dancing.

Xiang Huaizhi set up a party, tentatively invited him, and a few seconds later, the little spirit fox joined the party.

"Gegeee," the familiar voice in his earphones greeted him gently and cutely, "good evening."

Xiang Huaizhi was very curious—how did he make his voice sound like that? Did *Nine Heroes* also have a voice changer?

No, that couldn't be. Jing Huan had sent him a voice message on WeChat before.

Xiang Huaizhi logged into his WeChat, dug out the voice message, and listened to it again.

"Gege, I just went to soak in the hot springs. Remember to eat dinner on time! Mwah!"

The voice sounded identical to the one he heard on the computer, albeit a bit more muffled. Immediately, Xiang Huaizhi understood what this meant.

Lu Hang had gone to the closet to grab his clothes, walking in on the current scene. His eyes narrowed, his expression suggesting he seemed to be harboring some complicated feelings. "…Xiangxiang, I didn't expect you to be this kind of person. Is the kiss *that* nice to listen to?"

Xiang Huaizhi had only one earphone in. He exited WeChat. "It's not what you think."

"Oh, I know, I totally understand," Lu Hang said. "I wouldn't be able to take it either if someone acted that flirty with me every day. We're all men here, I get you."

Xiang Huaizhi gave up on explaining to him. "Get lost."

Jing Huan hadn't gotten a response. After confirming that his microphone was working, he called out again, "Gege?"

[Party] Yearning For: Here.

Jing Huan asked, "Gege can't talk?"

[Party] Yearning For: Mm, my roommate is here.

"Okay." Jing Huan's little spirit fox twirled around him. "The arena doesn't open for another two hours, did gege do all his dailies today?"

Xiang Huaizhi had slept all day, so naturally, he hadn't done them.

"Then you can take me to do them," Jing Huan said, "okay?"

Xiang Huaizhi didn't answer and merely took him to do the quests instead. On the way to the NPC, he couldn't help but shoot furtive looks at the little spirit fox behind him. After a period of careful observation, he confirmed two things:

First, his underclassman had no idea he was Yearning For. Second, his underclassman liked men.

Although Xiang Huaizhi wasn't gay, he respected other people's sexuality. Maybe Jing Huan didn't want to come out in real life hence why he projected his feelings onto a game character who was more in line with his fantasy. And, for better or worse, the game character happened to be Xiang Huaizhi's.

Xiang Huaizhi hesitated for a moment, then began typing.

[Party] Yearning For: Sweet Little Jing.

Jing Huan was in the middle of playing a single-player fighting game. He had just knocked a muscular man to the ground and was about to KO him when his eyes caught on the chat message and immediately switched back to *Nine Heroes*. "What's up, gege?"

[Party] Yearning For: What do you like about me?

The question came out of nowhere, leaving Jing Huan stunned, unable to react to that question.

Damn, is he going to say "I'll change" next?!

Jing Huan deliberated for a long time. Yearning For was also very patient, not pressuring him for an answer.

"I like..." Jing Huan said haltingly, "I like the way you talk. I like listening to your voice, I like your game character, I like skilled gameplay, I like..." *Did I miss anything?* Jing Huan licked his lips. "I super, really like everything about gege!"

Perfect! Utterly flawless!

Xiang Huaizhi choked. He shouldn't have asked.

When he didn't get a response from Yearning For, Jing Huan thought he was dissatisfied with his answer. "Every word that gege types…"

[Party] Yearning For: …

[Party] Yearning For: I get it. Don't say anymore.

Jing Huan sighed.

Too hard. Chasing someone is just too difficult. Especially when it's a narcissist who makes you list out all their good qualities.

After finishing their dailies, there was still an hour left before the arena opened, so Xiang Huaizhi called over Love is Sharing Noms and picked up some randoms to clear a dungeon first.

Love is Sharing Noms began chatting with Sweet Little Jing as soon as she joined the party.

[Party] Love is Sharing Noms: Jingjing, were the hot springs really niiice?!

[Party] Sweet Little Jing: So niiiiice~ [Rubbing belly]

[Party] Love is Sharing Noms: Who did you go with? Any flings?

[Party] Sweet Little Jing: Some friends and a senior.

[Party] Love is Sharing Noms: !! A SENIOR!!

[Party] Love is Sharing Noms: Is he hot?!

[Party] Sweet Little Jing: Hot!

[Party] Love is Sharing Noms: Daaamn, did you make any headway with him? Add him on WeChat? Did you wear a bikini?

[Party] Sweet Little Jing: …

Seeing this series of ellipses, an image of the other boy's embar-

 Chapter 09

rassed expression rose up in Xiang Huaizhi's mind, and the corners of his mouth unconsciously lifted. *Where would he get a bikini?*

[Party] Sweet Little Jing: No, no, no!

[Party] Sweet Little Jing: Actually, he's not that hot. Compared to gege, he's just dirt on the ground!!

Xiang Huaizhi took a long and deep breath.

[Party] Sweet Little Jing: Besides, how could I add other men's WeChat?! I'm very faithful, okay! I already have someone I like! Right here!! →→→

The senior who had, not too long ago, added him on WeChat stood frozen on Jing Huan's right.

[Party] Sweet Little Jing: And don't even think about bikinis! I'm not that open-minded! My legs are for gege's eyes only!! >.<

Sure, in a sense, this sentence is true, Xiang Huaizhi thought expressionlessly.

Love is Sharing Noms was already used to Sweet Little Jing's way of talking and sent several laughing stickers.

This was the random PUG party members' first time seeing a girl who could say such outrageous, flattering things with a straight face. They merely silently AFKed, lurking but not daring to speak.

[Party] Love is Sharing Noms: Ha ha ha, okay, I understand. By the way, did you open any Fate Stones today? Get anything good?

Jing Huan was stunned.

[Party] Sweet Little Jing: I didn't open any Fate Stones.

[Party] Love is Sharing Noms: Huh? Didn't Bishop Wood say he would give you 100 of them?

[Party] Sweet Little Jing: O.O How did you know...? I didn't take them. Too expensive, and I never get anything good out of them. [Almost crying]

[Party] Love is Sharing Noms: I saw it in the guild WeChat group chat, lol.

[Party] Sweet Little Jing: Guild group chat??

[Party] Love is Sharing Noms: Mhm, I think BrbOrNot mentioned it in the afternoon.

Jing Huan understood. Gossip king BrbOrNot must have spilled the beans about their conversation during the dungeon run.

He didn't really care. He was just about to heal Yearning For and buff his damage when he saw three words, "AFK," hanging above Yearning For's head.

With his target away, there was no need to continue buttering him up. Jing Huan crossed his legs, took a sip of coffee from the mug beside him, and switched back to beating NPCs in *King of Fighters*.

On the other side, Xiang Huaizhi picked up his cellphone. It had been a long time since he had opened the guild WeChat group; the number of notifications had already soared to 99+ unread messages.

After scrolling upward for a while, he found the part of the chat Love is Sharing Noms was talking about.

BrbOrNot: Goddamn, the guild officer is so generous. He heedlessly opened his mouth and offered to give Sweet Little Jing 100 Fate Stones!!

BrbOrNot: Will anyone gift me Fate Stones? If I get something good, it's yours. I just want to experience the excitement of opening them. My luck might be a bit better than Sweet Little Jing's, so I don't need 100; even ten would be enough. :)

 Chapter 09

Thousand Lights: The guild officer is wooing Sweet Little Jing. Who is pursuing you? [Doubtful]

Is Gege Big: So, um, out of curiosity, which guild officer are you talking about?

After their successful cooperation on the guild dungeon's first clear, Echoes of Spring had given Yearning For the Black Tortoise guild officer position in order to keep his party in the guild.

As soon as this question was raised, the guild group chat was silent for several minutes.

Bishop Wood: It's me, ha ha, but sadly she refused them. Does BON wanna play? I'll give you ten.

BrbOrNot: OMG, are you for real?

Bishop Wood: Yep, just don't mention this in the group chat again. I'm afraid it'll embarrass her. Look, she's not even talking now. [Taping mouth shut]

BrbOrNot: Deal! I'm in the main city, Guild Officer. [Shy]

Peach Cheese Stan: The guild officer thinks you talk too much, BON!

BrbOrNot: NP, as long as you give me Fate Stones, you can say whatever you want about me. [Shy]

BrbOrNot: Got the Fate Stones! Wishing Guild Officer and Sweet Little Jing a long and happy life together! Have a son soon! Be happy every day!

Xiang Huaizhi closed WeChat.

He had been in this server for a long time. Although he wasn't one to gossip, he still heard a lot of things, thanks to Lu Hang. One of which was, don't be fooled into pitying Bishop Wood for getting swindled out of all his money in an online relationship.

In fact, the most recent one had been his tenth in-game wife.

The number of marriages Bishop Wood had made even Lu Hang wave the white flag. One of Bishop Wood's strongest points was how he had ended things amicably with all nine of his previous wives. A few of those wives did vent in the *Nine Heroes* forum, but even then, they spoke positively about Bishop Wood; several even felt they "weren't good enough for him." Lu Hang once said Bishop Wood was the pinnacle of a scumbag.

Xiang Huaizhi glanced at the little spirit fox beside him. *Will Jing Huan become Bishop Wood's eleventh wife?*

Bishop Wood was an elegantly adorned, white-robed Warlock who, very recently, was neck and neck with Lu Hang for the top spot of the Sect Mastery rankings. He was quite strong, and his PK videos were also highly popular on the official website, just behind Xiang Huaizhi's own videos.

Moreover, Jing Huan had said, on more than one occasion, that he liked scumbags. Then, by that logic, didn't that mean Bishop Wood was exactly Jing Huan's type?

...Forget it, why am I worrying anyway? This isn't any of my business to begin with.

Xiang Huaizhi was about to look away when he saw the little spirit fox bouncing around him, using a Healing Spring to top off his health.

Their time was limited, so they were running low-level dungeons—the kind you could just AFK through.

[Party] Love is Sharing Noms: I thought you were AFK.

[Party] Sweet Little Jing: I'm still AFKing, but I've been keeping an eye on the game the whole time.

[Party] Sweet Little Jing: I will guard gege's health bar! [Heart]

Xiang Huaizhi paused, then lifted his hand to remove his AFK status and one-shot the boss with a critical hit from his sword.

The dungeon ended, and Xiang Huaizhi kicked all the other people, except for Sweet Little Jing, out of the party. He then led her to the entrance of the arena.

[Party] Yearning For: The arena will open in 10 minutes. I'm going to order take-out. Do whatever you want.

"I'm going to just AFK in the party then." Jing Huan was also perusing the take-out menus. "What are you eating today, gege?"

[Party] Yearning For: Not sure yet, what are you having?

"Yellow braised chicken!" Jing Huan said. "I've been craving it after being away for three days. The yellow braised chicken outside of our school is sooo delicious!"

[Party] Yearning For: Really?

"Mm!" Jing Huan carelessly threw out a promise that could never be realized, forcing a coquettish tone along with it. "If we get the chance, I'll treat you, gege."

[Party] Yearning For: No need.

Xiang Huaizhi searched for this yellow braised chicken restaurant on the take-out app and quickly placed an order.

As the arena's opening time drew closer and closer, more and more people gathered outside the arena. Noticing Love is Sharing Noms, Jing Huan went to greet her when a system announcement suddenly appeared in his chat channel on the right.

【System Announcement: Congratulations to Fae Bae from Mirage server for winning the most likes in the *Nine Heroes* singing competition. She has directly advanced to the semifinals; Congratulations to

Luo Baby from Distant Hearth server for winning second place for likes in the *Nine Heroes'* singing competition...】

[Megaphone] Ji Xiaonian: Congratulations, Faefae. Faefae is so awesome~

[Megaphone] I Like You: Faefae is the only player from our server to advance to the semifinals. Everyone, remember to go to the website and give her a like!

[Megaphone] Taptap~: As expected! After all, Faefae has REAL talent, unlike SOME people who rely on funny gimmicks to get likes.

[Megaphone] Fae Bae: Taptap, don't say that. Being funny is a talent as well. Thank you, everyone, for the likes and support. I'll work hard to win first place for the server~ [Patting head]

When Love is Sharing Noms saw these megaphones, she couldn't help but curse inwardly. Vagueposters were so passive-aggressive.

She opened Sweet Little Jing's chat, just about to offer her some comforting words—

[Megaphone] Sweet Little Jing: Don't need no man nor drama, don't @me.

[Megaphone] Long Road Ahead: That's right! If someone dares to drag Little Jingjing onstage again, we'd have to start charging an appearance fee!

Love is Sharing Noms quietly sat back.

Jing Huan had zero interest in megaphone drama. People who used this kind of method to argue were just creating a scene for people to gawk at. When it came to in-game matters, he preferred to speak through strength. If it wasn't because it was AFKing in the party was so boring, he wouldn't have even replied to that megaphone.

A line of yellow characters appeared on the screen; Fae Bae was

Chapter 09

trying to DM him again. However, since he had blacklisted her last time, she couldn't even send him a message.

Peace and quiet.

Their first few opponents, upon entering the arena, weren't strong. Jing Huan asked while they played, "Gege, why isn't Long Road Ahead fighting today?"

Since they were in the PK arena, Xiang Huaizhi finally unmuted himself. He deliberately lowered his voice. "He's doing the God of War quests."

Jing Huan was stunned. "He finished collecting all the materials that quickly?"

"Mm." Xiang Huaizhi asked, "Are you going to come kill the God of War when the time comes?"

"Yes! I definitely want to!" Jing Huan said excitedly. "Can gege take me along?

Xiang Huaizhi had already counted him as a party member. Hearing Jing Huan's pure joy, he couldn't help but smile. "Okay, I'll let you know when we set a time."

He was suddenly curious about what server and which sect Jing Huan used to play. Based on his gameplay, he must've been a quite a proficient player back then.

To properly express his elation, the little spirit fox went out of control: fluttering around Xiang Huaizhi back and forth and even blowing him a kiss.

Bishop Wood, who had just finished a match, bore witness to this scene and felt a pang of jealousy. After all, who could bear to watch the person they had been persistently flirting with lavish attention on another man?

Xiang Huaizhi finished buying potions and was about to queue up for another match when his friend chat suddenly lit up.

[Friend] Bishop Wood: God Xiang, let's talk.

[Friend] Yearning For: Go ahead.

[Friend] Bishop Wood: Can you give me your arena partner? I'll give you the Mage from my party. Double DPS is also pretty fun.

A slight frown touched Xiang Huaizhi's mouth.

[Friend] Yearning For: Ask her yourself.

[Friend] Bishop Wood: She's your fan. If I ask her to join me, she definitely won't want to...

[Friend] Bishop Wood: Dude, just don't take her to play with you. I can handle the rest.

[Friend] Bishop Wood: It'd be even better if you're willing to put in a good word for me. After all, you're the only one she'll listen to right now. If we end up together, you'll be the #1 matchmaker, [Kowtowing] and I'll definitely thank you properly... Oh right, aren't you collecting enchanted spirit orbs? If you help me, I'll give you one, how about that?

What an enormous sacrifice you're making, Xiang Huaizhi thought dryly.

[Friend] Yearning For: Don't need it, and I'm not interested in being a matchmaker.

"Gege," Jing Huan's dubious voice echoed from his earphones, "am I lagging? Why aren't you moving?"

"You're not, I'm coming." Xiang Huaizhi paused slightly, and then in a freak impulse, blurted out, "I might have to do something tomorrow, so I won't be able to make it. Do you want me to help you find a 2V2 teammate?"

 Chapter 09

"Aaah, don't bother, I don't want to play 2V2 with anyone else. If you're not here, I'll just play 1V1."

Of course, this was Jing Huan's embellished reason. The real reason was that his gear was trash while his rank was high. With Yearning For, they'd dominate the arena, but anyone else, he'd just be giving away points. If he was going to incur his teammate's hatred, it was better to not play 2V2 altogether.

Jing Huan ate another mouthful of rice. "What's gege doing tomorrow?"

After a brief silence, he heard the other party say, "I'm going out to eat."

Jing Huan wasn't sure if he was just imagining it, but Yearning For's voice sounded a bit off today. However, Jing Huan shrugged it off, saying, "Oh," and focused on the new PK match.

After finishing in the arena, Yearning For didn't rush to disband the party like usual. Instead, he took them through the teleportation portal to the Unknown Realm. It was a safe zone, often used for quests and shopping. Although players couldn't set up vending stalls, a lot of them liked to AFK here.

Two steps in, Jing Huan saw Fae Bae AFKing beside an Unknown Realm merchant, chatting with her besties.

Jing Huan couldn't help but curse inwardly, *Fucking hell,* when he read the names of the female players around her. They were all the players he had just seen blasting megaphones.

The girls who had been chatting so happily moments ago fell silent as soon as they noticed Jing Huan and Yearning For. It was obvious from a glance that they had migrated to their private chat.

The atmosphere turned awkward.

However, Yearning For led him over to stand in front of Fae Bae and stopped for a few minutes.

Unable to resist, Jing Huan asked, "Gege, what are we doing here—" He didn't get to finish before he saw a yellow line of text pop up in the game.

【Yearning For gave you Fate Stone x100.】

Jing Huan was taken aback.

[Party] Yearning For: Open them.

After Bishop Wood finished his arena matches, he felt bored and logged into YY to find someone to chat with. Unfortunately, since it was a workday, the guild's YY channel was mostly empty, leaving him no choice but to intrude on the private channel of his guild leader and vice guild leader.

Luckily, Regardless of Lovesickness was AFK, so Echoes of Spring didn't kick him out.

"Why do you think she's so...cold-hearted?" Bishop Wood couldn't help bemoaning about his Sweet Little Jing situation to her. He complained helplessly, "Look at how lively she is when she's with Yearning For, but when she's with me, she doesn't say a word."

Echoes of Spring sneered coldly. "This is why they say men are so cheap; you only want girls who are hard to get. Be honest: you just want to steal someone away from Yearning For, don't you?"

Bishop Wood choked, but he couldn't refute it. It was indeed because of Yearning For that he had started paying more attention to Sweet Little Jing.

"Let's keep things civil—no personal attacks." He paused. "It's not entirely that. Sweet Little Jing is very interesting on her own,

and she has many merits." Bishop Wood smiled, unbidden, and his voice gentled. "She has a cute personality, every word out of her mouth sounds coquettish, and she's pretty skilled... Most importantly, she's very down-to-earth."

Echoes of Spring's tone sounded rather conflicted. "Down-to-earth?"

"Mhm, I wanted to give her some Fate Stones this afternoon, but she refused, saying they were too expensive," Bishop Wood said with a smile. "She's totally different from other girls..."

Bishop Wood didn't even manage to finish his sentence before his voice vanished into thin air. Because right at that moment, notifications were flooding the chat box on the right side of his screen.

【System Announcement: Sweet Little Jing pries open the mysterious Fate Stone and obtains the Rainbow Stone x1! Congratulations, young hero!】

【System Announcement: Sweet Little Jing pries open the mysterious Fate Stone and obtains the Dragon Tongue x1! Congratulations, young hero!】

【System Announcement: Sweet Little Jing pries open the mysterious Fate Stone and obtains the Wool x3! Congratulations, young hero!】

And on it went.

Players had a chance to gain money, experience points, or items when they opened a Fate Stone, but the annoying thing about this was that as long as an item was gained, regardless if it was good or bad, the system would announce it.

For Sweet Little Jing, getting her pile of garbage broadcasted like this was akin to a public execution.

After a moment, Echoes of Spring deadpanned coolly. "Indeed. So down-to-earth."

"...Maybe she bought it on a whim?" Bishop Wood suggested. "She'd rather spend her own money than take mine. Isn't that even more precious?"

"I saw her when I passed by the Unknown Realm; she's in Yearning For's party." Echoes of Spring smiled. "And Yearning For was the party leader."

Only the party leader could interact with NPCs, and talking to them was necessary to trigger the purchase button for Fate Stones.

Bishop Wood was at a loss for words.

"It's not that she doesn't want your things, she only wants Yearning For's." For some strange reason, Echoes of Spring's tone held an admiring note. "From a certain angle, that is indeed quite down-to-earth."

Jing Huan originally had no plans to accept these Fate Stones. His goal was to ruin Yearning For's reputation—who was interested in these shitty Fate Stones?—but after Lu Wenhao's incident, Jing Huan had learned a valuable lesson: the more money his catfishing persona swindled, the deeper the emotional damage when the truth came out.

A hundred Fate Stones cost 2,000 yuan; anyone would feel some pain from that for a while.

Therefore, Jing Huan accepted the 100 Fate Stones, sending out a bunch of "AHHH," "Gege, why are you so good to me, QAQ" and "Gege, I can only pay you back with my body!"

However, lady luck chose to skip out on him. He got jackshit

 Chapter 09

from the 100 Fate Stones and ended up filling his inventory with useless trash instead. Just like that, all 2,000 yuan went down the drain.

Pay-to-win games deserve to go bankrupt sooner or later.

[Party] Sweet Little Jing: WAAAAAAAAH! QAQ

[Party] Sweet Little Jing: I'm going to delete this character as repentance!

[Party] Sweet Little Jing: My unlucky hands... I really should cut them off. [Lifeless]

[Party] Yearning For: ...It's not that bad.

[Party] Sweet Little Jing: I'm so unlucky, gege... T.T Should I go pray to Buddha?

[Party] Yearning For: It's a matter of probability. Opening another 100 should produce something good.

That gave Jing Huan quite a scare and he quickly unmuted himself. "Gege, don't buy any more, I won't open them!"

Yes, he wanted to empty Yearning For's bank account, but he also sure as hell didn't want this stupid game getting an easy 4,000 yuan.

Xiang Huaizhi's fingers stopped.

[Party] Yearning For: Don't want to open anymore?

[Party] Sweet Little Jing: [Frantically shaking head]

Only then did Xiang Huaizhi slowly close the purchasing interface.

These 100 Fate Stones could count as payment to Jing Huan for taking him in. The hot spring resort they stayed in that day cost at least four figures a night for a room. For someone with only a few hundred yuan of pocket money a week, who knew how long he had saved up for that trip? Moreover, he knew he had something to do with Sweet Little Jing's refusal of Bishop Wood.

After indulging the little spirit fox's Fate Stone addiction, Yearning For moved his fingers and used a flying charm to whisk her away. It was as if his "ex" and her bestie group didn't exist.

Meanwhile, the girls' private group chat had reached 99+ messages.

Ji Xiaonian: Isn't this Sweet Little Jing too arrogant?! Did she know that Fae Bae was AFKing here and intentionally came over with Yearning For??

Taptap~: That's most likely the case. This woman is so damn awful.

Fae Bae: Sigh, forget it. Let's not talk about this anymore. There's nothing between me and Yearning For now.

Little Mai: Probably not, right? Yearning For was the party leader, meaning he was the one who did it…

Ji Xiaonian: Little Mai, you just came back pretty recently, so you're not in the loop. This woman is really disgusting, she even buys likes!

Little Mai: Buys likes?

Ji Xiaonian: Yeah, she must have bought all the likes for her "Loyalty to the Country" entry! Several of my friends said their character's event interface showed that they liked the song, even though they hadn't voted at all.

Little Mai: Then report it to the GMs, and get her character properly banned.

Ji Xiaonian: That's why I said she's disgusting. She's afraid we might report her, which is why she made up an excuse to quit the competition first!

 Chapter 09

Taptap~: Puking.

Little Mai: So arrogant. And no one gave her trouble for it?

Ji Xiaonian: With her clutching onto Yearning For's thigh[1], who'd risk doing that? Didn't you notice? Even Regardless of Lovesickness has bowed her head. Now she can swagger through the entire server and no one has the guts to offend her.

Taptap~: Little Mai, your husband is the second-ranked DPS. He isn't that far behind Yearning For. You're the only one in this group who can help us vent our anger.

Ji Xiaonian: Exactly [Crying]. If you don't do something, this server will have to change its name to hers!

Little Mai: ...

Little Mai: Let me think.

The next day, Jing Huan went to class alone. Although it was blessedly quiet without Lu Wenhao and Gao Zixiang around, he was also bored. He yawned a dozen times in one class alone.

On his way home after class, messages began to pop up in his group chat.

Lu Wenhao: @Little Jing~, Huanhuan baby, have you finished class?

Little Jing~: ?

Gao Zixiang: Deliver us breakfast, and I'll be your beast of burden and Hao'er your wife in the next life.

Little Jing~: Fuck off.

Jing Huan had woken up late, so he hadn't even eaten his own

---

1   A Chinese saying referring to someone completely relying on someone else's strength to see difficult situations through.

breakfast. Forget bringing them food, all he wanted to do was go back and make up on sleep. After venting his frustration, he closed WeChat, finishing his rant off with two unfriendly stickers.

He walked toward the back gate and couldn't resist taking a peek as he passed by the basketball court. His eyes were instantly drawn to the wide shoulders of a guy who had his back to the fence.

The guy was wearing a black jersey for once. His hair was neatly cut and his exposed neck was clean and slender. At this moment, he was sitting with his legs apart, elbows resting on his knees, as he played on his cellphone.

Currently, Xiang Huaizhi was a little irritated.

After much difficulty, his foot had finally recovered, and his hands were itching to play basketball again. So, this morning, when he saw someone had pinged him in the group chat to play a game, he immediately agreed. He only found out upon arriving that two people couldn't make it due to emergencies, leaving their spots empty.

With so many other people on the basketball court, it wouldn't be any trouble to randomly grab a few of them to make a team, but he hadn't expected to find his sophomore neighbor with terrible sportsmanship also present. This killed off half of Xiang Huaizhi's enthusiasm.

Tsking, Xiang Huaizhi tried to come up with a reason to leave.

"Senior!"

Xiang Huaizhi jolted and whipped around. Jing Huan stood outside the chain-link fence, both hands curled around it. His eyes curved into crescents as he gazed at Xiang Huaizhi, his smile more revitalizing than the autumn wind.

 Chapter 09

"Morning, Senior." Jing Huan blinked. "Playing basketball so early?"

Xiang Huaizhi wasn't the only one to look over; the other guys around him also turned at Jing Huan's shout.

Brows furrowed, Xiang Huaizhi glanced in the direction Jing Huan had come from. "Mm. Just finished class?"

Jing Huan nodded. "Yeah, I'm planning to go back for a nap."

"Xiang-ge, who is this? A friend of yours?" The guy next to him stepped forward with a smile, greeting Jing Huan warmly, "Which department?"

"I'm a sophomore."

The guy stood in front of Jing Huan, hands on his hips, and asked, "An underclassman? That's great, can you play ball?"

"A little," Jing Huan said.

"That's good enough. We're short on people for this game, wanna fill in?"

Jing Huan looked at Xiang Huaizhi. "Are you playing too, Senior?"

Before Xiang Huaizhi could find an excuse to leave, the guy next to him had already jumped in. "Of course, Xiang-ge is playing. He's been sitting here waiting for a long time since we were missing one person. If you jump in, we can start right away."

"Oh, okay," Jing Huan agreed cheerfully. "But I want to be on the same team as Senior. If that's okay, I'll join."

Xiang Huaizhi's eyebrows rose slightly, and he swallowed down his excuse to leave.

The guy nodded and laughed. "No problem. Come join us."

Jing Huan stepped onto the court and started warming up

beside Xiang Huaizhi. He was dressed in casual clothes, but fortunately, he was wearing shorts and had sneakers on, so he could run easily.

Xiang Huaizhi glanced at Jing Huan's white sneakers. Above them were slender straight calves; a sharp contrast to the thick, muscular legs of the other dudes around him.

He tore his eyes away and said in a voice low enough that only the two of them could hear, "If you don't want to play, you can say no."

"Why wouldn't I?" Jing Huan gave him a quizzical look. The corners of his mouth curved up as he said, "I was planning on asking you out to play ball in the next few days anyway. Who would've thought we'd run into each other like this?"

Xiang Huaizhi was suddenly uncertain of Jing Huan's intentions. "Ask me out to play? Why?"

"Because I think you're really good at basketball."

"You've seen me play before?"

"Nope, but I've seen you catch the ball." Jing Huan raised his hand, mimicking his gesture from that night. "Cool!"

The corners of Xiang Huaizhi's mouth tilted up into a small smile. His face, usually cold and aloof, carried a bit of sharpness enhanced by his monolids. But when he smiled, that sharpness softened slightly.

The ten players split into two teams. Jing Huan and his team clustered together to discuss their respective positions. Xiang Huaizhi was the shooting guard, while Jing Huan was assigned as a forward.

Jing Huan guessed correctly; Xiang Huaizhi was really good at

Chapter 09

basketball, scoring two three-pointers right away, and giving their team a dream start of 6-0.

The number of spectators gradually increased around the court, the majority of whom were girls, who whispered amongst each other, their eyes locked on the two dazzling players on the court.

At 5'10", Jing Huan wasn't considered especially tall, but he could jump well, making him a competent forward. He dribbled the ball, watching the opposing team's forward closely.

Most of them seemed manageable, but one player—a tall, sturdy guy with a serious expression—looked difficult to deal with. Jing Huan thought for all of two seconds before he broke through to the right side, and the opponent immediately stepped up to defend.

As the guy jumped to block Jing Huan's shot, Jing Huan pivoted at the last second and launched the ball to the back.

None of his teammates, let alone his opponents, could react. Only Xiang Huaizhi, whether he anticipated it or just reacted quickly, caught Jing Huan's pass and shot yet another decisive three-pointer.

The ball went in. 13-2. A crushing lead.

Xiang Huaizhi raised his eyebrows, clearly not expecting the ball to go in. His skills were on point today. Just as he was thinking that, the opposing team called for a break.

The underclassman who was playing forward jogged over, still catching his breath.

"Senior, quick, high five!" Jing Huan extended his palm out toward him.

Xiang Huaizhi hesitated briefly before raising his hand. After

Jing Huan slapped him with a hard high five, he deliberately let his hand linger, rubbing his palm against Xiang Huaizhi's. Beaming, he said, "I'm hoping some of your skills rub off on me."

The boy's hand wasn't rough; it felt warm and soft—surprisingly pleasant to touch.

Xiang Huaizhi was still in a dazed stupor when Jing Huan pulled his hand away and sprinted back into position.

The break was soon over, and the opposing team made a substituition. The person guarding against Xiang Huaizhi was now the sturdy forward from earlier.

Jing Huan didn't think much of it. Xiang Huaizhi liked to shoot three-pointers, and although the guy guarding him was sturdy, he wasn't as tall as Xiang Huaizhi. His heavier frame also contributed to a clumsiness when jumping, so him blocking Xiang Huaizhi seemed unlikely.

But things were obviously not that simple.

The game continued. Two minutes later, Xiang Huaizhi received the ball again and he raised his hand as if he was going to shoot another three-pointer, but it was a fake—his real plan was to break through for a dunk. Just as he was about to make his move, something slammed hard into his chest, a sharp pain coursing through the spot where the opponent's elbow had struck him.

He knew it.

The guy defending against him wasn't just any player—it was the asshole from the neighboring dorm last semester, infamous for his dirty tricks. If it weren't for his great physique, he would've been kicked off the team ages ago.

Xiang Huaizhi grimaced and a slight groan escaped from his

throat, but he didn't stop. He changed his strategy, and instead of passing the ball, he went right for the three-pointer. The shot missed.

The ball thumped to the ground and was quickly snatched away by the opposing team. Xiang Huaizhi didn't say a word. He turned back to defend and coldly glared at the sturdy guy who merely shrugged and flashed an innocent smile at him.

At half-time, the score was 21-10, with Xiang Huaizhi's side maintaining an overwhelming lead. During the half-time break, Xiang Huaizhi, his expression dark, was about to confront the guy guarding him when someone snagged his wrist.

"Senior," said Jing Huan, "can we switch positions? I kind of want to play guard."

Xiang Huaizhi thought about the opponent's rough tactics and said, "Next time. It's already half-time, and I have experience in defending against him."

"I'm also very good at guarding," Jing Huan argued. "Let me try, okay? I'll just practice my technique. Worst comes to worst, we can switch back after a quarter."

Xiang Huaizhi hesitated, then finally relented. "Just one quarter."

When the two of them returned to the bench to rest, Jing Huan took out his cellphone and wiped off his sweat as he checked his WeChat messages.

Lu Wenhao: Fuck me @Little Jing~ how come you went off to play ball? Without even calling over your bros for the game?!

Little Jing~: How did you know I'm playing basketball?

Lu Wenhao: [Picture]

Lu Wenhao: The school group chat has been posting pictures of you and Senior Xiang nonstop, it'd be weirder not to know.

Jing Huan clicked to take a look. More than ten photos filled the chat, all focused on either him or Xiang Huaizhi. Everyone else was barely visible, blurred into the background.

Unfazed, he typed back: *Just playing casually.*

Lu Wenhao: But why are you with this guy? [Picture]

Lu Wenhao had circled the opposing team's shooting guard.

Lu Wenhao: This guy plays really dirty. Last time he jabbed a guy from the neighboring department so hard his brow split open.

Xiang Huaizhi heard the person next to him snort derisively and subconsciously glanced over, just in time to see the pink profile picture on his phone screen. The profile picture was familiar. The message, however, was anything but.

Little Jing~: Me? Fear him? You just park yourself in the school group chat and watch how daddy handles this later.

Xiang Huaizhi stared for a moment, then looked away.

As the third quarter began, Jing Huan stepped in front of the sturdy guy, rolling his shoulders and cracking his neck.

"You again?" The dude laughed when he saw him. "Did Xiang Huaizhi run away from my defense?"

Jing Huan smiled. "I heard that you're very good at basketball, and I wanted to see for myself."

The guy guffawed heartily. "No problem. Watch and learn."

A few minutes later, the sturdy guy got possession of the ball, thinking to dunk it to demonstrate his skills to the underclassman.

Confidence practically oozing out of him, he tried to break

Chapter 09

through, but the moment he took half a step, an elbow jammed viciously into his chest. Caught off guard, he let out a pained grunt, his legs buckled, and he crashed to the ground.

Everyone was stupefied and it took a few seconds for them to check on him. Only the culprit stood still; Jing Huan picked up the basketball from the ground and dribbled it a few times.

"You fucking—" The guy came to his senses. Face flushed, he glowered at Jing Huan. "You slammed into me?! On purpose?"

Jing Huan's jab hadn't been that strong. The dude had tried to shove him first, but the force rebounded back onto himself.

Xiang Huaizhi's brow furrowed as he stepped forward, just as Jing Huan, looking completely innocent, said, "I was just defending."

"Defending my ass!" The guy had finally regained his breath. "You knocked me down on purpose! That's a foul! Fuck..."

Xiang Huaizhi cut him off with a sharp look. "Watch your mouth."

Jing Huan didn't care. "So you *do* know that hitting people is a foul, huh?" A slight smirk tugged at his lips.

Xiang Huaizhi paused, his dark eyes staring at the person beside him.

So, he saw it. Was that why he asked to switch positions with me earlier and volunteered to defend against this asshole?

Dirty tactics on the court disgusted Jing Huan the most. There had also been someone in high school who had purposefully tripped Gao Zixiang during a game. Later, he and Gao Zixiang got revenge by stepping on their opponent's foot countless times.

An eye for an eye. It was a childish but effective method, because that person never dared to play ball with them again.

With so many eyes on him, the guy felt humiliated and stood up to retaliate. However, Xiang Huaizhi stood protectively in front of Jing Huan, blocking half of his shoulder.

"Xiang-ge, what he did counts as a foul. Not to mention, there should be a free throw, right?" the guy said through gritted teeth.

Xiang Huaizhi glared at him. "You got tired of slamming into people, so you started learning how to fake a fall?"

"Fake a fall…" The guy was stunned for a moment, then snapped, "Fake a fall my ass! *He* slammed into *me*!"

"With your two relative physiques…" Xiang Huaizhi paused. "He slammed into you?"

Jing Huan cocked his head questioningly.

As soon as Xiang Huaizhi said this, the people who came to help froze for a second. They instinctively glanced at Jing Huan and then back at the robust guy. Although Jing Huan's build wasn't considered delicate among guys, he did look much smaller compared to the other guy. Recalling the sturdy guy's aggressive basketball play style, a few people coughed, and released him.

"Forget it, forget it, it's not a big deal." Someone came to mediate. "A few bumps and scrapes are a given when you play basketball. Let's just keep playing, all right?"

"Fuck…" The sturdy guy cursed under his breath, but he also knew there was no point in him making a scene now. "Forget it."

Jing Huan was about to return to his guard position when someone grabbed his arm.

"Go back to your previous position," Xiang Huaizhi said.

"No," Jing Huan refused and insisted, "I want to play guard."

The words had barely left his mouth when Xiang Huaizhi sud-

 Chapter 09

denly reached out. Xiang Huaizhi's hand hovered over his head for a moment and then, as if afraid of dirtying his hair, finally rested on his back and gave him a gentle push forward.

"Go back," Xiang Huaizhi said. "Listen to me."

Jing Huan froze.

Xiang Huaizhi's hand was very big, and Jing Huan's shirt was thin, so he could clearly feel the warmth from his palm spreading slowly from his spine to the rest of his body. What had he been trying to do with the hand that had just been hovering over his head?

The others were already calling for him, giving Jing Huan little to no time to think. He shook himself. "Got it."

Because of the wide score gap and the earlier incident, their opponents had already lost their fighting spirit. In the last quarter, Jing Huan's side scored almost all the points, and in the end, they won by a large margin.

Jing Huan went to the bench and wiped off his sweat with a towel. He grinned at Xiang Huaizhi. "Senior, is that guy really part of the basketball team? Why do I feel like he's not that good? Even Lu Wenhao is better."

Xiang Huaizhi nodded in agreement. "He really isn't that good. The school coach most likely saw his good physique and decided to train him."

At that, Jing Huan couldn't help recalling what had transpired just now.

Xiang Huaizhi wiped his sweat, picked up his bottle of water, and was about to unscrew it when, all of a sudden, the person beside him wrapped his fingers around his wrist. Immediately, the scent of

shampoo mixed with a faint smell of sweat wafted into his nostrils.

Bewildered, he turned and saw the person next to him scoot closer, using his other hand to grab the bottom of his own T-shirt and yanking it up.

Beads of sweat slid over the boy's skin which was paler than that of most girls. When Jing Huan inhaled gently, the faint outline of his abdominal muscle became visible.

"Senior, you seemed to be looking down on me," Jing Huan said seriously. "I have abs too, you know, even if they're not that obvious."

Xiang Huaizhi stared at him for several seconds before stiffly looking away. "Mm," he said, carefully controlling the pace of his speech. "You're better than him."

"Obviously. I could dunk on him any time I want." It wasn't until after Jing Huan finished speaking that he felt something was off. Why did Xiang Huaizhi's tone sound like he was humoring a kid?

Jing Huan opened his mouth to respond but was interrupted when an unopened bottle of water was handed to him.

A girl with pigtails, wearing long sleeves and a short skirt, looked at Jing Huan shyly. She smelled sweet.

"Senior." She fluttered her eyelashes. "This is for you."

For both of them, girls giving them water bottles was a common occurrence. At the start of his freshman year, if anyone wanted to send water to Xiang Huaizhi, they would have had to wait in line. After half a semester of Xiang Huaizhi's cold refusals, however, this phenomenon gradually disappeared.

Xiang Huaizhi pursed his lips. He felt like the third wheel in this situation.

Jing Huan looked up and smiled. "Thank you, but it's all right, I have water."

"But I noticed you've already finished drinking it." The girl blushed and said, "That's why I just bought this, and it's ice-cold."

"Sorry. I don't like drinking iced water." Jing Huan pointed with his chin at the half-full bottle of water left on the bench. "And I have another bottle here."

The girl hesitated. "But that's Senior Xiang's..."

"We have a good relationship, so we don't mind sharing." Jing Huan wasn't lying; he often shared drinks with Lu Wenhao and Gao Zixiang, as long as their mouths didn't touch the bottle. "Right, Senior?"

Xiang Huaizhi raised his eyebrows slightly, and after a long interval, he finally replied, "Mm."

After the girl left, Jing Huan licked his lips. All that talk about water had left him quite parched. He scanned around but saw there were no unopened water bottles left.

Seeing his small movements, Xiang Huaizhi asked, "Thirsty?"

"A little." Jing Huan rubbed his stomach. "Well, Senior, I'm going to go first. Gonna grab something to eat by the school gate."

Xiang Huaizhi frowned. "You didn't have breakfast?"

"Not yet. I was planning to go back and take a nap." Jing Huan picked up his cellphone from the bench. "Let's play basketball together again sometime, Senior."

"Wait," Xiang Huaizhi called out. "Let's go together. My treat."

Without waiting for Jing Huan's reply, Xiang Huaizhi quickly explained, "As a reward for helping me win the game."

Ten minutes later, the two of them walked into the yellow braised chicken restaurant near campus.

Xiang Huaizhi's reasoning was simple: he'd treat Jing Huan to a meal thereby helping him save a bit on his living expenses.

"Senior, the yellow braised chicken here is really delicious!" Jing Huan split the chopsticks and handed them to him. "I order take-out from here all the time."

After a brief pause, Xiang Huaizhi took the chopsticks. "I know. Someone told me about this place before."

Jing Huan nodded sagely. "That person has good taste."

Xiang Huaizhi thought, *You're just tooting your own horn.*

After a few bites, Xiang Huaizhi remembered something. "How much did a night cost at the resort you stayed at last time? I'll transfer the room rate to you."

Jing Huan looked up. "Ah? No need—Lu Wenhao paid for the trip. I didn't spend a single penny."

The trip to the resort really had been Lu Wenhao's treat; Jing Huan had gifted him a pair of limited edition basketball shoes on his birthday. There were only a few hundred pairs in the world, and when Lu Hang laid his eyes on them, he almost burst into tears, nearly recognizing Jing Huan as his new dad.

Xiang Huaizhi nodded. *No wonder.*

Satiated, Jing Huan took out his cellphone and began typing one-handed while sipping his soup.

Feeling a vibration from his pocket, Xiang Huaizhi stopped chewing. A few seconds later…

 Chapter 09

Buzz, buzz...

Another two vibrations. Xiang Huaizhi's face was carefully blank as he pulled out his cellphone.

Little Jing~: Gege, are you up yeeet? >.<

Little Jing~: [Start bed sharing.JPG]

Little Jing~: When will gege get on today? [Tapping fingers together]

Xiang: ...In a bit.

Little Jing~: Okayyy. [Picture] Look, I'm eating yellow braised chicken right now!

The picture of the yellow braised chicken on rice appeared on his phone. Despite the two of them sitting across from each other, they were chatting through WeChat instead. This was the first time Xiang Huaizhi had found himself in this kind of situation.

He had originally wanted to head back before replying, but after seeing his own bowl and chopsticks displayed in the photo, something seemed to take hold of Xiang Huaizhi and he typed.

Xiang: Are you with friends?

Little Jing~: Yeeep.

Xiang Huaizhi couldn't help huffing out a laugh at the screen. Was he somehow infected by Jing Huan? How could he also act like he had multiple personalities?

He was just about to turn off his cellphone when the other party sent another message.

Little Jing~: Ah, don't misunderstand, gege, it's a female friend! >0<

Xiang Huaizhi's smile hardened.

Xiang: ?

Little Jing~: She's a very good senior. ^^

Xiang: ...

Finding himself suddenly friend-zoned, Xiang Huaizhi's heart was full of mixed emotions.

After they finished eating, the two of them walked out of the shop. Jing Huan's gaze lingered on the milk tea shop across the street. "Senior, do you want to drink some milk tea?"

Xiang Huaizhi rarely drank milk tea; he thought it was too sweet and cloying. He looked sideways at Jing Huan. "Do you want to?"

"Yes! I haven't had any for a long time." Jing Huan sighed, totally oblivious to how pitiful his sigh sounded to the person next to him.

"Then let's line up."

A moment later, Jing Huan was standing blankly in front of the milk tea shop, holding three cups of milk tea.

When it had been their turn to order, Xiang Huaizhi asked him what he wanted and he had casually answered, only to hear Xiang Huaizhi say to the clerk, "Three milk tea." Then he opened up Alipay, scanned the QR code, and paid for it all in one go.

He had thought that Xiang Huaizhi had wanted it all to himself, but after the milk tea came out, Xiang Huaizhi stuffed the three cups into his hands, said goodbye, and left.

Jing Huan tilted his head in confusion. *Did I look that thirsty?*

After putting two cups of milk tea into the refrigerator, Jing Huan sat in front of the computer. He shook his mouse, and the screen instantly lit up.

Just before going out, he had left his character in Penglai, who had now accumulated tens of thousands of experience points.

Chapter 09

The friend message icon kept flashing, and Jing Huan carelessly clicked it.

[Friend] Bishop Wood: Little Jingjing, it's so early.

[Friend] Bishop Wood: You AFK?

[Friend] Bishop Wood: Reply when you come back. [Cute]

[Friend] Sweet Little Jing: Ah, I'm not doing dungeons.

[Friend] Bishop Wood: You're just in time. It's not a dungeon, it's something else. Wait for me, I'll go find you.

[Friend] Sweet Little Jing: What's going on~ O.O

[Friend] Bishop Wood: Something big!

Jing Huan was frankly quite scared of Bishop Wood. No matter how many times he rejected him, the guy refused to go away.

Soon, the white-robed scholar arrived at his side, lightly waving a folding fan, looking gentle and elegant.

【Bishop Wood has invited you to join his party. Yes, No.】

Jing Huan clicked "Yes."

As soon as he joined the party, Bishop Wood's voice sounded out. "Little Jingjing, have you eaten yet?"

[Party] Sweet Little Jing: I have. Where are we going?

"Can't tell you. Anyway, it's not like I'm selling you to someone." Bishop Wood inquired, "You still can't use your mic?"

[Party] Sweet Little Jing: ...Yes.

As Jing Huan vacillated between leaving or staying, they passed by Yuelao's Temple. He broke out in a cold sweat, thinking that Bishop Wood was going to drag him in to get married.

He was so focused on Bishop Wood's route that he missed the player login notification on the right side of the chat box.

As soon as Xiang Huaizhi logged in, he received a player message notifying him that the gem he had ordered was ready.

He had ordered it for Jing Huan's ring. The higher the gem level on the ring, the higher the healing power for the Spirit Fox Den, making arena matches far more comfortable to fight in. After receiving the gem, Xiang Huaizhi opened his friend list.

Sweet Little Jing's name was lit up, indicating that the other party was online, but seeing as he hadn't sent him a message yet, he was probably AFK.

Xiang Huaizhi moved his mouse to Sweet Little Jing's portrait, checked the coordinates of the other party, and was preparing to go over to toss him the gem when he paused.

Moon Palace (19, 21).

What was he doing at the Moon Palace? That place was a scenic wilderness region, but it was a low-level area, so very few people went there.

While he was still wondering, he saw the coordinates of the other party change to Moon Palace (44, 102).

If he wasn't AFK, why didn't he send me a message after being online for so long?

Xiang Huaizhi headed to the main city teleportation portal, teleported directly to the Moon Palace, walking toward Sweet Little Jing's coordinates.

The black-robed man came to a halt.

Not too far ahead, beneath the full moon meteor shower stood a white-robed scholar and a little spirit fox with a big swaying tail. The two characters were very close, almost touching, looking incredibly intimate.

Chapter 09

With a soft swish, flowers blossomed under the scholar's feet—a player-made firework effect in the game. Hundreds of flowers of various colors was arranged into a heart shape with an enlarged "Jing" smack dab in the middle. Fireworks erupted from the four corners of this flower arrangement, lighting up the Moon Palace's night sky.

No matter how you looked at it, this looked like an extremely romantic date.

Hidden in the shadows, the black-robed man stood at the edge of the scene, an unwelcome intruder.

Xiang Huaizhi pressed his lips together.

In all the years that Xiang Huaizhi had played *Nine Heroes*, he never once touched the fireworks system. Never mind assembling fireworks, he didn't even know where to find the fireworks vendors.

By now, Jing Huan should have a very clear idea about Bishop Wood's intentions. Normally, Sweet Little Jing would have immediately left the party, but both Bishop Wood and the little spirit fox stood there, unmoving.

The two of them were obviously chatting in the party channel, but what could they be talking about?

Xiang Huaizhi thought that the person who had just been "sharing a bed" with him shouldn't have such a quick change of heart. Besides, judging from Bishop Wood's past relationships, he wasn't gay.

And yet, the little spirit fox stood right on top of the blossoming fireworks, showing no signs of leaving.

Should I tell my underclassman about Bishop Wood's romantic history?

As soon as the thought appeared, Xiang Huaizhi dismissed it; if Jing Huan really liked scumbags, Xiang Huaizhi would have unwittingly become a matchmaker for them.

Behind him, Lu Hang was about to vomit from running all his quests. He brokenly croaked, "This quest is so annoying; one step requires me to find ten NPCs. How long did it take you back then... Whatever, I'll order a cup of milk tea to refresh myself. Xiangxiang, you want one?"

"No," he said curtly.

Xiang Huaizhi suddenly remembered the three cups of milk tea he had bought for the little spirit fox. Was Jing Huan drinking the milk tea he had bought him while chatting with Bishop Wood under the moon?

He looked away and moved his fingers. The black-robed man sprinted out of the map and returned to the main city.

Why am I thinking about this so much? He and Jing Huan were neither kith nor kin, and he had no right to interfere with the other boy's affairs. Besides, Jing Huan had the right to choose. If Bishop Wood was his type, then that was just perfect. He wouldn't bother him in the future anymore.

With a heavy heart, Xiang Huaizhi consoled himself and opened his in-game inventory, his gaze falling on the gem lying resting inside.

If the little spirit fox really wanted to develop a relationship with other men, giving him the gem might no longer be appropriate.

This was also Jing Huan's first time seeing such extravagant fireworks. He stared vacantly at the heart-wrapped word "Jing" at his feet. He didn't react for a long time.

"It's pretty, right, Little Jingjing?" Bishop Wood asked, voice

gentle. "I just figured out how to make this. Took a lot of failed attempts."

"It's so pretty! I didn't know the fireworks system could be used like this!" Jing Huan exclaimed.

In the dorms, he'd seen Lu Wenhao set off heart-shaped fireworks for his wife before, but heart-shaped fireworks were so last season with tutorials flooding the forum. But this was the first time he'd seen someone write a word in the middle of a heart.

Bishop Wood smiled as soon as he heard his words. Finally, a glimmer of hope.

See? This young girl was so touched that she unmuted herself and spoke up.

"So long as you like it." He beamed. "If you want, I can make some for you every day."

"No thanks. All these flowers must've cost a fortune, right?"

One downside of assembling fireworks was all the various components and special effects were sold separately. Just making a large heart shape could cost around 200 yuan.

"Not much." Bishop Wood adopted a blasé air. "Each one costs a little over 500 gold, and along with the failed attempts, I think I spent around 800 gold." He knew exactly how to woo a girl. The first step was to let the other party know that he was willing to spend money on her.

Jing Huan was completely astonished.

Money was one thing, but the thought and care put into this flowery heart-shape was enough to move people. With this kind of skill, who *wouldn't* fall for him?

No wonder he couldn't stir Yearning For's heart—compared to Bishop Wood, he was nothing! Actions really did speak louder than words.

Jing Huan was still ruminating over this when his friend message icon suddenly flashed.

[Friend] Yearning For: .

Jing Huan started. When did Yearning For log on?

[Friend] Sweet Little Jing: [Heart][Heart][Heart] Gege!

[Friend] Sweet Little Jing: I'm so blind. I didn't see your login notification! TVT

Seeing these familiar stickers and kaomojis, Xiang Huaizhi released a breath he hadn't realized he had been holding.

[Friend] Yearning For: Just logged in. Want to run some dungeons?

After sending this sentence, Xiang Huaizhi opened up the dungeon list, pondering which one to choose.

Nine Heroes reset their dungeon challenge log weekly, but due to the overabundance, players rarely completed them all. Most opted for high-experience dungeons.

[Friend] Sweet Little Jing: Ah, gege, I'm not running dungeons today.

[Friend] Yearning For: ?

[Friend] Sweet Little Jing: I have something to do! >.<

Xiang Huaizhi reflexively glanced at Jing Huan's friend info. The coordinates hadn't changed—he was still at the Moon Palace.

[Friend] Yearning For: Got it.

He promptly closed both the chat box and dungeon list, expressionlessly opened a video app, and randomly selected a newly

Chapter 09

released movie. He had only watched a few minutes when the *Nine Heroes* icon on the taskbar suddenly lit up.

Someone had sent him a message in-game.

Ever since he met Sweet Little Jing, he had kept his messaging system enabled. This time, it was a level 43 alt character messaging him.

[Private] Secretly Pining: Are you there?

[Private] Secretly Pining: I'm Fae Bae, this is my alt. Don't block me just yet, I have a business proposition for you.

[Private] Yearning For: Go on.

[Private] Secretly Pining: Is your party going to go kill the God of War?

[Private] Secretly Pining: I know Long Road Ahead has been running the God of War quests, so I'd like to discuss something with you. Could you live stream your first-person POV of killing the God of War in my channel? I can pay you guys.

Despite *Nine Heroes'* long history, few parties could kill the God of War. Most parties managed the feat only after several wipes, and even then, just barely. The uncertainty deterred many from streaming killing the God of War as they feared public failure.

But the few times the God of War kills were live streamed, the viewer numbers soared into an astonishing range. So, when Fae Bae learned that Long Road Ahead was going to kill the God of War, she hatched this idea.

[Private] Yearning For: How would I give you a first-person POV?

[Private] Secretly Pining: Just take my character with you. I've already prepared my equipment.

Guide on How to Fail at Online Dating

Her backup team had worked around the clock for days, grinding for her equipment.

Apprehensive of Yearning For's rejection, she quickly added.

[Private] Secretly Pining: Don't worry about Sweet Little Jing. I'll split the money four ways, one for each party member, and I can give her a larger cut.

[Private] Yearning For: I don't need money.

[Private] Secretly Pining: ...You said you'd compensate me.

[Private] Yearning For: I can compensate you for your financial losses, but I'm not partying up with you.

Immediately afterward, Xiang Huaizhi turned on the setting to refuse messages from strangers.

Fae Bae, unable to get anything from Yearning For, went back to complain to Lu Hang.

"Tsk, I told Fae Bae that you wouldn't agree. Why'd she still message you?" Lu Hang said.

Xiang Huaizhi's head didn't even turn around. "Turn on the block strangers function."

"I'd never use that feature. What if some female admirerer comes knocking?"

"Don't worry. There aren't any."

"You never know. I mean, wasn't Sweet Little Jing basically that?"

Xiang Huaizhi felt as if he had been stabbed in his sore spot. It took a while for him to speak. "I meant that there aren't any girls who worship you."

"...Damn."

Lu Hang casually brushed Fae Bae off with a few words. Thinking it'd be boring to find the NPCs, he logged into WeChat on his

 Chapter 09

computer to chat with some guild members. On weekdays, the guild chat channel was relatively quiet; things were much more lively in the WeChat group chat.

"Fuck!"

Xiang Huaizhi heard a shout coming from behind him and frowned. He didn't even get a chance to ask before Lu Hang started talking.

"This fireworks display is really awesome. Bishop Wood is relentless. I surrender, I surrender to him completely. I'll let him have the title of the #1 scumbag in Mirage server. I don't even come close." Lu Hang clicked to enlarge the picture, murmuring, "So, you can use fireworks this way... I've learned something new."

Xiang Huaizhi glanced back. Bishop Wood had screenshotted the romantic scene from the Moon Palace today and shared it in the guild group chat.

He looked away, opened WeChat, and scrolled through the chat history.

Bishop Wood: [Picture] Aren't these fireworks cool?

BrbOrNot: Holy fuck, they're awesome!

Peach Cheese Stan: The guild officer is too OP! [Kneeling down]

Youth Chasing the Wind: Hold on, shouldn't we focus on the word "Jing" and Sweet Little Jing standing beside the fireworks?

Silent Affection: Did the guild officer finally get her?

Xiaoxiao: As expected, congrats to the guild officer! Looking forward to the wedding reception! [Smiling]

What followed was a screen full of congratulatory messages.

However, Bishop Wood did not speak again, while Sweet Little Jing never made an appearance.

"No wonder you didn't run any dungeons today," Lu Hang said after scrolling through the chat history, slapping the table. "Little Jingjing ran off with someone else!"

Xiang Huaizhi didn't say a word.

"Damn, is Sweet Little Jing going to form a fixed party with Bishop Wood now? Won't dungeon runs be boring from now on?" Lu Hang paused. "Is she still joining us for the God of War fight?"

"Don't know."

"*Haah*, it looks like they're going to get married," Lu Hang said. "As a former party member, what should I give her? Xiangxiang, what are you going to give Sweet Little Jing as a wedding present?"

"Don't know."

"But girls are sensitive. It's rare enough that she put up with your ass for so long," Lu Hang muttered to himself, sighing. "Wishing her happiness, I guess."

Xiang Huaizhi didn't respond. With a dark expression, he put in his earphones again and drowned out Lu Hang's murmurs with the movie's audio.

Jing Huan spent a whole afternoon in the main city's Temple of Heaven. By the time he finished, his eyes were glazed over.

He opened up Yearning For's chat box and sent out a "Gege," but there was no response. So, he opened up WeChat.

Little Jing~: Gege~

A few minutes later:

Xiang: ?

Little Jing~: What are you doing? Why are you ignoring me in-game? T.T

Xiang: ...Watching a movie.

Little Jing~: If you have the time, come back to the game!

Xiang: What's up?

Little Jing~: Something happened!

Little Jing~: A big thing!

Xiang: Coming.

Little Jing~: Mhm. I'll wait for you at Yuelao's Temple *^0^*!

Xiang: ...

Little Jing~: ...O.O What's wrong?

Xiang: Nothing, coming right away.

Getting married so soon?

Xiang Huaizhi turned off the movie, ignored the confusing feelings that were welling up in his heart, and directed his character to run to Yuelao's Temple.

Yuelao was a white-haired benevolent-looking old man holding a ball of red thread. Except for the little spirit fox currently sitting in front of Yuelao, the temple was empty.

Seeing him, the little spirit fox jumped up from the ground and brushed the dust off of her body.

[Current] Sweet Little Jing: Gege!

【Sweet Little Jing has invited you to join her party. Yes, No.】

Xiang Huaizhi hesitated, then joined her party.

What is he doing? Why isn't Bishop Wood here?

"Gege, what dungeons did you run today?" Jing Huan asked him.

"Something came up, I didn't do any." Xiang Huaizhi said. "...What are you doing?"

The other party member didn't respond and instead led him outside, leaving Yuelao's Temple.

They walked all the way to the party teleporter. The zone changed, placing them in Idle Pavilion's guild zone. Jing Huan led him to the stream they had visited before and disbanded the party.

Before Xiang Huaizhi could speak, a brilliant light flashed before his eyes.

Countless flowers blossomed out from the little spirit fox's feet, vibrant and colorful. The familiar pattern of a heart emerged, just like the one he'd seen in the afternoon. The only difference was that the word "Jing" had been replaced with "Xiang."

[Current] Sweet Little Jing: Tadaaaaaaa!!!

[Current] Sweet Little Jing: Giving gege Wednesday's gift! I super love gege today as well!

Jing Huan felt immensely satisfied with the trick he'd just learned. After seeing the fireworks display earlier today, he tossed a thousand gold to Bishop Wood as thanks and tuition for teaching him how to make the heart-shaped fireworks.

Copying someone else saved a lot of effort.

On the other end, Xiang Huaizhi watched the fireworks, silent for a long time.

Lu Hang passed by with a cup in his hand. He caught a glimpse of the screen and froze. "What the fuck? What's going on?"

Xiang Huaizhi snapped out of it, his mouth tugging up into a small smile. His tone carried traces of satisfaction and contentment that he seemed unaware of having.

"As you can see," he said, "she's still there. She hasn't run away."

Although the word "Xiang" was easier to piece together than

Chapter 09

"Jing," it was a challenge for someone like Jing Huan who struggled with such designs. Afraid that it would look too simplistic, he had also turned the "a" in "Xiang" into a heart.

Anyway, no matter how he looked at it now, it looked fabulous!

Yet, half a minute after the fireworks had been set off, the other person still hadn't reacted.

Jing Huan raised his eyebrows and probed hesitantly, "Gege, do you not like it?"

This was your daddy's blood, sweat, and tears! If you dare to say, "I don't like it," I'll fucking...

Jing Huan picked up the milk tea at his side and took a huge gulp.

...I can't fucking do anything about it. I'll just have to think of another way.

"Looks good," Xiang Huaizhi said. "You've been AFKing under the Temple of Heaven all afternoon for this?"

"Yeah. How did you know I was AFKing there?"

Xiang Huaizhi paused, then said, "I saw you."

At the sight of Xiang Huaizhi talking to Sweet Little Jing, Lu Hang rushed over, snatched the earbud hanging from one of Xiang Huaizhi's ears, put it in, and asked, "Little Jingjing, you made something so awesome! Did you save a fireworks template? Can you send me a copy?"

Jing Huan jumped. "Ah, don't have oneee." He had recreated everything from the screenshots taken earlier, carefully and painstakingly placing one flower after another.

"Then can you send me a screenshot? I'll save it to use for later," Lu Hang asked with a smile.

"Okayyy, I'll send it on WeChat."

"Nice. Good teammate!" Lu Hang said. "But uh, does Bishop Wood..." *Does he know you're doing this?*

Before Lu Hang could even finish speaking, the earbud was plucked out. Xiang Huaizhi took out a tissue, wiping it with a tissue, and slowly put it back in his ear. "If you don't finish your quests, don't even think about killing the God of War this weekend."

Lu Hang felt like he had one foot in the grave; that was how infuriated he was by Xiang Huaizhi's actions. "I wash my ears every day! They're as clean as a whistle! Why are you acting so disgusted?!"

"Because it's you."

Lu Hang threw himself back at his desk, scowling. Soon, Jing Huan sent him a screenshot of the fireworks on WeChat. Because he had just carelessly taken it, his and Yearning For's characters were in the frame.

After sending the photo to Lu Hang, Jing Huan dragged his mouse, and the little spirit fox twirled around the black-robed man.

Xiang Huaizhi wanted to say something when the game interface popped up a prompt.

【Sweet Little Jing wants to hug you. Yes, No.】

Nine Heroes had a whole menu of different character actions, including single-player actions and multiplayer actions. As a large social MMO game, it emphasized multiplayer actions, with hugging being one of them.

Idle and bored, Jing Huan clicking aimlessly around. He had browsed through a few fireworks posts, noting how closely the male characters posed in screenshots, each more intimate than the last.

After a few seconds of no response, he wanted to cancel the request. His mouse had just moved to the word "Cancel" when the action request interface suddenly disappeared.

He watched as the little spirit fox, hands clasped close to her chest, stood on the "a" heart in "Xiang," and coyly and affectionately leaned against the man in the black robe whose hand was wrapped around her waist. She kicked up a leg, her tail aloft in a picture-perfect display of girlish delight.

【You gently lean into the arms of Yearning For.】

It took a few seconds for Jing Huan's confusion to turn into giddy elation. He took a quick screenshot and rolled around, barely stifling a triumphant laugh.

Wait until you've succumbed to Daddy's charms. I'm framing this photo! In a nice frame! Mailed straight to your house! That'll drive you fucking insane!

Jing Huan licked his lips and sent another action request.

【You have sent a princess carry action request to Yearning For.】

Ten seconds later, Yearning For bent down and scooped up the little spirit fox. The little spirit fox buried her head into his chest, her tail flicking back and forth.

【You have sent a piggyback ride action request to Yearning For.】

After a moment, Yearning For squatted down, letting the little spirit fox gleefully clamber onto his back. Jing Huan's grin widened.

【You have sent a kiss action request to Yearning For.】

Two seconds later...

【Yearning For has rejected your kiss action request.】

[Current] Sweet Little Jing: ...

[Current] Sweet Little Jing: QAQ Sobbbbbbs!

 Chapter 09

If Lu Hang had turned around just then, he would've witnessed a revelation unfolding on his dear roommate's face pertaining to a certain *Nine Heroes* feature. As it were, he didn't; he was too busy studying the fireworks merchants under the Temple of Heaven to notice.

He had assembled his own fireworks before. In fact, the fireworks image that had been circulating on the forums for years was originally his. Thanks to his experience, what took Jing Huan an entire afternoon to complete, he finished in under twenty minutes. Satisfied, he took a screenshot of the template and sent it to the guild group chat.

Fluttering Firefly: Got it, thank you, boss.

BrbOrNot: Eh, isn't this the fireworks picture the guild officer posted today?! I asked the guild officer for the template, but he said he didn't save it! @Bishop Wood

Long Road Ahead: I pieced it together from Little Jingjing's screenshots. [Proud]

BrbOrNot: Awesome, but this heart looks a bit different than the guild officer's?

Long Road Ahead: Is that so? Maybe Little Jingjing modified it a bit?

BrbOrNot: What do you mean? [Surprise] Did Sweet Little Jing also make a fireworks display as a return gift?

Long Road Ahead: [Picture]

The guild was quiet for a few seconds.

Peach Cheese Stan: ?! Am I seeing it right? Why is this a picture of Sweet Little Jing and Yearning For??

Is Gege Big: You're seeing it right...

Silent Affection: We dare not say anything, we dare not ask.

BrbOrNot: @Sweet Little Jing what's going on ha ha ha?

Currently, Jing Huan was relentlessly sending action requests to Yearning For. Hug? Rejected. Hug and kiss? Rejected. A simple kiss on the cheek? Also rejected.

He clicked his tongue. *What, is kissing in the game considered taking advantage of you?!*

He was about to drop a few flirty lines when a WeChat notification popped up at the bottom right of his screen.

Sweet Little Jing: Huh, what's wrong? O.O

BrbOrNot: You actually set off fireworks in the guild zone with Yearning For?!

Sweet Little Jing: (///V///) Ah? We've been found out~ The guild zone is just prettier to set them in.

Fluffy Meatbun: Prettier than the scenery in Moon Palace zone? [Funny]

Peach Cheese Stan: And here we thought you were going to marry the guild officer. [Shutting up]

Sweet Little Jing: Ah, I do really want to marry gege, but he still refuses to accept me. >.< For now.

Peach Cheese Stan: ...

Peach Cheese Stan: I was talking about the guild officer, Bishop Wood.

Sweet Little Jing: ?!

Sweet Little Jing: How can I marry someone else?! [Frightened face] Bishop Wood and I are just friends~!

Bishop Wood: Holding the friend-zoned card while passing by, head held high.

Chapter 09

Peach Cheese Stan: lolololol.

BrbOrNot: Guild Officer, your plan isn't working.

Bishop Wood: Mm, the revolution hasn't been successful. Still need to work hard.

The group chat came to life again. Xiang Huaizhi glanced first at a few messages, then back at the game—only to discover the fireworks on the ground had already vanished.

He created a party. "Join the party."

Jing Huan snapped back to reality and hurriedly joined. He was about to ask him what they were going to do, when he saw Xiang Huaizhi leading him to the side of the guild cart driver. A moment later, the two of them were taken to the guild treasury.

【Guild Announcement: Yearning For paid the guild 40 gold of fees for commandeering the guild zone for 20 minutes.】

The guild chat channel exploded with question marks.

It had also taken Jing Huan aback, but before he could react, Yearning For had whisked him back to the main city.

【Yearning For gave you Gem x1.】

Jing Huan gaped at the item in his inventory. "Gege?"

"Embed it, and you'll have more healing output in the arena in the future," Xiang Huaizhi replied.

Jing Huan hesitated. A this level 10 gem like this would cost at least four figures if converted to yuan. It was *insanely* expensive.

Still, after a brief internal struggle, he accepted. "Okay."

Every five levels of gem granted random attribute enhancements to equipment. After Jing Huan embedded the gem, he linked his ring to the party chat.

"Gege, I rolled the best stats!" He was thrilled.

Xiang Huaizhi clicked on the ring, and indeed it did. "Mm."

"Thank you, gege." Jing Huan skillfully sent a kiss through his mic. "Gege, mwaaah!"

A brief silence followed. Then, Xiang Huaizhi said stiffly, "Don't kiss so casually."

Jing Huan, now a seasoned pro at shameless flirting, was unfazed. "What's the matter? It's not like I kiss anyone else." He paused for a bit. "Or do you simply think my kisses sound not good?"

That's not it.

Xiang Huaizhi's expression shifted slightly. After a moment, he eventually said, "The arena is about to open. Go and try out the ring."

"Okay." Jing Huan's attention was successfully diverted. Then he frowned, puzzled. "But gege, didn't you say you had something to do today so you couldn't play in the arena with me?"

Did I say that? Xiang Huaizhi thought back. It seemed like he had.

"It's not urgent," Xiang Huaizhi said after a pause. "I still have time for two matches."

"You'll lose points if you leave the arena halfway, forgeeet it." Jing Huan thought for a moment. "Gege, why don't we go to the dueling platform for a 1V1 match?"

The dueling platform, located in the center of the main city, was a place where people could spar freely. Victory or defeat had no impact on the ranks.

"All right."

Jing Huan pouted. "But gege's so strong, won't you kill me in one hit?"

Chapter 09

"I won't," said Xiang Huaizhi.

They soon arrived at the dueling platform. Since the arena had just opened, the place was practically deserted.

Jing Huan rubbed his hands excitedly. He had been dying to fight Yearning For one-on-one. After all, only in a duel could he truly gauge the other person's strength.

The second Xiang Huaizhi disbanded the party, he was dragged into the battle zone.

【Sweet Little Jing has initiated a sparring PK with you.】

Jing Huan finally understood why Yearning For had confidently said, "I won't" before.

The black-robed man stood quietly across from him, holding a plain white longsword. A very mediocre sword. A common grade piece of equipment. Yearning For had taken off his divine artifact.

Fuck! Is this scumbag looking down on me?!

[Current] Sweet Little Jing: QAQ Waaaaah, gege is so nice.

Xiang Huaizhi didn't respond, simply lifting his sword and rushing straight at him.

At the same time, in the guild WeChat group chat—

Echoes of Spring: Need someone for 2V2 in the arena, I'm a DPS healer.

Bishop Wood: Where's your wife?

Echoes of Spring: Out having fun. It'd be best if it were a Mage with some CC skills and good positioning.

Lately, Echoes of Spring and Regardless of Lovesickness had often been matched up against Yearning For and Sweet Little Jing. Since neither of them had any CC, they essentially lost every fight.

Is Gege Big: Vice Guild Leader, take me! God Xiang isn't playing in the arena tonight, so us two violent DPS will be unstoppable!

Echoes of Spring: How do you know he's not fighting today?

Is Gege Big: I was walking by the dueling platform and saw him and Sweet Little Jing doing 1V1 so I asked them.

Dueling platform? 1V1?

Echoes of Spring frowned. *Yearning For never goes to the dueling platform.*

After a moment of thought, she controlled her character and headed there.

When she arrived, there were quite a few people standing next to the dueling platform. It was much livelier than usual, and they were all watching the match.

Curious, Echoes of Spring entered spectator mode. She saw Sweet Little Jing on the ground, completely cut down. Her fox tail trembled pitifully in the dirt before going still, leaving only her summoning beast, the Nine-tailed Spirit Fox, standing. Nearby, Yearning For held a common-grade longsword and quietly stood by her side.

[Current] Sweet Little Jing: ...

[Current] Sweet Little Jing: Since gege has won me, I can only promise myself to him. [Wiping tears]

[Current] Yearning For: ?

[Current] Sweet Little Jing: I was doing a duel for marriage, after all. With so many witnesses present, I have no choice but to accept the outcome of the match. I swear I won't cheat. [Shy]

[Current] Yearning For: ...You didn't say that before.

[Current] Sweet Little Jing: No difference in saying it now~

[Current] Sweet Little Jing: Gege, what day should our wedding be? Whose family's house will we use for our marital home? Do you prefer baby boys or baby girls?

It seemed that the duel for marriage was already over.

Just as Echoes of Spring was about to leave spectator mode, she saw Yearning For abruptly sheath his sword on his back, recall his summoning beast, and then turn around, fleeing the PK zone without looking back.

Guide on How to Fail at Online Dating

Chapter 10

The next day in class, Jing Huan sat in the last row, headphones on, watching a video.

Lu Wenhao leaned back in his chair, hands dangling, and turned his head out of boredom. "Huanhuan, why are you holding your phone that close to your face this early in the morning?" When he saw what was on Jing Huan's screen, he did a double take. "What... are you watching?"

On the screen was a *Nine Heroes* PVP video. The black-robed man was brutally beating a tiger-headed player. The video's title read: "*Nine Heroes*' Top DPS Yearning For vs. Top Spirit Fox Den Player Eternal Descent."

"Watching PK," Jing Huan said without turning his head.

He simply couldn't figure it out. Although his equipment wasn't great, Yearning For had also switched to a set of common-grade gear. Yet, Jing Huan hadn't only lost—he hadn't even lasted three minutes.

Three minutes!!!

Jing Huan had never suffered such a humiliating defeat in all his years of playing *Nine Heroes*. Eternal Descent's weapon wasn't a divine artifact, judging from the glow of his equipment, but he was

still decked out in top-tier gear. Most *Nine Heroes* players who liked PVP had already seen this video, including Lu Wenhao.

He rewatched the clip with Jing Huan and clicked his tongue. "I've seen Eternal Descent's equipment; it's all burst damage[1] attribute purple gear. Even then, he still couldn't last ten minutes against Yearning For."

"Ten minutes?" Jing Huan checked the video timestamp. Sure enough, it clocked in at nine minutes and forty-eight seconds.

"Yeah, there's definitely some luck involved. The Spirit Fox Den moves fast, but God Xiang still managed to land seventy percent of his hits." Bewildered, Lu Wenhao asked, "But why are you watching PK videos all of a sudden? If you like PK so much, buy a character and come back to play."

Why, you ask? It's to study how to defeat Yearning For, of course!

Having chased after Yearning For for a while, Jing Huan felt that the easier path to revenge might be to just kill him off. Alas, his path to revenge was blanketed in thorns.

"Fuck buying a character. I don't have time to play." Jing Huan waved him off.

"You don't have time? What have you been doing lately? I checked last night, and you haven't been playing *LoL* or *PUBG*."

The video ended with the Spirit Fox Den getting slashed and sent flying by Yearning For. It was as if Jing Huan was watching himself from yesterday.

---

1   Burst damage attributes include things like: magical/physical damage, critical hit rate, critical damage, etc. These allow you to kill your opponent quickly instead of slowly chipping away at their health.

He frowned. "Spying on your daddy's stats?"

"It's not spying, I'm just looking out for my roommate. After you moved out and got your own place, you haven't been going out or gaming, so what are you doing all day?" Lu Wenhao said. "How about this? I have an alt character that I bought for event farming, why don't I give it to you?"

"No," Jing Huan said firmly.

"You're not going to take it even if I give it to you for free?!"

"Exams are coming up soon. I don't have the mental bandwidth."

Jing Huan wasn't lying; their exams were next week, and he hadn't started studying yet.

"Fine, we'll talk about it more after the exams." Lu Wenhao remembered something. "Have you not gone out recently because you've been secretly studying?"

Studying? These days, Jing Huan didn't even touch the textbook after leaving the classroom. Speaking of hitting the books, an inexplicable anxiety began to encroach on Jing Huan. "That's something only Xiang'er would do."

Gao Zixiang responded, "I haven't been either. However, I do plan to stay at the library all day tomorrow."

The three of them were internet addicts; if they stayed in the dormitory with a computer in front of them, they wouldn't be able to concentrate and study. Therefore, they all holed up in the library during exam season.

"Don't do tomorrow," said Jing Huan. "Let's just go this afternoon."

Gao Zixiang declined. "No can do, I have to video call my baby."

Lu Wenhao piped up, "I can't either, I have to clear dungeons with my wife."

Jing Huan had never been more relieved than in that moment to have moved out of the dormitory. Otherwise, he would have been subjected to these public displays of affection every day. In the afternoon, Jing Huan went to the library alone with his books. Most people had classes at this time, so there were plenty of empty seats in the library. He randomly picked a spot by the window, sat down, and pulled out his phone, intending to slack off a bit first. He opened up the group chat between him, Yearning For, and Long Road Ahead.

Little Jing~: [Knocking] Anyone here~

Long Road Ahead: Here, Little Jingjing!

Little Jing~: O.O How many steps have you completed for the quest?

Long Road Ahead: 73! The day after tomorrow, we can start the fight on time!

Little Jing~: Ooooo, great. Where's my gege?

Long Road Ahead: ...You just wanted to ask me this, huh?

Little Jing~: (#^.^#) He he, because gege didn't reply to my DM.

Long Road Ahead: Saw through you. :)

Long Road Ahead: He just came back from playing basketball. He's taking a shower, so he probably didn't see your message. He'll reply to you soon. By the way, Little Jingjing, I have something to talk to you about. Our God of War party is short a member, can I call Bishop Wood to fill in?

Little Jing~: Ahhh, that's fine with me.

Long Road Ahead: He he, okay, great. Bishop Wood's gear is pretty good. It'll save us some trouble if he's coming along.

Jing Huan closed the group chat and was about to move onto his Moments when his dormitory group chat popped up.

Lu Wenhao: [Picture]

Lu Wenhao: Huanhuan, aren't these shoes cool? Limited edition, dropping tomorrow at 8 a.m. on the official website!

Jing Huan opened the picture: the shoes were crisscrossed in simple yet stylish silver and white lines. But the most impressive part was the brand logo decorating the side of the shoe as it appeared to be crafted from a special material that made it black and shimmery.

Little Jing~: Cool! How much?

Lu Wenhao: Only a little over 8,000!

Little Jing~: AAAH, damn, buy it!!! >.<

Lu Wenhao: …

Eyes still on Jing Huan's emoticon, Lu Wenhao hissed to the person next to him, "Xiang'er, why do I feel like Huanhuan's texting style has been kind of girly lately?"

Last time, Jing Huan had even sent them a blushing sticker, which shocked the two of them to the point that they suspected his account had been hacked.

Gao Zixiang didn't even bother raising his head. "Say that to his face, and you'll know if he's girly or not."

Lu Wenhao silently shut his mouth.

Meanwhile, Jing Huan set an alarm for the shoe sale, preparing to get up early tomorrow to buy them.

"Senior?" a person behind him suddenly called out softly.

Jing Huan turned around. It was the girl who had tried to give him water at the basketball court last time. She had her long hair

 Chapter 10

loose, and was wearing a white shirt and jeans, clutching some books. Cheeks pink, the girl pointed to the chair beside him. "Can I sit here?"

Jing Huan blinked and surreptitiously put away his cellphone. "Of course."

When Xiang Huaizhi came out of the bathroom, he noticed he had four unread messages on his cellphone.

"In the ten or so minutes that you were in the shower, Little Jing-jing already sought me out," Lu Hang teased. "Hurry up and check if she had some kind of life-changing event that she wanted to talk to you about."

Xiang Huaizhi wordlessly unlocked his phone.

Little Jing~: Happy Thursday, gege!

Little Jing~: I'm in class, so sleeeepy. =0=

Little Jing~: What's gege doing? [Peeking]

Little Jing~: Gege, I have exams next week. I'm going to the library this afternoon to cram! I might not be able to run dungeons with you. QAQ

Lu Hang added, "By the way, I just asked Little Jingjing, and she said she didn't mind if Bishop Wood joined us, so I'll tell him he can come. He volunteered to help me; I really can't say no."

"Suit yourself."

"*Haah*, I actually wanted Echoes of Spring to fill in, since she could both DPS and heal, but she's not available..." Noticing the movements of the person behind him, Lu Hang paused. "Where are you going?"

Xiang Huaizhi put on a light jacket. "Returning some books."

"Returning books? Weren't you going to run dungeons this afternoon?"

"They're almost due," Xiang Huaizhi said concisely, grabbing a few books from the table. "I'm off."

"...Oh."

Because of his good looks, Jing Huan had received an innumerable number of confessions since he was young. He braced his head on one hand, holding the pen tip against his chin, pondering the best way to turn this underclassman down gently if it came to that.

This was the scene Xiang Huaizhi walked into: The boy was staring intently at the book on the table, while the girl beside him stole peeks in his direction. A ray of sunlight streamed through the window, casting a warm glow over the pair and making it seem like a scene right out of a romantic high school drama.

A handsome young man and a pretty young woman; no wonder onlookers couldn't resist stealing a glance at them. Just then, the girl seemed to have finally gathered her courage as she turned to say something to Jing Huan. He paused then offered a slightly apologetic smile.

Xiang Huaizhi looked away. Carrying his two books, he was about to find a random place to sit when he was spotted by his underclassman not too far away.

Jing Huan was initially surprised before he raised his hand in greeting. Since loud noises were prohibited in the library, Jing Huan mouthed, "Senior!"

Xiang Huaizhi hesitated before walking over.

"Senior, are you here to study too?" Jing Huan asked aloud when Xiang Huaizhi stood in front of him.

"Just returning some books," Xiang Huaizhi said, "and taking a look around."

Jing Huan looked at the books in his hand—all foreign classics.

"I'm here to study. Exams are next week, so I need to save myself." Jing Huan said. "Shall we sit together?"

Xiang Huaizhi glanced at the girl next to him.

"Ah, she said she was leaving," Jing Huan explained.

The girl's face turned redder. She scrambled to her feet. "Yes, I'm leaving now. Senior Xiang, please sit." Awkward and embarrassed, the girl fled with her books.

As Xiang Huaizhi sat down, he caught the faint sound of Jing Huan exhaling in relief. "What's wrong? You don't like this type of girl?"

Jing Huan looked startled. "You heard that?"

"Guessed it."

The shift in atmosphere had been unmistakeable as the girl's expectant expression gave way to disappointment. One glance was all it took to know a confession had been rejected.

"Sort of... It's mainly because I don't even know who she is. It would be strange to accept, right?" Jing Huan stretched languidly. Xiang Huaizhi's voice always made him think of Yearning For. He confessed with a wry smile, "Plus, I'm chasing someone else."

Eyelids twitching, Xiang Huaizhi asked calmly, "Really? Someone from our school?"

"No." He had no idea where in the world that guy was.

"What kind of person are they?"

Jing Huan was surprised, but recovered quickly with a smile. "No way, Senior, are you interested in this kind of thing?"

Xiang Huaizhi flipped a page in his book. "Just asking. You don't have to answer if it's inconvenient."

"It's not inconvenient." Jing Huan chuckled. "It's just that the person I'm pursuing isn't that great."

"Not that great?" Xiang Huaizhi tilted his head. There was a subtle shift in his expression as he looked at Jing Huan. "Then why are you pursuing them?"

Why else? Because there's another motive, of course.

Jing Huan just wanted to make something up and had no intention of elaborating. After all, he hadn't even told Lu Wenhao and Gao Zixiang about this so he couldn't possibly tell Xiang Huaizhi. Once his grand plan was accomplished, the matter of him masquerading as a girl would be forever sealed in the *Nine Heroes'* database along with Yearning For's character.

"Why else?" Jing Huan said naturally. "Because I like them, of course."

Xiang Huaizhi's expression grew complicated. "Even though they're 'not that great'?"

"Well, everyone has their type." Jing Huan turned to Xiang Huaizhi, amused. "Senior, you wouldn't look down on me because I have bad taste, right?"

Xiang Huaizhi's eyes dimmed. After a long pause, he responded stiffly, "No."

Jing Huan found it all quite intriguing; before his sophomore year, he had never even seen Xiang Huaizhi. But ever since their encounter in that stairwell, they seemed to keep running into each other. They bumped into each other while traveling. They crossed

 Chapter 10

paths again on the basketball court. And now, here they were, meeting once more at the library.

Thinking of the three cups of milk tea that Xiang Huaizhi had treated him to last time, Jing Huan wondered if he should buy a cup of coffee from the front desk to thank him. As he turned to ask, he saw Xiang Huaizhi reading with a serious expression, a frown pulling his lips down.

In truth, Xiang Huaizhi wasn't reading at all. He was trying to remember what he had done to earn the label of someone "not that great." After playing around with a multitude of possibilities, the only thing he could come up with was the incident with Fae Bae.

Should he set things straight in the game? Save himself from being regarded as a scumbag in Jing Huan's eyes? But if he explained everything, would Jing Huan still be so obsessed with him?

No way.

Thinking of Sweet Little Jing's bold remarks in the game, Xiang Huaizhi pursed his lips.

"Senior Xiang?"

Xiang Huaizhi snapped out of it and glanced over. "Hm?"

"Do you want some coffee?" Jing Huan asked. "I could grab a cup for you too."

"Mm." Xiang Huaizhi gathered his thoughts and stood up first. "I'll go buy it."

"You don't have to, I'll go…"

Before Jing Huan could finish, Xiang Huaizhi had already set his book down on the table and was already on his way to the front desk.

Jing Huan watched him leave, flabbergasted. His cellphone suddenly rang. Jing Huan tore his eyes away and opened his cellphone to take a glance.

Lu Wenhao: @Little Jing~ Huanhuan, are you in the library all by your lonesome? Why don't you come find us after you're done studying? I'm short a party member for my dungeon. [Shy]

Little Jing~: GTFO. I'm not lonely.

He held up his cellphone, took a picture of the book placed face down beside him, and sent it to the group chat.

Lu Wenhao: ???

Lu Wenhao: You really are seeing a girl behind our backs.

Little Jing~: Girl my ass, it's a guy.

Lu Wenhao: Besides me and Xiang'er, which other guy would go to the library with you?

Laughing, Jing Huan was just about to reply when he saw Xiang Huaizhi returning with two cups of coffee.

Xiang Huaizhi's broad shoulders and long legs gave him a first-class figure. When he walked, it was like he brought a gust of wind with him. There were hardly any girls around who didn't look at him with covetous expressions.

On impulse, Jing Huan point his cellphone camera at Xiang Huaizhi, and recorded a three-second video that he promptly sent to the group chat.

Lu Wenhao: Damn, you guys slept together just once, and your relationship is already this good?

Little Jing~: ?

Little Jing~: Don't say it so weirdly, I just happened to run into him.

 Chapter 10

Xiang Huaizhi obviously knew that he was being recorded. He put the coffee down on the table. "It's hot."

"Thanks." Jing Huan brought his focus back to the present and held up his cellphone to explain. "Lu Wenhao asked me who I was with, so I recorded a video for him."

Xiang Huaizhi glanced at his phone. Seeing the words "slept together once," he hesitated before averting his eyes. "Mm, it's fine."

The two of them stayed in the library all afternoon. It wasn't until the library's main lights flickered on that Jing Huan finally emerged from the sea of knowledge, struggling to drag himself back to shore.

He sighed and listlessly called out, "Senior."

Xiang Huaizhi asked, "Done studying?"

"I guess."

"Think you can pass the exam next week?"

"No."

Xiang Huaizhi stared at him.

"But I've done all I can do." Jing Huan closed the book. "Man proposes while God disposes; let's leave it all up to fate."

Xiang Huaizhi chuckled. This underclassman in real life was completely different from his in-game persona—as different as night and day—with only his optimism remaining the same.

It was already dark outside, and the two of them left the library side by side.

"Want to have dinner with me?" Xiang Huaizhi asked casually.

"Sure," said Jing Huan, "but I'm buying this time."

"No." Xiang Huaizhi paused for a beat. "I'm the senior, so I'll pay."

Jing Huan laughed and turned to face him. "If you put it that

way, I should be the one paying since I'm younger. You know, to show my respect to you."

Xiang Huaizhi frowned, wanting to say something else but Jing Huan interrupted him. "Senior, friendship is all about reciprocity. If you're always treating me, I'll feel too embarrassed to eat with you next time."

Xiang Huaizhi stared at him for a while and then gave up. "Sure."

They went to eat home-cooking style food. During the meal, Jing Huan occasionally pulled out his cellphone to type. Xiang Huaizhi appeared calm and collected as he drank his soup, when in reality, the cellphone in his pocket vibrated countless times.

After they had stuffed themselves, Jing Huan paid the bill and earnestly said, "Senior, let me know when you go to the library to study next time, and I'll keep you company."

Why would I need you to keep me company? It's a library; it's a quiet place by nature, Xiang Huaizhi thought but nodded outwardly. "All right."

"I'll head back first then, Senior." Jing Huan slipped his cellphone in his pocket but paused as he turned to leave. "Wait, Senior, can I address you another way from now on?" Calling him "Senior" all the time felt a bit awkward.

Xiang Huaizhi raised his eyebrows. "Sure."

"What should I call you then?" Jing Huan considered. "Huaizhi? Zhi-ge? Huai-ge?"

Xiang Huaizhi listened quietly, inexplicably feeling like none of these sounded right. "You can call me gege."

Jing Huan froze. "...Huh?"

His own words finally registered to Xiang Huaizhi. He also

stilled, but he quickly composed himself. "Since I'm older than you, isn't it very normal to call me gege?"

That made sense. Hesitant, Jing Huan tentatively tried it out: "…Gege?"

The voice was different from what Xiang Huaizhi normally heard; it wasn't as cutesy or sweet. Jing Huan was clearly a little embarrassed, his tone both restrained and shy, but Xiang Huaizhi still thought it was a huge improvement from when Jing Huan addressed him in-game.

After calling him that, Jing Huan felt that it didn't sound quite right. He laughed, face flushed. "Forget it, calling you that seems too mushy. I'll just call you ge or Xiang-ge?"

Xiang Huaizhi looked down, hiding his emotions. "Whatever you like. Let's go back."

"Gege!" Through his headphones, the girl's voice rang out, crisp and without any hesitation. "Gege, I'm late, *waaaaah*."

Xiang Huaizhi lightly clicked with his index finger, starting the dungeon. "It's fine."

[Party] Love is Sharing Noms: Little Jing, weren't you supposed to be free today? Why did you get online so late?

Having run dungeons together so many times, Love is Sharing Noms had her party members' schedules down pat.

[Party] Sweet Little Jing: I went to the library to study in the afternoon. Next week, I have an exam. QAQ

[Party] Love is Sharing Noms: That sucks, pat pat [Patting dog's head]

[Party] Sweet Little Jing: [Weeping]

 Chapter 10

[Party] Love is Sharing Noms: By the way, did you see tomorrow's update announcement?

[Party] Sweet Little Jing: I haven't had time to check. What, did a new event start?

[Party] Love is Sharing Noms: A new outfit is coming out!! And it's gorgeous!!

[Party] Sweet Little Jing: O.O! Wow, is it a limited edition?

[Party] Love is Sharing Noms: No, it's just a regular outfit. The point is, even though it's just a regular outfit, it's SO much more beautiful than the limited edition ones! The designer must've been resurrected just for tonight! [Knocking on a wooden fish] I sent you a picture in the WeChat group. Go look!

Since the outfit wasn't limited edition, Jing Huan didn't really care. Nonetheless, he opened WeChat and took a look. The outfit did look stunning, featuring a cute lantern design and even included a weapon pendant.

[Party] Sweet Little Jing: It's so pretty!! How much is it?

[Party] Love is Sharing Noms: 1,200 gold.

[Party] Sweet Little Jing: ???

[Party] Sweet Little Jing: [Waving handkerchief]

[Party] Love is Sharing Noms: It's not bad. It also comes with a weapon pendant, so it's like two items for the price of one.

[Party] Sweet Little Jing: It's too expensive. Forget it. I'll buy it later when I have money. [Wiping tears]

Buy my ass, Jing Huan cursed from the bottom of his heart. How could a stupid outfit cost 1,200 yuan?! Why didn't this shitty game just rob a bank instead of players' wallets?

The matter was quickly forgotten though, so when Jing Huan

logged into the game the next day and saw the system message, his mouth dropped.

【Unknown Realm shopkeeper: Congratulations, young hero! Yearning For has gifted you a set of Lantern Fairy attire. Please go to the Unknown Realm (118, 29) to claim your new outfit!】

Jing Huan blinked, reading the message several times. The gifter was indeed Yearning For, and the gift was indeed the new outfit.

But hang on… Yearning For actually gave him the outfit?!

Jing Huan was baffled.

He could see the ring as Xiang Huaizhi thanking him for his help with clearing the dungeons, and the gems for helping him in the arena fights, but what about the outfit?

Jing Huan pondered, his emotions a tangled mess. After several months of seeing no progress, finally, a faint glimmer of hope!

Jing Huan opened his friend list and saw that Yearning For wasn't online. But he was in a good mood; he hummed a few lines of a song, and had his little spirit fox bounce toward the Unknown Realm.

Since the new outfit was newly released, the area around the Unknown Realm shopkeeper was crowded with players eagerly waiting to buy it.

[Current] Ji Xiaonian: Black seems to look better. Faefae, which color are you buying?

[Current] Fae Bae: I bought one in every color [Cute]

Game maps were only so big, so it wasn't unusual to run into acquaintances. Jing Huan made his way into the crowd and was planning on leaving after getting his outfit, but due to the large number of players there to buy it, he still needed to queue to claim it.

 Chapter 10

[Current] Ji Xiaonian: You bought all seven colors?! You're so rich! QAQ

[Current] Fae Bae: Ha ha, Sheepy gifted them to me~

[Current] Ji Xiaonian: Damn, he's sooo generous. [Funny] You should accept him then.

[Current] Fae Bae: But I don't want to be in a relationship yet. I like where we're at right now.

It was only a few sentences, but everyone could catch her drift.

Jing Huan hadn't intended to eavesdrop on their private conversation, but unfortunately, they were chatting right behind him in the Current Channel.

He clicked his tongue. It seemed these days, you couldn't even be the fallback option without some family wealth.

[Current] Ji Xiaonian: Hey, you do you. I just think that he's way better than a certain someone.

[Current] Fae Bae: Why are you bringing that person up again? [Shutting up]

[Current] Ji Xiaonian: Oops, my bad. But those posts of you tearing Ranxin apart got bumped up again this morning. Rereading them made me sick to my stomach. [Vomiting]

Jing Huan froze just as he was about to claim his outfit. He immediately abandoned the queue and opened the *Nine Heroes* forum. Sure enough, the forum homepage was filled with posts about his jie.

【Ranxin is such a bitch, live streaming to delete friends.】

【Exposing Ranxin, the homewrecking side-chick from Mirage. Players in that server, beware.】

【Heard that Ranxin deleted her account out of guilt??】

The smile on Jing Huan's face slowly faded. He checked every single post and found they were all bumped by the same ID. Judging from their comments, they seemed to be latecomer catching up on the drama. They went through the posts, asking questions, with the other players quickly jumping in to answer them. With all this back-and-forth, the posts remained on the home page. Despite how many months had passed, the flaming still hadn't stopped.

Although this wasn't Jing Huan's first time reading these, it still made him see red. His eyes gradually froze over, turning indifferent, as he stared at the insults and humiliating comments on the screen.

After scrolling through all the posts, he closed the page and returned to the game, face expressionless.

Someone stopped Xiang Huaizhi right as class ended. "Hey bros, how about we play a round of ball before heading back?"

Before he could say a word, Lu Hang slung an arm around his shoulder and said, "Sounds good, it's been ages and I'm dying to play!"

Xiang Huaizhi shook off his hand. "You can go, I'm heading back to the dorms."

"Don't be like that, it's only ten o'clock. What are you going back for?" Lu Hang cajoled, "Come on, let's just play half a game."

"No," Xiang Huaizhi said firmly, grabbing his books with one hand. "I'm leaving."

Once he was back in the dormitory, Xiang Huaizhi put his books away and turned on the computer. Just after logging in, he received a system message.

【Unknown Realm shopkeeper: Your friend Sweet Little Jing has

 Chapter 10

rejected your gift. Please go to the Unknown Realm shopkeeper (118, 29) within seven days to receive your refund.】

He blinked. He instinctively opened and checked his friend list, and although Sweet Little Jing's name was quietly lit up, it was silent.

[Friend] Yearning For: ?

[Friend] Sweet Little Jing: ?

[Friend] Yearning For: You didn't want the outfit?

[Friend] Sweet Little Jing: I couldn't possibly spend your money.

[Friend] Yearning For: …

No kaomojis, no stickers. Even the period at the end of the sentence felt cold. Was he just imagining things?

Xiang Huaizhi frowned and typed tentatively.

[Friend] Yearning For: Wanna clear dungeons?

[Friend] Sweet Little Jing: No.

[Friend] Yearning For: What's going on with you?

[Friend] Sweet Little Jing: ?

[Friend] Yearning For: In a bad mood?

Yes, so it's better not to provoke your daddy right now.

Jing Huan pretended the keyboard was Yearning For and started stabbing the keys so hard they clacked.

[Friend] Sweet Little Jing: No.

[Friend] Yearning For: Then come clear dungeons.

[Friend] Sweet Little Jing: [Smiling] …I don't feel well and don't want to do it.

[Friend] Yearning For: Where do you feel unwell?

[Friend] Sweet Little Jing: Everywhere.

[Friend] Yearning For: Specifically?

Jing Huan was getting very annoyed with him very quickly.

Why are you asking?! Can you cure me?! Your main job is being a scumbag, but you moonlight as a doctor? Is that right?!

[Friend] Yearning For: ?

[Friend] Sweet Little Jing: …It's here.

[Friend] Yearning For: What is?

[Friend] Sweet Little Jing: My Aunt Flo.

Knowing Jing Huan's real gender, Xiang Huaizhi instinctively didn't make the connection.

[Friend] Yearning For: Your aunt? A relative?

[Friend] Sweet Little Jing: …

Xiang Huaizhi was about to type when an enormous wave of exclamation marks came crashing down on him.

[Friend] Sweet Little Jing: My period! Period!! My period came!! Do you understand what a period is?! Once a month! Abdominal pain and backache! Nonstop bleeding!! Do you understand!!! Huh?! How much clearer do I have to be?!

Xiang Huaizhi managed to pick out the words from the sea of exclamation marks and piece them together, but found himself, if possible, at even more of a loss. There were so many questions in his mind that they could only be summed up with one symbol:

[Friend] Yearning For: ?

It wasn't just Yearning For; even the *Nine Heroes* interface was an eyesore to Jing Huan right now. He promptly exited the game and went to bed. As he stared blankly at the ceiling, he thought, *What kind of bullshit did I just say?*

This was all because of Yearning For! His constant nagging had pushed Jing Huan into making such a stupid excuse!

 Chapter 10

After a moment, Jing Huan covered his eyes with his arms. What if that outburst had squandered all of his efforts over the past few months?

It probably didn't, right? Didn't people say to treat girls on their period like queens? Yearning For couldn't possibly be that petty, right?

Jing Huan rolled over, burying his face in the pillow.

Whatever! Vent first, worry later! Besides, it's not like he said anything out of line; at most, he maybe used one too many exclamation marks. If Yearning For truly was furious, then he just had a heart of glass.

All of a sudden, his cellphone vibrated.

Jing Huan let out a big sigh, and, without shifting positions, reached out and grabbed his cellphone off the table.

Xiang Huaizhi: You there?

It was Xiang Huaizhi. Jing Huan blinked and typed feebly.

Little Jing~: I'm here, gege.

Little Jing~: Oh... I typoed. What's up, Xiang-ge?

Xiang Huaizhi: Want to go play some night ball?

Little Jing~: No, I'm kind of sleepy so I was about to hit the hay.

Xiang Huaizhi checked the time. It wasn't even half past seven yet.

Xiang Huaizhi: You're sleeping so early. Do you not feel well?

Even though Yearning For had asked the same thing, Xiang Huaizhi's question didn't annoy Jing Huan.

Resting his chin on his pillow, he replied.

Little Jing~: No, just didn't get enough sleep last night. But once I sleep more, I'll feel better.

Little Jing~: [Muscle]

Xiang Huaizhi: Got it.

Lu Hang was still sweating when he returned to the dorm.

"It's really a pity you didn't come, Xiangxiang. You didn't see how intense the game was. There we were, neck-and-neck, always within one point of each other, and in the last three seconds, I made the game-winning shot!" In recalling this glorious moment, Lu Hang's chest was nearly bursting with pride. "I'm so awesome."

Xiang Huaizhi commented lightly, "You don't have to feel sorry for me. If I were there, the game wouldn't have been so intense."

Lu Hang couldn't refute that. He pulled off his shirt and tossed it into the dirty laundry basket, getting ready to shower.

"Lu Hang," Xiang Huaizhi suddenly called out to him, "let me ask you something."

"Go ahead, honorable sir."

Xiang Huaizhi frowned, hesitating. "If someone who's normally very clingy suddenly starts losing their patience with you—"

"Sweet Little Jing finally had enough of you?"

Xiang Huaizhi didn't reply. Lu Hang was shocked. "No way, I was just throwing that out there... Did Sweet Little Jing really turn against you?"

"No." Xiang Huaizhi kind of regretted asking him. "Forget it. Pretend I didn't ask."

Maybe he was just overthinking it. Other than typing a few extra exclamation marks and saying he was sleepy, Jing Huan hadn't acted that unusually. But why didn't he just say he was sleepy? Why did he have to say he was on his...

Chapter 10

Lu Hang could tell something was amiss from Xiang Huaizi's expression and waggled his eyebrows teasingly. Xiang Huaizhi had forcibly ended the topic, but Lu Hang wasn't going to let it go without adding his two cents in. "It's obvious what happened in that situation."

Sure enough, Xiang Huaizhi asked, "What's obvious?"

"She got tired of chasing. Gave up. The love's gone."

Xiang Huaizhi lifted a brow in question.

"A person's affection has limits. And if their feelings are not reciprocated, there's only so much they can take." Lu Hang had a deeply profound look on his face. "No one wants to be a simp[2] forever. You need to humor them sometimes."

Xiang Huaizhi didn't really understand, but he had a feeling Lu Hang wasn't saying anything good.

He frowned. "You're the simp."

Lu Hang shot him a bizarre look. "That's just a popular saying, I'm not actually calling Little Jingjing a simp."

Xiang Huaizhi retorted, "You stink, go shower."

Lu Hang bowed his head. "...Yes, my lord."

As Lu Hang grabbed his towel and walked into the bathroom, he thought, *Yeah, right. If Sweet Little Jing isn't your honorable self's simp, then I guess I fucking am.*

Jing Huan woke up early the next morning.

---

2 The original term 舔 狗 - tiǎn gǒu - translates as "licking dog" but it refers to someone who excessively flatters, prioritizes, or selflessly devotes themselves to someone they like, often without receiving affection or reciprocation in return. In short, it's a simp.

Out of habit, he picked up his cellphone, wanting to send a good morning message to Yearning For, but as soon as he opened WeChat, he received a message from his cousin.

Jiejie: [Photo] Do you like them, Huanhuan?

It was a pair of sneakers, brightly colored and stylish.

Little Jing~: Yes!

Jiejie: I'm glad. Then it was worth waking up early to line up and buy them for you. [Proud]

Jiejie: What's with your profile picture and WeChat nickname? It took me forever to find you in my contacts. [Face with tears of joy]

Little Jing~: ...It's nothing, I just lost a bet. Did you really line up just to buy them for me?

Jiejie: Of course. I stood in line until my legs were sore. Isn't your birthday coming up? I'll mail them to you.

Little Jing~: ? You're not coming back?

Jiejie: I'm going to be here for a while. I've found a job here.

The two cousins chatted for another half hour before they bade each other goodbye.

Jing Huan closed Liang Ran's chat and caught sight of Yearning For's profile picture out of the corner of his eye.

Good morning message? Fuck that.

Yesterday's bad mood had returned. Jing Huan cursed inwardly, angrily smashed the lock button, and got out of bed.

Yearning For and Long Road Ahead had a full day of classes today, and while Jing Huan didn't know if they were real college students, he was certain that, at least on Fridays during the day, those two wouldn't make an in-game appearance.

Chapter 10

Jing Huan logged into *Nine Heroes*. As soon as he did, all he saw were people flaunting the new outfit in front of him.

Jing Huan finally felt a twinge of regret. No matter how furious he had been yesterday, he shouldn't have rejected the outfit; he wasted the perfect opportunity to spend Yearning For's money!

Still, he really didn't care about the new outfit.

Using his mouse, he walked Sweet Little Jing over to the main city teleporter to do his dailies first. It was the busiest place in *Nine Heroes* since everyone liked to set up stalls, AFK, or form parties there.

[Current] Loving Life and Jiajia: Havoc in Heaven dungeon, join +++ our party, level 120-130, preferably DPS!

[Current] Qiao Yao: Looking for a husband~ I'm a voice-con, hoping to find a little gege with a nice voice. If our chemistry is good, we can video chat~~ [Blowing a kiss]

[Current] Young Luo: Qilin Mountain dungeon +, need a Spirit Fox Den.

[Current] Young Luo: Qilin Mountain dungeon +, need a Spirit Fox Den. Other sects don't +. Won't charge a carry fee.

Young Luo's message successfully caught Jing Huan's attention.

The Qilin Mountain dungeon was a five-player dungeon. Not only was the process cumbersome, but the dungeon also required 100 gold to open, with each party member typically contributing twenty gold. Truth be told, the rewards for this dungeon were lackluster—could even be considered terrible—but players ran it for one reason and one reason only: to trigger the hidden boss.

Defeating the hidden boss rewarded players with rare material

drops, so when this dungeon first came out, people scrambled to run it, only to be discouraged by the hidden boss's encounter rate. Most of them didn't even know what the Qilin Mountain hidden boss looked like. As time went by, the number of players running this dungeon gradually dwindled.

Jing Huan was also interested but solely because this dungeon had the rare materials he needed. But the second this idea came to his mind, he squashed it down. With his terrible RNG luck, it'd be easier if he just bought the materials.

The little spirit fox turned, about to leave.

【Young Luo invites you to join his party. Yes, No.】

【Young Luo has set you as a private chat recipient.】

[Private] Young Luo: Come join us. I won't charge you a carry fee.

[Private] Sweet Little Jing: …No, I'm not very lucky.

[Private] Young Luo: How do you know if you don't try? The team is full of high DPS, so it won't take long.

[Private] Sweet Little Jing: Why do you only need Spirit Fox Dens?

[Private] Young Luo: They can heal and seal. Very convenient.

Jing Huan had never heard of players bringing a Spirit Fox Den into a dungeon because it was "convenient."

[Private] Young Luo: Will you come? It'll just be an hour.

Jing Huan thought about it. Since Long Road Ahead and Yearning For wouldn't be back until the afternoon, he could save his dailies for later. He clicked "Yes," and joined the party.

After entering the dungeon, he took a casual look at his party list. He couldn't recognize any of the names except for one dual-wielding

Chapter 10

Rogue called Maimai's #1 Fan who was the second-ranked DPS on the Mastery rankings list.

Just as Young Luo had said, the party didn't have a healer. The only girl here was called Little Mai and she was playing a Mage. Jing Huan studied this loli for a long time. She looked familiar, but even after some head scratching, Jing Huan still couldn't recall where he had seen her before.

The five of them quickly entered the dungeon. Jing Huan was ready to coast through, but as soon as he tabbed back into the game, he realized something was wrong.

Both Maimai's #1 Fan and Little Mai were empty-handed.

[Party] Little Mai: My husband's and my weapons have no durability left. Can't use them, sorry.

Without weapons, the damage DPS sects' could deal was less than half of their usual output. Additionally, repairing the durability of purple equipment was very troublesome, and it was definitely too late to fix it now.

[Party] Maimai's #1 Fan: It's fine, let's just fight like this. We'll just be a little slower, that's all. Good thing we have a Spirit Fox Den in the party, right?

A slower monster kill speed meant they would take significantly more damage from the mobs, placing a heavier burden on the healer.

Jing Huan was at a loss. He had intended on coasting through this dungeon—how did he end up working like a slave?

[Party] Maimai's #1 Fan: Hey, you're getting carried for free. Putting in some effort is more than fair, don't you think?

Jing Huan frowned. The party leader had been the one to ask *him* to join. Why was he framing it as him freeloading to save money? But Jing Huan wasn't going to kick up a fuss over running a dungeon.

[Party] Sweet Little Jing: 1.

Just then, the guild's WeChat group flashed.

Bishop Wood: @Sweet Little Jing, want to run a dungeon?

Jing Huan casually took a screenshot of the battlefield and sent it to the group chat.

Sweet Little Jing: I'm already in a dungeon.

Bishop Wood: Why are you in THIS dungeon? You basically get no experience points.

Sweet Little Jing: I want to see if I can get it to drop some centipede legs. [Aggrieved]

Bishop Wood: Ha ha ha, good luck with that.

Spirit Fox Dens weren't dedicated healers, so their healing output was nothing in comparison to Putuo Mountains. As the only healer in the party, Jing Huan couldn't go AFK especially as the dungeon's difficulty increased toward the end. Clearing this dungeon was much more exhausting than fighting in the arena.

[Party] Sweet Little Jing: Little Mai, are you there?

[Party] Little Mai: Ah.

[Party] Sweet Little Jing: Are you not wearing any armor? Why are the monsters dealing so much damage to you?

"She found out," the girl said in a private YY chat, surprised. "How did she see through us?"

"It doesn't matter." The man's voice was indifferent. "So what if she found out? Just say whatever."

[Party] Little Mai: I just checked, and my armor also has no durability left.

Chapter 10

Not checking your gear's durability before running a dungeon was peak irresponsibility, since it unnecessarily increased the burden on your party members.

Jing Huan didn't respond. They've already come this far; at this point, saying anything more would be superfluous.

Finally, two hours later, they cleaned up the last trash mob and were ready to fight the boss. Jing Huan breathed a sigh of relief and sat up, back straight, to welcome the boss in the final battle.

A line of yellow characters appeared:

【You've been dismissed from the party by Young Luo.】

Jing Huan gazed at the system prompt without reacting for several seconds.

[Current] Sweet Little Jing: ?

The other four party members ignored him and charged straight into battle, with the "in combat" indicators appearing over their heads.

Frowning, Jing Huan entered spectator mode. He saw Little Mai's #1 Fan and Little Mai standing side-by-side, the weapons in their hands shining brightly and magnificently.

Jing Huan finally realized—he had been played. After making him heal and working him to the bone for two hours, they kicked him from the party right before the boss battle.

If you didn't kill the boss, the dungeon wouldn't count as completed, meaning this dungeon was essentially moot for him. In all his years of playing *Nine Heroes*, this was the first time Jing Huan encountered such a thing.

How fucking disgusting.

He didn't know that the most disgusting part was yet to come.

Twenty minutes later, the boss fell to the ground and a system prompt appeared.

【Dungeon party: Young Luo and his party fought to defeat the Baizu King and found the Centipede Spirit's invitation on him!】

They had triggered the hidden boss.

Jing Huan was forcibly sent to the Centipede Spirit's cave by the system. He never expected that his first time seeing this dungeon's hidden boss would be under such circumstances.

Jing Huan put his hands on the keyboard. It was time to bring out his alter ego: *Nine Heroes'* Legendary Trash-talker.

Back when he played *LoL,* he often got into flaming matches with his teammates. With his fast typing speed, he never lost an argument. Trash-talking wasn't going to change anything, but at least it made him feel better.

To hell with keeping the harmony, Daddy's not indulging you anymore.

He typed a line of words and was about to send it when another prompt popped up in the chat channel.

【Dungeon party: Ji Xiaonian has joined the party.】

Jing Huan's hand froze.

Ten seconds later, Ji Xiaonian appeared in his field of view and joined Young Luo's party. Without saying a word, the five of them entered combat with the hidden boss.

Jing Huan took a deep breath, silently deleted all the words in the chat box, and teleported out of the zone. He opened the marketplace, browsing back and forth for a long time, and bookmarked several pieces of purple equipment. Then, he added them all to the shopping cart, checked out, and paid—all in one go.

Chapter 10

The guild WeChat group began to flash again.

Bishop Wood: [Picture] @Sweet Little Jing, Little Jingjing, why aren't you in this picture?

The battle screenshot Bishop Wood sent over showed Ji Xiaonian killing the hidden boss with the other members of her party.

Sweet Little Jing: I got kicked when we reached the boss.

Bishop Wood: ??

Peach Cheese Stan: ??? What??

Echoes of Spring: What happened?

Sweet Little Jing: It's fine.

Sweet Little Jing: I'll handle this. But to avoid causing trouble for the guild, I'll leave the guild and group chat first.

Without waiting for a response, Jing Huan left the group chat and, in the next second, the guild. He opened his friend list and called on an old friend.

[Friend] Sweet Little Jing: You there?

[Friend] OFF!: Here meimei, what's up?

[Friend] Sweet Little Jing: Tail a few people for me. Let me know when they're alone or in a party of three or less. I'll give you 500 gold if you follow them for two days.

[Friend] OFF!: What are you up to? [Surprise]

[Friend] Sweet Little Jing: Killing people.

Even clay figurines were refined with fire, and he had never been one to let others walk all over him. Moreover, after two days of being in an awful mood, he desperately needed to vent.

[Friend] OFF!: ...Okay, send me the IDs.

Jing Huan sent all five IDs.

[Friend] OFF!: Listen, meimei... you'd be fine dealing with the

others, but Maimai's #1 Fan is the second-ranked DPS in the server. Even three of you might not be enough to take him down. Why don't you just focus on the other four?

[Friend] Sweet Little Jing: I don't need you to teach me how to kill people. :D

A chill inexplicably crawled down OFF!'s neck at the sight of the emoji at the end of her sentence.

[Friend] OFF!: Okay, understood.

Since all five players were in the same party, it was natural for them to run some other dungeons.

At 3 p.m., Jing Huan was boosting his Nine-tailed Spirit Fox's cultivation points when OFF! finally had some news for him.

[Friend] OFF!: They just finished the Havoc in Heaven dungeon and then disbanded the party. The other three are in a safe zone, while Little Mai and Maimai's #1 Fan are doing a couple's quest.

[Friend] Sweet Little Jing: Okay.

[Friend] OFF!: I'll help you keep an eye on Ji Xiaonian. She's always moving around so she might leave the safe zone soon.

[Friend] Sweet Little Jing: Don't bother, just follow Maimai's #1 Fan and his wife.

[Friend] OFF!: ??? Meimei, you won't be able to kill them. Be careful! The tables could turn on you and you might be the one dying and lose your equipment!

[Friend] Sweet Little Jing: Can you just be an emotionless reporting machine?

[Friend] OFF!: Okay, I'll give you an update every minute.

Jing Huan unsummoned his Nine-tailed Spirit Fox and changed into his gear with the highest movement speed attributes. Of course,

Chapter 10

he knew that he had no hope of killing that damn couple, but he could still sneak attack them. Both were glass cannon DPS, so as long as he sealed them quickly and dodged their summoning beasts' skills, killing one of them wouldn't be too difficult.

As he made his way toward the coordinates that OFF! had reported, he devised his plan of attack. Soon, he arrived at the Moon Palace. Jing Huan licked his lips and was about to check the coordinates when a prompt popped up, blocking his view.

【Yearning For has invited you to join his party. Yes, No.】

Jing Huan was stupefied and reflexively checked the time. Oh, it was 3 p.m.

Jing Huan's hands moved faster than his brain, and by the time he realized it, he was already in Yearning For's party. He blinked, unsure of what to say, and ended up blurting out, "Gege."

Yearning For led him forward. Shaking himself out of his daze, Jing Huan couldn't help letting out a silent "Fuck." He had asked OFF! to report their coordinates for nothing.

"Why are you online?" Jing Huan's voice trailed off. "Weren't you supposed to have class all day today?"

His party member finally reacted; Yearning For's voice sounded unusually deep. "Mm."

What do you mean by "mm"?

With his window of opportunity to kill gone, Jing Huan was consumed with regret. He crossed his legs and propped his chin on his hand. "Gege, yesterday, I…"

【Attention! Party leader Yearning For has initiated a forced PK against player Maimai's #1 Fan.】

Jing Huan paused, confused.

The battle began so abruptly that it startled not just their two opponents, but Jing Huan as well.

[Current] Little Mai: ?!

[Current] Maimai's #1 Fan: What's the meaning of this, God Xiang? [Doubtful]

Jing Huan returned to his senses and asked uncertainly, "Gege, what are we doing..."

"Killing people." Xiang Huaizhi sounded no different than usual, as if they were merely running dungeons. "Who do you want to kill first?"

Hands resting on the keyboard, Jing Huan didn't speak for a long time.

Xiang Huaizhi was also in no hurry. He leaped up and blocked Maimai's #1 Fan's dual blades slashing toward Sweet Little Jing with his saber. He asked, "Is the person who kicked you from the party here?"

"No, the party leader is someone else." Jing Huan hesitated. "Gege, how did you know I was kicked?"

Xiang Huaizhi replied, "I saw it in the WeChat group."

Meanwhile, Little Mai's panicked voice came through on YY. "Honey, didn't you say that Yearning For wouldn't care about her?"

"It's okay, didn't you see that all he's done is defend?" Maimai's #1 Fan shook off his surprise. "I'll talk to him."

[Current] Maimai's #1 Fan: Hey, say something. What's going on? Did your hand slip and you clicked the wrong thing?

Their battle had not gone unnoticed by surrounding players.

[World] No One Like You: Fuck!!! Moon Palace (81, 99)!! God Xiang and Maimai's #1 Fan are fighting!!!

 Chapter 10

[World] Petal Dance: I saw it too! It's a team PK battle! Maimai's #1 Fan brought his wife, and God Xiang brought Sweet Little Jing!!

[World] Peach Cheese Stan: ?! I'm rushing to the scene right now!

[World] I've Got a Cat~: Is it true? The two of them are finally fighting?! Are they competing for the top DPS rank??

[World] Drunk in the Mortal Realm: What... What do you mean "compete"? Maimai's #1 Fan isn't anywhere close to Yearning For's level. Are the previous commenters joking? I'm more interested as to why Sweet Little Jing is involved. Again!

[World] Alt123: I know, I know! I got some juicy gossip from a Mirage server QQ group! Sweet Little Jing joined Maimai's #1 Fan's party as a PUG player in the afternoon and got kicked when they reached the boss. The most rage-inducing thing was that they triggered the Qilin Mountain's hidden boss, and Ji Xiaonian got the loot.

[World] I've Got a Cat~: ...At this point, I can't tell if Sweet Little Jing is lucky or unlucky. I still don't know what the Qilin Mountain hidden boss looks like.

[World] You're My Guide: I'm just curious... Why would Sweet Little Jing even think about joining Maimai's #1 Fan's party? [Sweating]

[World] This Servant Withdraws: ^

[World] Drunk in the Mortal Realm: Okay, now I'm convinced there's a different owner behind Sweet Little Jing's character.

Every server had griefers; while they didn't necessarily have to be the strongest player, they were definitely the most pretentious. And Maimai's #1 Fan was a well-known griefer in the Mirage server.

If he liked a piece of equiment, no one else could take it. If he sent out a megaphone, no one dared to retaliate. If he was gathering materials, others had to wait their turn.

Someone once offended him during a dungeon run, so he sabotaged the boss fight in retaliation and hunted the player down for a week. That player quit the game within a few days.

This was not the first time Maimai's #1 Fan has done this kind of griefing; Sweet Little Jing was merely another victim added to his list.

The players in this server had long grown accustomed to it. Of course, there were a few who couldn't stand this, but Maimai's #1 Fan had deep pockets; he owned four or five god-tier characters. The only person in the server who could stand on equal footing with him was very low-key and generally didn't get involved in such things.

If you couldn't afford to provoke him, it was best to avoid him. Over time, players in the server began taking a a detour whenever they spotted him.

Today, however, Yearning For had finally appeared.

Moved by the sight of such a phenomenon, the players of Mirage couldn't resist commenting.

[Megaphone] Clear Pond: Did God Xiang finally have enough? Is he going save us commoners?! Kill him! KILL HIM! AAAAAH!!

[Megaphone] Clinging to Pingzhi: What are you all getting excited about? Have you all forgotten about the drama with Yearning For already? This is just a dog-eat-dog situation, let's not act as if he's some kind of hero.

[Megaphone] Is Lovesickness Bitter: To be fair, Yearning For might be a scumbag in relationships, but since it has nothing to do

 Chapter 10

with us, it's none of our business. It's not like he's bullied the weak, right?

Jing Huan looked away from the megaphones. "Gege, has Maimai's #1 Fan done this kind of thing before?"

Xiang Huaizhi switched to a longsword. "I don't know. Maybe." He had never paid attention to this person.

Seeing no response from Yearning For, Maimai's #1 Fan thought he might have muted the Current Channel text chat. He turned on his in-game microphone. "What's going on, bro?"

Still nothing.

He was still wondering when Yearning For suddenly charged forward with his saber. They had no time to react; the blade pierced Little Mai, and bright red numbers popped up as her health bar instantly dropped, leaving only a third left.

Little Mai was frightened. "Honey, what kind of damage is this?"

"It's okay, baby, we can beat him." Maimai's #1 Fan gritted his teeth. "He brought a useless Spirit Fox Den with him; it's basically two against one. Buff your magic damage."

Maimai's #1 Fan had never partied up with Yearning For before. Additionally, since he liked to play 2V2 matches with his wife, while Yearning For focused solely on playing 1V1, this was the first time the two had ever faced off. Although he had watched many of Yearning For's videos, the latter's actual strength was still a mystery to him. Nonetheless, Maimai's #1 Fan was very confident in his equipment; the only difference between him and Yearning For should be just a single divine artifact weapon.

Long ago, he had made plans to send out thousands of megaphones and host a server-wide banquet for all the players in Mirage

the day he obtained a divine artifact weapon and became number one on the Mastery rankings.

But soon, Maimai's #1 Fan abandoned that idea. After being slashed by Yearning For's crit combo again, his health was down to a mere seventeen percent.

"Yearning For, are you using a script[3]?!" Maimai's #1 Fan turned on his microphone, gnashing his teeth. "Almost every single one of your attacks landed! You can't be this accurate even with a fucking script!"

The onlookers couldn't hold back any longer.

[Current] Peach Cheese Stan: God Xiang has always had an unbelievable hit rate. Besides, how could he use a script on his god-tier account? He'd be permanently banned if it were true!

[Current] Alt123: Maimai's #1 Fan's positioning is so shit, even I could hit him, let alone God Xiang. What's the issue here?

[Current] Pure Snow: I don't think he's using a script either. Yearning For's PK videos are always on the official *Nine Heroes* website recommendations. If he used a script, how could the GMs not have noticed?

[Current] Sweet Little Jing: Facts! Just because you can't beat my gege, now you're slandering him?? What kind of man are you!! [Fury]

[Current] Petal Dance: ?

[Current] Alt123: ??

[Current] Taste and Like It: ? Can you focus on playing PK?

---

3   A script is a set of "automated commands" or a program that performs actions for you. Maimai's #1 Fan is accusing Yearning For of hacking.

[Current] BrbOrNot: 【Song share—"What Kind of Man" by Jay Chou】

The outcome of this battle was never in doubt. In less than ten minutes, only a low-health Maimai's #1 Fan remained on the other side. Yearning For had already knocked Little Mai to the ground.

On their side, Sweet Little Jing barely took any damage thanks to her fast movement speed, and Yearning For's health bar was always full due to Sweet Little Jing's healing.

"Yearning For," Maimai's #1 Fan spoke through his microphone again. Just when everyone thought he was going to rant, he suddenly lowered his voice. "Kill me, but let my wife go. It was my idea to not let Sweet Little Jing kill the boss. This has nothing to do with her."

Jing Huan was taken aback. Maimai's #1 Fan really cared about his wife...but there was absolutely no way Little Mai didn't have a hand in today's incident. He finally remembered where he had seen Little Mai before; she was the loli chatting with Fae Bae near the Unknown Realm shopkeeper that day.

Jing Huan frowned. He was no saint; he didn't buy Maimai's #1 Fan's act, but he was not so sure about Yearning For.

Weren't scumbags like central heating? They warmed up ambiguous partners, they warmed up their wives, and they could even warm up other people's wives...

[Current] Yearning For: Is your wife the only one who can feel wronged?

The reticent man finally broke his silence.

With that, Yearning For stabbed Maimai's #1 Fan with his saber and, before anyone could react, sent his corpse flying out of the zone. The fallen Little Mai had also disappeared.

Jing Huan stared blankly at Yearning For's words, his ears inexplicably warming. By the time he came back to his senses, the black-robed man had already sheathed his saber and returned to his side. They could barely see the other's characters due to the sea of people surrounding them.

[Current] Pure Snow: That was the duel between the top DPS and the second-best DPS? Lame.

[Current] Youth Chasing the Wind: Pure Snow, you're wrong. Our server only has a top DPS, there is no second-best.

[Current] Not Your Cup of Tea: Hmmm… "Is your wife the only one who can feel wronged?"? Why do I feel like this sentence sounds a bit odd?!

Xiang Huaizhi then realized that what he just said was pretty ambiguous.

[Current] Fallen Blossoms: Is your wife the only one who can feel wronged…then, my wife can't feel wronged?

[Current] Peach Cheese Stan: Shit, that's right.

[Current] Drunk in the Mortal Realm: Fuck, it really does seem like that's what it's implying?!

[Current] Sweet Little Jing: (*·Δ·*) !!! DOES IT?!

[Current] Drunk in the Mortal Realm: …

[Currently] Not Your Cup of Tea: …

[Current] Pure Snow: ?

[Current] Alt123: Can you stop with all your lurking?

Xiang Huaizhi's furrowed eyebrows slowly relaxed, the corners of his lip curving up. Before Sweet Little Jing could continue to spew nonsense, he flew away with her.

Xiang Huaizhi initially wanted to bring them to the guild zone,

but since Jing Huan had left the guild, they were turned away by the guild coachman. So, he took them to Petal Valley.

All throughout, the little spirit fox was unusually quiet, obediently following him as they flew back and forth. Even when they landed at the waterfall in Petal Valley, Sweet Little Jing remained expressionless.

Was she still angry? That made sense—Xiang Huaizhi had been furious enough to attempt a solo killing spree.

He pressed the push-to-talk key and opened his mouth to speak.

"Hubbyyy," The little spirit fox next to him dragged out the last syllable in a flirty, shy, and overly cutesy voice. She cupped her face with both hands and performed a shy character action.

Xiang Huaizhi coughed violently.

On the other side, Jing Huan was seconds away from fucking exploding from embarassment.

But... Hm, how should he describe this feeling?

He was both embarrassed and thrilled—embarrassed for addressing him this way, but thrilled that Yearning For had finally taken the bait.

Since this incident had nothing to do with Fae Bae, Yearning For technically didn't need to get involved and could have just ignored it.

And yet, he still came.

Jing Huan's upper lip curled into a disparaging smile. *Just you wait, scumbag. Me calling you "hubby" will eventually shorten your lifespan by ten years.*

His headset was quiet for a long time, until finally, a faint crackling sound broke the silence.

Guide on How to Fail at Online Dating

"You... Don't call me that randomly." Yearning For's voice was slightly hoarse.

Jing Huan pouted. "But you just called me your wife."

Xiang Huaizhi denied it. "No, I didn't."

Jing Huan said, "That's what you meant though."

"No, it wasn't," Xiang Huaizhi deflected.

The other side went quiet. A few seconds later, the little spirit fox's character action changed to crying.

What a quick mood swing.

Xiang Huaizhi suddenly thought of something. After a pause, he asked, "Are you feeling better today?"

"What?" Having just killed some people, Jing Huan was, yes, in a much better mood. There was nothing more satisfying than solving things with your fists!

Xiang Huaizhi said lightly, "Your Aunt Flo."

Jing Huan twitched. *Fuck.*

He was so overjoyed that all of the nonsense from yesterday had been completely forgotten.

It was a bit vulgar for two guys to discuss such a topic. Uncomfortable, Jing Huan said, "Of cooourse I'm all better. It's already over."

Xiang Huaizhi acknowledged him with an "mm," then continued, "If this happens again, come find me first."

Jing Huan was baffled. "But this happens to me every month..."

Xiang Huaizhi sighed. "I mean, you getting bullied."

Jing Huan's headset was high quality; Yearning For's slightly heavier breathing sounded like he was blowing in his ear, making it itch.

Chapter 10

He raised his hand and rubbed his ear. "If I come to find you, will you help me vent?"

"Didn't I just do that?" Xiang Huaizhi glanced at the coordinates an informant had sent him. The other three people in that party were still in the safe zone.

"Then can I offer myself to you?"

No response.

Jing Huan fought down a laugh. He was about to continue his flirtatious advances when out of the blue, Yearning For asked, "Do you like me that much?"

It took a while for Jing Huan to recover from his surprise.

"Yes." He blinked rapidly. Yearning For's tone seemed to be hinting at something.

Wait... What does that question mean? Are we finally going to get together?! Can I finally move on to the next step of my plan??

Jing Huan's heart was pounding with excitement, but once again, Yearning For fell silent, and did not speak for a long time.

Squashing down his emotions, he called out, "Gege?"

At long last, Yearning For responded. His tone sounded the same as usual. "Got it."

Jing Huan was stupefied. "What do you mean 'got it'?"

Rather than letting him shift his focus to a stranger in the game, it's better that he likes me, Xiang Huaizhi thought.

How many online relationships ever worked out? The internet was virtual; what you saw was only what others *wanted* you to see. If nothing online was real, how could genuine affection—let alone, love—exist?

Moreover, if other men discovered that their online girlfriend was actually a guy, forget acceptance—he'd be lucky if they didn't turn hostile. Lovers turning against each other—the pain would be agonizing.

Let Jing Huan focus his feelings on me. At least I won't take them seriously and he won't get hurt. Once Jing Huan finds the right guy...

Xiang Huaizhi stopped that train of thought.

"I mean that I'll take responsibility for your feelings. As long as you're willing, you can come to me for anything in the game from now on."

Without thinking, Jing Huan said, "Then I want to marry—"

"Except for marriage."

Xiang Huaizhi had a vague premonition that if they got married, a certain aspect of their relationship would change.

At the other end, Jing Huan sat cross-legged, staring confusedly at the laptop he was holding.

What does this guy mean? He'll be responsible for my feelings, but marrying me is out of the question? Then what the hell is he taking responsibility for?

There was a crackling sound in his headset, and Yearning For spoke again. "But if, one day, you fall for someone else..." Xiang Huaizhi paused and continued indifferently, "This agreement will be void."

Jing Huan's eyes widened as it hit him.

Fuck! This scumbag is so shameless!! He doesn't want to take responsibility; he just wants to string me along and play around with me for a bit!!!

When Jing Huan remained silent, Xiang Huaizhi thought he must've misunderstood him. "I'm not saying that you can't like other people."

Jing Huan cursed out Yearning For a thousand times in his heart, then started typing. He was afraid that if he turned on his mic, he was going to cuss him out aloud.

[Party] Sweet Little Jing: How could I possibly like anyone else besides gege? T.T

Xiang Huaizhi nodded, under the impression that he had gotten his message across. "For now, try not to leave the safe zone when I'm not here."

Maimai's #1 Fan's personality would never allow him to silently swallow his anger after being killed like that. Who knew what trouble he might try to cause?

[Party] Sweet Little Jing: It's okay, I'm not afraid of him at all. >.<

And Jing Huan truly wasn't. Maimai's #1 Fan's equipment may be high-tier, but his skills were trash-tier—a typical pay-to-win player. He believed the reason behind *Nine Heroes'* popularity and longevity was because frugal but skilled players could still compete against pay-to-win players. At the same time, not spending any money at all wouldn't work either.

"You really have no fear," Xiang Huaizhi said and glanced at the little spirit fox beside him. "When did you buy all this new gear you're wearing?"

The little spirit fox no longer had just one glowing ring. She was adorned with a purple whip and a gourd that emitted a white light at her waist—even her belt was purple.

Xiang Huaizhi's question initially took Jing Huan by surprise and then he remembered this full set of equipment had been bought in a fit of anger.

[Party] Sweet Little Jing: I...

[Party] Sweet Little Jing: I just got really mad at the time! QAQ

"Where did the money come from?"

[Party] Sweet Little Jing: My living expenses...

"Your living expenses were enough to buy all of this?"

What? What kind of strange conversation is this? Jing Huan felt like he was being audited by his wife.

[Party] Sweet Little Jing: Yes, I overspent~! I can only afford to eat steamed buns this month!

Xiang Huaizhi choked. He didn't expect there would actually be someone who would skip meals for the sake of playing games.

"Why are you only typing and not talking?" Xiang Huaizhi picked up his cellphone. "I'll lend you some money. How much do you need?"

Jing Huan nearly tripped over his words as he scrambled to say,

"Huh? No, you don't have to! I still have money on my meal card. Anyway, I'm actually trying to lose weight right now."

"You're not fat. You don't need to lose weight."

The voice channel went quiet for a moment.

Jing Huan asked, "How do you know I'm not fat?"

Xiang Huaizhi paused for two seconds before innocently saying, "I'm just guessing."

You smooth talker!

"You reallyyy don't have to, gege. The meat buns at our school are really delicious. They have thin skins and are stuffed with lots of meat and only cost one-fifty each!" Jing Huan paused. "Besides, we're not in *that* kind of relationship, so how can I spend gege's money? If you really care about me, gege, why not fulfill another dream of mine? Let's go to Yuelao's Temple—"

"Okay." Xiang Huaizhi put down his cellphone. "Then you can just eat at the cafeteria."

Jing Huan was just about to whine a bit when his friend message icon suddenly lit up.

【Unknown Realm shopkeeper: Congratulations, young hero! Bishop Wood has gifted you a set of Lantern Fairy attire. Please go to the Unknown Realm (118, 29) to claim your new outfit!】

Shocked, Jing Huan instinctively sent a "?" to Bishop Wood.

[Friend] Bishop's Wood: A consolation gift. [Patting head]

Instead of replying to him, Jing Huan turned on his microphone and asked, "Gege, can we go to the Unknown Realm?"

"Why?"

"I want to return the new outfit Bishop Wood sent me."

Nine Heroes' gifting system had a peculiar rule: if a gift was left with the Unknown Realm shopkeeper for more than half an hour, a service fee was charged. This was euphemistically called a "storage fee." While it wasn't much, Jing Huan had no desire to spend that money.

Without saying another word, Yearning For led them out of Petal Valley. Once they arrived in front of the Unknown Realm shopkeeper, Jing Huan left the party and quickly returned the outfit.

[Friend] Bishop Wood: It's just an outfit.... You still don't want it?

[Friend] Sweet Little Jing: I appreciate your gesture~ No need to spend any money. O.O

Just a few seconds after he sent that reply, his friend message icon lit up once more. Jing Huan thought it was Bishop Wood responding, but when he clicked it open, it was the system's all too familiar pink message box.

【Unknown Realm shopkeeper: Congratulations, young hero! Yearning For has gifted you a set of Lantern Fairy attire. Please go to the Unknown Realm (118, 29) to claim your new outfit!】

The hell? Are these two gifting addicts?

[Friend] Yearning For: Just take it.

[Friend] Sweet Little Jing: I can't keep accepting such expensive things from you...

[Friend] Yearning For: ?

[Friend] Yearning For: If you return it, I'll just give it to Long Road Ahead.

[Friend] Sweet Little Jing: Thank you, gege. Gege, do I look good in it?

 Chapter 11

Jing Huan changed into his outfit. He originally didn't want to scam Yearning For out of this 1,200 yuan, but since the scumbag *insisted* on giving it to him, could Jing Huan really be blamed for his lack of morals?

[Friend] Yearning For: Mm. Have you done your dailies today?

[Friend] Sweet Little Jing: ...If you hadn't brought it up, I would've completely forgotten about them. QAQ

[Friend] Yearning For: Join the party, I'll help you do them.

Jing Huan gladly jumped at the opportunity to slack off and quickly joined his party. After half an hour's work, he opened a food delivery app and was pondering what to order, when his sister-in-arms came looking for him.

[Friend] Love is Sharing Noms: Stupid Jingjing! [Angry] What's going on? How could you quit the guild? And not even reply to my WeChat messages!!

Jing Huan was startled, surprised. He opened WeChat and saw that he really had received quite a number of messages.

[Friend] Sweet Little Jing: My WeChat glitched and didn't send me any notifications! QAQ I had a conflict with Maimai's #1 Fan and was afraid of dragging the guild into it, so I quit.

[Friend] Love is Sharing Noms: That wouldn't have mattered. There was already bad blood between Maimai's #1 Fan and our guild.

[Friend] Sweet Little Jing: O.O Oooh what kind of bad blood?

[Friend] Love is Sharing Noms: Can we do a WeChat call? I'm eating, so typing is a pain.

[Friend] Sweet Little Jing: Sure.

Jing Huan turned off the in-game microphone and started a WeChat voice call with Love is Sharing Noms.

"He previously killed a didi from Idle Pavilion, and drove him to quit the game. He also quarreled with Echoes of Spring, causing a lot of unpleasantness. But this was before you started playing, so it makes sense you didn't know. Also, a lot of people in the guild don't like him," Love is Sharing Noms said. "We were all discussing how we could help you get revenge this afternoon."

Jing Huan was surprised. "Help me get revenge?"

"Yeah, Guild Officer Bishop Wood even secretly went to find Maimai's #1 Fan, and God Xiang himself spoke up," Love is Sharing Noms said.

Jing Huan kind of regretted quitting the guild so hastily. "Ah… what did gege say?"

"I'll send you a screenshot on WeChat."

Jing Huan immediately picked up his cellphone.

【BrbOrNot: Really? Did she really quit? Was that necessary…

Youth Chasing the Wind: Seriously unnecessary. It's not like we're afraid of trouble.

Peach Cheese Stan: So, will Sweet Little Jing return to the guild?

Echoes of Spring: I'm on holiday with Regardless of Lovesickness. We'll handle it when we get back tomorrow.

Bishop Wood: This Maimai's #1 Fan… We've tolerated him once before, and now he's messing with our guild again. Don't worry, I'll get justice for Little Jing, for sure.

BrbOrNot: Good! Guild Officer is mighty!

Yearning For: @Bishop Wood, she's my party member, I'll deal with it by myself, no need to bother you.】

Jing Huan read Yearning For's words over and over again. Eventually, he asked, "Did gege say anything else?"

"That's it, just that sentence." Love is Sharing Noms clicked her tongue. "God Xiang is super cool when he talks now. He's totally different from before."

"Before?"

"Yeah, when he was with Fae Bae…" Love is Sharing Noms stopped midway through her sentence.

Jing Huan then remembered Love is Sharing Noms and Fae Bae used to be good friends. He unconsciously straightened up and asked curiously, "What was gege like when he and Fae Bae were together?"

Love is Sharing Noms hemmed and hawed. "Oh, you know…"

"Tell meee," Jing Huan wheedled. "I promise not to talk about it!"

"Like any normal couple, nothing special." Love is Sharing Noms thought for a moment. "They were just on mic together for like ten hours a day."

They had that *much to talk about?* Jing Huan let out a few dry chuckles. "How do you even know about this?"

"Faefae liked showing off their relationship, so a lot of people knew," Love is Sharing Noms said. "They had matching WeChat profile pictures. Yearning For used to always post her photos on his Moments; she even sent me screenshots… But it looks like God Xiang has changed his WeChat profile picture now?"

Jing Huan's thoughts flitted back to his own rejected friend request, and his smile tightened further. Yearning For's Moments were also wiped clean; it was obvious he had deleted everything after their breakup.

"Matching profile pictures, huh…" he muttered.

Recalling all of the public displays of affection she had endured, Love is Sharing Noms couldn't shut her mouth: "Yeah, God Xiang even used to call Faefae 'baby' and 'wifey.' Can you imagine?"

Jing Huan's throat felt tight.

What did Yearning For usually call him? He couldn't think of anything other than "Sweet Little Jing."

No fucking way... Yearning For had actually talked to someone for ten whole hours, had matching profile pictures, and even called her "baby"? Jing Huan simply couldn't connect any of this behavior with the person currently leading him around.

Moreover, how dare you? How dare you change your profile picture and post on Moments for someone else, but when it comes to me, you can't say anything nice?!

Jing Huan suddenly felt displeased—*very* displeased—to the point that he lost his appetite.

Only after she finished talking did Love is Sharing Noms realize she had probably said too much. "But...God Xiang treats you well too! See, he even helped you kill someone."

"What about Fae Bae? Did he ever help her kill anyone?"

Hearing the dejection in the other person's tone, Love is Sharing Noms rushed to reassure, "No! During the time they were together, they barely played in the arena."

"They didn't fight in the arena?" Jing Huan was puzzled. "Then, what did they usually do?"

"Some dungeons, sightseeing, taking pictures..." Love is Sharing Noms coughed. "Stuff like that."

Jing Huan froze. *Damn it! This guy clearly knows how to do it all! Why is he always acting so cold and distant in front of me then?!*

Chapter 11

After hanging up, Jing Huan sat in his chair, his desire to order take-out completely vanished. The more he thought about it, the stronger his ire grew. *Yearning For was a goddamn hypocrite!*

[Party] Yearning For: Are you there?

[Party] Sweet Little Jing: ...I'm here.

[Party] Yearning For: Why'd you turn off your mic?

Because daddy doesn't want to talk to you, you double-standard dog.

[Party] Sweet Little Jing: I didn't. I was just in a voice call with Nomnom.

Xiang Huaizhi paused mid-water sip.

[Party] Yearning For: Are you two close?

[Party] Sweet Little Jing: Of course~ We're party members after all.

[Party] Yearning For: .

Unlike Bishop Wood, Love is Sharing Noms was a girl, and if Jing Huan switched to liking her...

That wouldn't be so bad, Xiang Huaizhi thought expressionlessly.

After finishing their dailies, the two of them stood beside the NPC in the main city, neither saying a word. After a long interval, Xiang Huaizhi finally pulled himself out of his thoughts and was just about to type when his party member called out a pitiful "Gege."

"Hm?"

"You promised me that, I could come to you for anything related to the game from now on," Jing Huan said, "right?"

"Mm."

"Then...can you take some pictures with me?"

Xiang Huaizhi was a little startled. "Pictures?"

"Mm!" Jing Huan said unabashedly. "Pictures of us in a kissing pose!"

After a pause, Xiang Huaizhi asked, "What do you want to do with those?"

Jing Huan didn't know, but he did know he still wanted to take them.

"I just wanna," Jing Huan said. "Is that okay, gege?"

Ten minutes later, the two arrived at the Moon Place, and stood right in front of the full moon.

【Sweet Little Jing wants to kiss you. Yes, No.】

Xiang Huaizhi's mouse hesitated between the two options before he finally, while holding his forehead, clicked "Yes."

The little spirit fox tilted her head, her fox tail swaying to and fro, gently planted a kiss on the corner of his mouth. Flowers bloomed in front of them, and the moon shone down, illuminating the two in its light. There were even a few moon rabbits randomly gamboling around at their feet in the midst of this beautiful scene.

He stared at the scene for a few seconds, and his hand unconsciously pressed the screenshot key.

"Gege," the female voice said, discontented, "can you call me... Well... baby?" His voice grew smaller toward the end of the sentence.

Xiang Huaizhi choked; it felt like something was stuck in his throat. After a long while, he managed to squeeze out: "What?"

"Just call me that in-game!" Jing Huan forced himself to sound justified. "Th-this counts as something related to the game too..."

"No."

 Chapter 11

"Why not!" Jing Huan was disgruntled. "Gege, you're going back on your word!"

Xiang Huaizhi chuckled. "Who makes this kind of request?"

"I do!" Jing Huan said. "Just call me that, gege! It won't cost you a thing."

"No way."

"Once! Just ooonce!" Jing Huan said. "Just once would be good!"

Xiang Huaizhi remained obstinately tight-lipped.

Jing Huan turned on his recording device while he tried to come up with a way to persuade Yearning For to agree. He was going to record Yearning For saying "baby" and, once the truth was revealed, bombard his inbox with it every day!

At Yearning For's silence, Jing Huan whispered cutely, "Gege, I…"

"…Baby."

The word—unexpected, unfathomable—caught Jing Huan wholly off-guard.

The guy spoke very fast, but very clearly. His voice was already pleasant to listen to with its low and hoarse timbre, but combined with the helplessness and indulgence in his tone… No one could listen to it without feeling their heart flutter.

Jing Huan even had a brief delusion—as if they were really in an online relationship, as if he really liked Yearning For, as if he was truly courting him.

It felt like ages before Jing Huan recovered from hearing "baby." His cheeks were slightly hot, and his throat was dry. He grabbed a glass of water and took a swig.

Gotta give that scumbag credit where credit's due… He actually has some game.

It took Jing Huan a while before it hit him: he hadn't. Actually. Recorded. It!

"Gege, I...I didn't hear it just now," Jing Huan said quickly. "Can you say it again?"

Xiang Huaizhi retorted, "If you didn't hear me, how do you know I already said it?"

Well now, aren't you suddenly being so clever?

Jing Huan wailed, "Waaaaah, do it again, one last time!"

"No."

"Gege..."

"Don't be coy, it won't work," Xiang Huaizhi said, voice rough. "I'm going to go AFK, message me on WeChat if you need anything."

Immediately afterward, Xiang Huaizhi grabbed his cup and got up to get some water. He had just filled it when the dormitory door suddenly opened.

"I'm exhausted. I never should've picked the same courses as you; every Friday is like hell." Lu Hang walked in, face wan. "You even left early today. Do you know how bored I was sitting all by myself? You left like a tornado, I thought your account got hacked again."

Lu Hang originally had a lot more to say, but when he saw his roommate's face, he stopped.

"You..." Lu Hang frowned and leaned forward. "Why's your face red?"

Xiang Huaizhi pushed his face away and spat out an expressionless "hot."

Lu Hang had seen Xiang Huaizhi's face red before; who wouldn't

be flushed after playing basketball? However, this was the first time he'd seen the pink color spread all the way to his ears.

After some ruminating, milk tea in hand, Lu Hang cheekily asked, "You weren't watching some porn, were you?"

Xiang Huaizhi's eyelids didn't even twitch. "Fuck off."

Lu Hang laughed and said, "Just kidding, did you help solve Little Jingjing's problem?"

"Mm."

"How'd you do it?"

"Killed them."

"Killed…" Lu Hang collapsed onto his computer desk, stunned. "K-killed them?! Killed who?!"

After downing half a cup of water, Xiang Huaizhi refilled it again. "Maimai's #1 Fan."

Lu Hang felt like the floor had fallen underneath his feet. It was already surprising enough that Xiang Huaizhi cut class for Sweet Little Jing, but to actually help her kill someone? In all the years that he and Xiang Huaizhi had gamed together, Xiang Huaizhi had only killed two people: one was Fae Bae, and now the other was Maimai's #1 Fan—both of whom had been killed for Sweet Little Jing.

Lu Hang's expression was complicated. After a while, he came to a sudden realization. "So, Xiangxiang, you…really like girls like Sweet Little Jing, huh?"

Mystery solved; he finally knew why his dear roommate had never dated anyone all these years.

To be honest, girls like Sweet Little Jing were practically extinct these days. Nowadays, girls were fiercer than boys and their thoughts were particularly hard to grasp. Someone so sweet, clingy, and fond

of acting cute... The only person Lu Hang knew with that kind of personality was Sweet Little Jing. His dear roommate's taste was indeed special.

Xiang Huaizhi gave him an indifferent look. "You've got that much free time?"

"Nope, nope." Lu Hang wisely shut up. "I'll finish the last part of the quest now, and we can fight the God of War first thing tomorrow morning!"

Xiang Huaizhi ignored him and went back to his computer. The little spirit fox was still in his party, their two characters overlapping, unusually intimate.

The calm expression on Xiang Huaizhi's face slipped slightly, and he could feel a headache brewing.

Why did I just say that?

Xiang Huaizhi had no idea what had possessed him to call Jing Huan that. In all his life, he had never addressed anyone so intimately before, let alone to another man.

That night, Lu Hang finally finished the God of War quest and rejoined the dungeon party.

"This quest is really fucking inhumane," Lu Hang griped. "I'm almost running myself into the ground; a single step of the quest requires traveling to a dozen NPCs. I hope the GM has some sense and gives me something with good attributes. I really don't want to do this a second time."

Love is Sharing Noms said, "That's probably unlikely. I don't think anyone has ever gotten a divine artifact on the first try."

Jing Huan asked, "Gege, how many times did you kill the God of War before you got your divine artifact?"

Xiang Huaizhi replied, "Three times."

Envy surged through Jong Huan. Three times, one time; what was the difference? There were countless servers that had been live for ten years without ever seeing a divine artifact drop.

After some thought, Lu Hang agreed. "Then, I'll lower my expectations. I won't hope for a one-shot miracle; I'd be fine with three times too. I'll go to Lanshan Temple to pray later." Lanshan Temple was a game zone in *Nine Heroes*—a simple temple that had several quest NPCs surrounding it.

Xiang Huaizhi scoffed. "Praying to a Buddha statue made up of a bunch of data?"

"It's the thought that counts, you know!" Lu Hang said. "I've heard many people say that praying in that zone really works."

Lu Hang grew bored and leisurely clicked open his *Nine Heroes'* social center to browse around.

Nine Heroes' social center, similar to QQ's Space and WeChat Moments, allowed users to post text and pictures, and see posts from friends. Lu Hang's female friends often posted photos there.

Lu Hang went through his feed, liking each photo, and accidentally swiped past a game screenshot. He frowned, feeling like he had seen something of great importance and slowly swiped back to it.

After a while, Lu Hang called out tactfully, "Xiangxiang."

"Speak."

"You kissed Little Jingjing?"

Xiang Huaizhi's hand slipped, and his attack missed its mark, the longsword barely grazing past the boss's face. "It's called a character action."

Lu Hang dutifully corrected himself. "You actually did a kissing character action with Little Jingjing?"

Xiang Huaizhi gave up on correcting him and frowned. "How did you know?"

"Little Jingjing put it on her social center homepage, didn't you see it?"

Xiang Huaizhi really hadn't. He had very few in-game friends and never posted any game updates. The social center button was essentially rendered obsolete. He opened his homepage and refreshed it, Jing Huan's update showing at the top of his feed.

【Sweet Little Jing: ٩(≧ ≦*)۶ Love gege forever! [Picture]】

The picture was of the two of them kissing in the Moon Palace that afternoon. There were several comments and likes below it, and Xiang Huaizhi scrolled down.

[Love is Sharing Noms]: Ewwww~

[BrbOrNot]: It's over. My guild officer Bishop Wood has no hope now. Tch, I even bet someone that you'd change your mind. I lost big time.

[Peach Cheese Stan]: BON, how are you everywhere? Sooner or later, God Xiang is going to hunt you down.

[Bishop Wood]: Little Jing, hurry and reply to my DM. [Going to cry]

Xiang Huaizhi closed Sweet Little Jing's homepage and opened his own. Naturally, he had no posts on it, but there were countless comments, all of which were from Fae Bae, and all filled with flirtatious banter.

Without batting an eye, Xiang Huaizhi deleted all the comments.

Chapter 11

Early the next morning, Lu Hang got up before his alarm rang, thrumming with excitement. While he didn't dare wake up Xiang Huaizhi, his eagerness to kill the God of War was a strong motivator, so after some dawdling, he held a medium-sized concert in the dormitory using cups, bowls, tables, and chairs.

Xiang Huaizhi woke up from the noise, his brows heavily furrowed. "If you keep banging those cups on the table, I'll throw you out the window."

Lu Hang cleared his throat and sang out, "Daddy! Daddy! Daddy! Good daddy, good daddy, I have a good daddy!" Receiving no reply nor reaction from Xiang Huaizhi, he switched gears and begged, "Daddy, get up and help me kill the boss for a divine artifact. Your son has been gathering materials for months, and has been looking forward to this very day."

"I don't have a son like you." Xiang Huaizhi raised his hand to shield his eyes. "What time is it now?"

"It's nine, daddy."

"No one will be online this early anyway."

"They're online, daddy," Lu Hang said with a big grin. "I woke them all up on WeChat."

Xiang Huaizhi's eyes slowly cracked open. "You woke everyone up?"

"Yes, daddy."

Xiang Huaizhi said with the utmost sincerity, "You're really wicked."

"If something happens to them in the future, no matter the time, I'll be the first to arrive at the scene!"

Xiang Huaizhi didn't bother arguing. He felt around his pillow

and found his cellphone. He checked it, and sure enough, there were two messages.

Little Jing~: Gege, are you awake?

Little Jing~: [Rubbing eyes]

Xiang Huaizhi casually shot off a reply, then groggily threw off his blankets, and got out of bed to wash up. When he logged in, the other four were already in a party waiting for him. Since they were helping him, Lu Hang naturally provided all the potions.

He said, "Xiangxiang, tell everyone which potions they should bring, and I'll toss it at them."

Once all the potions were distributed, Xiang Huaizhi asked, "Bishop Wood, what attributes do you use?"

"Resistance and seal hit rate," Bishop Wood replied.

"Switch to speed and seal hit rate. We have enough healing." Xiang Huaizhi swept his eyes to the little spirit fox beside him. "Sweet Little Jing, what are you using?"

"Using..." Jing Huan's voice carried obvious traces of sleepiness, "speed and seal hit rate."

"Mm," Xiang Huaizhi said. "Let's start the battle. Follow my lead. The faster we kill it, the sooner we can rest."

At 1 p.m., a post appeared in the *Nine Heroes* forum, and within a few minutes, the players had shot it up to "hot."

【Yearning For's party in Mirage server has defeated the God of War in 62 minutes, setting a new record, video included.】

In a private room at an internet café, Jing Huan lay on the table, yawning while listening to Lu Wenhao and Gao Zixiang's dual commentary.

Chapter 11

Lu Wenhao exclaimed, "Holy shit, God Xiang's combo... Seven-hit combo, how the hell did he do that?"

Gao Zixiang added, "Those two Warlocks are also awesome, you can see they have a very high sealing hit rate, and the mobs are all tightly CCed by them."

"But I still think that Spirit Fox Den is pretty hardcore. Look at her! She's only taken a few hits. Being able to dodge attacks like that for a whole hour is OP," Lu Wenhao said, frowning. "But why are her Healing Springs only supporting God Xiang? Everyone else in the party is relying on the Putuo for heals."

"Spirit Fox Dens aren't really healers anyway, but her seals are spot on. She's the one dealing with all the special mobs that spawn each round. Her role was probably to seal the special mobs, and healing God Xiang was just extra." Gao Zixiang clicked his tongue. "Stop watching. Even if you took away this Spirit Fox Den's healing ability, she'd still be a hundred times better than you."

"You fucker, are you taking the chance to diss your daddy again?"

Scowling, Jing Huan lifted his face up from his makeshift nest, and asked, "Can you guys be quiet for a while?"

Gao Zixiang looked at him, puzzled. "Huanhuan, what's wrong with you today? How'd you manage to get sleepy at an internet café?"

After he finished killing the God of War, Jing Huan belatedly remembered he had promised his roommates he'd play *PUBG* with them. Worried that a nap would lead to insomnia at night, he decided to come out, but it didn't work, because he was obviously still sleepy.

"I didn't sleep well," he said, irritated. "Do you guys want to play or not? If we're not playing, I'm going back."

Lu Wenhao hurriedly reassured, "We're playing, we're playing. Huanhuan, just wait a bit more, there's only ten minutes left in the video. Want to watch with us?"

"Nope." Jing Huan yawned again and abruptly stood up.

"Don't go." Gao Zixiang's hand shot out to stop him. "I'm setting up the VPN now."

Jing Huan pushed open the door of the private room. "I'm going to the bathroom to wash my face."

In his current state, he'd likely get wrecked when he played later.

They were at the best internet café near the school, but the school was in a remote location. While it was still the best around, it was considered small by city standards.

Jing Huan wasn't picky about most things, but the restrooms were simply too small—there were only two, one for men and one for women. The hallway leading to the restroom was also very narrow. Two big guys couldn't walk side by side without squeezing past each other.

Jing Huan navigated the narrow hallway to the sinks in the men's restroom. He saw a used paper towel left by the faucet and frowned, losing the courage to even touch the faucet taps.

They should avoid coming to this internet café in the future.

Just as he was about to leave, he noticed four small black specks near his shoes, seemingly moving. Because they were in the shadows, he couldn't see them clearly and instinctively bent down slightly to take a look.

Xiang Huaizhi walked into an internet café, and upon seeing him, the receptionist's eyes brightened. "Hello, need a computer?"

 Chapter 11

Xiang Huaizhi asked, "Can I use your restroom?"

A passer-by had accidentally smeared ice cream on his sleeve and arm a few minutes ago. The sticky feeling was uncomfortable, so he wanted to wash it off.

The receptionist nodded quickly. "No problem. Go straight and turn left. It's the furthest door on the left."

"Thank you."

Xiang Huaizhi walked into the hallway and glanced down at his sleeve. The chocolate ice cream had already ruined his white sleeve.

Xiang Huaizhi stood outside the closed men's room and waited. He was debating whether or not to throw the shirt away after he got back when he heard frantic footsteps coming from inside the restroom.

Before he could react, the restroom door in front of him burst open, and a guy rushed out, looking terrified out of his wits.

Seeing who was sprinting out, Xiang Huaizhi was stunned. "You..."

With his escape route blocked in front, and the giant monster coming at him from the back, Jing Huang, without hesitation, jumped right onto the other person.

"GE! COCKROACH!! COCKROACHES!" Jing Huan was in full panic mode. He was practically strangling Xiang Huaizhi as he stepped on his shoes frantically. His words were garbled and incoherent. "FOUR! FOUR!! FOUR OF THEM!!! HUGE! COCKROACHES! TH-THEY CAN *FLY*!"

First, Xiang Huaizhi got hit in the face, then he had his neck tightly squeezed, and finally, his feet were stomped on. Even now, the other person's feet were still on his shoes.

Xiang Huaizhi had never held anyone this closely before, and Jing Huan's cold arm pressed against his neck, the sensation intense.

He looked at the four rapidly moving black bugs on the restroom floor, and his eyelid twitched twice. "Mhm, I see them. Four of them."

Goosebumps exploded all over Jing Huan's body and he reflexively tightened his chokehold.

Smelling the scent of soap on Jing Huan's body, Xiang Huaizhi said hoarsely, "Get down, I'll close the door."

Jing Huan choked out, "No way, ge. I'll die if I get down. Like instant death kind of die."

Xiang Huaizhi could hear his voice trembling. Was he really that scared?

"Then stand on my feet. I'll take two steps forward, close the door, and then we'll leave."

The silence from Jing Huan couldn't be more doubtful.

"I promise they won't touch you."

Jing Huan didn't speak. After a long time, Xiang Huaizhi felt him nod slowly into his shoulder.

He closed the door, and Xiang Huaizhi could feel the young man hugging him sigh with relief, and then start breathing heavily.

After a brief hesitation, he placed his palm on Jing Huan's back and gave him two light pats. "Are you okay?"

Jing Huan's scalp tingled. "Did they come out?"

"No, they're all inside. I saw them."

Two minutes later, Jing Huan squatted outside the hallway. It took a long time for him to recover and compose his emotions.

"Well," he looked up, apologetic, and said, "Sorry, ge, I bumped into you again."

His eyes, even the tip of his nose, were red.

Xiang Huaizhi stared blankly at him. "Are you...really afraid of cockroaches?"

"Yeah." It wasn't a big deal, so Jing Huan was honest. "When I was a kid, we went back to my hometown where I accidentally got locked in an abandoned house for a whole day. Since then, I've been really afraid of bugs... It totally clashes with my tough guy image, huh?"

Snuffling, Jing Huan raised his hand to show the distance between his fingers, and said with a smile, "Those cockroaches were so close to my shoe just now, and they even flew toward my face. I was *this* close to dying..."

Xiang Huaizhi looked at Jing Huan's red eyes, and for some reason, his heart twinged slightly.

Jing Huan suddenly seemed to remember something and glanced down. His stomach dropped. "Oh fuck... Ge, are your shoes like this because I stepped on them?"

Xiang Huaizhi's white sneakers were covered in his footprints, clearly indicating just how hard he had been trampled on.

Jing Huan was instantly overwhelmed with guilt. "Oh no, did I ruin them? Ge, do your feet hurt? Can you still feel them?"

Xiang Huaizhi's mind cleared. "They don't hurt, you're light."

"I'm over 150 pounds, ge." Jing Huan squatted and shuffled closer to his feet, his eyes fixed on Xiang Huaizhi's shoes. "Should we have you checked out at the hospital?"

"No need."

"Then why don't you take off your shoes and I'll massage your feet for you?"

Xiang Huaizhi's throat tightened. "No need. It's fine…really."

Jing Huan finally gave up a few minutes later. "Then, if you start feeling uncomfortable, you have to tell me. I'll take responsibility."

"…Okay."

Jing Huan stood up. "By the way ge, did you come here to play too?" Without waiting for Xiang Huaizhi's answer, he scanned around. "Are you alone? We have an empty seat in our private room. Wanna join us? I'll pay for your computer time. Lu Wenhao and Gao Zixiang—you know them—are also there."

Xiang Huaizhi had no plans on going. They weren't close enough to sit and game together.

"We'll game for the afternoon, go for dinner together after, and then play some night basketball in the evening." Jing Huan gazed at him expectantly. "How about it, ge?"

A pause, then Xiang Huaizhi turned around. "What's the private room number? I'll go set it up."

"Number three, but I'll come with you, I did say I'd pay for your computer time." Jing Huan hurried to catch up to him. He'd only walked two steps, before suddenly sidling closer to Xiang Huaizhi, and sniffed. "Ge, you smell so sweet."

"Got ice cream on me."

"No wonder…" Jing Huan looked at his own clothes, which now also had some chocolate stains. He laughed. "It actually smells pretty good."

Xiang Huaizhi didn't turn around, only lightly responding with an "mm."

Chapter 11

There's no need to throw away this shirt, he thought. *I can still wear it after I give it a good wash.*

Even though the Gao Zixiang and Lu Wenhao had claimed there was only ten minutes left in the video, they were still on the webpage when Jing Huan returned.

Gao Zixiang, who was wearing only one earphone, didn't even turn his head at the sound of the door opening. "Huanhuan, just two minutes left, really! Go log in first, we'll be right there!"

Xiang Huaizhi glanced at Lu Wenhao's computer screen and paused. It was showing the video of them defeating the God of War earlier that afternoon.

Reflexively, Xiang Huaizhi looked at the person in front of him. Did these two roommates know that he was actually Sweet Little Jing?

"Fuck off, you guys don't need to come—I'll play with someone else," Jing Huan said disdainfully.

Hearing the footsteps behind Jing Huan, Gao Zixiang turned around and was surprised to see who it was. "Senior Xiang, why are you here? Did you also come here to play?"

"Mm," Xiang Huaizhi said, looking away from the screen. "Is it okay if I join?"

Before they could answer, Jing Huan had already taken a seat and casually pulled out the chair next to him. "Xiang-ge, sit here. Ignore them."

"Of course it's fine," Lu Wenhao said. "Senior, are you alone? Lu-ge didn't come out?"

Xiang Huaizhi nodded. "He's busy."

During this great weekend, Lu Hang had absolutely shit all to do. Currently, he was wrapped up in his blankets, completely knocked out cold.

After the battle video finished playing, Lu Wenhao sighed ruefully. "Some teams take sixty minutes to kill the God of War, while we take sixty minutes to wipe."

"When you get as good as this Spirit Fox Den, then our party won't wipe," Gao Zixiang said coolly. "Healing Springs are a cooldown skill for other people. For you, it's a lucky break. Getting just one heal is like winning the jackpot."

Lu Wenhao sneered and countered, "You don't even have half of Yearning For's DPS, and you think you could get exclusive Healing Springs like those of Sweet Little Jing? Are you worthy?"

Xiang Huaizhi shot a surreptitious look at the person next to him. Jing Huan appeared nonchalant, completely slouched in his chair as if their conversation had nothing to do with him.

"Fine, then I won't mention Sweet Little Jing." Gao Zixiang's gaze swept over to Jing Huan, finding his next target. "Let's talk about Huanhuan! Look, Huanhuan hasn't played *Nine Heroes* in years, but that day at that internet café, he played better than you—and he was just playing casually."

Lu Wenhao silently chanted to himself, *Don't get angry, don't get angry*[1]. If he got sick from anger, he'd be walking right into Gao Zixiang's trap.

"I'm not going to argue with you," Lu Wenhao said as he closed

---

1   Lu Wenhao is starting to recite—莫生气 - Mò Shēng Qì (Don't get angry)— a famous Chinese poem that advises people to let go of anger and embrace a peaceful mindset, often printed on fans and used by the elderly.

 Chapter 11

the webpage. He realized, too late, he had neglected to check something. "Oh shit, I forgot to see what kind of divine artifact the Warlock got as the drop in the end."

"Trash," Gao Zixiang said. "I checked the forums, and they said it had the most basic attributes. Its glow isn't even as bright as purple gear."

Lu Wenhao nodded. "Then I'm relieved."

Jing Huan opened *PUBG*, urging Xiang Huaizhi. "Come on, ge, log on."

PUBG was so popular that Xiang Huaizhi had obviously tried it before. He entered his account credentials from memory and logged in.

"Wait, Senior Xiang." Lu Wenhao was reminded of something and leaned forward, full of smiles. "I heard from Lu-ge that your *Nine Heroes* account is super impressive. Since we're all here, could you show me just how good you are?"

The words came out of Xiang Huaizhi's very naturally. "I sold the account already."

Lu Wenhao looked regretful. "I see... Okay then."

Soon, all four of them entered *PUBG*'s squad interface. Jing Huan and Xiang Huaizhi wore the game's default outfit, while the other two were decked out in flashy gear—sunglasses, masks, and scarves.

Xiang Huaizhi said, "I haven't played for a long time so I'm a bit rusty."

"It's okay," said Jing Huan. "We're all noobs."

At first, Xiang Huaizhi thought he was merely being modest, but he quickly realized this underclassman was being completely honest.

Within half a minute of landing, all three of his teammates were all knocked out by the same player in the nearby factory area.

They really were noobs.

Xiang Huaizhi was speechless. He wordlessly reloaded his gun and switched the game to first-person view.

"Aaaaaah!" Jing Huan exclaimed in frustration. "I fired several shots! Were you two just watching from the sidelines?!"

Lu Wenhao immediately refuted, "Bullshit! Those shots were clearly mine!"

"They were definitely from me, okay?!" Gao Zixiang protested as well. "I emptied a whole magazine; there's no way I missed every shot!"

They argued for a while but in the end, they still couldn't figure out who actually landed a hit. Since he had already been killed and turned into a loot box, Jing Huan leaned closer to Xiang Huaizhi.

Seeing that Xiang Huaizhi was still lingering in the area where the three of them had been killed, Jing Huan hurriedly said, "Ge, you should hurry and leave. Their whole team landed here."

"Mm," Xiang Huaizhi acknowledged but didn't seem inclined to leave. "What colored outfit was the guy who killed you wearing?"

"White!"

"Light gray!"

"Purple!"

The three of them answered in unison.

Xiang Huaizhi thought, *All right, I'll get rid of the purple one first.*

Jing Huan initially thought the game would end soon, and was

already making plans to land in a less populated area next match—at the very least, he wouldn't get turned into a loot box right after landing. But then he saw Xiang Huaizhi rush into the factory with an M762 and wipe out the entire opposing team in thirty seconds.

Jing Huan watched the scene unfold, mouth slightly agape. *You call this rusty?*

By the time the game ended, Xiang Huaizhi had single-handedly wiped out two teams, plus a few stragglers, for a total of twelve kills. Although they didn't win the game, it didn't stop him from becoming a legend in the eyes of all the members of Dorm 312.

"Goddamn!" Lu Wenhao exclaimed as soon as he snapped out of his dazed stupor. He changed his way of addressing Xiang Huaizhi. "Mr. Xiang, you're incredible… even better than those streamers!"

Gao Zixiang nodded hastily as well. "For real. And you were being so modest just now…"

Xiang Huaizhi opened their profiles and took a look: they were really quite low-ranked.

Very tactfully, Xiang Huaizhi said, "Judging by your outfits, I thought this was a high-ranked match."

Jing Huan quipped, "Who knew it was just two flashy noobs."

Lu Wenhao cursed, "Fuck, like you're any better!"

Jing Huan raised his eyebrows. "I'm different. At least my performance is consistent with my appearance."

Xiang Huaizhi's mouth unconsciously tugged up into a faint smile. *He's actually quite proud of himself.*

Suddenly, his cellphone vibrated. Xiang Huaizhi checked it.

Guide on How to Fail at Online Dating

Lu Hang: Xiangxiang, why are you taking so long at the convenience store? Bring me back some hot and sour noodles, okay? QAQ

Xiang: Order takeout yourself.

Lu Hang: Don't be like that. T.T I'm too lazy to go downstairs and get it. >.<

Xiang: ?

Xiang: Why are you using those emoticons?

Lu Hang: Oh, I noticed you seem to like the ones Little Jingjing sends, so I'm willing to change myself for you.

Xiang: Buy it yourself, I won't be back until tonight.

Lu Hang: Why, where are you going? O.O

Xiang: Internet café.

Lu Hang: ??

Lu Hang: Why are you going to an internet café? Am I not flirty enough for you? Is gaming with me in the dorm not fun?

Xiang: Yes.

Xiang: Don't use those emoticons anymore, they don't suit you.

Lu Hang: ...

The four of them spent the whole afternoon gaming at the internet café, and was so thoroughly glued to their screens they even ordered delivery for dinner. It was only when the clock struck nine did they reluctantly log off. It was too late for night basketball, so that plan was scrapped.

It was already mid-autumn, and the temperature had steadily dropped. As soon as Lu Wenhao pushed open the door of the internet café, the cool wind hit him, making him shiver and get goosebumps all over. Except for Jing Huan, all of them wore short sleeves.

 Chapter 11

"It's so damn cold. Lu Wenhao and I are going to get something hot to warm up," said Gao Zixiang. "Are you guys coming?"

Jing Huan didn't really want to go. He glanced at Xiang Huaizhi who also shook his head.

"Then, I'll head off with Xiang-ge." Jing Huan also felt a bit cold, and he shrugged. "It's on the way home anyway."

After they left, Xiang Huaizhi asked, "You don't live in the dorms?"

Jing Huan shook his head. "No, I'm renting a place outside."

He's living so frugally, and yet he still rents a place?

"The school always cuts the water and power, so I don't want to live there." Jing Huan added jokingly, "And I can't stand Lu Wenhao's stinky socks."

After some thought, Xiang Huaizhi understood. Although their dormitory conditions were decent, most of the guys were pretty careless and lazy. Cleaning the dorm once a week would count as a win to them, so cockroaches and mice were common visitors.

It was the weekend, and with how cold the evening had turned, there weren't many people on the path to the back gate, and even fewer street vendors. The two men walked side by side along the roadside, their shadows stretching long under the streetlights.

Another gust of cold wind hit, and Jing Huan instinctively shrunk back. He turned to Xiang Huaizhi and said with a smile, "I didn't expect you to be so good at *PUBG*. You're even better than those gaming companions."

Xiang Huaizhi asked, "Gaming companions?"

"Yeah." Jing Huan explained, "They're people you pay to play games with."

Guide on How to Fail at Online Dating

Xiang Huaizhi of course knew what gaming companions were; he was just puzzled. "You've hired gaming companions?"

"Yeah, I'm a noob so I hire them often," Jing Huan said frankly.

After a few more steps, Xiang Huaizhi tossed out a casual question. "Do you hire male or female companions?"

Immediately, Jing Huan said, "Definitely guys."

Having expected this answer, Xiang Huaizhi glanced over at him. The wind blew Jing Huan's hair back to reveal a clean and full forehead, making him look neat and refreshing.

"But I haven't hired gaming companions much lately," Jing Huan said, looking straight ahead, "I'd be better off joining Xiao Yan's team—he's both reliable and exciting."

"Xiao Yan?"

"Yeah, a male streamer on StarfieldTV. He's really good. The viewers all call him Yanyan. You haven't heard of him? He's pretty popular."

"No." Xiang Huaizhi seldom watched live streams.

"He plays just as good as you," Jing Huan instinctively complimented Xiang Huaizhi. "And he's very good-looking—but not as handsome as you."

Xiang Huaizhi's eyelids drooped a little. "Is that so?" There was a subtle nuance in his tone that went unnoticed by Jing Huan.

"Mm, I've sent him gifts before, although it was just a few thousand yuan—nowhere close to what his whale supporters spend. But he still reaches out to me to play games pretty often," Jing Huan said with a wink. "What can I say? I'm just that popular."

Xiang Huaizhi was a little speechless. All Yearning For had received from Jing Huan were some fireworks that were worth about

Chapter 11

three figures. But this male streamer had received gifts that cost thousands of yuan?

A long couple of minutes passed. Xiang Huaizhi then asked calmly, "Don't you regret spending all that money?"

Jing Huan, feeling fidgety, absentmindedly swung his hands back and forth. "It's fine, I really like the streamer."

There was a brief silence beside him before Xiang Huaizhi asked, "Do you still like him?"

"I do," Jing Huan confessed. He'd occasionally watch Xiao Yan's stream to kill some time when he got bored running dungeons.

Xiang Huaizhi's eyelids twitched slightly, and his expression shifted just a bit.

Okay. This guy is actually two-timing. Then, why doesn't he just cling to the male streamer? Why me?

Jing Huan sighed. "But ever since Xiao Yan got into a relationship, he rarely streams anymore."

That explained why he had turned his attention to him; the other guy was already taken.

When he thought about it, Xiang Huaizhi realized that, in all the times they had met in reality, Jing Huan had never voluntarily mentioned Yearning For in front of him. The only time he brought him up, he had dismissed him with a casual "the person's not that great."

Jing Huan had spoken for a long time without getting a response. He looked up at him slightly and asked, "Ge?"

Xiang Huaizhi lowered his eyes, suppressing his emotions. "Mm."

"Were you listening to me just now?"

"I was."

"Then why didn't you say anything?"

"I was just thinking about how strong that streamer must be." *So strong that even though he's dating someone now, you still can't forget about him.*

"Actually, he's just all right. He's pretty quiet, not as naggy as other gaming companions," Jing Huan said casually. "But I prefer playing with you. If you were a gaming companion, I'd hire you every day."

"I don't want to be a gaming companion," Xiang Huaizhi said suddenly.

Jing Huan nodded. "I know, I was just saying that..."

"But if you want to play, you can reach out to me anytime," Xiang Huaizhi added.

Jing Huan smiled. All of those hints he had dropped had been for this! "Really? But I'm such a noob, wouldn't playing with me be frustrating?"

"No." Xiang Huaizhi paused. "But I have one condition."

"Hm?"

"When you play with me, you can't bring any gaming companions. Or the streamer." Xiang Huaizhi's tone was steady as usual. "I don't like gaming with strangers."

Jing Huan's smile widened. "With you around, why would I need to hire gaming companions?"

Here he goes again with his sweet talk.

Just then, Jing Huan's right hand, which was swinging around carelessly, accidentally grazed against his. The back of their hands touched, making a gentle brushing sound.

Xiang Huaizhi froze slightly and was about to move his hand

 Chapter 11

away, but the person beside him caught his wrist before he could do so.

"Ge, your hand is so cold." Jing Huan naturally wrapped his hand around his. "Let me warm it up for you."

Feeling the heat from his palm, Xiang Huaizhi's throat tightened, and he wanted to pull away. "You don't have to…"

"It's okay, I have good circulation, so my hands are always warm in the winter. Lu Wenhao and Gao Zixiang often get me to warm them up." Jing Huan gently rubbed his hands. He looked up, and smugly asked, "Feels good, right?"

The warmth spread from his fingertips to the rest of his body, making every cell in his body feel like they were on fire.

Xiang Huaizhi looked at him, quietly noting the unusual rhythm of his heartbeat. He tried to keep his tone neutral, but when he spoke, his voice was much deeper than usual.

"Mm," he said. "It feels good."

Guide on How to Fail at Online Dating

Chapter 12

As soon as Jing Huan woke up on Monday, he noticed that someone in the dormitory group chat had been constantly @ing him. Squinting, he began slowly scrolling through the chat history.

Lu Wenhao: Oh fuck! Anyone on!!

Lu Wenhao: @Little Jing~ @Gao Zixiang

Lu Wenhao: URGENT! Someone respond @Little Jing~

Gao Zixiang: Holy fuck, can you pay attention in class and stop disturbing your roommate's sleep? I was literally jolted awake by you.

Lu Wenhao: FINALLY, someone's here, I was fucking suffocating.

Gao Zixiang: If you have shit to say, spit it out.

Lu Wenhao: 【Link share - Campus BBS -*AAAAH I photographed Xiang Huaizhi and Jing Huan! They were doing things!!!*】

Seeing his name, a completely confused Jing Huan frowned and clicked the link.

The photo had been taken at the main building where he and Xiang Huaizhi stood beside each other, illuminated by the streetlights. He was holding Xiang Huaizhi's left hand, smiling

happily. It was from the night he helped warm Xiang Huaizhi's hands.

So what? What's wrong with this photo?

Jing Huan blankly kept scrolling down.

3L: They're real! They're real!!

7L: Damn, does anyone have any insider info? Please share the details.

10L: I knew something was off about them!! Look how handsome they are! How could they not have girlfriends if they were straight?!

Wait... Jing Huan seemed to realize something and sat up slowly.

20L: Thanks, OP. My roommate confessed to Jing Huan twice and got rejected both times. For a long time, she was a total mess, but now she's better and sincerely wishes him and Senior Xiang a long and happy life together.

37l: Is OP from the photography club? The photo is so beautiful, they look so sweet...

79l: Our school actually has a gay couple! And they're both so handsome! Damn, I'm swooning! I'm going to show this off to my high school roommates!!

155L: I also heard that Xiang Huaizhi defended Jing Huan on the basketball court. I guess they were dating this whole time?

No, he *defended Xiang Huaizhi. Get that right!*

Realizing that he had focused on the wrong thing, Jing Huan shakily scrolled down further.

173l: Haha, good thing I'm smart. The moment I saw Jing Huan,

Chapter 12

I knew he had to be gay—and a cute, sunny little 0[1] at that! That's why I didn't even bother pursuing him, even though I liked him. But I never would've expected Xiang Huaizhi, of all people, to be his partner.

Sunny, cute, little, 0—he understood each word individually, but what the hell did they mean together?

After scrolling through the entire post, Jing Huan didn't know whether he should be angry or find it funny. He closed the site and returned to the group chat.

Little Jing~: Can we trace the IP address on the BBS post?

Gao Zixiang: Calm down. Don't automatically jump to doxxing people.

Little Jing~: What the hell... What's going on? I just warmed up Xiang Huaizhi's hands a bit.

Looking at all these comments, someone who didn't know any better might've thought that he and Xiang Huazhi had been caught in bed together.

Lu Wenhao: I don't get it either, it's just holding hands... I held your hand every day last winter, so how come no one said we were dating?

Little Jing~: ?

Gao Zixiang: No duh, people aren't stupid.

Lu Wenhao: ???

Lu Wenhao: What do you mean? I might not understand what you're saying, but I know you must be badmouthing me.

Gao Zixiang: It's all about looks. Get it?

Lu Wenhao: No.

---

1   Chinese slang for bottom is 0, while tops are 1.

Gao Zixiang: When two good-looking people hold hands, it's called a perfect match. Anyone who looks at them will think they're a couple.

Lu Wenhao: Stop talking.

Gao Zixiang: If a good-looking person holds hands with an ugly person, that's called charity, brotherhood, or a friendship forever and ever.

Lu Wenhao: ...I'm definitely going to settle this with you today once and for all. Just wait, I'm coming back with a knife.

Jing Huan had been feeling quite down but watching these two idiots chat lightened his mood a lot. He opened his chat with Xiang Huaizhi.

He typed: *Ge, someone took a photo of me warming your hands that night, and it got posted on the school BBS. QAQ*

Just as he was about to hit send, Jing Huan paused, his eyes catching on the emoticon he had added at the end.

What kind of shit habit is this... He removed the emoticon, and sent it.

Xiang Huaizhi: Saw it. Do you care?

Jing Huan was stunned. He was the one who had taken the initiative to hold someone else's hand, why would he care?

Little Jing~: No... It's just that I made you look bad.

Little Jing~: How about I go to the BBS to explain?

Xiang Huaizhi: I don't care either.

Xiang Huaizhi: I'm busy right now. Let's talk about it next time.

The chat ended quickly, and Jing Huan was left holding his cellphone, feeling a bit perplexed; so, should he explain the situation or not?

 Chapter 12

Before he could think too much about it, his cellphone vibrated.

Xiang: Awake yet?

Little Jing~: Awake, gege. \ \ ^ 0 ^ / /

Xiang: Get on the game.

Jing Huan checked the time. It wasn't even 10 a.m. yet; were they going to run a dungeon this early?

His sleepiness was already dissipated by the BBS post, so he obediently replied, "Okay" and got out of bed.

After washing up, he logged into the game and AFKed in the main city, wanting to order breakfast first to fill his stomach. He didn't even get to open his food delivery app when a system prompt popped up.

【Yearning For invites you to join his party. Yes, No.】

As Jing Huan clicked "Yes," he wondered if he should turn off the share coordinates display in his friend info. With his location exposed all the time, it left him no privacy.

He moved his mouse to Yearning For's information, and as expected, he couldn't see his coordinates.

"Good morning, gege." Jing Huan noticed a good chunk of his friend list was gray. Neither Love is Sharing Noms nor Long Road Ahead were online. "Looks like it's just us two?"

"Morning," Xiang Huaizhi replied and took him out of the city.

Jing Huan, still drowsy from waking up minutes ago, didn't speak nor type. He was curious to see where Yearning For was leading him. After a few zone transitions, they arrived at Petal Valley.

Jing Huan had to ask. "Gege, are we on a date—"

"No," Xiang Huaizhi cut him off. "Top off your health."

That surprised Jing Huan. He moved his hand to refill his health bar, a vague guess taking form in his mind.

Jing Huan still hadn't seen anyone yet when they reached Petal Valley's most beautiful waterfall, but a message popped up in the chat channel.

[Current] Ji Xiaonian: I love you too! Forever and ever. I'll never leave or abandon you. [Heart]

Ji Xiaonian stood under the cherry blossom tree, a refined scholar next to her. The two characters looked like they were on a date: they were dressed in matching couple outfits, and had their arms wrapped around each other in a tight embrace. They made for an extremely lovey-dovey image.

Jing Huan faintly remembered seeing the scholar's name on the server's rankings list, but he didn't make much of an impression. But, of course, that wasn't important. He didn't think Yearning For brought him here to eat dog food[2]. Sure enough, he didn't even have to ask when a line of yellow text appeared.

【Attention! Party leader Yearning For has initiated a forced PK against player Ji Xiaonian!】

Jing Huan stared, nonplussed.

Ji Xiaonian obviously noticed them too, but unfortunately, Yearning For's hands were too quick. She had no time to run away.

[Current] Ji Xiaonian: ???

[Current] Ji Xiaonian: Are you crazy? Are you ambushing me??

---

2 Chinese slang for single people (single dogs) watching couples do lovey-dovey stuff together.

 Chapter 12

Xiang Huaizhi didn't respond and simply threw out a Celestial Binding Rope, entrapping Ji Xiaonian and giving her no chance to escape.

[Current] Ji Xiaonian: I have nothing to do with that matter. Are you going to camp me every day? You only know to bully women. Truly shameless! [Vomiting]

[Current] Ji Xiaonian: Scumbag. [Despise] Disgusting. [Vomiting] Cheating couple. [Spitting]

Ji Xiaonian's specialty lay in spewing out sarcastic and mocking quips. In no time, the entire chat channel was filled with her messages.

Jing Huan's entire vision turned red. He slammed the keyboard, hammering out a heap of words to fire back.

"No need to argue with her," Xiang Huaizhi said.

Jing Huan paused. "How did you know…"

"Your keyboard is very loud." Xiang Huaizhi's voice was calm, completely unaffected by Ji Xiaonian's words.

Jing Huan blinked and silently deleted all the words in the chat box. *Wow, have I lost my mind? Did I want to defend Yearning For just now?!*

[Current] Ji Xiaonian: What, did I hit the nail on the head? Too scared to talk?

At this moment, the scholar on a date with Ji Xiaonian finally spoke up.

[Current] Moonlight with You: Yearning For, aren't the two of you being bullies, ganging up like this to kill one woman?

[Current] Yearning For: You can form a party.

Those words immediately shut Moonlight with You up. A forced

PK allowed players to make temporary parties; if Moonlight with You truly felt like they were bullying her, he could've easily partied up with Ji Xiaonian to fight back.

Yearning For's words reminded Ji Xiaonian of this, and she immediately went to DM him.

[Friend] Ji Xiaonian: Baby, join my party! Let's take down Sweet Little Jing and destroy her gear!

[Friend] Moonlight with You: …That's not a good idea.

[Friend] Ji Xiaonian: ??? She brought someone to kill me. What do you mean it's not a good idea?!

[Friend] Moonlight with You: But what if we can't kill them?

[Friend] Ji Xiaonian: How would you know if we don't try?

[Friend] Moonlight with You: …

[Friend] Moonlight with You: It's just that… Baby, I'm trying to climb the Wealth rankings, so I have a lot of in-game currency on me. If I die, I'll lose a lot of money…

[Friend] Ji Xiaonian: ?

[Friend] Moonlight with You: Niannian, look at Sweet Little Jing's gear. None of her items are worth as much as mine. Why bother fighting them?

[Friend] Ji Xiaonian: So you're just going to leave me like this?

[Friend] Moonlight with You: No, how could I leave you? I'll wait for you at the respawn point, and then I'll take you to buy some outfits after, okay?

When Ji Xiaonian didn't respond, Jing Huan asked, "Will they party up?"

Xiang Huaizhi replied, "Probably not."

Jing Huan was stupefied. "Why not?"

Chapter 12

"The Wealth rankings list refreshes today. Moonlight with You should have a lot of gold on him."

"That's the reason?" Jing Huan frowned. "He's going to ignore his wife, let her get killed, all because of a bit of money?"

Xiang Huaizhi paused. "If it were you, would you care?"

"Of courseee," Jing Huan answered without thinking. "If gege ever got killed, I'd accompany you to the respawn point. We live under the same roof and die in the same grave! Death can't tear us apart!"

"There's no need to accompany me to the respawn point," Xiang Huaizhi said leisurely. "I won't die."

Jing Huan stared wordlessly. *This person doesn't have a single romantic bone in his entire body.*

The person broke their silence just then.

[Current] Ji Xiaonian: If you're going to kill me, get it over with.

Jing Huan then realized that only the three of them were in the area; Moonlight with You had disappeared at some point. Ji Xiaonian did not say anything more, and when she was knocked to the ground, Jing Huan even felt a little sorry for her. After the battle ended, only he and Yearning For remained.

"Maimai's #1 Fan is out of the safe zone," Xiang Huaizhi said. "Was killing him last time enough?"

"Ah...it's fine, he hasn't tried to bother me since then." Something occurred to Jing Huan. "Gege, how did you know that Ji Xiaonian left the safe zone?"

"Saw her while doing my dailies."

"I see." Jing Huan sighed. "She's kind of pitiful. Her husband doesn't even care that she got hunted down."

"Mm."

"Forget it. Why am I sympathizing with her?" Jing Huan calmed down. "When I was being hunted down, I didn't even have a husband!"

Xiang Huaizhi looked away.

"And I still don't have one!!!"

Xiang Huaizhi led him back, to end this conversation. Jing Huan was certainly not going to let this go, and blurted out, "Gege, marry me!"

"Not marrying you."

"Why not!"

Because you're a guy. The words popped into his mind, startling Xiang Huaizhi. He couldn't pinpoint what was wrong, but he knew that his thoughts…had traversed into a strange place. A very strange place.

He subconsciously glanced at the back of his hand. The warmth from Jing Huan's palm seemed to linger from that night.

"Because," Xiang Huaizhi paused slightly and said, "I see you as a friend."

…What?

Your daddy has been flirting with you for months. Coyness and acting cute aside, I've called you gege so many times I feel like throwing up. Now, you're telling me you just see me as a friend? Let me tell you, it's pretty damn hard being your friend!

Jing Huan inwardly cussed him out—maybe he should just trick

Chapter 12

Yearning For into revealing his address, and go over there to perform a real-life PK. Even if he had to spend fifteen days at the police station, it'd still be better than running barefoot after this train every day. Or so he thought.

[Party] Sweet Little Jing: [Falling to the ground and spitting out blood]

[Party] Sweet Little Jing: T.T I'm not even a meimei... WAAAAH!!

He had switched to typing, on account of his rage bubbling up to his lips and preventing him from speaking.

[Party] Yearning For: ...

[Party] Yearning For: If you want to be a meimei, that's fine too.

How about I become your ancestor instead?

Jing Huan took a few deep breaths and comforted himself. Being a meimei was better than a friend; at the very least, there was a chance to further develop their relationship.

[Party] Yearning For: I'm going to go do dailies. Go play by yourself.

Go play by yourself. Like he was ordering around a little kid.

[Party] Sweet Little Jing: No, I want to chill in gege's party!

[Party] Sweet Little Jing: I'm just waiting for my food delivery anyway. I haven't had breakfast yet, and I'm too hungry to move. QvQ

Xiang Huaizhi checked the time and then summoned his mount. "Whatever you want." He sent Jing Huan a ride-sharing invite. "Get on."

It was Jing Huan's first time seeing Yearning For riding a mount. In *Nine Heroes*, mounts were not dissimilar to outfits in that they

did not provide any bonus attributes, nor did they increase movement speed; players had to purchase the speed buff separately. When this system first came out, players cursed the developers and their families for a month. Moreover, riding a mount hid the player's weapon; using mounts thus became scarce. Yearning For, who owned the most dazzling and eye-catching weapon across all servers, was even less likely to use a mount.

Jing Huan clicked his tongue. *How vain!*

The food delivery arrived in record time. Jing Huan took a bite of the fried dough stick and was considering whether to find a movie to pass the time when his friend message icon lit up.

[Friend] Echoes of Spring: Are you there?

[Friend] Sweet Little Jing: Yep!

[Friend] Echoes of Spring: The dungeon progress is about to reset. If you don't return to the guild, Yearning For will have to clear guild dungeons with other female players.

[Friend] Sweet Little Jing: ?

[Friend] Echoes of Spring: In the few days since you've left the guild, a lot of people have come to me saying that they want to join Yearning For's party.

[Friend] Sweet Little Jing: I've applied to rejoin the guild! Approve it!! [Angry]

【Guild Announcement: Welcome Sweet Little Jing to the Idle Pavilion Guild!】

[Guild] Peach Cheese Stan: Welcome, welcome!!

[Guild] BrbOrNot: Welcome back!

[Guild] Love is Sharing Noms: Tossing out flowers!

[Guild] Bishop Wood: Welcome mwaaah. =3=

Chapter 12

[Guild] Long Road Ahead: Little Jingjing is back~

[Guild] Sweet Little Jing: Mm, if I didn't come back, gege would've run guild dungeons with other women. QAQ

[Guild] Long Road Ahead: Understood.

[Guild] Bishop Wood: It's okay, I can still take you~

[Guild] Echoes of Spring: Now that you're back, I have a special announcement to make. As the largest guild in the server, Idle Pavilion doesn't cause trouble but we also do not fear it. Everyone should actively contribute to the guild, and as the vice guild leader, I'll be responsible for everyone. In the future, if any issues arise, please consult with me in a timely manner. Acting impulsively and quitting the guild when something happens isn't only bad for you, but also detrimental for the guild's image.

Jing Huan instantly felt like a scolded elementary school student. However, Echoes of Spring's words, albeit blunt, made sense; he really had acted rashly when he left the guild.

[Guild] Sweet Little Jing: All right, I won't leave the guild next time. [Wiping tears]

[Guild] Echoes of Spring: ?

[Guild] Echoes of Spring: Let's not have a next time.

[Guild] BrbOrNot: But I'm really curious… Why hasn't Maimai's #1 Fan made any moves yet? In the past, you would've been hunted by assassination squads all over the server by now, right?

[Guild] Silent Affection: Are you crazy? What assassination squad would dare target one of Yearning For's party members?

[Guild] Sweet Little Jing: (/ / / V / / /) With gege around, I'm definitely not afraid of him.

Xiang Huaizhi silently read the guild chat; he had no intention of participating in the conversation.

"Still not done with your dailies yet?" Lu Hang swiveled around. "We're all waiting for you two so we can clear dungeons."

"Almost done."

From the angle he was sitting at, Lu Hang could just barely make out the chat channel. He teased, "What are you lurking for? Not going to say anything?"

Xiang Huaizhi looked away. "What's there to say?"

"So heartless."

Xiang Huaizhi ignored him and moved to turn in the quest. The cellphone on the table suddenly rang, and he paused as he took a quick glimpse at the caller ID. He typed "taking a call" in the game, then took off his headset and answered it.

A girl's voice yelled through the phone, "Xiang Huaizhi!" Her voice was so resonant that even Lu Hang could faintly hear it.

Xiang Huaizhi could already feel his temples throb—signs of an incoming headache. He held the phone a good distance away and said helplessly, "How many times have I told you to not use my full name?"

When Jing Huan returned from throwing out the trash, he saw his friend message icon blinking incessantly.

Long Road Ahead: Little Jingjing, something happened!

Long Road Ahead: Xiangxiang is on the phone with another girl!

Sweet Little Jing: ?

Sweet Little Jing: QAQ How could this be! With who?!

 Chapter 12

Long Road Ahead: I don't know. I only heard a girl's voice. Xiangxiang even asked her to call him by his nickname!

Sweet Little Jing: ...Could it be...his girlfriend...

Long Road Ahead: No way, Xiangxiang doesn't have a girlfriend. I live with him every day—wouldn't I know?

Jing Huan reflexively bit his thumb. *Yearning For actually let someone else call him by his nickname?!*

Crisis! Huge, massive crisis!

Baffled as he was, he also felt annoyed. Why did it feel like Yearning For treated both the girl on the phone and Fae Bae a hundred—no, a thousand—times better than himself?

Up until today, he had always thought he and Yearning For had successfully reached the golden stage of "ambiguity," which was just a step away from becoming an official couple. And yet, Yearning For said he just saw him as a friend.

Although Jing Huan had never been in a relationship before, he knew that if a guy felt even the slightest *anything* in his heart for a girl, he would never say something like "I see you as a friend." After everything he had done, he was still stuck at the starting point.

Jing Huan couldn't help but start to reflect on his methods thus far. Were they truly effective on Yearning For? Was he focusing his efforts in the wrong direction?

[Friend] Sweet Little Jing: Road-ge, could you check things out for me...

[Friend] Long Road Ahead: What do you want to check? The girl's identity? I can do that.

[Friend] Sweet Little Jing: Not that. T.T I want to know what type of girl gege likes.

It's okay; wherever I fall, that's where I'll get back up. He could pretend to be whatever kind of girl Yearning For liked.

[Friend] Long Road Ahead: ?? There's no need to worry, you're definitely his type.

[Friend] Sweet Little Jing: ...?

[friend] Sweet Little Jing: Really? But just now, gege said he only sees me as a friend. [Wailing]

[Friend] Long Road Ahead: Damn, he told you that? You two have already made that much progress?

Jing Huan slowly typed out a question mark.

[Friend] Sweet Little Jing: Much? [Lifeless]

[Friend] Long Road Ahead: Yeah. Look around, does he have any other friends in the game besides me?

[Friend] Sweet Little Jing: ?

Could this really be the case?

[Friend] Long Road Ahead: Really, just keep doing whatever you're already doing. It won't be too long before you win Xiangxiang over.

Jing Huan frowned; somehow, he didn't quite believe him. But aside from Long Road Ahead, he really didn't have anyone else who could give him advice about Yearning For.

Jing Huan hesitated for a moment, then replied with a "good luck" sticker.

I'll just continue doing what I'm doing for now and see how things go.

After class the next day, Jing Huan declined Lu Wenhao and Gao Zixiang's invitation to play basketball, and headed toward the

Chapter 12

back gate alone. He was going straight back to his apartment to video call his mom. After sending his mom a text message, he looked up and saw a familiar figure walking out of the men's dormitory.

Xiang Huaizhi was wearing a loose black T-shirt, looking relaxed. Although it looked like clothes he would usually wear in the dorms, he somehow managed to stand out more than anyone around him.

Holding a pair of shoes by the laces, he strolled toward the trash can waiting on the right side of the dorm entrance, the sneakers swaying by his side. Jing Huan recognized the shoes right away—they still had imprints of his own shoes from a few days ago.

"Ge, you're throwing them away?"

Xiang Huaizhi paused, and he looked back to see the underclassman behind him who was currently staring guilty holes into the shoes he was carrying.

Xiang Huaizhi had already walked all the way up to the trash can, so there was no point in denying it. He made an affirmative noise. "They're old and worn out so I've been meaning to toss them."

"Aside from the footprints, they still look pretty new..." Jing Huan was the type of person whose sneaker collection couldn't even fit in one room at his family home. He wouldn't dare to make claims about anything else but considered himself a connoisseur of sneakers. The style of these shoes looked vaguely familiar; he couldn't remember the specifics, but they definitely weren't cheap.

He looked away from the shoes and met Xiang Huaizhi's eyes. "Ge, let me replace them for you. What model are they? What size do you wear?"

"No need," Xiang Huaizhi refused. "They're limited edition, so you can't buy them anymore."

As soon as he said "limited edition," Jing Huan finally remembered these shoes had been released by a certain brand last October. Even the thought of stepping on and scuffing up limited edition shoes like these sent a sharp pain through his heart; he couldn't even begin to imagine what Xiang Huaizhi must be feeling.

Jing Huan wanted to offer money, but how could he compensate him for something like this? The market price of the shoes right now would be much higher than the original retail price, and Xiang-ge definitely wouldn't accept his money.

Jing Huan's dazed appearance made him look a bit silly. Xiang Huaizhi glanced at him, his lips curling slightly into the faintest of smiles. He raised his hand to toss the sneakers into the trash can, so as to save Jing Huan from his inner turmoil.

Seeing this, Jing Huan immediately took a few steps forward, trying to stop him.

Worried that Jing Huan might bump into the trash can, Xiang Huaizhi instinctively reached out and pressed his palm against Jing Huan's forehead. His fingers curled slightly, grasping Jing Huan's head as if holding a basketball, but without exerting any force.

Both of them were taken aback.

Jing Huan recovered first. "Ge, don't toss them. Let me clean them. I'm great at scrubbing shoes, I can guarantee I can make them spotless."

Xiang Huaizhi decisively tossed the shoes into the empty trash can. The shoes made a dull clanging sound as they hit the bottom.

"I told you it's not necessary," he said, casually ruffling Jing

Chapter 12

Huan's hair a couple of times before withdrawing his hand. "I'd been meaning to replace them anyway; this has nothing to do with you. Just got out of class?"

Jing Huan was a little bewildered to have his head suddenly rubbed. "Mm..."

Xiang Huaizhi didn't think he did anything out of the ordinary. What was the problem with an upperclassman tousling an underclassman's hair?

"Then you should go back. The weather doesn't look good; it's going to rain soon."

"Okay." Jing Huan licked his lips and let out a small laugh. "Ge, are your hands clean? You were holding your shoes just now."

"The one that touched you was clean."

"I don't believe you," Jing Huan joked. "You're getting back at me."

Before he could finish speaking, Xiang Huaizhi raised his left hand, palm out in front of him. The faint scent of soap wafted into his nose, fresh and pleasant.

Feeling Jing Huan's breath on his hand, Xiang Huaizhi pulled away. "Believe me now?"

Jing Huan was perplexed. What was up with his ge today? Why was he getting so handsy?

He pursed his lips and blinked. "I believe you...ge."

It wasn't until Jing Huan's video call with Mama Jing that he discovered some of his hair was sticking up.

The video connected, showing a woman with refined makeup and dressed in a sleek, tailored suit, her hair pulled back without a single strand out of place. Her eyes and brows bore some resemblance to Jing Huan's.

Seeing Jing Huan's movements, the corner of the woman's mouth quirked up slightly. "Did you have a windstorm at your school?"

"Not really." Jing Huan looked around at her surroundings. "Mom, it's so late. Are you still at work?"

"Mm, just finishing up the last bit of work, then I'll head home." Jing Huan's mom closed the file. "How have you been lately? Are you getting used to the new place?"

Every time the mother and son pair chatted, it was always in a question-and-answer format.

"I have a few days off coming up soon, so I was thinking I'd visit you with your dad." After a pause, Mama Jing went right for the main point. "And really, you had a break last month, so why didn't you come home?"

"It's not my fault, Gao Zixiang and Lu Wenhao insisted on dragging me to the hot springs resort." Jing Huan shifted the blame.

"Zixiang had a way of making you go along even though you didn't want to?" Mama Jing twirled her pen and raised an eyebrow. "Be honest, have you been dating someone recently?"

Jing Huan didn't hesitate. "No, how could that be possible…"

"Then, what have you been busy with lately?" Mama Jing started keeping score. "You used to call me once a week; how many times have you called since the semester started?"

I've been preoccupied with trying to get a scumbag to fall in love with me.

Jing Huan said, "I've just been busy with something. I promise I'll call you every day from now on."

 Chapter 12

"No, that would be annoying." Mama Jing glanced at the calendar on the table. "Your dad and I will visit you on the eighth of next month."

"Okay, you guys can come whenever you want," Jing Huan said. "Do you want me to come pick you up at the station?"

"No need. We'll drive there and take a few days to do some sightseeing around the area while we're at it. Your dad has already booked the hotel room."

...Visiting me was just an afterthought, huh?

After hanging up, Jing Huan moved at a snail pace and turned on the computer. As soon as he logged into the PC version of WeChat, he saw that he had 99+ unread messages in the guild group chat. He was used to it; there were over 200 active people in this chat, each one chattier than the last. Several hundred messages could easily be sent in just one class period.

Jing Huan logged into the game and sent a message to the person at the top of his friend list.

[Friend] Sweet Little Jing: Gege, I'm here. [Blowing a kiss]

This process had become a habit for him. In *Nine Heroes*, the friend list was sorted by intimacy level, with the highest at the top. Each time they did a battle while in the same party, the intimacy level would increase by one. Therefore, the person with the highest intimacy level for Jing Huan was Yearning For. It was also currently high enough for them to get married in the game.

Jing Huan leaned back in his chair and lazily typed.

[Friend] Sweet Little Jing: Gege, our intimacy level is already 3,300. When will you marry me and take me home?

[Friend] Yearning For: My intimacy level with Long Road Ahead is 9,999.

That was the maximum intimacy level for regular friends. Unless you were married, it didn't matter how many battles you fought together, your level would still be capped at 9,999.

[Friend] Sweet Little Jing: But he can't marry you. Even if we go by queue positions, it's my turn! [Pounding table]

[Friend] Yearning For: Come to the dungeon.

[Friend] Sweet Little Jing: Come marry me.

[Friend] Yearning For: Main city teleporter.

[Friend] Sweet Little Jing: Old Moon Temple, Yuelao.

[Friend] Yearning For: Be good.

Half a minute later, the little spirit fox reluctantly walked to the main city teleporter. As soon as he joined the party, he heard Love is Sharing Noms chatting with Long Road Ahead.

"Why haven't you been gathering the God of War materials lately?" Love is Sharing Noms asked.

"Girl, please spare me. Don't mention the God of War to me right now," Long Road Ahead said. "If you bring it up again, I'll throw myself off the cliff in Petal Valley."

Jing Huan helpfully suggested, "Actually, it's better to jump off the cliff in Endless Peak. In Petal Valley, you need to jump off the cliff twice to die, but you just need to do it once at Endless Peak."

"I pass info to you every day, and this is how you treat me? Little Jingjing, you're so cruel," Long Road Ahead bemoaned.

Jing Huan hurriedly explained, "It was just a suggestion. I couldn't bear to see you jump twice."

"Pass info?" Xiang Huaizhi repeated.

 Chapter 12

Realizing that he had slipped up, Lu Hang coughed and changed the subject. "Anyway, we're still short for a person. I'll go find someone. We really need to get a regular party member; it's awkward to always have to bring in a random player."

Xiang Huaizhi knew that the info being reported was likely about him, but he didn't bother prying. "Mm."

He opened his equipment tab, meaning to check the remaining durability of his gear when a prompt popped up.

【xoxoYuyu has added you as a friend.】

Xiang Huaizhi dismissed it without a second thought. Adding friends was a one-sided affair; as long as he didn't reciprocate and add them back, they'd remain off his friend list. Dozens of friend request notifications flooded in almost daily, but he had grown accustomed to ignoring them long ago.

But a few seconds later, the other person sent a message.

[Stranger] xoxoYuyu: Xiang Huaizhi!!!

[Stranger] Yearning For: ...

Xiang Huaizhi opened up xoxoYuyu's profile: a level-capped female warrior with no guild who had numerous empty slots for cash shop outfits. It looked like a character freshly bought from the marketplace. He didn't need to think too hard to guess who it belonged to.

Long Road Ahead's call-out in the World Channel led to many players adding him. A few minutes into looking through his temporary friend list, he asked, "What sect should we recruit? Healer, DPS, or CC?"

Love is Sharing Noms replied, "Recruit a DPS. It'll be faster to kill with two of them."

"Okay—"

"Don't recruit anyone," Xiang Huaizhi interrupted them. "I have someone coming."

Those words sent everyone into a dumbfounded state.

Jing Huan, who had been playing on his phone while lounging against his lumbar cushion, immediately stiffened and sat up straight.

Who could Yearning For call over? Didn't everyone say he had no friends?

Lu Hang was also puzzled. "Who?"

Xiang Huaizhi didn't answer. "Give me party lead."

Lu Hang obeyed and Yearning For led the party toward the wilderness. They made their way to one of *Nine Heroes'* high-level wilderness maps called Senluo Palace.

Senluo Palace was a level 150 wilderness map whose rewards were only negligibly better than the other max-level maps. Players rarely came here to grind for experience, so the map was teeming with ferocious mobs; you couldn't walk two steps without triggering a battle.

Jing Huan couldn't stand the silence. "Gege, where are we going now?"

"Picking someone up."

Five minutes later, Jing Huan finally saw another player on the map.

An empty-handed female warrior stood motionless in a crowd of wild mobs. Aside from the most basic outfit and a scabbard hanging by her waist—the unique symbol of a female warrior—she did not have a single piece of equipment on her.

The rest of the party also caught sight of her, and Long Road

 Chapter 12

Ahead muttered, "Is she trying to die, running around naked like that in this wilderness map? It would be quicker to just jump off the cliff in Petal Valley."

【xoxoYuyu has joined the party.】

Lu Hang's mouth dropped open.

"Xiang... Gege!" Upon recalling Xiang Huaizhi's earlier threat, xoxoYuyu changed her way of addressing him midway through his name. She complained, "What took you so long? I was almost pecked to death by these crows! If you came any later, you would've had to pick me up at the respawn point!"

Gege... The two spectators in the party turned simultaneously to stare at Sweet Little Jing.

"Who told you to stand there?" Xiang Huaizhi said.

Jing Huan's heart sank. *What's going on? How can you let her call you gege!*

"Well, what else could I do! I appeared here as soon as I logged in! Did the original owner of this character do it on purpose?" xoxoYuyu defended herself, angry. "I don't have any Flying Flags or Blue Teleports, so I couldn't leave at all. This is too much!"

Xiang Huaizhi led the party back to the teleportation point. "Why did you come to this server?"

"To play with you. My guild in the other server disbanded, so it's boring over there."

"I don't have time to play with you."

"You do. I don't care, I'm sticking with you no matter what!"

xoxoYuyu let out a *harumph* before greeting the party members. "Hello everyone. Thank you for looking after my gege. Let's play together from now on!"

What the hell is this? What's with this empress addressing the harem-like statement!!

Jing Huan was glaring so hard at Yearning For's character, he was practically shooting daggers into it. The other person didn't say anything to refute xoxoYuyu's "gege" statement.

Lu Hang remained quiet for a while before he finally spoke, "Sure, let's do that."

"Gege, this character doesn't have any gear. Buy me some," xoxoYuyu quickly spoke up again.

"Buy it yourself," Xiang Huaizhi said dismissively.

"My card is maxed out this month. Buy it for me!" xoxoYuyu whined. "If you buy it, I'll do whatever you say!"

Jing Huan sneered. *Save your breath, girl. I've used this trick a million times. If Yearning For had fallen for it, I would've given birth to a basketball team of kids for him by now...*

"You'll do whatever I say?" Yearning For repeated uncertainly.

He's...hesitating? You're not allowed to hesitate, you fucker!

"Whatever you say!" xoxoYuyu said. "If you say one, I won't say two! If you say go left, I won't go right! If you say..."

"Add everything to the shopping cart," Xiang Huaizhi coolly cut her off, not wanting to hear her bootlicking, "and then send me the link."

The fuck! The hell's going on?! Jing Huan's milk tea suddenly did not taste so sweet.

Love is Sharing Noms quickly DMed him, asking who on earth this xoxoYuyu was and if he had heard of her before. Jing Huan didn't reply because he was also just as confused.

 Chapter 12

How did this become a reunion of old friends? How did they become gege and meimei? And why is he paying for her entire shopping cart?!

xoxoYuyu zoomed back. "Gege, I've picked everything. Hurry up and pay for it so we can start the dungeon run together!" She wouldn't have been able to return so quickly if she had had to browse through all the equipment; she must've prepared the list in advance.

Yearning For responded, "Done. Pick it up."

A few seconds later, the female warrior in the party was fully equipped, a purple glow wrapped around her from the gear she was wearing. A full set of purple gear must've cost at least five figures.

Jing Huan was thoroughly unsettled. He quickly opened up Yearning For's chat box.

[Friend] Sweet Little Jing: Gege, who is she...

[Friend] Yearning For: Meimei.

The reply came in less than three seconds. Not a moment of hesitation.

Jing Huan was immediately incensed. *What meimei! Why is it another meimei! Why do you have so many meimei! And saying it so straightforwardly! Fuck! You scumbag! Die! Just die!!!*

Jing Huan furiously pounded on the keyboard, typing out every swear word he knew into the chat box. After reaching a hundred words, he took a deep breath and calmly deleted everything.

No, he couldn't ruin everything now. He knew that but the fury couldn't be abated; Jing Huan had never felt this resentful before. It felt like something was stuck in his chest, frustration rampaging around inside him.

All of a sudden, the little spirit fox in the party stopped moving.

Xiang Huaizhi raised an eyebrow and was about to remind him to keep playing.

[Friend] Sweet Little Jing: Behind every successful man, there can only be one meimei.—Lu Xun[3]

[Friend] Yearning For: ?

[Friend] Yearning For: Lu Xun never said that.

[Friend] Yearning For: What do you mean?

[Friend] Yearning For: ?

His message sank like a stone into the sea, and Xiang Huaizhi frowned. Did he go AFK to deal with something?

Just as he was about to type, Lu Hang spoke first, "Everyone get ready, the boss is coming up."

"Wait a second, the Spirit Fox Den isn't here," Xiang Huaizhi said.

All right. That "Spirit Fox Den" title was like pouring a hundred barrels of oil into the fire blazing in Jing Huan.

He held in his rage and muttered, "I'm here."

Xiang Huaizhi frowned. "If you were here, why didn't you reply?"

"I...just came back," Jing Huan said, and then instinctively added, "gege."

He wanted to take back that word as soon as it left his mouth. *Why the fuck did I call him gege!*

"Gege?" xoxoYuyu blanked a bit then asked, "When you said gege, are you referring to *my* gege?"

---

3   A prominent Chinese writer, essayist, and critic, Lu Xun is considered one of the most influential figures in modern Chinese literature.

 Chapter 12

"Yeah." Jing Huan paused. "Can't I?"

xoxoYuyu asked, "Why are you calling him gege?"

Took the words right out of my mouth. Jing Huan gave a dry laugh and retorted, "Why are *you* calling him gege?"

"Why shouldn't I call him gege?" xoxoYuyu said. "He's precisely my gege."

"What a coincidence," Jing Huan said. "He's also my gege."

Baffled, xoxoYuyu asked, "But he only has one meimei…?"

Jing Huan huffed out an exasperated laugh. "What, did you engrave that on his face? Does it say 'xoxoYuyu's exclusive gege' there? So no one else can call him that?"

Everyone in the party was getting whiplash from this "gege" and "meimei" talk. No one knew how to chime in.

xoxoYuyu asked, shocked, "Ge, who is this person?"

Xiang Huaizhi had a feeling he knew what was happening, but he was also not entirely sure. After a moment, he hesitated and said, "xoxoYuyu is my mei…"

Enraged, Jing Huan cut him off sharply, "I know she's your mei!"

"My tangmei[4]."

"So what if she's your tangmei?! Whatever! You have so many meimei, you don't need to introduce each one to me…" His words came to an abrupt halt.

The party voice chat was silent for ten whole seconds.

Bullseye. Xiang Huaizhi was first amused then took the time to explain to Jing Huan, enunciating each word as slowly as possible. "My father's younger brother's daughter."

---

4   A term for a younger female cousin on the dad's side of the family.

...Did I ask for an explanation?! You think I didn't learn this in kindergarten?!

Jing Huan's face flushed scarlet as he recalled his conversation with xoxoYuyu just now. He wished he could just crawl into a hole in the ground and spend the rest of his life sealed inside it. He was embarrassed beyond belief and subconsciously covered his face with his hands, his cheeks burning. "Ohhh... Hello, cousin."

It was Xiang Huaizhi's turn to be speechless.

At first, xoxoYuyu was shocked, but when she recalled the girl's tone when talking to Xiang Huaizhi, she understood. She had grown up playing with Xiang Huaizhi; she knew how attractive her cousin was and how indifferent he usually was, especially toward girls.

For a while, she'd even wondered if Xiang Huaizhi was gay—a suspicion that earned her a scolding from her parents when she voiced it once during a meal. But now, Xiang Huaizhi had a girl who called him "gege" in his fixed party, plus their relationship seemed quite good.

xoxoYuyu was now *very* interested. "What did you call me?"

Jing Huan flinched, feeling even more fucking awkward. He rubbed his hair fiercely, then leaned back in his chair.

What are you thinking, getting into an argument with a young girl...

"I...called you the wrong thing," he stammered. "I'm sorry."

"It's okay," xoxoYuyu said. "Are you real-life friends with my ge, or just in-game friends...?"

"Female Warrior, go to the back and do some combos," Xiang Huaizhi interrupted their conversation. "You, give me a Healing Spring."

Chapter 12

xoxoYuyu quietly clicked her tongue. "All right, all right, I got it."

Jing Huan said nothing more, quietly moving forward to place a Healing Spring. After the cooldown reset, he circled to the back of the boss and fully healed xoxoYuyu as well.

Five minutes later, the boss fell to the ground, and the party was teleported back to the main city. Xiang Huaizhi did not linger and headed toward the dungeon emissary to go to the next dungeon.

"Aw, another dungeon?" xoxoYuyu pouted. "Let's do something fun."

Xiang Huaizhi replied, "Go by yourself."

"Why are you like this..."

"Cousin, what do you want to do?" Lu Hang asked. "This gege will take you."

Lu Hang had met xoxoYuyu twice before, but had never spoken to her, which was why he didn't recognize her voice.

"Don't call me that," xoxoYuyu said. "Anything but dungeons. We can spar in the dueling platform, open a couple Fate Stones, or find players for some Ten Thousand Yuan matches."

Officially called the Life and Death battle in the game, the Ten Thousand Yuan match was a system-monitored PK between two parties with a gambling setting. The in-game betting cap was very low, so players usually raised the stakes privately and started the bets at 10,000 yuan, hence the name Ten Thousand Yuan match. There was always a match on in Jing Huan's old server since the players loved starting shit. However, these matches were rare in the Mirage server. Players in this server preferred to do ambushes in the wilderness maps.

It seemed like this cousin was also a pay-to-win player, whose only interests were PK and spending money.

"No can do, we live in a harmonious society, so no fighting," Lu Hang said. "How about I take you sightseeing after this dungeon?"

"What kind of grown man goes sightseeing?" xoxoYuyu said disdainfully. "That's too girly."

Lu Hang clamped his mouth shut.

xoxoYuyu checked the time. "Gege, why don't you come with me to the arena later?"

Xiang Huaizhi wasted no time in rejecting her. "Not playing with you."

"Why!"

"I already have a partner."

"Who is it?"

"Spirit Fox Den."

Hearing her cue, the Spirit Fox Den said magnanimously, "It's okay, don't worry about me. You guys go ahead."

xoxoYuyu was quiet, pondering. Moments later, she opened her friend chat.

[Friend] xoxoYuyu: Ge, what's your relationship with this Sweet Little Jing?

[Friend] Yearning For: Children shouldn't concern themselves with such matters.

[Friend] xoxoYuyu: I'm only two years younger than you?!

[Friend] xoxoYuyu: Are you two married?

[Friend] xoxoYuyu: You probably aren't since you haven't put up the couple titles.

 Chapter 12

[Friend] xoxoYuyu: So, are you just starting an online relationship? Planning to get married? Or are you just a situationship?

It was like she was tossing stones into the sea. Xiang Huaizhi's game character kept moving.

[Friend] xoxoYuyu: If you don't reply, I'll just ask her myself. [Smiling]

[Friend] Yearning For: Return all the gear I just bought you.

[Friend] xoxoYuyu: Why are you like this!

Xiang Huaizhi knew his cousin wasn't one to stay quiet. He was certain that once her curiosity got the better of her, she would ask Jing Huan.

[Friend] Yearning For: We're just regular friends.

[Friend] xoxoYuyu: Since when do regular friends call you gege??

[Friend] Yearning For: Since when did you get so nosy?

[Friend] xoxoYuyu: I've always been nosy.

[Friend] Yearning For: New Year's is coming soon.

[Friend] xoxoYuyu: ???

[Friend] Yearning For: If you still want to have a pleasant New Year at home, don't bother her.

xoxoYuyu was shocked.

The two had been together since childhood. Who knew how many of her secrets Xiang Huaizhi was privy to, but he had never used them for blackmail material—until now. What was more, he was doing it for an online friend.

xoxoYuyu became all the more certain: there was something going on between them!

Jing Huan didn't know that he had become the topic of conversation between the two cousins. Every time he remembered the

earlier conversation, he felt like dying from embarrassment and yet, he couldn't stop thinking about it.

In the end, it was a WeChat notification sound that saved him. He felt like he had been granted a reprieve and immediately snatched up his phone. No matter who was looking for him, he would talk with them for several hours, clutching them with a vice-like grip.

Counselor: Are you there?

Never mind. Jing Huan closed the chat, eyes glazed over. He was better off wallowing in embarrassment instead.

Counselor: I know you're there. What's with your profile picture?

Counselor: Come out, there's something I need to discuss with you.

Little Jing~: I just saw your message. What's up, teacher?

Counselor: Have you been attending classes properly this week?

Little Jing~: Come on, sir. Have I ever skipped class?

Counselor: [Smiling]

Little Jing~: [Smiling]

Counselor: All right, let's talk business. Did you know our school is having an evening gala at the beginning of next month?

Little Jing~: Nope.

Counselor: I had bad luck in the lottery, so now our class has to put on a program and a stage play. You need to participate as well.

Little Jing~: ?

Handle your own affairs. You drew the lot, so you *perform it. Why can't you understand such a simple principle,* sir*!*

Chapter 12

Little Jing~: I've never acted in a stage play before. You should ask someone else, sir.

Counselor: You're the first person I put on the list. You don't need to be good at it. You can just stand there. But I heard from Wenhao that you're quite good at singing?

Little Jing~: Sir, you believe his nonsense? He also claims he loses weight every day.

Counselor: ...

Counselor: Don't insult your classmates. As the face of our class, you must go on stage. Besides, the other students in the class will be more motivated when they see you participating. Come to the classroom on Saturday, and we'll see what role we can give you.

They talked about this matter for over half an hour, and by the end of it, the counselor couldn't stand it anymore and started listing all the classes Jing Huan had skipped in the past few weeks. Jing Huan had no choice but to surrender. The thought of performing in front of his classmates was humiliating.

When stage actors took the stage, it was a performance. When he went on stage, it was a comedy. He had an enormous bone to pick with Lu Wenhao, so as soon as they finished the dungeon, he fired off an "I'm logging off, bye-bye" and left the party.

Before he could follow through on his message, his friend message icon flashed.

[Friend] Yearning For: Not going to the arena tonight?

[Friend] Sweet Little Jing: O.O Weren't you taking your cousin?

[Friend] Yearning For: I'm not.

[Friend] Sweet Little Jing: That's not very nice, is it...?

[Friend] Yearning For: It's fine, come to the arena entrance.

Jing Huan hesitated but still went. What could he do? His hands were tied; being a simp was just that humbling.

Halfway through the match, Xiang Huaizhi vaguely noticed that something was off. "What's wrong with you?"

"Hm?" Jing Huan jumped. "Did I mess up?"

"You're not talking."

Jing Huan sighed. "It's nothing, the counselor just came to talk to me."

"You got caught skipping class?"

"How could that be!" Jing Huan said. "He just asked me to perform for the school's anniversary next month."

School anniversary? Xiang Huaizhi thought for a moment. There did seem to be something like that.

"What's there to worry about?"

"I don't want to go. I can't act, and I'm not interested in singing." Jing Huan added smoothly, "I only want to sing for gege."

"Then sing."

"I... Huh?" Jing Huan was dumbstruck.

Xiang Huaizhi asked, "Didn't you say you wanted to sing for me?"

That was just bullshit flattery! Meant to be said and forgotten! There's no after-sales services here, okay?!

Jing Huan chuckled awkwardly. "We're playing in the arena right now, gege. It's not exactly convenient..."

"This match is about to end, you can go AFK."

I dug my own grave. Jing Huan wished he could go back in time two minutes, knock himself out, and drag his past self away from the computer. Having reaped what his words had sown, Jing Huan

 Chapter 12

steeled himself, opened his music app, and looked at his playlist: "Sailor[5]," "The Ordinary Road[6]," "Cao Cao[7]."

None of these were songs girls would sing. *AAAAAH.*

"What...what does gege want to hear?"

Xiang Huaizhi raised an eyebrow. "There's even a song request service?"

You bet. There's even a full-service package to kill, dress your corpse, and bury you—a free all-in-one service. Do you want it?

Jing Huan had no idea how forced his tone sounded as he politely expressed, "I might not know the songs you request."

Xiang Huaizhi chuckled. It wasn't like he really wanted to hear him sing with a voice changer; he just thought that he shouldn't indulge Jing Huan's sweet-talking habit too much. Liking someone didn't mean that you had to please their every whim. While it was fine with him, but if it was someone else, wouldn't Jing Huan be bullied to death?

Xiang Huaizhi's mouth unconsciously tightened, and his smile fell.

"Forget it." After topping off his health, Xiang Huaizhi continued

---

5   水 手 - Shuǐ Shǒu - A famous Taiwanese song by Zheng Zhihua (郑 智 化), released in 1992. The song tells the story of a sailor giving heartfelt advice to a boy about perseverance, resilience, and what it means to become a real man.

6   平凡之路 - Píng Fán Zhī Lù - A hit song by Pu Shu (朴树), released in 2014. It served as the theme song for the road trip movie *The Continent*.

7   曹操 - Cáo Cāo - A song by Singaporean singer JJ Lin (林俊杰), inspired by the historical figure Cao Cao, a prominent general and politician from the Three Kingdoms period, released in 2006.

matching opponents and said, "How about next time? The next match is about to start."

Jing Huan had been in the middle of searching for songs guys liked to hear girls sing on Baidu when he heard this, and he blankly responded, "Oh..."

With how quickly this guy's mood changed, he must've been an actor in a past life.

The next day, in the classroom:

"Daddy, Daddy, I'm sorry. Really, really sorry." Lu Wenhao clasped his hands together, bowing to the person beside him, the flesh on his arms trembling as he did so. "I truly didn't expect he would make you perform in a stage play."

"You didn't expect, my ass." Jing Huan glowered at him. "You're done for. Don't even try to run away after class."

"I really didn't know! He asked me how your singing and dancing were, and I said your singing was okay, but your dancing was deadly..."

Jing Huan eyed him suspiciously. "So what role did he give you?"

"Ah?" Lu Wenhao blinked innocently. "Xiang'er and I are in the props group."

Gao Zixiang still had a conscience and nodded. "It's true, I was beside them when they were chatting."

Great.

With nowhere to vent, Jing Huan was forced to bite back his frustration.

Halfway through class, Jing Huan's eyelids grew heavy. Unable to focus, he took out his phone to play with. Before opening his game, he messaged Yearning For.

Chapter 12

After five rounds of Tetris, he still hadn't received a reply. Jing Huan switched back to the chat window and angrily poked the other person's profile picture a few times.

Not replying to your daddy again!

He didn't notice that his seatmate had been staring at him for a long time, a frown on his face.

"Huanhuan," Lu Wenhao finally couldn't hold back and leaned in to ask him, "aren't we good bros?"

Jing Huan didn't even turn his head, too focused on stacking blocks. "Depends."

Lu Wenhao paused. "When I was in an online relationship before, weren't you the first one I told?"

"It's not like I really wanted to know."

"Just answer me, damn it!"

"...I guess."

"Then be honest with this ge now," Lu Wenhao asked seriously in a hushed tone. "Are you dating someone? Don't worry, I'll keep it a secret!"

That momentary slip in concentration caused the horizontal block fell, blocking the two empty spaces Jing Huan had carefully arranged. He turned his head, frowning in confusion. "Are you still half asleep?"

"Nope, wide awake," Lu Wenhao said. "But I mean, just look at yourself right now. You look like someone who's head over heels in love."

Jing Huan's brow scrunched in bafflement.

Lu Wenhao held up a finger and started listing them out. "First, you switched to WeChat ten times while playing your game."

"Bullshit," Jing Huan interrupted. "I can't wait for a friend's message?"

"You don't even check your mom's messages that often. Okay, okay, just hear me out." Lu Wenhao put up another finger. "Second, you rush back to your apartment after every class. You're rushing back to voice chat with your girlfriend, right?"

...*Fuck, he actually guessed half of it right.*

"Third, you changed your profile picture, and your Moments' vibe is different," said Lu Wenhao. "You changed it for that girl, right?"

...*Shit, this time he got ninety percent of it right.*

"Fourth, your way of texting has been weird lately too, with exclamations and cutesy stuff getting thrown in." Lu Wenhao raised his thick eyebrows cryptically. "You learned that from her, didn't you?"

"Fifth, when she didn't reply to your message just now, your face nearly turned as black as charcoal. In conclusion, she must be your girlfriend or at least someone you like…"

Jing Huan coldly cut him off, "If you keep counting in my ear, I'll print out a photo of your ex-online lover and frame it in your family shrine."

Lu Wenhao finally shut up.

After class, they all left the classroom together, deep in discussion on whether they wanted to go downtown over the weekend.

"Lu Wenhao?"

All three of them looked back and saw Lu Hang and Xiang Huaizhi standing behind them. Xiang Huaizhi was looking down at his cellphone, and upon hearing that name, slightly lifted his eyes.

Chapter 12

Lu Hang smiled. "I could tell it was you guys from a distance. Where are you heading?"

"Going to grab some food." Lu Wenhao asked, "Lu-ge, what are you guys doing here?"

"They moved our class to this building, and we just wrapped up," said Lu Hang. He held out the basketball in his hand in offering. "How about it? Want to play for a bit?"

"Sure," Gao Zixiang agreed, then hesitated. "But won't the basketball courts already be full at this time?"

Lu Hang winked at him. "I had someone save us a spot, let's go."

Xiang Huaizhi put his cellphone in his pocket. "You guys go ahead; I won't be joining."

"I'm not going either," Jing Huan immediately chimed in.

Lu Wenhao seemed to know no fear as he asked, "Why? Are you rushing back to voice chat again…"

Jing Huan brandished a fist at him.

Lu Wenhao hurriedly hid. "My bad, my bad, I'm just joking."

They went downstairs, and the five of them split into two groups again. As he walked alongside Xiang Huaizhi, Jing Huan couldn't help but sneak glances at his shoes.

"What's the matter? Want to step on it again?" Xiang Huaizhi asked.

Jing Huan shook his head vigorously. "No, no." After a few steps, he sensed something was amiss and looked around.

"What's wrong?" Xiang Huaizhi asked, noticing his movements.

Jing Huan's expression was complicated. "Um, ge… Don't you feel like a lot of people are staring at us?"

Xiang Huaizhi didn't notice. He was used to being the center of attention, so he couldn't tell if today was any different from the usual. "Don't think so."

Jing Huan wondered. "Maybe it's just my imagination then."

When they reached the men's dormitory, Jing Huan was about to say goodbye, but the person beside him didn't stop and continued walking ahead. He was stunned. "Ge?"

Xiang Huaizhi stopped. "Mm."

"You're not going back to the dorms?"

"We already walked all the way here," Xiang Huaizhi said matter-of-factly. "Let's have lunch together."

The two of them visited that same yellow braised chicken restaurant again. During the meal, Jing Huan took out his cellphone and discovered that Yearning For had already replied to him. Glancing at the timestamp, he saw it had been sent right after he got out of class. He must've missed the notification while walking.

After they finished eating, Jing Huan was about to pay the bill, but Xiang Huaizhi, having already scanned the code, beat him to it.

"Let's go," Xiang Huaizhi said.

Jing Huan blinked, cellphone still in hand. "Oh...okay."

As they left the restaurant, they caught sight of the same milk tea shop from last time.

Xiang Huaizhi asked, "Want some milk tea?"

"Sure..." Jing Huan quickly said, "I'll buy it myself!"

Xiang Huaizhi walked to the back of the line. "I'm getting coffee too."

Ten minutes later, Jing Huan stepped out of the milk tea shop

 Chapter 12

with three cups of milk tea again. He stood by the roadside, confused. Why did this feel like...déjà vu?

Xiang Huaizhi strolled up to him with his coffee, and said, "I'm heading back now."

"Oh, okay...wait a sec!" Jing Huan freed a hand to grab his clothes. Xiang Huaizhi turned back, looking questioningly at him.

Jing Huan snapped out of it. "Can we talk over there for a bit?"

The two of them sat down in the milk tea shop's outdoor seating area. Jing Huan put his milk teas on the table and got straight to the point. "Ge, do you need help with something?"

Xiang Huaizhi didn't understand. "What?"

"I mean..." Jing Huan sat up straight. "If you need help with something, just say so. You don't need to...go through all these steps."

Xiang Huaizhi realized that Jing Huan's thought process was a bit different from everyone else.

He couldn't help chuckling and was about to answer when Jing Huan leaned in close and asked him in a low voice, "Do you like one of the girls in our class?" At Xiang Huaizhi's quizzical expression, Jing Huan added, "Don't be shy, ge. I'm no stranger to this kind of thing; I'll definitely help you. Which girl is it? I might not be too close with the girls in our class, but I can probably help you get her number."

When he didn't receive a response from Xiang Huaizhi, Jing Huan grinned, a rather amusing notion hitting him. "I never expected someone as great as you would worry about pursuing someone."

Guide on How to Fail at Online Dating

A smile still playing on his lips, the young man took a sip of his milk tea. Xiang Huaizhi frowned as he stared at him, his gaze subtle, his thoughts indiscernible to those around him. After a while, he found his voice. "I'm not trying to pursue anyone."

"Ah."

"And I don't need anyone's number," Xiang Huaizhi said calmly as he stood up, holding his coffee. He looked down at Jing Huan with slightly drooping eyes. "I simply wanted to treat you to a meal. There's nothing else to it, no ulterior motive. You don't need to overthink it."

That same night, Lu Wenhao once again shared a post from the campus BBS in the group chat where he and Xiang Huaizhi had been photographed again. Maybe it was because he was mentally prepared, but Jing Huan wasn't as surprised as he had been the first time. Seeing the triple-digit comment count, Jing Huan couldn't help but click his tongue.

What are university students thinking about all day instead of studying?

This time, there were several photos of them walking on the road, sitting in the restaurant, lining up to buy milk tea... All of that was documented.

Little Jing~: Why don't these people go to a media studies university?

Gao Zixiang: Can't be helped. Shipping two guys is popular nowadays.

Little Jing~: ...

Jing Huan studied the photos again.

 Chapter 12

Little Jing~: Is my ge really that much taller than me? Did these girls just decide to photoshop his legs longer but not mine?

Gao Zixiang: Nah, Senior Xiang really is a bit taller than you.

Lu Wenhao: How come you call him ge, ge, ge so easily? I'm older than you too, you should also call me ge.

Little Jing~: GTFO.

On Saturday, Jing Huan reluctantly went to the sports field. Since they couldn't move the desks and chairs in the classrooms, they didn't have enough space to rehearse there, so they had to find another place.

When the counselor saw him, he raised his chin and said, "You're here?"

Jing Huan originally wanted to trudge over to Lu Wenhao and Gao Zixiang's side, but turned around at the counselor's voice.

He smiled sweetly. "Yes, teacher."

As soon as Jing Huan arrived, the girls around him immediately began fussing over their appearance, constantly stealing glances at him.

"Not bad, you're not late." The counselor's expression then shifted, turning complicated. He shot Jing Huan a meaningful look. "Come with me for a moment."

The two walked off to the side of the goalpost. Jing Huan stopped chewing his gum. "Teacher, if we keep walking, we'll leave the sports field."

The counselor stopped, checking to make sure their conversation wouldn't be overheard before allowing himself to relax.

"You..." It was the first time the counselor had encountered this kind of situation, so he struggled to know where to start. "Are you dating someone?"

Jing Huan frowned. Why was everyone asking him this question?

"Teacher, I'm already twenty. Even if I was in a relationship, I wouldn't be considered too young to date, right?"

Without preamble, the counselor went for the kill. "You and Xiang Huaizhi… Is it true?"

Jing Huan almost swallowed his gum. "It's not… how could it be possible? What are you thinking?"

"I don't care if it's true or not, but since you're in my class, I have to remind you." The counselor had a solemn look on his face as he continued, "Dating is fine, but you must be careful about health and safety…in all aspects, understood?"

When Jing Huan came back, Lu Wenhao asked curiously, "Huan-huan, what did the counselor say to you?"

Jing Huan tossed out a vague answer. "He told me to…perform well." He couldn't possibly tell Lu Wenhao that the counselor actually thought he and Xiang Huaizhi were together. And even cautioned them.

Tch. He subconsciously rubbed the back of his neck. *What kind of situation was this?*

Jing Huan's role was soon decided. The counselor had said he just needed to make an appearance, and that was literally it. He was going to play a bodyguard, an extra role with almost no lines. All he needed to do was stand in the corner of the stage.

When Lu Wenhao heard, he nodded and sarcastically said, "The role sounds *so* tough to perform. No wonder the counselor specifically called you for a private meeting."

The rehearsal began. Everyone, except for Jing Huan, had a job

to do; even Lu Wenhao and Gao Zixiang were busily preparing props. Idle and bored, Jing Huan sat in the audience stands and fiddled with his cellphone.

As Xiang Huaizhi strolled back to the dormitory with his newly purchased broom, the cellphone in his hand began vibrating nonstop.

Little Jing~: Gege~ [Sticking head out]

Little Jing~: It's 10 a.m. If gege is still sleeping, he'll become a [Pig's head].

Little Jing~: [Today I also put my smol heart with gege.JPG]

This person's sticker collection was steadily growing.

Xiang: Here.

Little Jing~: Whatcha doing? >o<

Xiang: Just had breakfast, heading back to the dorms.

Little Jing~: Oh.

Little Jing~: [Photo] I'm watching my classmates rehearse.

Xiang Huaizhi opened the picture and saw that it was the school's sports field.

Xiang: You're not rehearsing?

Little Jing~: I don't have any lines. I'm just going to be acting as a mascot, but the counselor won't let me leave. I'm so bored just sitting here.

Little Jing~: Whenever I'm bored, I think of gege.

Jing Huan couldn't help but snigger after sending this message. *It's so fucking cheesy and sweet, what guy can resist that? I am truly the best.*

As expected, Yearning For sent over a string of ellipses. Hearing the girls in front of him chatting, Jing Huan casually copied and pasted their conversation into his texts.

Little Jing~: Also, the playground is sososo sunny. I didn't put any sunscreen on, I'm going to tan... TVT

Yearning For didn't reply after that.

Jing Huan played a game on his phone while wondering, *Was that too much cutesiness again?*

"Jing Huan."

Jing Huan instinctively looked up and saw Xiang Huaizhi standing in front of the audience railing, holding a broom. Initially surprised, he quickly closed his game that he was about to clear the level for and walked forward a few steps, facing Xiang Huaizhi across the railing.

"Ge." Jing Huan leaned against the railing. "What are you doing here?"

"Buying a broom. The one in the dorms broke." Xiang Huaizhi asked although he already knew the answer, "What about you?"

"I'm watching the rehearsal. That's our class over there."

Xiang Huaizhi nodded. "Aren't you getting too much sun from sitting here?"

Jing Huan said indifferently, "It's okay. Real men aren't afraid of the sun." He didn't notice the subtle expression the person in front of him had. He asked, "Ge, what program is your class doing?"

"Not doing anything. We're just the audience."

Jing Huan immediately turned green with envy.

Feeling a piercing gaze behind him, Xiang Huaizhi looked back, just managing to catch the gaze of another young man. Jing Huan had also noticed. He sighed. "That's our counselor."

Chapter 12

Xiang Huaizhi averted his gaze. "He seems to be staring at me."

"Mm," Jing Huan replied, leaning his elbow on the railing and propping his chin up with one hand lazily. "He thinks we're dating."

Xiang Huaizhi unconsciously tensed.

"I don't know who it is, but they clearly have nothing better to do all day than secretly take pictures of others. If I catch them, I'll beat them to death." Jing Huan seemed to finally notice the broom in Xiang Huaizhi's hand. "But ge, why did you bring that all the way over to the sports field? Isn't your dorm on the other side?"

"I," Xiang Huaizhi paused briefly, "was on the way to see my advisor."

Their short conversation was cut even shorter when they heard the counselor shouting from afar, calling Jing Huan over. After saying goodbye to his underclassman, Xiang Huaizhi left the sports field carrying his broom, taking the small path around the sports field back to the dormitory. He hadn't walked very far when his phone rang; the caller ID showed it was his cousin Xiang Yu.

"Ge!" Xiang Yu said excitedly. "I heard next weekend is your school's anniversary!"

Xiang Huaizhi didn't even blink as he lied, "It's not."

"I wanna go!" Xiang Yu said. "You should show me around." Just as Xiang Huaizhi was about to refuse, she put on a pitiful act. "You see, I've always wanted to go to Mancheng University, but I didn't get in… I just want to take a look now! Stroll around a bit! Touch things! Is that too much to ask!"

"That's what you get for not studying hard in high school," Xiang Huaizhi replied coldly.

"Waaah gege, take me with youuu! Mwah mwah!"

Xiang Huaizhi's eyes twitched. "... Who taught you to talk like this?"

"Lu Hang. He said that learning from Sweet Little Jing would be effective."

"Since you two are so close, you should let Lu Hang take you." His said, Xiang Huaizhi hung up.

Chapter 13

Xiang Huaizhi

Jing Huan

Xiang Yu still showed up at the school anniversary, utterly heedless of Xiang Huaizhi's words.

Lu Hang's club had a performance, so he didn't have time to accompany her. Although Xiang Huaizhi complained, he still took her for a tour around the school and had a meal with her. Xiang Yu had a lively personality, an endless stream of chatter flowing out of her mouth as she bounced along the way.

As they came out of the supermarket with Xiang Yu holding a popsicle, she said, "Xiang Huaizhi, I heard that there's a performance in the small auditorium tonight. Take me there to see it, 'kay?"

"We'll see." Xiang Huaizhi glanced at the popsicle in her hand. "If you catch a cold from eating that, don't come crying to me."

Knowing that Xiang Yu was coming, Lu Hang had already given two tickets to the small auditorium to Xiang Huaizhi early on. After they finished their meal and dessert, the two headed toward the small auditorium. Halfway there, Xiang Huaizhi's cellphone in his pocket started vibrating incessantly. He took out his cell phone to check his messages.

Xiang Yu peeked at the screen. "Sweet Little Jing?"

"Mm," Xiang Huaizhi said while typing.

Xiang Yu licked her popsicle and muttered, "I can't believe this is your type…"

Xiang Huaizhi put away his cellphone and returned her gaze steadily. "What kind of girl do you think she is?"

"Well," Xiang Yu had always been very blunt with her words, "a green tea bitch? Fake? Likes to act cute?" She hurriedly tacked on, "I mean on the surface. Once you get to know her, you realize she's not too bad. But she doesn't make a great first impression, so it's no wonder a lot of female players in the server don't like her."

"A lot of female players?" Xiang Huaizhi's eyes narrowed. "Who complained to you?"

"Quite a few… You wouldn't know this, but when they see me partying up with Sweet Little Jing, they DM me to badmouth her. Most of them are using alt characters."

Xiang Huaizhi said shortly, "Just turn off DMs from strangers."

As soon as they stepped foot in the small auditorium, Xiang Yu said she needed to go to the restroom, so Xiang Huaizhi waited for her in the hall outside the auditorium.

"*Daaamn*, Huanhuan, your outfit looks so fucking lit."

"How much wax did you use on that hair?"

"What's it to you? Just compliment me on how handsome I look and we're good."

A clatter of footsteps came from outside the door, and Xiang Huaizhi subconsciously turned his head as he heard a familiar voice.

Lu Wenhao and Gao Zixiang each held a wooden bench in their hands, talking to the young man sandwiched between them. Jing

 Chapter 13

Huan was wearing a black suit today. The fitted suit outlined his figure which was usually hidden under loose clothing, drawing attention to his long and straight legs. The usually sunny and cheery young man exuded a more mature aura today, and yet, it didn't feel unnatural.

"I prepared the outfit myself. The one that the counselor gave me was too small and way too tight…" Jing Huan's words trailed off midway as he met Xiang Huaizhi's gaze.

Lu Wenhao said, "I guess the counselor gave you his own suit."

"I think so too." Jing Huan patted him on the shoulder. "I saw someone I know, you guys go ahead first."

Jing Huan strode over to Xiang Huaizhi, slipping his hands into his pockets. He put on a serious expression and raised his eyebrows at Xiang Huaizhi, but the cold mien didn't last three seconds before it was melted away by his grin.

"Ge," he said, "am I handsome?"

Xiang Huaizhi lowered his gaze. Jing Huan hadn't buttoned up his suit jacket, revealing a white shirt tucked into black pants that accentuated his slim waist. Although he had abs, he was still thin.

"Mm," Xiang Huaizhi said, "you're handsome."

Jing Huan was very satisfied with his answer. He laughed lightly before looking around him. "Where's the girl?"

"What girl?"

"Didn't they say you were showing a girl around the school?"

"That's my tangmei." Xiang Huaizhi paused. "How did you know?"

"Lu Wenhao told me. He said there were eyewitnesses on BBS claiming they saw you cheating on me." Since Xiang Huaizhi didn't

Guide on How to Fail at Online Dating

seem to mind, Jing Huan didn't care much either; he even found it somewhat amusing. "Some people even said we were a BE[1]."

Xiang Huaizhi did not reply.

Jing Huan wanted to say more, but the ringing of his cellphone derailed his thoughts. He took it out of his pocket, and after checking the caller ID, didn't answer it.

He clicked his tongue. "Ge, I'm heading in first; the counselor's looking for me. Are you here to watch the performance too?"

"Mm."

"Then be sure to look for me. I'm the seventh to perform, I'm going to be standing in the very corner." Jing Huan turned around and cheekily said, "But you're not allowed to make fun of me."

When Xiang Yu came out, all she saw was the back of a young man hurrying away into the distance.

"Xiang Huaizhi, I'm ready." She flapped her hands around to shake off the water. "Shall we go in?"

Xiang Huaizhi tore his eyes away and intoned deeply, "Mm."

Xiang Yu took out her cellphone from her bag and was prepared to start recording whenever the occasion called for it when the young man at her side suddenly called her name. "Hm?"

Xiang Huaizhi frowned. "What does BE mean?"

The school anniversary gala was divided into two groups—one for the art students, and the other for everyone else. Out of the twenty programs, fifteen were taken by the art students, and the remaining five were drawn from various classes across the school.

Overall, the evening gala was quite entertaining. Given Mancheng

---

1   Bad ending for a couple.

 Chapter 13

University's open atmosphere, the show kicked things off with a hot dance routine performed by several attractive and stylish dance students. It livened up the mood in an instant.

Even Xiang Yu was practically drooling as she watched, captivated. She was frantically recording the performances with her cellphone. Meanwhile, her cousin sat still beside her, eyes trained on his cellphone as he played with it, not even lifting his head up once, as if he were living in his own world.

After the first six performances, the first non-art student group took the stage. Seeing it was a stage play, Xiang Yu disinterestedly leaned back against her seat cushion. She was about to share the recording with her friends when she noticed the perpetual light emitting from the phone next to her suddenly vanish.

Xiang Huaizhi put away his cellphone, casually crossed his arms in front of him, and began to earnestly watch the performance.

She couldn't resist sending a message to complain to her friends.

【My ge is seriously such a boring guy.】

【He didn't look up at all when he had a bunch of beautiful women doing a hot dance in front of him, but as soon as someone brings a few tables and chairs for a stage play, he's all alert.】

Xiang Yu was happily chatting away when she noticed the girls around her start to show signs of restlessness. As a woman herself, she understood this atmosphere all too well—it meant an idol or a handsome guy was about to make his appearance.

Sure enough, as soon as she looked up, she caught sight of the pretty boy in the suit standing in the corner of the stage.

She quickly fished out her glasses from her bag and put them on. When she got a clear view of his looks, she excitedly grabbed Xiang

Huaizhi's sleeve, softly screaming. "Aaaaaaah! That guy in the suit! He's so hot!"

Xiang Huaizhi yanked his sleeve away and ignored her.

Jing Huan played an emotionless bodyguard, his only lines being "yes" and "okay." The way he just stood there was almost mascot-like. What the performance lacked in excitement, a hot guy could easily make up for—a trick the counselor was very familiar with.

The stage play was very short, lasting less than ten minutes. When it came time for the curtain call, Jing Huan's stern expression finally relaxed, his mouth curving into a smile. His eyes finally pulled away from the leading actor and to the audience.

It was unclear who he was looking at but whoever it was caused him to smile wider, and he winked.

Xiang Yu managed to come back to her senses after Jing Huan left the stage.

"Ge!" She grabbed Xiang Huaizhi's sleeve again. "That pretty boy in the suit...h-he looked like he winked at me just now!"

Xiang Huaizhi didn't pull back his sleeve this time. He looked down as he felt his cellphone vibrate in his pocket. Voice serene, he said, "Don't get too excited. He wasn't winking at you."

Whether it was meant for her or not, Xiang Yu happily accepted the wink and was floating on cloud nine for the rest of the night.

After the gala ended, the cousins walked out of the small auditorium side by side. Xiang Yu halted as they reached the gate.

"Xiang Huaizhi," a blush painted her cheeks as she declared, "I've decided! I'm going to go backstage and get that guy's phone number."

Xiang Huaizhi slowed his steps. He said bluntly, "You can't."

"Why?" Xiang Yu caught up with him. "Does he have a girlfriend already?"

"No."

"Then why not!" she whined.

Xiang Huaizhi frowned, his brain unable to think of a reason right on the spot.

Xiang Yu asked, "Is it because he's not a good person? Is he a player? Or…"

"He has someone he likes," Xiang Huaizhi interrupted.

"Really?" Xiang Yu was shocked but nonetheless plowed on. "It's okay. So long as he doesn't have a girlfriend, I still have a chance. Is the person he likes also at Mancheng University? What year are they in? Are they good-looking? What's their name? Do you have any pics?" When Xiang Huaizhi didn't respond, she continued her rapid-fire questions, "Ge, are you listening to me? Who exactly does he like?"

Me. The person he likes is me. The words suddenly popped into Xiang Huaizhi's mind, causing him to stop in his tracks. His emotions burst out along with the thought, overwhelming all his senses and leaving him somewhat at a loss.

Jing Huan liked him.

Ignoring Xiang Yu's chatter, Xiang Huaizhi mulled over the information in his mind over and over again, savoring it carefully, and came to a startling realization: he felt satisfied, at ease…and even a little pleased.

Even though Jing Huan had finished his performance long ago,

the counselor refused to let them leave, insisting that they stay backstage to help out. After he moved the props, Jing Huan sat by the window, soaking up the breeze. He loosened his tie and unbuttoned the top two buttons of his shirt, and only then did he finally feel a bit cooler.

Lu Wenhao walked in, carrying a table, and said, "Finally, finished moving this shit… Who are you trying to seduce sitting there like that?"

The unbearable heat made Jing Huan irritable. "Seducing your ancestors."

Lu Wenhao chuckled and brought a chair over to sit next to him. "I think the counselor just brought us in to do the grunt work; we even had to carry the musical instruments. How inhumane."

Jing Huan nodded in agreement. "We should trick him into treating us to a late-night snack someday. Where's Xiang'er?"

"It's girlfriend check-in time." Lu Wenhao stretched his arms. "Everyone's leaving, so we should get out of here too before we get roped into cleaning up the venue. Let's grab some barbecue before heading back."

Jing Huan opened his mouth to agree but then seemed to remember something. He took out his phone. "Wait a sec."

"What for?"

"My ge is here too," said Jing Huan. "I'll ask if he wants to join us for some barbecue."

"Your ge…" Lu Wenhao paused. "Xiang Huaizhi? Seriously, you're that close?" *You're even inviting him out for a late-night snack?*

"You've asked that twice," Jing Huan said without looking up.

Guide on How to Fail at Online Dating

"Besides, he's right here at the auditorium, and it's not like I'm asking you to treat him."

"Do I look like someone who cares about money?" Lu Wenhao said. "But I thought you two would, you know, keep your distance."

Jing Huan glanced at him, bewildered. "Why would we keep our distance?"

"Isn't the campus BBS spreading rumors about you two?"

Jing Huan brushed it off. "So what? It's not like it's true anyway. Let them say whatever. What am I supposed to do? Reach through the screen and beat them up?"

If I had that ability, Yearning For would've died 8,000 times by now.

Lu Wenhao replied, "What if, one day, the BBS starts spreading rumors about you and me..."

"Fuck off," Jing Huan cut him off without raising his head.

Lu Wenhao snapped his mouth shut.

It took a while for Xiang Huaizhi to reply. He declined Jing Huan's invitation, saying he had to take his meimei home. The three of them traipsed over to a barbecue place near the school where Lu Wenhao ordered a dozen skewers with a wave of his hand.

Jing Huan gnawed on a chicken wing, legs crossed. Chin propped up on his hand, Gao Zixiang studied him and said very seriously, "Huanhuan, you should drop out of school and debut as an idol. Hao'er and I will definitely be your number one fans."

Jing Huan was too busy savoring the delectable taste on his tongue to bother responding.

Lu Wenhao nodded rapidly. "Yeah, I'll even sell all my game

 Chapter 13

accounts to help support your idol career. But how would he debut?"

Gao Zixiang said, "Join those reality survival trainee shows or trainee programs. There are plenty of those."

"Holy shit, you're so smart. I'll check out how to sign up tomorrow... Huanhuan, what are you doing!" Lu Wenhao stopped talking as he quickly reached out to protect his plate of food.

Jing Huan took a bite of the beef skewer he had just nabbed. "I figured you must be full since you're spewing out so much bullshit."

Gao Zixiang laughed and took a sip of his alcohol. "By the way, someone in the guild chat just said that our server is going to merge."

The two people beside him paused, unable to react right away.

"What? Server merging?" Lu Wenhao asked.

"Two servers," Gao Zixiang clinked his glass with him, "merging into one."

"What the hell?" Lu Wenhao was flabbergasted. "What, why? Isn't our server pretty active?"

Gao Zixiang said, "That's what *you* think. The status bar of every other server except ours have been red recently, right? That's because, these days, everyone's playing mobile games instead. *Nine Heroes'* traffic has been declining. I heard the developers are already working on a new expansion."

This was the first time Jing Huan had heard about the server merging news as well.

Eyes nearly popping out, Lu Wenhao asked, "Has *Nine Heroes* ever done something like this before?"

"No. That's why our server's going to be the first; we're essentially

the guinea pigs," Gao Zixiang said. "I think the news is pretty legit, but we just don't know which server we'll merge with."

"Merging servers..." Lu Wenhao pondered for a moment, then said eagerly, "Hold on, if the servers are merged, doesn't that mean we have to redistribute the territories? The server battle parties will have to compete, right? Not to mention, the guild rankings and the other ranking lists..." He got increasingly passionate. "Then won't things get really heated?"

The two chatted animatedly beside him, but Jing Huan's attention span lasted only so long before he ducked his head and resumed eating his late-night snack. Server merges were a common practice in other games; as new servers opened up, old players eventually left, with the new players preferring the new servers. It was only a matter of time before a server died off. The fact that *Nine Heroes* had been in operation for ten years before introducing server merging was already quite an accomplishment.

After finishing their late-night snack, Jing Huan went home, took a shower, and slowly opened the game.

[Friend] Yearning For: Why are you so late?

[Friend] Sweet Little Jing: Good evening, gege. I just went out to have dessert with my girlfriends. ^0^

[Friend] Yearning For: Mm, how was the performance?

[Friend] Sweet Little Jing: I outshone all the beauties. [Shy]

[Friend] Yearning For: ...

[Friend] Sweet Little Jing: Too bad gege couldn't see it. QAQ

[Friend] Yearning For: I can imagine it.

[Friend] Sweet Little Jing: Hmm??

[Friend] Yearning For: Where are you? I'll take you to do dailies.

 Chapter 13

After joining the party, Jing Huan took a sip of hot milk to wash away the taste of barbecue in his mouth. He was about to speak but got distracted by some commotion happening at the bottom of his screen.

[Megaphone] Ji Xiaonian: I see through it all now, this is what your love amounted to.

[Megaphone] Ji Xiaonian: I guess I loved the wrong person.

[Megaphone] Ji Xiaonian: If I had known this would be the outcome, I would've rather not met you.

What is this girl talking about? Jing Huan licked the milk off his lips and looked through the World Channel chat in confusion.

[World] Is Gege Big: The fuck is this BS?

[World] Peachy Belle: ... [Sweating]

[World] Frost: Throwing a guess out there, a divorce!

[World] Peach Cheese Stan: It's here! The divorce drama segment I've been looking forward to the most!

[Megaphone] Ji Xiaonian: I once thought you would give me all the tenderness in the world, but I never imagined you wouldn't even have the courage to save me from the villains' evil clutches.

Jing Huan had just crossed his legs and was getting ready to enjoy the drama when he saw the last sentence. He immediately deflated.

Face twisted into a complicated expression, he said, "Gege, look at Ji Xiaonian's megaphone. That last sentence... Doesn't it sound like she's talking about us?"

Xiang Huaizhi glanced at it and reassured him, "No."

[Megaphone] Ji Xiaonian: It's just the Wealth rankings list... Is money and social prestige that important to you?

The two "villains" in the party fell silent instantly.

Ji Xiaonian kept spamming megaphones as if her life depended on her sharing all her feelings with the world. Every server had people like this; this wasn't Jing Huan's first time seeing such a scene. Aside from the gloom he felt when they were mentioned, he still found it quite entertaining to read.

"What are you doing?" Yearning For suddenly asked on the mic. "Why aren't you talking?"

"I'm reading the megaphones, gege."

Xiang Huaizhi wasn't particularly fond of perusing those, but since megaphones couldn't be muted, he caught a few lines.

[Megaphone] Ji Xiaonian: Online love is too fake. I hope my fellow sisters will keep their eyes peeled and not fall in love carelessly. Just so you know, the person you like may not be who you imagine them to be.

Xiang Huaizhi frowned slightly and then asked, "Hm, what do you think after reading them?"

Do I really need to give my opinion on megaphones?

"I think," Jing Huan said, dead serious, "no man in the world is better than gege!"

Xiang Huaizhi paused mid-sip. No matter how many times he heard her say stuff like this, he still couldn't get used to it.

"Really?"

"Yes!" Jing Huan said firmly. "My gege is the best in the world!"

Xiang Huaizhi was silent for a moment before relaxing.

Yeah, getting used to this would be strange.

The *Nine Heroes* players kicked up a fuss on the forum for several

Chapter 13

days following news of the server merge. Most of them were opposed as merging servers would not only combine the ranking lists, it would also completely disrupt the server's in-game economy.

Jing Huan had heard Lu Wenhao and Gao Zixiang ranting about it for a week.

Lu Wenhao asked, "Which unlucky server do you think we'll merge with?"

Gao Zixiang dropped his chin in his hand. "How would I know? Hey, is our server the only one that got the news? How come the other servers aren't complaining?"

"Yeah, they're not really. I even checked the other day, and our server really does have the lowest traffic in the entire game. Fuck, how did we not notice before?"

Jing Huan wasn't interested in the conversation. He was currently occupied with texting Yearning For.

Little Jing~: Gege, I heard that *Nine Heroes* is implementing server merging.

Xiang: It was bound to happen.

Little Jing~: Hehe. I still have 20 minutes before class ends. When will gege be back in the dorms? I want to do dailies with gege~ ヾ(≧≦*)ﾉﾞ

Xiang: I have something to do today. Won't be logging on.

Xiang: Won't be able to go to the arena either.

Little Jing~: T.T... Okay then, I'll wait for gege to come back.

After class, Jing Huan went home, opened up *Nine Heroes*, spent half an hour completing his dailies, and then teleported back to the main city. He stood next to some insignificant NPC for some time before he realized: he didn't know what to do next.

Jing Huan frowned. *What did I usually do?*

Do dailies with Yearning For. Run dungeons with Yearning For. Fight in the arena with Yearning For. Occasionally, he'd pester Yearning For to take him sightseeing and snap some screenshots.

Fuck. Jing Huan, you've lost your sense of self.

This won't do. As soon as he taught Yearning For a lesson, he was going to buy a DPS character, thus returning to his former self—the one who slaughtered everyone in his path.

Jing Huan needed to find something to do. As he wandered near the party-finding area, his friend message icon flashed.

[Friend] Bishop Wood: Little Jingjing, what are you doing?

[Friend] Sweet Little Jing: Looking for a quest bus[2] near the party finder area. O.O

[Friend] Bishop Wood: Wow. Pretty gutsy of you to join a PUG bus.

It hadn't been a concern for Jing Huan at first, but now that Bishop Wood had brought it up, he hesitated.

[Friend] Sweet Little Jing: Ha ha… Do you need something?

[Friend] Bishop Wood: Since your teammate isn't here, why don't we fight in the arena together? My teammate also isn't coming tonight.

[Friend] Sweet Little Jing: How did you know gege isn't here…

[Friend] Bishop Wood: The arena opens in two minutes, and he's still not online.

[Friend] Sweet Little Jing: Ehhh.

[Friend] Bishop Wood: We're just fighting in the arena together. You can't expect to only do PK with Yearning For for your entire

---

2   This is a carry request to help you through a specific quest.

life, right? Besides, partying with him won't help you improve your skills.

His words took Jing Huan aback, but Bishop Wood wasn't entirely wrong. Yearning For's individual skills were too superior, so partying up with him meant Jing Huan's occasional mistakes didn't have much of an impact. Over time, he would not only become complacent but also dependent.

[Friend] Sweet Little Jing: ...Okay, fine. Where are you?

[Friend] Bishop Wood: ^^ Come to the arena entrance.

Today was Mama Xiang's birthday, so Xiang Huaizhi had specially come home to have dinner with her. Mama Xiang didn't like seeing him in front of the computer all day, so he had left his laptop behind.

After eating and drinking their fill, Mama Xiang and her best friends went to play mahjong. Xiang Huaizhi sat on the sofa and checked his cellphone, but there were no messages. When he opened WeChat, the Idle Pavillion guild group chat jumped to the top, showing 99+ unread messages.

【BrbOrNot: What are these two doing in that little hidden room!!】

Xiang Huaizhi didn't usually check the guild group chat, but for some inexplicable reason, he found himself clicking on the group chat after seeing the message preview.

BrbOrNot had posted a screenshot of a locked room in the guild's YY. There were only two people in it. One was Bishop Wood who had an orange vest badge. The other was Sweet Little Jing, who, just a few days ago, had obediently whispered in his ear, "My gege is the best in the world."

People really couldn't stay in their comfort zone forever. This was a fact Jing Huan had to come to terms with after losing two consecutive rounds. He looked at all the points he had lost, feeling heartbroken.

It wasn't like Bishop Wood was bad, but a duo of two CC classes was harder to fight with compared to a support and a DPS—their damage output just couldn't compare. Although Jing Huan was fully geared now, his summoning beast's quality wasn't high. The Nine-tailed Spirit Fox's grade wasn't up to par, with the opponent killing it in just two hits.

The two were sent flying out of the PK arena by Regardless of Lovesickness and Echoes of Spring. Bishop Wood was about to comfort his teammate when his friend message icon lit up.

[Friend] Echoes of Spring: Did you two party up tonight so you could donate points? Philanthropists, aren't you?

[Friend] Bishop Wood: Why didn't you go easy on me?!

[Friend] Echoes of Spring: My wife is pushing for 4,000 points. Why are you with Sweet Little Jing again?

[Friend] Bishop Wood: I didn't want to play since my teammate wasn't online tonight, but then I noticed Yearning For wasn't online either, so I called her up. [Smirking]

[Friend] Echoes of Spring: I suggest you disband the party right now. When she's with Yearning For, she gains points, but when she's with you, she's rushing to lose them. The more matches you two play, the more she'll appreciate Yearning For.

Bishop Wood let out a short and angry laugh, sending a contemptuous sticker in response.

Jing Huan had been talking into the microphone at length before realizing he hadn't pressed the push-to-talk key and Bishop Wood

Chapter 13

hadn't heard a single word. He didn't use YY often and wasn't used to the software's default hotkey. He slowly pressed F2. "Maybe you should find another teammate, Bishop Wood?"

Bishop Wood pleaded, "Don't leave. I was just underperforming in the last two matches. I'll help you gain points in the next couple matches."

"It's not you," said Jing Huan. "I'm just too noob, and your points are too high. It's not worth it to queue with me."

After promoting more team-based competition, the arena recently added a new rule: when high-ranking players partied up with low-ranking players in ranked arena matches, the points gained from winning were reduced by twenty percent, while the points lost were increased by twenty percent.

"It doesn't matter, I just want to queue with you." Bishop Wood paused slightly. "Besides, weren't you always partying up with Yearning For? He's the highest-ranked player in the server."

Jing Huan's movements paused. That was true. However, because they rarely lost their matches, he had never considered that, and Yearning For never brought it up either.

Worried she might leave, Bishop Wood warned her, "Get ready."

"Oh...all right."

As they entered the arena matchmaking screen, Bishop Wood cleared his throat. "By the way, Little Jing, the Realm of Lovers event is coming up soon. Do you want to do it together? I'll carry you."

Jing Huan repeated blankly, "Realm of Lovers?"

Bishop Wood had forgotten that Sweet Little Jing was a *Nine Heroes* newbie; based on her skills, he always had the impression she was a veteran player. "It's the year-end event in *Nine Heroes*, similar to the Valentine's Day and Qixi Festival events. However, the Realm of Lovers event is specifically designed to raise intimacy levels. If you complete all 100 steps, you can earn a Lovers' Brocade Pouch accessory that lasts for a year. It'll look great hanging on your outfit."

Jing Huan then remembered. This event was quite popular among players—especially female players. Who wouldn't want to have a high intimacy level with their partner?

In the game, the higher the intimacy level a couple had, the stronger their exclusive couple skills became. While these skills could never surpass a sect's exclusive skills, they were still top-tier when it came to showing off affection. But this event also had an obvious drawback.

"The quests are time-consuming, and they give very few experience points. God Xiang probably won't do them, right?" Bishop Wood chuckled. "If I remember correctly, he hasn't done them in these last few years."

Jing Huan agreed with Bishop Wood; after all, Yearning had never participated in something like this before. The only person who might actually look forward to such an event would probably be Lu Wenhao.

Just after declining Bishop Wood's offer, his cellphone chimed. It was the group chat that Long Road Ahead had set up before, which now had five people in it.

Little Road Never Gets Lost: @Little Jing~, Little Jingjing, I love you so much! Come out quickly and let gege give you a kiss!!

Nomnom: ?

 Chapter 13

Little Jing~: ??? Gege is still in the group, don't get touchy with me!

Little Jing~: [Shoo shoo, I'm getting shivers.JPG]

Little Road Never Gets Lost: I saw the contribution you've made to this party. I'll always remember you.

Little Road Never Gets Lost: Little Jing, don't fight in the arena with Yearning For anymore. Just go with Bishop Wood! Drain all his points for me!! With you around, he'll never surpass me!!

Fuck. Jing Huan felt humiliated. He had once been a formidable figure in his old server. Back then, who in his guild of over a hundred people didn't address him as ge?

Now, he had become a burden—and a huge one at that. It was all Yearning For's fault! If it weren't for him, how could he have fallen from grace like this!

Little Jing~: You just want to trick me into leaving, so that gege can help boost your rank. :)

Little Jing~: 【Song share—"I Won't Fall for Your Tricks."】

After dropping the song link into the chat and seeing no sign of Yearning For, Jing Huan opened their DM, habitually seeking some attention.

Little Jing~: Missing gege~ [Drawing circles]

After sending that message, he skillfully selected a few cute stickers and sent them all at once.

Xiang: Mm.

Jing Huan paused, just about to lock his phone screen. *Why had he replied so quickly?*

Little Jing~: O.O Gege! I thought you weren't here.

Xiang Huaizhi casually draped his long legs over the sofa's armrest, resting his head on his hand. His eyes were calm and unfazed, lost in thought.

If you thought I wasn't here, why send me messages?

Xiang: Just finished dinner.

Little Jing~: I've eaten too~ I'm playing in the arena right now. ~\(≧▽≦)/~

Xiang: I know.

Little Jing~: Huh? How did you know??

Xiang: ...

Xiang: Just checked the guild group chat by chance.

"Little Jing, heal up my summoning beast a bit." His teammate's voice came through the headset. "What are you doing? Why aren't you moving?"

Looking up, Jing Huan started, realizing they were already in a match. He reflexively locked the cellphone. "Ah, coming."

Xiang Huaizhi held his cellphone, quietly waiting for a few minutes.

Silence from the other side. There wasn't even a sticker from the person who usually responded within milliseconds.

Papa Xiang sat on the sofa next to Xiang Huaizhi, newspaper in hand. "Why the long face? Dinner wasn't good?" He lowered his voice. "Your mom's only hobbies are cooking and playing mahjong now. No matter how bad it tastes, you must endure it. Don't let her notice."

Xiang Huaizhi lowered his eyes and tossed his cellphone aside. "That's not it."

Just then, Mama Xiang's voice came from the mahjong room. "Dear!"

 Chapter 13

Papa Xiang immediately sprang to his feet and dashed over to the mahjong room's door. "What's wrong?"

"Go to the snack street and buy us some chicken feet."

Papa Xiang frowned. "I'll order delivery for you."

Mama Xiang retorted, "That shop doesn't do delivery."

Looking extremely reluctant, Papa Xiang was about to nod when a voice came from behind him.

"I'll go." Xiang Huaizhi stood up, grabbing his coat from the sofa. He hesitated for a moment, but ultimately stuffed his cellphone into his pocket. "How many portions should I get?"

Once Xiang Huaizhi left, Mama Xiang looked at her husband and asked reproachfully, "Did you nag him again?" Having raised him since he was a child, she could tell at a glance her son wasn't in a good mood.

"I didn't even say anything," Papa Xiang protested.

Xiang Huaizhi strolled down the road carrying two bags of chicken feet. The cellphone in his pocket had been vibrating the entire way, but he stared straight ahead. He had no plans to check it.

As he passed by the supermarket, Xiang Huaizhi decided to make a quick stop and buy some bread for tomorrow's breakfast. While checking out, the girl in front of him was on the phone. They weren't standing too close, but Xiang Huaizhi could still hear her conversation.

"Hmph, he sent me more than twenty messages and called several times... I'm not going to bother with him... Who told him to get so close to another girl! He clearly promised to only play games with me, but then he turns around and ranks up with another support girl! No way—this time I'm going to leave him hanging, so he realizes his mistake!"

Xiang Huaizhi twitched.

As soon as he left the supermarket, Xiang Huaizhi took out his cellphone and started going through the messages he had just received, as if doing so would somehow set him apart from the girl just now.

Little Jing~: I just got sent into a fight. [Kitty rolling around]

Little Jing~: Waaaaah gege, I lost so many points tonight...

Little Jing~: I'm the most pitiful person in the world now.

Little Jing~: Can't win fights, and gege is gone too. T▽T

Little Jing~: 【Screenshot】

In the screenshot, the little spirit fox was doing a crying character action. The scene behind the little spirit fox was a random wilderness map. Xiang Huaizhi frowned and glanced at the time. It was just past 8:30 p.m. The arena should still be open.

Jing Huan sat in front of the computer, his head lolling to the side as he leaned his cheek against his hand, idly scrolling through a video app. A WeChat notification popped up at the top of the screen, so he immediately stopped and opened the notification.

Xiang: Weren't you fighting in the arena?

Little Jing~: Bishop Wood's teammate just came online, so I found an excuse to leave~

Little Jing~: I can't bear to lose all the points that were painstakingly earned while gege carried me. QAQ

He made it sound so nice, as if he wasn't the one just handing out points in the arena.

Xiang: How many points do you have now?

 Chapter 13

Little Jing~: 2,422...

Xiang: So you lost sixty.

If only Yearning For hadn't laid it out so plainly. Jing Huan's heart ached.

Little Jing~: WAAAAAH! ~~(>_<)~~

After crying, Jing Huan felt something was off again.

Little Jing~: Huh? Gege, how did you know how many points I had before?

Little Jing~: Gege, you've been stalking my points!!!

He wasn't on the Mastery rankings; if someone wanted to know how many points he had, they'd have to input his ID at an NPC to check.

Xiang Huaizhi's pace slowed down slightly. After a while, he started typing.

Xiang: I wanted to see how far you were from 3,000 points.

Xiang: But now, it seems that you're not particularly interested in the 3,000-point reward.

Little Jing~: Ah??

Xiang: Otherwise, why would you queue with Bishop Wood to give away points?

Little Jing~: He's the one who invited me...

Xiang: You decided to go just because he invited you?

Jing Huan was a little dazed with surprise. He blinked, slowly typing out the word "I," but then stopped. He quickly scrolled up and down, reading their conversation multiple times.

Was he imagining things? Why did this feel...oddly like jealousy?

Didn't Long Road Ahead used to give away points all the time too? Yearning For had never said a word about it then.

An abrupt and absurd thought came to him. Jing Huan instinctively dismissed the possibility of such a notion, but he couldn't help teasing Yearning For.

Little Jing~: Gege.

Xiang: ?

Little Jing~: Are you feeling jealous? >0<

Sure enough, just after the message was sent out, the name at the top of the screen changed to "Typing..."

Even through the screen, Jing Huan could practically picture the other person vehemently trying to deny it, and for some reason, found it oddly amusing. He stared at the screen, curious to see how Yearning For would respond.

A minute went by. Then five. A whole ten minutes passed, and all that appeared was "Typing..."

Jing Huan's eyebrow lifted. *Damn? Seriously, bro? I was just teasing you, you're not really writing an 800-word essay to scold me for being presumptuous, are you?!*

Twelve minutes later, Jing Huan, lower lip caught between his teeth, decided to break the deadlock. He opened the keyboard, typing slowly: *Gege, I was just saying that—*

Buzz.

Xiang: No.

Xiang: Just don't ask to party up with me again if you're going to fight in the arena with other players. I'm not in the habit of wiping other people's asses.

Jing Huan blinked, gawking at these two lines of text on his cellphone screen. The tone was harsh and brusque. As he continued

staring at it, the corners of his mouth suddenly lifted, a grin growing on his face until finally, he burst out laughing.

That's all you managed to type in twelve minutes?!

Jing Huan cheerfully picked up his cellphone, and tapped on Yearning For's profile picture twice with his finger.

Scumbag, oh scumbag. If you didn't feel even the tiniest bit of flutter in your heart just now, I'll marry you.

Jing Huan had never been in a relationship, but he had seen a besotted pig run around before.

Lu Wenhao often did stuff like that in the dorms, clutching his cellphone anxiously and peppering the air with questions like, "Oh my fucking god, how am I supposed to reply to that?!" After agonizing for a few minutes, he would reply to his wife with a lovestruck face, saying, "Oh, got it."

As time went on, Jing Huan was no longer mystified by how Lu Wenhao got scammed back then.

Xiang Huaizhi returned home and placed the chicken feet on the coffee table beside the mahjong table.

"Thank you darling, what took you so long?" Mama Xiang winked at her son as she played her tile.

Xiang Huaizhi was instantly reminded of Jing Huan winking at him in that suit. The young man's eyes were pure, clean, and beautiful, his posture elegant and composed. Back then, all of the girls in the audience seemed to be watching him.

Xiang Huaizhi snapped out of his thoughts, softly responded with an "mm" sound, greeted Mama Xiang's besties, and then turned to go to his room. As soon as the door closed, the conversation at the mahjong table turned to him.

"I haven't seen him for a while, and Little Xiang just keeps getting more handsome. He really took after your looks."

"Yeah, he's so tall and such an excellent student. If my child were even half as outstanding as Little Xiang, I can't imagine how much less I'd worry."

Mama Xiang took a sip of tea and slowly shook her head. "What's the use of being handsome? He's already in university but I haven't seen him date a single girl. I'm envious of you all, getting to experience the thrill of watching your kids fall in love for the first time."

Xiang Huaizhi went back to his room, changed clothes, and slipped into bed. After standing on the road for ten minutes, his fingers were still cold from the biting freeze of the late autumn night.

His cellphone vibrated. He lifted it up to read.

Little Jing~: Waaaaaah...

Little Jing~: From now on, I'll never mess around with men who aren't gege. Gege, don't be angry with me anymore~ T∇T

Xiang Huaizhi's eyebrows furrowed, his expression shifting minutely. He had almost admitted it back then. When he stood outside the supermarket entrance, he had typed "yes" in the input box and had stared dazedly at that word for a long time before pursing his lips and deleting it.

Something was out of control. He could feel it.

His thoughts nearly consuming him, Xiang Huaizhi was pulled out of that confusing mire when his cellphone gave two gentle buzzes.

Little Jing~: So long as gege is alive, I belong to gege.

Little Jing~: After gege dies, I'll be gege's little widow. ˇ(≥ ≦*)o

Xiang Huaizhi was pretty sure that wasn't how the original

Chapter 13

saying[3] went. The crease in his forehead deepened further. He didn't understand how this guy, who usually appeared so well-behaved and serious, could be so flirtatious online.

Xiang: I didn't get angry at you.

Xiang: Do you usually talk like this in real life too?

Little Jing~: How could that be!!!

Little Jing~: No matter where I am, I only talk to gege like this~ =3=

Xiang: ...

Xiang: It's late. Go to bed.

Little Jing~: It's only 9 p.m., gege. Are we really going to just sleep now? >.< Don't you want to chat a bit more...

Jing Huan had logged into the desktop version of WeChat earlier. He was ready to strike while the iron was hot and ratchet up his flirting.

Xiang: Chat about what?

Jing Huan's heart leaped with joy, and he immediately started typing: *Why don't we do a voice chat—*

Xiang: Video call?

Jing Huan froze. *What? I dare you to say that again to your daddy. In the dead of night! A man alone with a woman! You want me to video call you?! Damn... You scumbag! You have vile intentions!!!*

Jing Huan took a deep breath and told himself to calm down.

From a certain point of view, the fact that Yearning For has started to showing interest in his appearance could be seen as

---

3   The original saying would've gone like this: When I'm alive, I'm gege's, and when I'm dead, I'll be gege's ghost (rather than widow).

278

progress. *Bullshit! Where am I supposed to find a girl to video call this scumbag!!*

Jing Huan subconsciously glanced at his legs. If he added a slimming filter, he might pass for a girl. But...Jing Huan's gaze moved upward and stopped on his baggy black boxers.

If his hands accidentally shook and exposed his boxers, wouldn't he be killed on sight?

Not good, not good.

Xiang Huaizhi took a sip from his glass of water, watching the "Typing..." indicator repeatedly appear at the top of the chat. Thinking he teased him enough, he moved to end the topic.

Little Jing~: Ahhh... I also want to video call gege.

Little Jing~: But I'm not wearing any clothes right now...

Little Jing~: [Covering face][Shy]

Xiang Huaizhi spat. Coughing hard, he expressionlessly grabbed a paper towel and wiped the water off of himself. *How could I forget that I shouldn't drink water while chatting with this person?*

Jing Huan deftly sent, "You're so mean" and "Gege's a bad guy," and laughed so hard the voice-activated lights within his vicinity lit up.

Stupid scumbag, you just want to flirt with me over a video call, huh? Well, BRING IT ON. Who's afraid of who!!

Little Jing~: Ah, gege, don't misunderstand, I normally sleep like this cuz it's a bit more comfortable. QvQ

Xiang Huaizhi dabbed his clothes dry, thinking, *It's normal for guys to sleep naked.* But the image of the sliver of skin on Jing Huan's small, slender waist that he had revealed on the basketball court kept resurfacing in his mind, and he couldn't shake it off.

Chapter 13

I'm going insane.

After his shower, Jing Huan crawled into bed with his cellphone, waiting for Yearning For's reply. He was even thinking about how he would respond if Yearning For really wanted to have a flirty video call with him.

Just as he was about to ask Lu Wenhao for advice, a new message popped up in their chat. It was two voice messages. Jing Huan clicked play and held his cellphone to his ear to listen.

"Okay, I'm going to sleep. Make sure to cover yourself with a blanket."

The next day, Jing Huan was back in Yearning For's party. The two stood next to the teleporter, waiting for the arena to open. Long Road Ahead and xoxoYuyu had also formed a party beside them.

[Current] Long Road Ahead: Yuyu, your ge's outfit looks good today.

[Current] xoxoYuyu: Huh? It looks the same as usual...

[Current] Long Road Ahead: Isn't there an extra big green hat[4]?

[Current] xoxoYuyu: Ohhhhh, I see it. Poor guy.

[Current] Yearning For: ?

[Current] Sweet Little Jing: Long Road Ahead, stop trying to drive a wedge between us! I didn't cheat on my gege!!

[Current] Long Road Ahead: Uh-huh, you just played a few arena matches with another guy and lost a few points. It's all good. ^^

---

4   戴 绿 帽 子 - Dài Lǜ Mào Zi - In Chinese slang "wearing a green hat" refers to being cuckolded or having one's romantic partner cheat on them.

[Current] Long Road Ahead: Xiangxiang already told me that he's chosen to forgive.

Xiang Huaizhi picked up one of his slippers and hurled it at him.

Lu Hang quickly paid the price for his speech. That night in the arena, he encountered Xiang Huaizhi three times in a row.

"Daddy!" Lu Hang hollered at the top of his lungs. "Daddy, it's all my fault. Please show mercy, sir! Let me win one round, I'm begging you!"

Xiang Huaizhi ignored him and ruthlessly knocked him to the ground.

[Current] xoxoYuyu: Sister-in-law, [Crying] please show mercy.

The little spirit fox immediately froze.

[Current] Sweet Little Jing: [Nodding]

Xiang Huaizhi paused. "Why are you holding back? Don't you want to reach 3,000 points?"

"I do," Jing Huan said pitifully, "but I want to be Yuyu's sister-in-law even more."

Xiang Huaizhi: "..."

Xiang Huaizhi questioned, "A casual 'sister-in-law' won you over that easily?"

"Mhm," Jing Huan said, voice gentle. "If you call me 'wifey' once, I'll even give you my character."

Xiang Huaizhi swiftly eliminated his cousin, bringing this conversation to a quick and decisive end.

Lu Hang lost several matches in a row and fumed, "Dammit! I lost over fifty points in one night! It's almost as much as what Little Jingjing lost the night she cheated on you!"

Xiang Huaizhi threw his other slipper at him.

 Chapter 13

Lu Hang expertly dodged it, his outrage growing the more he thought about it. "This won't do; you made me lose so many points, you're coming with me to play *PUBG* so I can kill people and vent my frustration!" It just so happened that they had completed their dungeon runs for the week and had nothing else to do.

"It was your own lack of skill."

"So what! I'm weak, and that's my justification!" Lu Hang opened the group chat. "I'm going to call out in the group chat and invite two more people to join us."

"Wait." Xiang Huaizhi stopped him. His tone sounded normal. "Just call one person, I've got two here."

"Ah? That's perfect, Nomnom also said she wants to come." Lu Hang quickly opened the *PUBG* client. "Who did you call? Send me the name, I'll invite them."

Xiang Huaizhi let out an "mm" when something occurred to him just as he started his ping booster[5] program. "Do you have any extra *PUBG* accounts?"

When Jing Huan received the invite, he hurriedly opened the *PUBG* client, rushed to the in-game cash shop, and quickly bought a flashy skirt. As he paid, he couldn't help but be moved by his own dedication.

Be the most diligent scammer to scam the scummiest of scumbags.

Half a minute later, a harmless-looking female student in a white blouse and gray miniskirt appeared in the game interface.

---

5   A program that people use to lower the latency when playing online games. Examples that most people use are WTFast and Mudfish. They're VPNs that lower your ping latency to improve your performance by reducing the delay in your keyboard actions.

Shocked, Xiang Huaizhi looked up to confirm the ID. *Ah, it was "Just Be Happy."*

"'Just Be Happy…'" Lu Hang subconsciously sounded out Jing Huan's in-game name. "Little Jingjing, you're quite the optimist, huh?"

Jing Huan laughed shyly, secretly relieved that his past self hadn't chosen "Your Daddy Jing." Otherwise he would've had to create a new alt account today.

"Gege." As soon as they entered the waiting area, Jing Huan bounded over to Yearning For and had his character wiggle his head about. "I'm so noob at this… You have to protect me, *waaah*."

Lu Wenhao once said that men typically didn't like overly strong women. The weaker you were, the stronger a man's protective instinct became.

As expected, Xiang Huaizhi said, "Mm. Don't stray too far from me later."

"It's fine, we're just playing for fun," Lu Hang said. "With two girls, we probably won't be the last squad standing anyway."

Three minutes later, Love is Sharing Noms wiped out an entire squad with a shotgun. She sauntered over to Lu Hang, who had been knocked down by the enemy. As she reloaded her gun, she looked imperiously down at him. "What were you saying just now?"

"That Xiangxiang and I are counting on you two to carry us to win the match," Lu Hang said with a straight face. "Jiejie, please revive me."

Xiang Huaizhi landed on another building. He knocked down his opponent with a submachine gun and looked back at the person who had been following him this whole time.

Chapter 13

Amused, he remarked, "You don't have to stick this close to me."

Do you think I want to!!

Jing Huan responded pitifully, "Gege, I don't have a gun."

Xiang Huaizhi paused, then threw the other gun he had slung around his shoulder to him.

After clearing out the enemies in the town, the four of them got in a car and headed toward the safe zone.

Love is Sharing Noms glanced at the gun on Jing Huan's back and laughed. "Jingjing, why are you still carrying an S686? This gun is pretty useless in late-game. Why didn't you pick up any of those rifles that were all over the place earlier?"

"Gege gave me this gun. I don't want to swap it out." Jing Huan said, stubborn.

Xiang Huaizhi stayed quiet.

Love is Sharing Noms said, "Ah, sorry for asking."

Long Road Ahead said solemnly, "I already guessed it a long time ago; that's why I didn't ask."

When they arrived at another town, Jing Huan jumped out of the car and heard a voice through his headset: "Come here."

Xiang Huaizhi didn't name anyone specifically, but everyone knew who he was calling.

Jing Huan happily scampered over to his side. "What is it, gege?"

Xiang Huaizhi threw a fully loaded rifle on the ground. "Use this one."

Jing Huan didn't expect Yearning For to give him a gun and was momentarily rendered speechless. There was no such thing as brotherhood in this game. When he played *PUBG* with his dormmates in

the past, getting gun attachments depended on how fast you clicked on it, or on hiding the fact that you found one. The only time he had seen someone give away attachments or guns to their teammate was when Lu Wenhao was trying to coax a girl.

"Why aren't you picking it up?" Xiang Huaizhi tossed out another gun. "Or do you prefer this one?"

Fuck. This scumbag is even more skilled than Lu Wenhao!

Jing Huan snapped out of his stupor and randomly picked up a gun. "Thanks, gege."

Xiang Huaizhi didn't say much. H picked up the other gun and walked away. Watching him depart, Jing Huan blurted out, "Wait."

Xiang Huaizhi paused. "What is it?"

What kind of question is that? I'm giving you a return gift. Duh.

Jing Huan thought for a moment and pressed the C key to crouch down.

"Gege, come here," he whispered. "I want to tell you a secret."

Xiang Huaizhi replied, "This is the squad voice chat, I can hear you just fine from where I'm at."

Jing Huan whined, "Nooo, come here, please."

Xiang Huaizhi wavered. He already had a vague idea as to what this person wanted to do. A few seconds later, he walked over to Jing Huan and crouched down beside him. Jing Huan put his gun away and shuffled closer to him until the two were almost stuck together.

The female character in front of Xiang Huaizhi tilted her head as if she was whispering to him.

"The secret is..." Jing Huan whispered quickly, "...I like you."

...As expected.

 Chapter 13

Xiang Huaizhi felt a slight squeeze in his heart. A small leap. The tips of his ears tingled. *What kind of secret is this?*

He was quietly surprised by how much he enjoyed the prickling sensation in his fingertips. It took him some time before he found his voice again. "What did you say? I didn't hear you."

Jing Huan's cheeks were also a little hot, but he attributed it to shyness. After all, this was a normal reaction when honest people like him lied.

"I said, I like…"

Bang, bang, bang, bang, bang—

Several shots rang out, cutting him off.

Lu Hang couldn't take it anymore and started wildly shooting at the wall. "Holy fuck! I already got blinded in the arena, and now I'm getting blinded by your PDA in *PUBG* too!" He cursed, "Can't you guys play fair?!"

After they finished that *PUBG* match, Lu Hang felt like he had been force-fed a mouthful of lovey-doveyness. Frustration still bubbling up inside him, he immediately exposed them in the guild group chat after turning off the lights and getting into bed.

Long Road Ahead: Damn it! Secret? What secret?! What were Nomnom and I? Chopped liver?!

BrbOrNot: Ha ha ha ha, who told you to invite them?

Peach Cheese Stan: You did this to yourself.

Sweet Little Jing: OMG, Long Road Ahead, you were eavesdropping! >.<

Long Road Ahead: ???

Long Road Ahead: I'll k*ll you.

Sweet Little Jing: Aaaaaaaah gege. QAQ

Yearning For: Mm.

Sweet Little Jing: Long Road Ahead wants to k*ll me!!

Lu Hang looked up and saw this dear roommate was in the same position as him: lying on his side, cellphone in hand. He couldn't resist asking, "Why are you just looking at the screen and not saying anything? Are you that repressed?"

Xiang Huaizhi didn't look up. "I did say something."

"Yeah, only after Little Jingjing called for you." Out of the blue, Lu Hang asked, "When are you two going to get married?"

Xiang Huaizhi paused in his typing. "Why would we get married?"

Lu Hang was stunned. "Because you're already together... shouldn't the question be, why *wouldn't* you? What, can't spare the 100 gold marriage fee? I'll pay for you."

Hearing the first part of Lu Hang's words, Xiang Huaizhi's heart stirred slightly, but his voice remained even as he insisted, "We're not together."

"Not..." Lu Hang sat up. "Not together? Then what were you two whispering about just now?"

Xiang Huaizhi replied, "They've always been this way."

"True, she's always been like that, but you also walked over. Didn't you crouch in front of her yourself to listen..."

Xiang Huaizhi silently stared at his cellphone screen, seemingly focused but in actuality, Lu Hang's words went in one ear and out the other. Indeed, he had walked over, and it wasn't out of helplessness or compromise. He had wanted to go over there, wanted to get closer, wanted to know what secrets that person had to tell him and only him.

 Chapter 13

Lu Hang was still mumbling on the other side, "You even gave her guns—not just one, but two of them! Usually, when I ask for a couple bullets, you tell me to pound sand."

Xiang Huaizhi was listening absentmindedly and was about to interject when he saw a familiar pink avatar appear on the screen.

Sweet Little Jing: Question for everyone~ When will the Realm of Lovers event start? (^▽^*)

Regardless of Lovesickness: I heard it's at the end of the month.

Lu Hang continued, "And there was that thing with Maimai's #1 Fan—"

"What's the Realm of Lovers event?" Xiang Huaizhi interrupted him.

"Huh?" Lu Hang did a double take. "You've got to be kidding me, you don't know what that is? It's that event where you can increase the intimacy level between spouses."

Xiang Huaizhi of course knew what the event entailed; he just didn't know that was its name. He let out an "oh" and continued reading the guild group chat messages.

Jing Huan had already started chatting with the guild members. He didn't often speak up in the guild group chat, but whenever he did, he had a knack for drawing out the lurkers. That was just how he was—he could easily hit it off with whoever he wanted.

BrbOrNot: @Sweet Little Jing, heard that Bishop Wood took you to the arena and was giving away points for the entire night. You didn't cut ties with him?

Sweet Little Jing: How do you know everything...

Bishop Wood: @Echoes of Spring, help me kick BON out. He's

gossiping and even trying to sow discord between me and Little Jingjing.

BrbOrNot: Come on. What even is your relationship?

Sweet Little Jing: We're just friends...

Bishop Wood: For now. Who knows about the future? [Shy]

Sweet Little Jing: ??

BrbOrNot: Speaking of that, why were you two alone in YY that night? The *Nine Heroes'* voice chat isn't enough for you two anymore??

Bishop Wood: Don't ask. Asking means you want to be sent to jail.

Sweet Little Jing: He said the game couldn't recognize his microphone.

Love is Sharing Noms: And you believed that...

Lu Hang was also reading the group chat and piped up, "Bishop Wood is really brazen."

Xiang Huaizhi had already closed the guild group chat and was beginning to DM the pink profile picture.

Xiang: No class tomorrow?

Little Jing~: Still have class, two of them in the morning. T∇T

Xiang: Then go to sleep.

Little Jing~: Okaaaay gege. o(*°∇°*)o Let's sleep together~~

Little Jing~: Nuzzle nuzzle.

Xiang Huaizhi read the last two messages over and over again before replying with a curt "goodnight." Then, he got out of bed, grabbed the water from the table, and downed half of it in one go.

In the guild group chat:

 Chapter 13

BrbOrNot: Can't believe Sweet Little Jing fell for such an obvious lie. What does that tell us?

Peach Cheese Stan: It means if you keep babbling, God Xiang will hunt you down tomorrow.

BrbOrNot: That's not gonna happen. If God Xiang wanted to kill me, he would've done it a long time ago. They've been quiet for so long, so there really must be nothing going on.

Bishop Wood: Ha ha, you're right.

Sweet Little Jing: That's because my gege is a good person! Not chatting with any of you anymore! (╯ ` □')╯ ╱┻━┻

BrbOrNot: Nooo, keep chatting.

Sweet Little Jing: No! Gege urged me to go beddy-bye! Wave wave~

Is Gege Big: ?

BrbOrNot: ...

Long Road Ahead: ...???

Lu Hang looked at the person opposite his bed, expression complicated.

What kind of relationship game is my roommate playing? I kill for you, help you rank up, give you guns, listen to your whispers, and urge you to sleep—but we're just friends?

Jing Huan went to a restaurant with his roommates over the weekend. The atmosphere at the dinner table was so heavy it was practically palpable. The two guys sitting across from him had their heads down as they furiously shoveled food in their mouths.

When Lu Wenhao raised his hand to ask for a fourth bowl of rice,

Jing Huan finally put down his chopsticks. "Are you planning to eat the restaurant's entire supply of rice tonight?"

"You don't understand." Lu Wenhao grabbed the rice from the waiter. "We need to build up our strength."

"Why? You're already overflowing with it," Jing Huan said. "What's going on?"

Gao Zixiang wiped his mouth with a napkin. "The server merge announcement is coming out tonight."

"Tonight? Is that confirmed?" Jing Huan raised an eyebrow. "Which server are you merging with?"

"Don't know yet." Gao Zixiang looked at his watch. "The announcement comes out at eight. Ten more minutes left."

Lu Wenhao mumbled through a mouthful of food, "The servers will shut down at midnight and reopen at eight in the morning. It's going to be a brutal fight. We probably won't have time to go out to eat for the next couple days."

Jing Huan didn't think it was so bad. "Isn't server merging a good thing? It's more fun when there are more people." Their server wasn't particularly popular. Since they kept matching with the same people in the arena, it could get dull at times.

"Yeah." Gao Zixiang sighed. "After the merge, the wilderness maps will probably be littered with corpses. If it's not the assassination squads stealing business from each other, it'll be the guilds fighting for the top spot."

At 7:59 a.m., a cellphone lay quietly on the dining table while Lu Wenhao and Gao Zixiang, their faces serious, nervously refreshed the official *Nine Heroes* website continuously.

Jing Huan chucked. "Is that really necessary?"

 Chapter 13

"You don't understand. Our guild leader said that we must secure the potion material farms in the main city," Gao Zixiang said. "If the server we're merging with has a strong guild, we'll be fighting nonstop."

"Holy shit!" Lu Wenhao suddenly saw a new game announcement, excitedly grabbing onto Gao Zixiang's sleeve. "It's out, it's out! Hurry up and open it, holy shit!"

"Don't fucking rip my clothes," Gao Zixiang snapped. "I was about to click on it, jeez."

So inexperienced. Jing Huan scoffed and sipped his tea to cleanse his palate.

" 'To enhance our players' gaming experience, we are officially launching the server merging system… The first *Nine Heroes* server merge will be the following servers: Match Made in Heaven'—Shit, that's our server—" Lu Wenhao cursed as he read it, " 'and Mirage?' "

Jing Huan nearly choked to death on his tea.

Lu Wenhao frowned. "Mirage? Why does that server name sound so familiar?" He and Gao Zixiang exchanged looks, and then stared at the person opposite of them.

Jing Huan covered his mouth, coughing so hard his neck turned crimson. *Fuck. Motherfucking dammit. Is the universe screwing with me?!*

Gao Zixiang patted his back, trying to soothe him. He wore a complicated expression. "Is it really worth getting this worked up over the server name?"

Jing Huan, with his ears still burning red, shook his head. "No, I…"

Lu Wenhao finally remembered and slapped the table. "Fuck! Huanhuan, don't you worry. Your jiejie is our jiejie! We couldn't help you before because we weren't in the same server, but an opportunity has now fallen into our laps. I'll make sure to deal with God Xiang... No, Yearning For, properly!"

Jing Huan sputtered, "That's really not necessary..."

"Hao'er is right!" Gao Zixiang nodded frantically. "He needs to know that bullying a girl comes with consequences, and bullying our jiejie means his death!"

Jing Huan began, "Actually, it's not that serious..."

"And what about the one who spammed megaphones insulting your jiejie? Should we kill them too?" Lu Wenhao punched the air. "Just say the word!"

Jing Huan tried again. "Really, there's no need..."

"Exactly!" Gao Zixiang echoed excitedly. "Huanhuan, if you're still not satisfied, I'll get you an account, so you can join us and kill them yourself. How does that sound?"

"I might not have the time..." Jing Huan finally managed to catch his breath after his coughing fit. He gently reminded them, "I appreciate your intentions, but let's be real: can you even kill Yearning For?"

"Come on, why are you looking down on us?" Lu Wenhao said. "We might not be able to beat him one-on-one, but if we gather a party, we can do it, right?"

Jing Huan was about to say, that's not quite fair, but he found himself swallowing his words back down.

What was so unfair about it? Since when was killing someone about *fairness*? If it weren't for the fact that he couldn't physically

operate all the characters, he would've bought five of them to corner Yearning For with.

And yet...he felt there was something undignified about a five-on-one battle; it edged on too much bullying. He must've been influenced by all the times he had been hunted and chased down... Yes, that had to be it.

Jing Huan said earnestly, "Even so, you guys can only kill him once, and after that, Yearning For will be on guard. What happens if he forms a party and retaliates?"

"No big deal! We're still part of the server's battle party. How could we let him kill us?" Lu Wenhao snorted coldly. "If he hunts us back, even better. We'll win one out of ten times, and if we blow up his divine artifact, wouldn't that be even more awesome?!"

Jing Huan thought to himself, *What are you talking about, 'once every ten times'? You guys probably couldn't even kill him after twenty tries.*

The care he had shown his two good friends hadn't been in vain. For the rest of the meal, they discussed seventy-two different ways they could kill Yearning For. Jing Huan, the person actually involved in the matter, sat across from them, unable to get a word in.

Before parting, Gao Zixiang patted him on the shoulder and solemnly said, "Don't worry, Huanhuan. We're bros; we'll help you get revenge. Just wait for my good news."

Jing Huan allowed himself to be patted. Afterward, he returned home, his thoughts in turmoil. He flopped down on the sofa and slowly opened WeChat. The guild group chat had already exploded because of the server merging news.

Echoes of Spring: I had someone look into it, and they discovered the top guild in the Match Made in Heaven server is Limitless. Their guild leader has parties already organized and primed to ambush us at any moment. So, once the server opens tomorrow, don't leave the safe zone alone! Do your dailies in parties! At the same time, we can't just sit around and wait for our deaths. We cannot allow them to take the main city potion material farms, and we cannot let them seize the top guild title! I've already arranged assassination squads and posted the list in the group chat. Everyone, please take a look. This is a critical moment, and I hope we can all work together to help the guild overcome this challenge! @Everyone

Echoes of Spring was also a ruthless person. Less than an hour after the server merge announcement came out, and she had already arranged the assassin squads. It was clear neither side had any plans of negotiating peace.

There were many more messages below, but Jing Huan couldn't be bothered to read through them all.

Fuck. Shitty *Nine Heroes*. Ten years—they hadn't merged servers in ten years, and they decided to do it *now*?

He lay on the sofa in a trance for a while. When he came to his senses, he saw he had already opened up his DM with Yearning For. Their last conversation was before dinner; Yearning For had mentioned he was going to play basketball, and Jing Huan had replied with a heart and red lips emoticons. Since he had already opened the DM, he had to say something.

Sweet Little Jing: Gege, our server is going to merge with Match Made in Heaven…

Sweet Little Jing: Judging by what the vice guild leader said, it

 Chapter 13

looks like our guild is going to fight with the top guild from that server. I'm so scareeed, aaah... T∇T

As soon as he sent the message, a notification appeared above, indicating the other party was speaking. Ten seconds later, the voice message came.

"I know." The guy sounded slightly out of breath, but his voice was deep and steady as always, standing out amidst the background noise. "What are you afraid of? As long as I'm here, no one can kill you."

...Stupid scumbag. You can't even protect yourself, how can you protect me? Jing Huan silently mocked, then played the voice message again.

Guide on How to Fail at Online Dating

When Jing Huan woke up the next morning, his WeChat was already flooded with messages from his two group chats. He checked the time: just a few minutes past eight. The server maintenance should have just wrapped up.

Unsurprisingly, the guild group chat had 99+ unread messages again, and even his dorm group chat had 40+ messages. He couldn't understand why those two, who were together 24/7, could still hold cringeworthy conversations in the group chat every day.

Jing Huan had to blink several times before his bleariness gradually went away. Still rather sluggish, he opened the dorm group chat.

It turned out his roommates weren't just chatting about whatever came to mind. All 40+ messages were game screenshots.

【Is Gege Big, coordinates (19, 41) Penglai.】

【BrbOrNot, coordinates (129, 18) Main City.】

【Sweet Luoluo, coordinates (99, 83) Unknown Realm.】

The list continued.

Instantly, Jing Huan was on high alert.

Fuck... These are all of my guild members' coordinates.

Little Jing~: What are you guys doing?

Lu Wenhao: Killing people, of course. The alts are already set up; we're just waiting for them to leave the safe zone. Why are you up so early?

Little Jing~: ...Some store downstairs is playing music, it's noisy.

Gao Zixiang: I envy you. We got up at 6:30 a.m.

Little Jing~: ??

Gao Zixiang: We were afraid that *Nine Heroes* would fuck us over and open the server early, and we'd be left in the dust.

Lu Wenhao: Good thing we thought ahead! We got to log in as soon as the server opened. Everyone else is still in the login queue, ha ha ha!

Little Jing~: Why can't they get in? It's just two servers merging. It can't be bad enough that you have to queue, right?

Lu Wenhao: Wrooong. There are a bunch of people from other servers here just to watch the show. Since you're awake, why not come help us? My wife's account just so happens to be free.

Little Jing~: ...Nah, I'm going back to sleep, see ya.

After shooting off that message, Jing Huan immediately opened up the guild group chat. It was also exploding with coordinate screenshots.

Echoes of Spring: Attention everyone: don't do dailies today. Those with parties, please group up to protect our guild merchants. Those without a party, don't leave the safe zone! Thank you for your hard work! To compensate you all, I'll distribute guild bonuses starting today and throughout the rest of the week!

Echoes of Spring's call to arms received an overwhelming response, and everyone was ready for battle. The thrill of gaming

was all about excitement, and now that excitement had come knocking on their door, the guild members were all pumped up.

Jing Huan also enjoyed the excitement. The thought of competing for territory after the server merge was exhilarating. That was, if his two dumbass roommates weren't in the enemy guild.

When he remembered their audacious words last night, Jing Huan could feel a migraine starting to build. He had considered confessing to them yesterday, asking them not to interfere in matters between him and Yearning For. However, as soon as he thought about what he had done in the past few months, that thought was immediately vanquished.

He was taking his secret—pretending to be a woman, acting coquettishly, and sending seductive thigh pics from the hot springs to flirt with a guy online—to the grave. And if someone else were to find out, well, they would have to go to the grave with him too.

His phone vibrated slightly, pulling him back to reality.

Xiang: Text me when you wake up.

Little Jing~: I'm here! Morning gegeee. ~\\(≧▽≦)/~

Xiang: Morning, are you playing today?

Little Jing~ : Not sure, the guild chat looks terrifying... T▽T Is gege going to?

Xiang: Mm.

Xiang: I promised Echoes of Spring I'd help her seize the main city's potion material farm.

Each major map in *Nine Heroes* had its own potion material farm, allowing only one guild per farm. The farm in the main city had the highest quality. Prior to the server merge, the harvesting rights for

Chapter 14

this particular potion material farms had always belonged to Idle Pavilion.

The farm harvesting rights changed every two months. Only the guild with the highest funds during selection week could secure the main city's potion material farm. Guild funds couldn't be directly purchased with real-life cash; instead, they could only be earned through guild merchants trading with NPCs across various maps, with a maximum of ten merchant positions in a guild available at any time.

In short, to seize the main city's potion material farm, you needed to protect your merchants while hunting down those of the enemy guild during selection week.

Xiang: It's okay if you don't want to play. I already talked to Echoes of Spring so you don't have to come.

Little Jing~: Nooooo, I want to stand with gege through thick and thin. Gege, wait for me, I'll log in after I freshen up~ [Kiss kiss]

"Is Little Jingjing coming or not?" Lu Hang was collecting potions. "If she isn't, we'll have to find another party member."

Xiang Huaizhi typed on his keyboard. "She's coming."

"Sounds good." Lu Hang looked at the server merge announcement at the top of the game, muttering, "Match Made in Heaven... The server name sounds kind of familiar."

Xiang Huaizhi paid him no mind. Lu Hang knew quite a few people from the game, having played in other servers before Mirage and attended offline events. It wasn't surprising the server name sounded familiar to him.

Until a megaphone popped up in the game—

Guide on How to Fail at Online Dating

[Megaphone] Half a Lifetime: Where are the Idle Pavilion people? Are you all hiding in the safe zone??

Half a Lifetime? This name sounded familiar. Xiang Huaizhi frowned and clicked open the other person's information.

Half a Lifetime, Level 150, Spirit Fox Den.

Spirit Fox Den... Xiang Huaizhi had just vaguely recalled something when he heard the person behind him shout, "Oh, holy shit—"

"Aren't they Lu Wenhao and Gao Zixiang?" Lu Hang slapped the table and cackled. Afraid that Xiang Huaizhi wouldn't remember, he reminded him. "It's those underclassmen we met at the resort! Hey, weren't you watching them run a dungeon? Half a Lifetime is Lu Wenhao, the pudgy one!"

Xiang Huaizhi was just slightly startled and instinctively glanced at the WeChat interface on the side.

"What a small world!" Laughing, Lu Hang opened Half a Lifetime's profile and added him as a friend. "Tch, I have to go talk to him. How dare he holler at his senior..."

"Don't." Xiang Huaizhi stopped him. Seeing Lu Hang's puzzlement, he pursed his lips. He struggled to make up a plausible excuse. "...We're opposing guilds right now. If you say something, it'll just put them in an awkward situation."

If they found out that Lu Hang was Long Road Ahead, then his cover would be blown as well. After all, both his real name and his in-game name shared two characters[1], and his voice was too similar—

---

1 向淮之 - Xiàng Huái Zhī, 心向往之 - Xīn Xiàng Wǎng Zhī - Yearning For. So the 向 (Xiàng) and 之 (Zhī) are shared between his name and his in-game name.

 Chapter 14

it was much too obvious. He wasn't ready for Jing Huan to know his real identity just yet.

"What awkward situation? We can just bury the hatchet."

Voice calm, Xiang Huaizhi asked, "Then, who should have the right to harvest the main city's potion material farm?"

Lu Hang was taken aback. "Us, of course!"

It was then that he realized there was no easy way to resolve the situation. Both guilds combined had around 400 members, and each guild was responsible for its own. They couldn't just give in. As strong members in each of their respective guilds, fighting was inevitable.

"Then what should we do? Just pretend we don't know them?" Lu Hang asked. "That wouldn't be right. I mean, they even took us in before."

Xiang Huaizhi pondered for a moment. "We'll talk about it after this is over. This fight won't last long. A month at most."

"Is...is that okay?" Lu Hang was immediately won over by Xiang Huaizhi's suggestion and answered his own question. "It seems okay. When the time comes, I'll act like I just found out about this. It shouldn't be too obvious. All right, let's just avoid them when we fight later. We don't have to acknowledge them but we definitely shouldn't kill them."

Xiang Huaizhi let out a perfunctory hum. No wonder Jing Huan kept sending him crying stickers when the server merge was mentioned yesterday. His dormmates probably didn't know he was playing a female character, nor that he was pursuing a man in the game.

Jing Huan skipped breakfast in favor of turning on the computer.

The guild's YY voice chat currently had over 180 people. With today being the weekend, most of the guild members were there and discussing the deployment strategy for later.

"Why are there only 180 people in the voice chat?" Bishop Wood asked. "Aren't 200 people online in the guild?"

"It's fine. For now, we can catch all those spy alt accounts hiding in our guild. I'll kick them out later," Echoes of Spring said serenely. "Trading opens at nine so there's twenty minutes left. Everyone, go form your parties. Their guild has two strong parties, and I've posted their IDs in the public chat. If you encounter them, don't engage—leave them to my and Yearning For's parties to handle."

Jing Huan logged into the game as he listened. As soon as he entered *Nine Heroes*, a party invite popped up.

【Yearning For invites you to join his party. Yes, No.】

It startled Jing Huan a little, but he immediately clicked to join.

"Gege." His voice was a little raspy since he had woken up not long ago. "I saw you as soon as I logged in. Guess today is my lucky day."

Xiang Huaizhi led him to the main city and threw a bunch of high-tier potions at him. "I watched you log off yesterday."

Jing Huan's brain was a bit slow to catch up. "Wha…?"

"I was waiting for you," Xiang Huaizhi said. "It has nothing to do with luck."

Jing Huan had logged off in a wilderness map yesterday. Trading with NPCs hadn't opened yet, so assassins from both guilds had been hunting the wilderness maps for lone guild members. Just in case someone decided to make Jing Huan a target, Xiang Huaizhi came to get him.

Chapter 14

Jing Huan blinked, silently digesting this information. Yearning For had been waiting for him to log in?

When silence followed on the voice chat, Xiang Huaizhi realized he'd said too much. He hurried to add, "I was just picking up a party member. Even if it were Long Road Ahead stuck on a wilderness map, I'd still go get him."

He gave Jing Huan little time to think as he dragged the others into the party.

"Aaaah, this is so exciting. I can't wait anymore." xoxoYuyu was practically vibrating with excitement. "How much longer until trading opens?"

Love is Sharing Noms replied, "We're in the last few minutes."

"Let's find a spot first," Lu Hang said. "We'll go to the Silk Road since it's a place all merchants must pass through."

The Silk Road map was teeming with players—members from both Idle Pavilion and Limitless filled the area, joined by alt characters from various guilds and servers, all drawn here to witness the thrilling chaos of battle.

Even though Jing Huan was a veteran, this was the first time he had seen such a sight in the game. He couldn't help but sit up straighter in anticipation.

[Megaphone] Half a Lifetime: Idle Pavilion, you have three minutes to surrender. [Smug]

Why did Lu Wenhao sound like an idiot? People who spouted this kind of shit right before a big battle didn't survive more than two chapters in a novel. He longed to tell his dormmate to tone it down, but he was afraid of giving himself away, so he gave up on that idea.

At 9 a.m. sharp, the fierce battle began, and the Silk Road was reduced to a battlefield. Xiang Huaizhi was about to go after the enemy guild's merchants when he saw Half a Lifetime was walking at the front, exuding on a grandiose air as he led his party toward them.

Xiang Yu was ready to fight, but for some reason, her ge suddenly turned and ran, putting himself out of Half a Lifetime's attack range.

She stared blankly. "Ge, isn't Half a Lifetime part of their main parties? Why aren't you engaging?"

Xiang Huaizhi said shortly, "I saw their guild's merchants. We're going to prioritize killing them."

Jing Huan had just breathed a sigh of relief when his WeChat chimed.

Lu Wenhao: @Little Jing~, Damn it, Huanhuan, I was so close to getting to Yearning For, but he turned around and ran as soon as he saw me! What a coward!!

Little Jing~: ...In that case, it's probably better to just let it go.

Lu Wenhao: ?

Lu Wenhao: Don't worry, I won't let him get away. Just wait: today, your bro will teach him a lesson he won't forget!

Teach him a lesson my ass. Stay away from me, thank you very much.

Unfortunately, God didn't hear Jing Huan's prayer. The two parties still clashed three hours later.

"Fuck! Why are they still chasing us?" A bewildered Lu Hang muted his microphone to ask Xiang Huaizhi aloud. "Who initiated the battle?"

 Chapter 14

Xiang Huaizhi's lips pursed. "They did."

Lu Hang fell silent. If they launched a counter-kill attack, there was a high chance Lu Wenhao and Gao Zixiang would lose their equipment.

Xiang Huaizhi glanced at the little spirit fox next to him. Since entering combat, Jing Huan hadn't said a word, his movements noticeably panicked. Meanwhile, the opponents stuck to the ruthless strategy of targeting the healers first, attacking the Putuo Mountain and Spirit Fox Den relentlessly.

"Fuck man, what kind of situation is this?" Lu Hang scratched his head. "What now? Should I just reveal our names and get them to back off?"

Xiang Huaizhi dodged one of the enemy's skills and quickly threw a health potion to the little spirit fox.

"No." He hesitated for a moment before making a quick decision. "Do as I say."

Lu Wenhao was once again immobilized by the opposing Spirit Fox Den. He swore loudly.

"If you were half as accurate as her, we wouldn't be struggling this much," Gao Zixiang said only to have a large chunk of his health taken out by Yearning For's sword. He immediately retreated. "Tch, I don't think we can win this."

"That Spirit Fox Den is definitely using cheats! I'm going to report her later!" Lu Wenhao fumed. "We might not be able to but, dammit, we have to try! What if we get lucky? Besides, I don't think Yearning For's playing well today. He's taken a lot of damage from you."

Twenty minutes later, their health points were nearly depleted, and they were almost out of health potions.

"Even if he plays like shit, his equipment is still more than capable of crushing us." Gao Zixiang sighed. "Forget it, let's first decide on what to do if we lose our equipment."

"I don't care," Lu Wenhao said. "I'll compensate the other three if they lose their equipment."

Their healer's mana had been exhausted, and the enemies clearly noticed. Yearning For quickly switched to a saber and charged straight for them. Just when everyone thought the healer was doomed, something unexpected happened.

The black-robed man sprinted, saber aimed right for the healer, when he froze in the middle of the map. The pause was so abrupt, no one had time to react.

Gao Zixiang's shock didn't last long. With a rare opportunity standing still in front of him, he unleashed a combo attack on Yearning For. Yearning For didn't even make any attempts to dodge, taking all the damage head-on.

Jing Huan came back to his senses and quickly healed him up, tentatively calling out, "Gege?"

"Oh crap." xoxoYuyu turned on her microphone. "Long Road Ahead just messaged me. He said their dorm lost power."

Jing Huan then noticed their party's Warlock also hadn't moved in a long time. When a *Nine Heroes* player unexpectedly lost connection, there was a ten-minute delay before they could log off, and for those in combat, that delay happened only after the battle ended. This meant Yearning For's character was stuck in the game until this battle was over.

Chapter 14

"What do we do now?" Love is Sharing Noms asked as she healed the other two.

"It's fine," xoxoYuyu said composedly. "Our enemies haven't healed themselves up in a while, so they're probably out of potions. With me just DPSing, we should be fine."

No sooner had she finished speaking, the enemy healer suddenly chugged a mana potion and began diligently healing their party members again.

xoxoYuyu was shocked. "Did I remember wrong?!"

Jing Huan frowned. He had also been keeping an eye on the opponent's potion usage. Each player could only carry twenty potion slots, so the healer's potions should've been used up by now.

"Ha ha ha, bet you didn't expect that, did you?" Lu Wenhao turned his voice chat to All so he could taunt them, "We had someone deliver us potions. Get ready to *die*!"

Had his roommate's voice always been this punchable?

xoxoYuyu fought back immediately, spitting. "*Ptui*! You have some damn nerve saying that! Do you have no fucking shame?"

"There's no rule against having potions delivered during a wilderness map PK, is there?" Lu Wenhao countered. "How can a girl swear like that? By the way, why aren't your party leader and Warlock moving?"

xoxoYuyu spat out, "We decided to go easy on you seeing how pitifully noob you guys are."

Jing Huan heaved a sigh. He wanted to tell xoxoYuyu to stop wasting her energy. Words that would've incensed other men merely bounced right off Lu Wenhao.

As expected, Lu Wenhao smirked. "Disconnected, huh? Tsk tsk tsk, that's what you call divine retribution; evil gets its just deserts!"

WeChat suddenly chimed and Jing Huan shot a quick glance at it.

Xiang: Run.

Before Jing Huan could reply, Bishop Wood's voice came through his headset.

"Hello ladies," Bishop Wood said. "Yearning For asked me to come get you. Leave your party and join mine, and I can take you back to the main city with my Invincibility Medallion." A special item obtained by completing quests, an Invincibility Medallion gave a player temporary immunity for five minutes.

xoxoYuyu was reluctant and did not want to give up. "We can kill them off!"

"No, you can't." Bishop Wood said calmly. "Their guild members are using alt characters to deliver potions. There's no way you can win when it's three against five."

Love is Sharing Noms asked, "What about God Xiang and Long Road Ahead?"

"Two people dying is still better than five," Bishop Wood said gently. "Leave the party and come with me. Don't waste your time on them. There will always be another chance to get revenge."

xoxoYuyu hesitated at length before sulkily relenting. "Okay."

Seeing them retreat, Lu Wenhao let out a cackle. "What's this? You were so fierce a moment ago, but now you're running away with your tail between your legs?"

Chapter 14

"If our party members hadn't disconnected, you'd have been toast already!" xoxoYuyu yelled.

Lu Wenhao guffawed. "Luck is also a part of one's strength, you little coward, nyahahaha."

"You'll pay for this!" xoxoYuyu shouted then hurriedly joined Bishop Wood's party.

Jing Huan continued casting Healing Springs as he watched the man standing still and stuck in the middle of the map take a harsh thrashing.

"Bishop Wood," he suddenly said, "how did you know my gege disconnected?"

"He DMed me to come save you guys." After pulling the other two into the party, Bishop Wood urged her, "Hurry and leave! I'll bring you back."

Jing Huan hesitated for half a minute, his hands simultaneously casting skills while he dodged Gao Zixiang's attacks.

"I'm not going," he quickly decided. "Take the other two."

Bishop Wood was stunned. "Why?"

Why else? I want to see Yearning For die with my own eyes!!!

Jing Huan said seriously, "What if gege logs back in?"

Bishop Wood was speechless. "The chance of that happening is slim to none. By the time they get to an internet café, the battle would be long over."

Bishop Wood spent a few valiant minutes trying to persuade her but she was stubborn and refused to change her mind. With the time limit of the Invincibility Medallion quickly running out, he had no choice but to bring the other two back to the main city.

Jing Huan was preparing to go AFK and wait for death when he heard Lu Wenhao call out softly, "Is that Sweet Little Jing-meimei?"

It's your daddy. Jing Huan expressionlessly typed a smiling emoticon.

[Current] Sweet Little Jing: ^^ He he.

Gao Zixiang's hands never stopped moving even as he scolded Lu Wenhao. "Hurry up and seal her! Why are you flirting with her? Saw an opportunity to mess around while your wife isn't here?"

"Don't rush me, I just want to chat with her a bit." Lu Wenhao continued using the All voice chat. "Sweet Little Jing-meimei, why aren't you running away?"

[Current] Sweet Little Jing: Don't wanna.

Lu Wenhao exclaimed, "You're pretty gutsy! This ge admires you!"

Damn it, why does this guy have so much shit to say when killing someone?

[Current] Sweet Little Jing: ^^ He he.

"Sweet Little Jing-meimei, I'm actually a huge fan of yours," Lu Wenhao said. "Really! I listen to your rendition of 'Loyalty to the Country' all day."

[Current] Sweet Little Jing: ^^ He he, thanks.

"You're welcome." Lu Wenhao snapped his fingers. "Meimei, how about this: why don't you sing it for me live and I won't kill you. How does that sound?"

[Current] Sweet Little Jing: ?

Lu Wenhao sniggered. "But I wouldn't mind if you sing

something else like "Meow, Meow, Meow," or "Shape Up." Whatever you like…"

What Jing Huan wanted to do was buy a suona[2], storm back to the dormitory, and blast it unceasingly into Lu Wenhao's ears. Lu Wenhao babbled on for the next few minutes. Impatient and not wanting to waste any more time, Gao Zixiang knocked down the two disconnected players.

"Sweet Little Jing-meimei, sorry. If you want to blame someone, blame yourself for taking up with the wrong man."

Wrong. I blame myself for having two dumbass roommates.

Jing Huan watched helplessly as the opposing Mage's Thunderstrike blasted the little spirit fox to smithereens. The game screen shifted, dumping him back in the respawn point. Jing Huan felt a little disoriented. He hadn't been back here ever since he joined Yearning For's party.

The respawn point was crowded with people. From a quick glance, Jing Huan saw they were either from their guild or from the Limitless guild, and amongst them, the most eye-catching figure of them all was one who wielded a dark, long sword: Yearning For.

Before Jing Huan could see how much gold and experience points he had lost, his cellphone rang.

Lu Wenhao crowed, "Mwa ha ha ha ha, Huanhuan, your bro has avenged you! I killed Yearning For! Am I awesome or what?!"

Jing Huan said flatly, "Awesome."

---

2   The suona - 唢呐 - suǒnà is a traditional Chinese double-reed wind instrument with a loud, piercing sound often used in festive occasions such as weddings and temple fairs, as well as funerals and other ceremonies. It was a subtle death threat.

"You don't sound very happy!" Lu Wenhao complained. "Didn't you hear what I said? I killed Yearning For! Annihilated him!"

"A-annihilated?" Jing Huan repeated haltingly.

"Yeah! Ah, too bad you weren't there." Lu Wenhao shook his head and clicked his tongue. "I even chased their party's Spirit Fox Den around the entire map. They were completely powerless to fight back!"

The completely powerless Spirit Fox Den said, "He he."

Oblivious to Jing Huan's odd tone, Lu Wenhao cheerfully offered, "Want to see the screenshots?"

"What screenshots?"

"The in-game ones, of course. I took more than a dozen of 'em!" Lu Wenhao said, chortling. "I have complete 360-degree, no-dead-angle screenshots of Yearning For falling to the ground. I'll send you a few so you can have a good laugh."

Jing Huan's face was twisted into a complicated expression. He didn't know what to say.

The screenshots of Yearning For's corpse on the ground arrived as soon as he hung up. The black-robed man lay in a crumpled heap on the ground, his long sword fallen from his hand and barely glowing.

After staring at the screenshots multiple times, Jing Huan finally confirmed one thing: he didn't feel happy that Yearning For had been killed.

It was quite strange. After all, his initial purpose for reinstalling *Nine Heroes* was to see Yearning For fall dead over and over again. Could this uncomfortable feeling be because he wasn't the one who personally killed him? Jing Huan absentmindedly pondered, glancing at the in-game chat channel from the corner of his eye.

 Chapter 14

[World] Maybe Someday: Are these damn players from Idle Pavilion and Limitless blind? I'm just an innocent bystander! Why are you killing me, fuck!!

[World] Background Noise: Don't go to the Silk Road for the time being. Those guys are out for blood and they don't give a crap as to which guild you're from...

[World] Fate Stones Hurt: Holy shit, is that actually Yearning For at the respawn point?? Am I just hallucinating from my all-nighter??

[World] Suddenly Looking Back: You're not hallucinating. The Limitless players killed Yearning For. But since you've been awake until now... I suggest you go to sleep soon to preserve your life.

[World] Peaceful or Not: You're kidding? You're saying Yearning For couldn't beat people from Limitless? Then Idle Pavilion must be fucked.

[World] Fated With You: Idle Pavilion has more than just Yearning For's party! Echoes of Spring's party is also strong. I'm still rooting for Idle Pavilion!

[World] Alt888: Not surprised. Yearning For's skills have always been mediocre. I just watched the whole battle, and his positioning was simply garbage... He's only so OP because he has a divine artifact. What a poser.

[World] BrbOrNot: Better than a loser who creates an alt to badmouth others passive-aggressively. [Smile]

[World] YaMo: He was really killed? Is Match Made in Heaven's server's battle party that impressive? Why haven't I heard of them before?

[World] Seaweed Maiden: Yearning For and Long Road Ahead were only killed because they disconnected. All you haters can disperse now.

[World] Alt888: Oh, so now we're bringing hater and fan culture into gaming? I bet they're just saying they were AFK because they lost and feel ashamed.

Alt888 managed to successfully stir the chat channel into a chaotic quagmire all by themselves.

Jing Huan scanned through a few more messages, and then he muted the World Channel chat. These people must have too much damn time on their hands, going out of their way to create alts for the sake of causing trouble. How senseless and malicious.

He moved his mouse, and the little spirit fox spun around Yearning For. It wasn't until after she had completed the twirl that Jing Huan realized what he had done. *Hold on. The scumbag isn't even here, who am I trying to please? Habits are the worst!*

Jing Huan had just turned to leave when a system notification popped up.

【Your friend Yearning For has come online.】

...Huh?

...Huh???

Jing Huan was stupefied, but the little spirit fox wasn't—she had taken two steps before whipping around and bolting back to Yearning For's side.

[Current] Sweet Little Jing: ?

[Current] Yearning For: ?

[Current] Not My Cup of Tea: ?

Chapter 14

[Current] With You: ...?

[Current] Just One Ladle: ??

The players who had merely been pretending to be AFK confusedly played "Follow the Leader" as they typed question mark after question mark.

【Yearning For invites you to join his party. Yes, No.】

After Jing Huan clicked "Yes," the two of them formed a party at the respawn point, but they didn't immediately teleport away.

"Gege," Jing Huan said after a moment. "Is it really you?"

"Mm," Xiang Huaizhi murmured, "just got power back."

Jing Huan opened his mouth but words failed him. At last, he let out a weak "oh..."

Xiang Huaizhi also didn't speak. All of a sudden, he asked, "Why didn't you leave earlier?"

Jing Huan was about to answer but he apparently had more to say. "Weren't you going to be my little widow? Why did you die with me instead?"

Jing Huan's ears turned red. *Your. Little. Widow? Did I ever say that? I never said that. This scumbag is really shameless. Even in death, he's still expecting me to be his widow and mourn for him.*

While he was cursing up a storm in his heart, the person at the other end of his headset spoke again—all to annoy him. "Hmm?"

"I...changed my mind at the last second," Jing Huan explained slowly. "What's so good about being a widow? I'd rather be a happy ghost couple with gege."

Jing Huan glanced at the system announcement. He had lost gold and experience points. The money wasn't a huge deal, but the lost

experience points, more than thirty million of them, made his heart hurt a little. It would take him a week to grind back every last one of those experience points.

"How much did you lose?" Xiang Huaizhi asked.

"Not much, just about eighty gold," Jing Huan said listlessly. "But I lost over thirty million experience points though."

【Yearning For gave you 100 gold.】

Jing Huan immediately threw the money back. "What are you doing?"

Xiang Huaizhi threw the money once more, but this time, it turned into 300 gold. "We wouldn't have lost if I didn't get disconnected."

For a fleeting moment, Jing Huan felt a twinge of guilt. If it wasn't for him, Lu Wenhao wouldn't have engaged Yearning For in a fight. However, that smidgen of guilt was quickly brushed off.

After a moment of thought, Jing Huan kept eighty gold for himself, and threw the rest back. "I don't want the extra, gege."

Xiang Huaizhi didn't insist. "I'll help you grind back the experience later."

Jing Huan was silent for a long time before he finally said, "Okay."

The battle between Idle Pavilion and Limitless went on for three days straight with no signs of abating. The Silk Road was still bustling, and assassination squads from both guilds were on high alert across various wilderness maps. However, the intensity of the battles was no longer as high as it was on the first day since everyone had other real-life commitments and couldn't stay online 24/7.

To address this, Echoes of Spring compiled stats of when the

 Chapter 14

guild members were online and organized various parties according to those stats. Jing Huan and his party were assigned to cover the time slot from 7:00 p.m. to 10:00 p.m.

As soon as class ended that day, Lu Wenhao hooked his arm around Jing Huan and pulled him close, putting him in a headlock.

"Huanhuan, you heartless little thing, you can't just abandon your bros just because you got a girlfriend!" he scolded. "How many days has it been since you Netflix and chilled with us?"

"When have I ever Netflix and chilled with you guys?" Jing Huan said but didn't break free from his hold. "And how many times do I have to repeat myself? I don't have a girlfriend."

Gao Zixiang stuck his hands in his pockets. "Then, why are you rushing back home after class every day?"

To kill your guild members, duh.

"To watch the *LoL* matches. Don't you know that season nine has started?" Jing Huan felt his throat itch, coughed, and lazily asked, "Didn't you guys have that server merge? Why do you have so much free time every day?"

"Our guild has arranged duty shifts, so the two of us have the noon shift." Lu Wenhao smirked. "I heard Yearning For scheduled his shift to be in the evening to avoid us. I'm thinking of asking the guild leader to swap time slots."

Why did he have to bring it up? At the mention, Jing Huan mourned the loss of his thirty million experience points.

"There are so many people in your guild, you can't just swap shifts at will. Don't make a fuss." Jing Huan patted his hand. "Let go, I need to go back."

Lu Wenhao didn't move. "Come on..."

"Jing Huan."

Hearing someone call him, Jing Huan turned around with considerable effort. It was Xiang Huaizhi who stood behind him. He chuckled. "Ge?"

Xiang Huaizhi frowned, staring intently at their positions. After a while, he asked, "What are you guys doing?"

Lu Wenhao greeted him cheerfully, "Hello, Senior."

Xiang Huaizhi didn't even spare him a look, uttering an icy "mm."

"Nothing, we just got out of class." Jing Huan patted Lu Wenhao's chubby hand again, this time with some force. "You damn... Let go already."

Lu Wenhao released him, feigning hurt. "You've changed. You used to let me hug you all the time."

Jing Huan laughed. "Fuck off, when did I ever let you hug me? You two better hurry up, or there won't be any seats left in the cafeteria."

"Jing Huan," Xiang Huaizhi said again.

"Hm?"

Xiang Huaizhi had wanted to invite him to dinner, but when he remembered they had Silk Road duty soon, the words on the tip of his tongue changed to, "Let's head back together?" The two men walked toward the back gate, their shoulders touching.

Lu Wenhao rubbed his belly. "Xiang'er, let's go too. If we wait any longer, we really won't get to eat... What are you looking at?"

Gao Zixiang watched the two leave. He frowned. "Nothing. It's just a bit strange."

Lu Wenhao was puzzled. "What's strange?"

"Senior Xiang seemed to be...I don't know...quite cold toward us?"

Lu Wenhao laughed. "Isn't he notoriously cold to people?"

"But he's very good to Huanhuan."

Lu Wenhao choked. "I suppose... But Huanhuan has always been very likable. Maybe Senior Xiang likes him too and that's why he's good to him."

Gao Zixiang returned Lu Wenhao's gaze, expression conflicted. He had initially brushed it off but his roommate's words sent his imagination running wild.

"Why are you looking at me like that?" Lu Wenhao asked, baffled. "Are we still eating or what?"

Gao Zixiang gave up trying to have a conversation with him. "Yes, yes, eat until you drop, let's go."

When Jing Huan logged into *Nine Heroes*, his party members were already there waiting for him.

[Party] Sweet Little Jing: Waaaaah, sorry for being late. QAQ

"It's okay, Xiangxiang also just came back." Lu Hang stretched. "Why aren't you using your mic?"

[Party] Sweet Little Jing: My throat doesn't feel too good today.

Maybe he had strained it from talking so much these past few days, but there was something wrong with his throat. It was nothing serious—a tickle in his throat and the occasional cough. The other reason why he wasn't using his microphone today was because he didn't feel like putting on the cute act. He was closed for business.

Xiang Huaizhi paused. He hadn't noticed anything different in Jing Huan's voice a few minutes ago.

"Have you taken any medicine?" Xiang Huaizhi asked.

[Party] Sweet Little Jing: Nope. Gege, it's just a bit of a cold from the change in seasons. It's nothing serious.

"You should be careful then. It's been really cold here lately. I even have to use a blanket in the dorm." Lu Hang then offhandedly asked, "Where do you live, Little Jingjing?"

Jing Huan began, "I live…"

"Do you all have everything?" Xiang Huaizhi led them toward the Silk Road, subtly cutting Lu Hang off. "Keep an eye on your health later; don't worry about saving your potions. If you need more, just ask me."

Lu Hang would never miss a chance to take advantage of his dear roommate. "Do you have any extra Spirit Restoration Incense too?"

Xiang Huaizhi threw him five Spirit Restoration Incenses, successfully shutting him up.

Fearing that Yearning For would seek revenge against Lu Wenhao, the Limitless guild leader had deliberately assigned Lu Wenhao to the noon shift. With no scruples now, Xiang Huaizhi became unstoppable, cutting down everything in his path. He never returned to the respawn point again. In just three days, more than a dozen "God Xiang's Brilliant Gameplay Highlights" videos appeared on the forum.

"Why are there only 'God Xiang's Brilliant Gameplay' and no 'God Road's Brilliant Gameplay'?" Lu Hang grumbled. "How come none of these netizens have eyes that can appreciate true beauty?"

Chapter 14

Love is Sharing Noms sighed. "How much longer will all this fighting go on? I still want to do the Realm of Lovers event. It's been out for two days already."

Lu Hang asked curiously, "Who are you doing it with?"

"With one of my alt characters," Love is Sharing Noms said. "I just want that limited edition outfit."

To complete the Realm of Lovers event quests, players needed to find various NPCs in the wilderness maps. However, with assassin squads camping every wilderness map, it was near impossible to complete the event quests without incident.

Lu Hang pondered. "It should be soon, I guess. We already have way more guild funds than them."

At 10:00 p.m., the five of them got off their shift on time, not lingering any longer than necessary.

They had wiped out seven parties today. When their party returned to the main city, Jing Huan couldn't help but twist his neck from side to side, feeling utterly drained. As luck would have it, it seemed he really had caught a cold.

Xiang Huaizhi was about to take Jing Huan to do dailies when he noticed the little spirit fox was the first to leave the party.

[Friend] Yearning For: ?

[Friend] Sweet Little Jing: What's up gege~

[Friend] Yearning For: Are you doing dailies?

[Friend] Sweet Little Jing: I will.

[Friend] Sweet Little Jing: But can you wait a bit? I want to go downstairs for a moment.

[Friend] Yearning For: What for?

[Friend] Sweet Little Jing: To buy medicine.

Guide on How to Fail at Online Dating

Xiang Huaizhi's fingers paused slightly, then he typed: *Go ahead.*

"Echoes of Spring mentioned this in the guild group chat." Lu Hang stood up and stretched his body. "But Limitless seems to be on the verge of defeat. They're currently in negotiations with the other guilds, hoping to form an alliance against us. Think any of them will work with them?" Lu Hang waited but when no response seemed forthcoming, he turned around. "Xiangxiang?"

Xiang Huaizhi said blandly, "Don't know."

Lu Hang checked the time and threw on a coat. "It's still early, so I'm going to go next door to play some cards. Don't lock the door."

His roommate left, and Xiang Huaizhi was alone in their dormitory. He sat up straight, but a few seconds later, he let go of the mouse and leaned back in his chair. The room was completely silent, and in that moment, his feelings became clear.

Their school was in a remote location, and had only two pharmacies nearby: one at the front gate, and one at the back.

I want to go downstairs. I want to see him.

Xiang Huaizhi wasn't surprised by this idea, but when these feelings had begun growing inside of his heart, he couldn't quite pinpoint.

His cellphone on the table vibrated slightly.

Little Jing~: Fuck, the pharmacy downstairs is closed... Where exactly is the one at the front gate again??

【Little Jing~ recalled a message.】

Xiang: ?

Little Jing~: I pressed the wrong sticker, gege~ [Cute]

 Chapter 14

Xiang Huaizhi lowered his gaze, and he opened the sticker packs. He rifled through them but couldn't find one that he wanted to reply with. In the end, he just crammed his cellphone into his pocket.

Jing Huan's feet dragged as he left the pharmacy with his medicine. The cold wind slapped his face, and he immediately sneezed. Rubbing his nose, he looked up and spotted Xiang Huaizhi standing by the bus stop.

Both hands stuffed in his pockets, Xiang Huaizhi looked quietly back at him. For one bizarre second, Jing Huan got the impression he had been waiting for him.

Jing Huan dismissed that outlandish notion and instinctively walked toward Xiang Huaizhi. "Ge, why are you here? Waiting for someone?"

Xiang Huaizhi shook his head. "Doing a night jog."

A night jog in this cold weather? The moment winter greeted their city, all Jing Huan wanted to do was curl up in his blanket and never emerge.

"No wonder you're in such good shape," Jing Huan praised sincerely. "Well then, I'm heading back first. Keep at it."

"Let's go together." Xiang Huaizhi fell into step beside him, expression unchanged. "I'm done jogging anyway."

But sir, you don't look like someone who just finished a jog.

Jing Huan was confused but didn't press further. "Okay."

"Did you catch a cold?" Xiang Huaizhi glanced at the pharmacy bag in his hand.

With a laugh, Jing Huan said, "Yeah, I was careless."

"It's been getting colder lately. Be sure to keep warm."

"You as well, ge."

Xiang Huaizhi noticed Jing Huan searching their vicinity. "What are you looking for?"

"Nothing, I'm just checking if anyone is taking pictures of us." Jing Huan stopped looking around. Despite the nasal sound due to his being sick, his tone still held a mischievous note. "If I catch them, I'll beat them up."

Xiang Huaizhi tilted his head, lowering his gaze to stare at him. From his angle, he could see the curve of Jing Huan's nape. He wasn't even wearing a scarf, leaving his slender, fair neck fully exposed. The memory of Lu Wenhao looping an arm around Jing Huan's neck flashed through his mind, and a small wrinkle appeared between his eyebrows.

"Does it bother you?"

The question took Jing Huan by surprise and he turned around. "Hm?"

"The photos being taken," Xiang Huaizhi said. "Does it bother you a lot?"

"Not really." Jing Huan licked his lips. "I just don't like being photographed, that's all. It's weird."

Xiang Huaizhi nodded, and then, as if he just remembered something, asked, "By the way, how's it going? The thing with the person you like?"

It took Jing Huan a long time to remember exactly what Xiang Huaizhi was talking about. The lie he had told was already out there, and he couldn't reel it back in, so all that was left for him to do was continue spinning it. "Nothing much, haven't caught them yet."

Chapter 14

It was true to some extent.

"Do you like that person a lot?"

Jing Huan turned to stare at him.

Xiang Huaizhi felt a little flustered at Jing Huan's scrutiny, but his face betrayed none of his inner emotions. "What's wrong?"

Jing Huan laughed, his eyes curving into crescents. "Nothing, I just noticed that you seem quite interested in the person I like."

"Just asking since it came to mind," Xiang Huaizhi said. "It's okay if you don't want to talk about it."

"Yeah, I like them." Jing Huan affirmed in a relaxed voice. "Why would I pursue them if I didn't like them?"

The streets were almost empty save for a few people. On the outside, it seemed like the two men were friends based on the casual chitchat between them. Only Xiang Huaizhi knew he was being confessed to.

A secret, subdued joy rose within him, along with an indescribable restlessness. He wanted to come clean and reveal his identity as Yearning For. He wanted to ask Jing Huan what exactly it was that he really liked about him, and then ask him whether the real-life version of himself was more appealing than his in-game character.

Jing Huan exhaled a breath of warm air, complaining, "But I'm getting tired of pursuing them lately."

Xiang Huaizhi flinched and turned to look at him. "Hm?"

"No matter what I do, I'm not getting anywhere with them. It's getting a bit frustrating," Jing Huan said half-jokingly and half-seriously. "I don't want to pursue them anymore."

I might as well buy five in-game accounts to kill him with. That'd be quicker, not to mention, more satisfying.

Xiang Huaizhi's heart sank, and even his footsteps grew a bit heavier. "You're giving up?"

Instead of answering, Jing Huan asked his own question, "Ge, have you ever pursued anyone before?"

Jing Huan's eyes were especially bright in the dim light. Xiang Huaizhi held his gaze for a moment before looking away. "No."

Jing Huan nodded. The wind must've muddled him; how could a guy like Xiang Huaizhi ever be the pursuerer?

Xiang Huaizhi pursed his lips and wanted to continue his line of questioning when he realized they had already reached the back gate.

"Ge, my apartment is right here, so I'll go up first." Jing Huan waved at him. "Good night."

It wasn't until the young man's figure disappeared into the building that Xiang Huaizhi snapped out of it. In those brief minutes, all that filled his mind was that one sentence: "I don't want to pursue them anymore."

Jing Huan got home, poured himself a cup of hot water, and took some medicine. Afterward, he climbed into bed with his laptop and pulled the blanket up to his shoulders. After some shifting around to find a comfortable position, he looked up and realized the two characters in the game were motionless. The two of them, one in front of the other, stood quietly together near Qingxuan Terrace.

Jing Huan disabled following mode and twirled around Yearning For twice.

[Party] Sweet Little Jing: Gege?

No response. Maybe he had to go do something. Jing Huan

 Chapter 14

didn't mind. He rolled over and lay in bed playing with his cellphone.

When Xiang Huaizhi returned to the dormitory, Lu Hang was sitting on his bed searching for something.

"Where'd you go so late?" Lu Hang turned, looking at him with a perplexed expression.

Xiang Huaizhi didn't bother making up another excuse, so he just used the same one as before. "Night jog."

That did nothing to alleviate Lu Hang's confusion. "It's half past ten, and you went on a night jog? Wearing that thick jacket?"

"Can't I?"

Lu Hang frowned and said, "Sure, you can." *You could even go for a night flight if you wanted.*

He found his wallet and stuffed it into his pocket. "Xiangxiang, I'll be staying next door tonight. I've made plans to play cards with them all night. Don't miss me too much."

Xiang Huaizhi nodded. "It'd be best if you played for the whole week."

"How could I bear to be away from you for that long?" Lu Hang said as he opened the door. Halfway out the door, he didn't forget to add, "You just wait! I'll treat you to a nice meal tomorrow with the money I'm going to win."

Xiang Huaizhi didn't hear him clearly, having just put on his headset. "Close the door."

He saw the person in his party had disabled following mode and was standing beside him. He opened the chat channel where there was a message from Jing Huan calling him gege. The time stamp indicated it had been sent ten minutes ago.

Guide on How to Fail at Online Dating

Jing Huan was woken up by his cellphone clattering to the ground. His eyes snapped open, confused, the corners of his eyes tinged red from sleepiness. The light above him beamed down on him, and he couldn't help but squint his eyes. It took a while for him to fully wake up.

Jing Huan turned over, his hand scrabbling around on the floor for his cellphone until he finally managed to find it. As soon as he picked it up, he checked the time.

4:23.

What the hell? He slept all the way into the afternoon?!

He gently rubbed his eyes, then unlocked the phone to read his messages.

Xiang: I felt like going to the supermarket. I just got back.

It was sent at half past ten last night.

Little Jing~: Gege, I fell asleep last night. QAQ Good afternoon...

The top of the chat quickly displayed the "Typing..." indicator. Jing Huan lay still, quietly waiting for him to reply.

Xiang: Afternoon?

Xiang: It's 4:30 a.m. right now.

Thunderstruck, Jing Huan yanked open the curtains and scanned outside... Oh. So, it was.

Little Jing~: I got it wrong!! TVT

Little Jing~: ...But gege, it's already 4:30 a.m. Why are you still awake?

Xiang Huaizhi didn't know the answer to that either. However, he wouldn't force himself to sleep. Since he didn't have any classes tomorrow, he brought his laptop to bed and selected a movie at

Chapter 14

random. Just as he started the second one, his cellphone screen lit up.

Xiang: I was watching movies. Why are you awake?

Little Jing~: My cellphone fell on the floor and scared me awake…

The tight corners of Xiang Huaizhi's mouth relaxed slightly as he imagined the scene.

The temperature had dropped sharply these past few days. Rain began to fall. In his hopeless endeavor to get himself to fall asleep, Xiang Huaizhi hadn't turned on the lights. The glow from his computer and cellphone were the only light sources in the room.

Xiang: Mm, you should go back to sleep.

Little Jing~: Okay, gege should also go to sleep soon. Good night.

It was the second good night tonight.

At first, Xiang Huaizhi typed out an "mm," but then Jing Huan's words from earlier tonight rang in his ears. After a while, he ducked his head and deleted the "mm."

Xiang: Good night.

Xiang: Put your cellphone away. See you tomorrow.

This should be warm enough, right? Xiang Huaizhi had never intentionally changed his attitude toward anyone before, so he was feeling a little uncertain. His fingers wavered over the sticker options.

Little Jing~: (*°∇°*)??

Little Jing~: Okay, nuzzle nuzzle.

Xiang: Mm.

Jing Huan looked at this "mm" and wondered if he was dreaming. Did Yearning For know what "nuzzle nuzzle" meant? He used to ban him from sending kissing stickers!

Maybe it was the loud noise the cellphone had made when it hit

Guide on How to Fail at Online Dating

the ground, or perhaps the rain was a little raucous, but Jing Huan couldn't fall back asleep. He rolled over. The laptop in front of his pillow was still on, and he noticed that Yearning For had taken them to Penglai. Their two characters stood on a bridge at the top of the map. It was a rather isolated location, but they were were somehow surrounded by a crowd.

Seeing that BrbOrNot was also next to them, Jing Huan instinctively opened the guild's WeChat group chat. Sure enough, he saw his name after scrolling just a bit.

BrbOrNot: 【Screenshot】 These two are already at a point in their relationship where they just AFK grind exp as a party in Penglai?!

Peach Cheese Stan: …If, one day, any of our guild officers have the irresistible urge to kill BON, please don't involve the rest of our party. The others are innocent. Just kill him.

BrbOrNot: That's not going to happen. Guild Officer Bishop Wood is so easygoing, Yearning For doesn't check the group chat, and Sweet Little Jing also wouldn't blame me. [Shy]

Bishop Wood: Don't be so sure about that. [Cleaver]

Silent Affection: They're in such a secluded spot, how did you know they were AFKing there?

BrbOrNot: I saw it while browsing the forum. One screenshot and there's already over 200 posts. God Xiang is seriously badass.

Jing Huan had long gotten used to BrbOrNot's antics. His heart was completely tranquil as he opened the forums.

BrbOrNot was right. The original poster of the thread had indeed only posted a single screenshot, opting to blur out their own character. He quickly skimmed through the posts.

Chapter 14

11L: What's strange about this? Our server's full of couples AFKing as a party in Penglai. PDA galore.

12L: The key point is that these two aren't a couple.

33L: What's the point of posting this? Wasting forum resources? We already know Sweet Little Jing is always clinging onto Yearning For. It's old news.

38L: ...But Yearning For's the party leader. Doesn't this mean Yearning For was the one who brought Sweet Little Jing to Penglai?

47L: Replying to 38, who knows how coy and needy Sweet Little Jing acts in private? I guess Yearning For probably got annoyed by her pestering and gave in.

Jing Huan closed the forum thread. Although he had always tried to convince himself by saying he wasn't Sweet Little Jing, it was clearly unsuccessful since posts like these still made him angry. Sleep was going to be impossible tonight.

A few seconds later, in a fit of rage, he tabbed back to the game interface and pressed the "Leave party" button. He'll just say he got disconnected tomorrow. With his excuse prepared, he controlled the little spirit fox to make her way to Penglai's exit.

[Friend] Yearning For: ?

[Friend] Sweet Little Jing: ...

Why are you, Mr. Yearning For, still awake and staring at the game?

[Friend] Yearning For: Weren't you going to sleep?

[Friend] Sweet Little Jing: ...The rain outside was too noisy. I couldn't go back to sleep.

[Friend] Yearning For: Then what are you planning on doing?

[Friend] Sweet Little Jing: IDK, maybe just stroll around.

[Friend] Yearning For: It's past midnight, do you want to do today's dailies?

Dailies, dailies, dailies... Do you know anything else other than dailies?! Boring scumbag!

[Friend] Sweet Little Jing: Don't want to. These past few days have been nothing but fighting and dailies. I don't want to see the sect master anymore. QAQ

[Friend] Yearning For: Then who do you want to see?

[Friend] Sweet Little Jing: Want to see gege. (*^▽^*)

The black-robed man on the bridge was already moving when Jing Huan sent those words.

【Yearning For invites you to join his party. Yes, No.】

...Fuck, I was just being polite. I didn't actually want to see you, man!!

Sweet Little Jing's escape had only lasted a scant two minutes before she was caught and dragged back into the party again. Jing Huan wanted nothing more than to screenshot the invite and shove it in those haters' faces on the forums.

It's your God Xiang who keeps inviting me every day, okay?! I'm not the one trying to party up to AFK with him!!

Because he hadn't spoken for a long time, Xiang Huaizhi's voice was a bit hoarse. "Not sleeping anymore?"

"Mm, I really can't sleep," Jing Huan said. "Weren't you watching a movie, gege?"

"Already closed it." Instead of returning to the bridge, Xiang Huaizhi led him toward the exit.

"Where are we going?" Jing Huan asked.

Chapter 14

"Running a quest."

So you didn't hear me say "I don't want to" just now, did you?

Whatever, Jing Huan thought while resting his chin on his hand. There wasn't much to do in the middle of the night anyway. Yearning For guided him back to the main city and all the way to the teleporter. Just as Jing Huan was about to start a movie to pass the time, he noticed the game scene suddenly change, signaling that they had entered a special zone.

The *Nine Heroes* developers had clearly put in a lot of effort. Each special event came with a unique event zone, and the Tree of Fated Bonds where they currently stood under was one of them. And it was here, they could take the Realm of Lovers quest. Before Jing Huan could react, the quest had already been accepted.

【Fairy of Fated Bonds: I heard that Rumo [Petal Valley (12, 11)] has always held a deep admiration for the Scholar [Main City Bookstore (12, 22)]. Please help her deliver a bouquet of peach blossoms to the scholar.】

Yearning For took him to the general store to buy peach blossoms. Jing Huan couldn't stand the silence and called out, "Gege..."

"Mm."

"Do you know what event this is?"

"Realm of Lovers."

Maybe he misunderstood something. Jing Huan tactfully said, "The experience points rewarded for this event are very low."

"I know." Xiang Huaizhi pressed his lips together. "You don't want to do it?"

Jing Huan blinked. *No, not really.* The process was so cumbersome,

and the rewards were absolute shit. Who would want to do this kind of quest? It was a complete waste of time!

"I want to." He laughed while rolling his eyes. "I want to do it with gege."

Xiang Huaizhi's Adam's apple bobbed. He quietly led Jing Huan to the wilderness map to track down the Scholar.

【Scholar: Miss Rumo is so thoughtful. Please help me deliver this letter to her.】

【Rumo: Ah, this really is his handwriting. [Blushing] So my wish was heard by the Fairy of Fated Bonds? Thank you. Please tell him I received the letter.】

【Scholar: Thank you for your hard work, young heroes. I just bought a hairpin on Long Street and thought it would be perfect for Miss Rumo. Please pass it on to her for me.】

【Rumo: What a beautiful hairpin! I've read his letter, and this is my reply. Along with this letter, please also help me give another peach blossom to Scholar-gege.】

Jing Huan paused, narrowing his eyes.

If you're asking us to deliver flowers, you should at least compensate us the money for peach blossoms. Am I your carrier pigeon? Do you two not have legs or something? What kind of crappy event is this?

Jing Huan was too exasperated to complain. After going back and forth several times, they finally reached the final confession scene of the quest.

【Rumo: This is a lock of my hair. Please deliver this and the letter to the Scholar.】

Chapter 14

Jing Huan breathed a sigh of relief, thinking that this idiotic quest was finally coming to an end.

【Scholar: (Surprised) Wh-what? Miss Rumo actually has such feelings for me?】

No, duh?! Why else would she send you flowers? Or keep sending you letters?! Jing Huan found it funny and laughed out loud. He couldn't help but tease, "I also have the same kind of feelings for gege."

Xiang Huaizhi paused when he heard this. The impatience that had accumulated while doing this tedious quest gradually faded away.

【Scholar: What should I do? I don't have romantic feelings for Miss Rumo.】

Jing Huan was once again full of questions. *If you felt nothing for her, why did you reply to her letters? Why give her the hairpin?*

【Scholar: It's like this... Because Miss Rumo bears so much resemblance to my late wife, she holds a special place in my heart. I truly didn't expect such a misunderstanding to happen... These are the peach blossoms and letters she sent me. Please help me return them to her. I really can't accept her feelings.】

Well, damn. The Realm of Lovers event quest had a bad ending. Didn't expect anything less from *Nine Heroes*.

After finishing the quest, Jing Huan looked at the experience points. They had been running back and forth for nearly ten minutes and only earned a few thousand experience points for their efforts. What a damn waste of time.

After handing in the quest, Jing Huan tentatively spoke up, "Gege, this event quest gave so little experience points."

"Mm." Xiang Huaizhi glanced at the quest reward details. "But the intimacy level shot up." With one event quest done, their intimacy level had increased by twenty points.

"So what?" Jing Huan said lazily. "It's not like you're going to marry me. Our intimacy level can only reach 9,999, max."

Xiang Huaizhi stopped moving his mouse. He lifted his eyes slightly and stared, transfixed, at the little spirit fox's tail. After a long interval, he asked, "When do you want to get married?"

"Your intimacy level with Long Road Ahead is also 9,999. Even if we grind intimacy levels to get to that point, there's no difference between him and me in gege's eyes... Huh?"

Jing Huan's eyes widened, suspecting that the sound of the rain outside had affected his hearing. He slowly tugged on the earphone cable, pulled the microphone right next to his mouth, and asked uncertainly, "What did you just say?"

Xiang Huaizhi suddenly recalled Jing Huan's scent—the faint smell of shampoo, carried by the wind and into his senses.

"I asked, when do you want to get married?"

Glossary

Guide on How to Fail at Online Dating

Xiang Huaizhi

Jing Huan

Guide on How to Fail at Online Dating

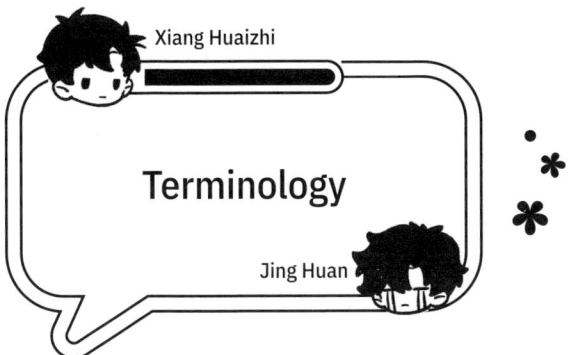

Terminology

AFK: An acronym for "Away from Keyboard," typically used in online settings and gaming. It can mean that someone is physically away from their computer, or it can also indicate that the game is minimized and they are "away from the game."

AFK Grinding: This can mean that the game has an "auto-battle" feature, where you can have your character automatically fight for a certain amount of turns while you are free to do anything else. This could also mean actively grinding but it requires low effort, such that you can do something else like browsing the internet while playing.

Alt: Short for "Alternate account," it is a secondary character created by a player for purposes of farming or to pretend to be a different person.

AoE: An acronym for "Area of Effect." It refers to any ability, spell, or action that affects multiple targets within a specific range, instead of just a single target.

 Glossary

Attributes: Specific stats, bonuses, or effects that enhance an item's performance or grant additional abilities to the user. These are things that influence a character's effectiveness in combat by modifying their damage, skills, healing output, etc.

Blind: This refers to attempting a dungeon, boss battle, quest, or any in-game activity for the first time without prior knowledge, preparation, or external guides (i.e. videos or tutorials). Players typically like to do this for newly released content.

Booster: A booster is typically a hired individual who plays your account for you to either farm, grind, increase your rank, level you up, or do anything that you specify. It's generally a paid service people use to maintain or increase their character rank/status.

Buff: A temporary effect that enhances a character's stats or abilities, such as increased health, damage, speed, healing, etc.

Camping: The act of staying in a specific location, often for a long period of time, to achieve a goal such as gathering resources, waiting for enemy spawns, or targeting other players to PK them.

Carry: Refers to a scenario where a skilled or powerful player (or party) helps a less experienced, under-leveled, or weaker player to complete content (a quest, a dungeon, etc). This term can also describe a player who performs exceptionally well in a party, so they "carry" the party to victory.

CC: An acronym for "Crowd Control," and is someone whose role in a party is focused on controlling their enemy by preventing them from moving, casting spells, etc.

Cooldown: The waiting period after using an ability, item, or skill before it can be used again.

Crafting: The process of creating items such as weapons, armor, potions, tools, or other in-game items using materials gathered in dungeons, wilderness maps, or other methods.

Dailies: This refers to daily quests, dungeons, or any task that reset every 24 hours, allowing players repeated opportunities to earn rewards. This encourages players to regularly log in to do them every day. If something resets every week, it is called "weeklies."

Debuff: A temporary or permanent negative effect applied to a character or enemy that weakens their stats or abilities.

Direct Message (DM): This is a private communication channel between players, anything that is considered a one-on-one conversation is a DM. This includes things like in-game private chats, whispers, or when you message a single person.

DPS: An acronym for "Damage Per Second," which in gaming means, someone whose role in a party is focused on dealing damage to their enemy.

 Glossary

Dungeon: A party-based instance where players face challenges, enemies, and bosses, often for rewards like gear and experience.

Equipment: This refers to the items a character wears to enhance their abilities, stats, and performance. This includes weapons, armor, accessories, and tools and is important to a player's gameplay.

Experience Points: A numerical measure of a character's progress toward leveling up, earned through completing quests, defeating enemies, or other in-game activities.

Farming: The intentional and repetitive collection of specific resources, items, or materials. It is used interchangeably with "grinding" except typically for loot.

Gear: This is a more casual way to refer to a player's worn equipment.

Grinding: Repetitive actions like killing enemies, doing quests, or crafting to gain experience, resources, or items.

Health Points: The numerical representation of a character's life. When health points reach zero, the character dies and needs to respawn.

Inventory: A character's personal storage space for holding items such as gear, weapons, crafting materials, quest items, potions, etc. There is often a limited amount of inventory slots, and excess needs to be stored in a storage box.

Loot: Items, gear, or currency that is dropped by enemies or obtained from completing quests, challenges, or dungeons.

Level: A level in *Nine Heroes* represents a measure of the character's progression, strength, and overall experience points in the game. Levels are gained by earning experience points.

Leveling: The process of advancing a character's level by reaching the required experience points through activities like completing quests, defeating enemies, or participating in events. Leveling a character increases a character's stats, unlocks new abilities, and can unlock new maps or zones.

Main: Short for "Main Account," which is the primary character that a player focuses on, and usually plays on a game.

Mana Points: A resource used to cast spells or activate abilities. Mana is consumed when using abilities and can regenerate over time, or with the help of items or skills.

Marketplace: An official buying and selling platform in *Nine Heroes* that allows players to spend real-life money for in-game items.

Merchant Union: In *Nine Heroes*, this is where players sell their in-game items to other players for in-game currency.

Glossary

Mob: A mob, short for mobile or mobile object, is a computer-controlled non-player character (NPC), or an enemy that players fight.

Mounts: Rideable creatures or vehicles that allow players to move faster (compared to walking) across the game zones. They are often used for aesthetic purposes.

NPC: An acronym for "Non-playable character." These are characters programmed by the game developers to have specific roles, actions, and dialogue. A player can normally interact with them, they can be quest givers, merchants, etc.

Party: A small group of players who team up to complete objectives, often sharing experience points and loot. In *Nine Heroes*, a party is typically considered 2-5 people.

Potions: Consumable items that provide temporary benefits or restore health points or mana points. Once it is used, the resource is gone.

Pickup Group (PUG): A group of players assembled randomly, where people normally don't know each other. It typically occurs through an in-game matching system or by opening up a party recruitment.

PvP: Player vs. Player gameplay where players compete directly against each other in combat or objectives. In *Nine Heroes* this is called "Player-Killing (PKing)."

Rarity: Equipment in *Nine Heroes* is categorized into tiers, often denoted by color codes or labels. These include Common (White), Uncommon (Green), Rare (Blue), Epic (Purple), and Legendary (Orange). There are also low-tier and high-tier consumable items, like potions.

Respawn: A a character, enemy, or resource reappears in the game after being defeated, used, or gathered.

RNG (Random Number Generator): In gaming, RNG is a system that creates unpredictable outcomes by using algorithms to generate random probabilities. It determines events like loot drops or critical hits by rolling virtual numbers within predefined probabilities.

Sect: A sect in *Nine Heroes* is a specific character archetype or role that determines the abilities, skills, and playstyle of a player's character (similar to that of a typical gaming character class). Players choose a sect as part of their character identity.

Skills: Special abilities or actions that a character can perform, often tied to their sect or role. These are used in combat, crafting, or other gameplay, and can be unlocked as the character levels up.

Stats: Short for statistics, stats are numerical values that represent a character's performance and capabilities in specific areas such as attack power, defense, speed, healing effectiveness, critical hit chance, health points, mana points, etc.

Storage Box: A game feature that allows players to store excess items, gear, or resources they do not want to carry in their character's inventory. It is an extended storage space, often found in specific locations, and must be accessed at that location to store or withdraw items to and from the inventory.

Support: It is a role that is focused on supporting the party rather than dealing damage to an enemy as their main purpose, for example, by buffing the party or debuffing the enemy, healing their party, or CCing their enemy. Of course, they can also deal damage.

Teleporting: This is an ability to instantly transport a character or party from one location to another within the game. It's faster than walking, riding, or other forms of travel.

Wilderness/Town/Arena Map: This represents the game's specific zones that a player can traverse. For example, The Riverside of Bianliang is a wilderness map, it's an open-world area zone where players can go to kill monsters. Another example is the Main City, as a Town Map, which is a safe zone where players rest.

Wipe: When an entire party is defeated in combat during a dungeon. This typically resets the dungeon and the party can try again from the beginning, or a save point.